FOREVER LOVE

The long-building fire finally caught and the flames of desire flashed around them. Pressed against him, she felt the hardness of his body and the rock-hard proof of how he wanted her. They moved to the bedroom he now occupied and undressed each other hastily, each breath catching in their throats.

"I came out to check on you when you didn't come back," he said. "I don't want anything to happen to you."

She stroked the back of his head. Then she drew his mouth to hers and he kissed her so hard her mouth hurt. She clung to him as if she were drowning. Her melting softness filled him with glory and his solid muscular hardness filled her with feelings of security.

The patter of rain against the windowpanes soothed them both. They were in this world but not quite of it. Each felt the other's passion as his or her own.

BOOK YOUR PLACE ON OUR WEBSITE AND MAKE THE ARABESQUE ROMANCE CONNECTION!

We've created a customized website just for our very special Arabesque readers, where you can get the inside scoop on everything that's going on with Arabesque romance novels.

When you come online, you'll have the exciting opportunity to:

- View covers of upcoming books

- Learn about our future publishing schedule (listed by publication month and author)

- Find out when your favorite authors will be visiting a city near you

- Search for and order backlist books

- Check out author bios and background information

- Send e-mail to your favorite authors

- Join us in weekly chats with authors, readers and other guests

- Get writing guidelines

- AND MUCH MORE!

Visit our website at
http://www.arabesquebooks.com

FOREVER LOVE

Francine Craft

ARABESQUE
BET BOOKS

BET Pubications, LLC
www.bet.com
www.arabesquebooks.com

ARABESQUE BOOKS are published by

BET Publications, LLC
c/o BET BOOKS
One BET Plaza
1900 W Place NE
Washington, DC 20018-1211

All Kensington Titles, Imprints, and Distributed Lines are available at special quantity discounts for bulk purchases for sales promotions, premiums, fund-raising, and educational or institutional use. Special book excerpts or customized printings can also be created to fit specific needs. For details, write or phone the office of the Kensington special sales manager: Kensington Publishing Corp., 850 Third Avenue, New York, NY 10022, attn: Special Sales Department, Phone: 1-800-221-2647.

BET Books is a trademark of Black Entertainment Television, Inc. ARABESQUE, the ARABESQUE logo, and the BET BOOKS logo are trademarks and registered trademarks.

First Printing: September 2001
10 9 8 7 6 5 4 3 2 1

Printed in the United States of America

This book is dedicated to my beloved "other." May we be there for each other throughout our lives.

To Herschel and Mario—lovers extraordinaire.

ACKNOWLEDGMENTS

I wish to acknowledge the superb help always given to me by Charlie K.

To June and Bruce Bennett, who help me above and beyond the ordinary

To the Aruba Tourist Office—ever charming

To Wayne Ketcham, a security specialist, who couldn't have been more helpful

Minden, Maryland

One

Francesca Worth turned as a warm late August breeze caressed her voluptuous body. It was early afternoon and she walked along a woodland path, admiring the lush green foliage that would change to red and gold in a couple of months. Sunlight sparkled on leaves that were still wet from a morning rain. She paused a moment to admire a bluejay sitting on a low-hanging branch of a pale-barked sycamore tree. Smiling to herself, she reflected that she was happy enough to skip like a child, and then laughed aloud.

But the laughter froze in her throat when she saw the man on the path, no more than twenty feet ahead of her. Tall, heavy, with reddish-brown hair and copper skin, he stared at her malignantly, and her glance was compelled to the snub-nosed revolver he held.

"No, Trey! Don't!" she managed to gasp to her ex-husband, knowing that her words would be useless. Fear closed her throat and made her eyes feel as though they would jump from their sockets. Her limbs were encased in ice, yet her inner body burned with fury to protect herself. Her brain was on fire.

She wasn't going to let him kill her without a

fight! As she prepared to zigzag toward him the way she had learned in self-defense classes, a tall man burst from the woods to Trey's right and grabbed his arm.

"Drop the gun, Hudson," the stranger barked. "I won't let you hurt her."

Trey cursed the stranger and fought, but he was overmatched. The stranger took the gun, trained it on Trey and commanded him, "Don't move!" And, blessedly, Trey didn't move.

Hot tears of relief flooded Francesca's face. Her desert-dry throat began to gather moisture, and she moaned deep in her throat.

Who was the stranger? She had seen this man somewhere.

Coming awake, Francesca heard herself moan again and sat up, looking around her. She slept under a dark blue blanket and had clutched it around her. She then threw it back.

Drawing a deep breath, she sat up and slung her long, shapely legs over the side of the bed and looked at the black digital clock with its blue dial face. Two o'clock in the morning, and she knew she could sleep no more that night. It was not the first time she had suffered a night of short sleep lately.

Running her fingers through her very dark brown, soft, corkscrew-curled hair, she reflected on her dream. Trey had called her the day before.

"I just wanted to know that you're okay," he had said in his smooth, oily voice.

She grew tense just thinking about him. Tense and angry.

"And you wouldn't know any reason I might not be all right?" she came back with.

"No, I wouldn't. I haven't run into you much in the

past few months. I'll always keep up with you, Fran. In some part of me, you'll always be my wife."

Francesca had clenched her teeth. "I'm *not* your wife, Trey," she had said evenly. "Not anymore."

She stroked her walnut-brown arms that had a peppering of goose bumps on them. That was the trouble with Trey, she thought, he didn't live in the real world. In his world, things were the way he wanted them to be.

Quite unbidden, the stranger in the dream came to mind. She racked her brain trying to remember where she had seen him before. She couldn't remember. An involuntary smile tugged at her face, and warmth spread through her. He was certainly attractive.

But as quickly as it had come, the smile vanished. She got up and went to her mahogany chest of drawers and gingerly picked up a letter she had left on top two days before, the day it had come. *Why bother?* she asked herself. The envelope contained only a scrawled note: *Just thought you'd like to know.* This was written on a large, yellow Post-it note and attached to a news clipping about a woman who had been murdered. There was no way of knowing what newspaper it had come from.

Why had she kept this one out? Francesca wondered. There were five other clippings that had come to her in the prior four months. Three from newspapers and three from what looked like detective magazines. And attached to each clipping was the same-size yellow Post-it note: *Just thought you'd like to know.*

Then she realized what she had denied: The woman in this clipping she held resembled her with her dark mane of hair and an oval, walnut face. Both she and the woman had almond-shaped eyes. They even had similar expressions. Shuddering, she refolded the clipping with the Post-it note and slipped it back into the envelope.

For a moment, she started to put the envelope in the drawer with the others. Then, hesitating, she took the others from the drawer. Expelling a harsh breath, she made up her mind. She was going to talk with someone at the police station again before going in to work.

She had thought the first letter was a prank, possibly sent by Rush, the angry young man she had replaced at the radio station. She had taken the second letter in to the police station and a nice young sergeant had advised her that he was sorry, but there was nothing they could do. No direct threat had been made.

He had asked about her marital status, and she had told him about Trey, how he sometimes called and stopped just short of harassing her.

"It seems you've come up against the clever type that's so damnably hard to get our hands on. Believe me, I'm sorry. Keep us posted, because you never know when he'll overstep his bounds."

She was a reasonably strong woman, but the letters had shaken her. With her throat nearly closed with fear, she had offered her hand to the young sergeant because she suddenly needed someone to hang on to.

Now Francesca brushed back a few tears. She hadn't told her father about the letters. He had never liked Trey. She had told Holly, her coworker and best friend, and Holly had been vividly sympathetic.

"I always knew somehow Trey would turn out to be a bastard," Holly had glumly said.

In the kitchen, Francesca drew the blinds, expecting every window to shatter with gunfire. She made herself a cup of hot chocolate sweetened with stevia, a natural sugar she had begun to use. She put a dollop of whipped cream left over from dessert the night before in the cup and sat sipping the thick chocolate. She was wide awake now. She willed her hand to stop shaking. Her nerves screamed, and she couldn't wait for morning to come.

Telling herself to relax, she looked around. The luxury of her house was far beyond her means, although she made a very good salary. When she married Trey, she had owned the house. He had had it rebuilt. Now there were touches of luxury everywhere.

The pine-paneled kitchen was her favorite room. She walked around it now. Her hands still shook, and she spilled a little of the chocolate and wiped it up with a napkin.

Her morning show at WKRX, Minden's radio station, began at nine-thirty, and she needed to be at her best. No question about it, she loved doing the show. She worked in the community with everything that mattered, and she had a huge fan base.

Carrying her chocolate, she went into her home studio. It had been Trey's idea to make it state of the art. Now the ivory-and-raspberry paneled walls welcomed her. The microphones spoke to her. She was a performer from the heart.

Turning on the radio, she sat down. WKRX didn't begin broadcasting until six o'clock. She switched to another station and soft rock music filled the air. Nervously, she rubbed her fingers along the plush of the chair she sat in. The mirror across from her reflected her rigid, frightened face. Once, she thought, she had been so fearless.

It was a dream, she told herself. Dreams happened. Their meaning was often obscure. She shuddered. That gun had been so real. The cold, hostile stare on Trey's face had been so real. That had been the way he looked when—

She leaned forward, her face in her hands. She didn't want to think about that. What happened then had driven her to file for a divorce. Nothing could have stopped her. The judge had been lenient; he hadn't tried to stop her after realizing that she needed to be free of this man for her own protection. Except, she thought dully, she was free, and she still wasn't protected.

The first song on the radio finished and "Killing Me Softly" came on. Roberta Flack's huskily beautiful voice surrounded her. She got halfway up to get another station, then slumped back. That had been one of her favorite songs. Now it seemed too threatening. Was Trey trying to softly kill her with his devious moves? There was little about him that was soft.

Minden's police station was a large, redbrick structure, nicely landscaped. Chief Wayne Kellem believed in community policing, and he drove his staff to be the best they could be.

As Francesca walked into the station house, a sergeant sat at the front desk. His nameplate said he was KEITH BEAUMONT. He glanced at his watch, and his square, brown face lit up. Eight-fifteen.

"Good morning, ma'am. What brings you here so early?"

"Good morning. I—need to talk with someone. I talked with you once before."

"I remember you. Sorry I couldn't help. Why are you here this time?"

"It's still about the stalking, if you could call it that."

He nodded sympathetically and stood. "Lieutenant Ryson is still here. He's got a way with cases like yours. He's had more success than the rest of us have. Just come this way, ma'am."

She followed him down the short corridor to a door at the end of the hall. A tall, dark walnut-hued man stood up as they entered and came around from behind his desk. He extended his big hand, which she took. His grasp was warm and strong, and small electric thrills shot through her.

Her breath caught in her throat. *He* was the man in her dream last night, the one who had rescued her. How could this be? She racked her brain for information. The pressure of his hand was warm, steady, comforting.

As the sergeant left, the tall man said, "I'm Lieutenant Jonathan Ryson."

His smooth baritone voice left her even more breathless. That voice said he was a man who cared.

"I'm Francesca Worth." Her tone was even. She didn't sound as though she were scared to death. It was a bad dream, that was all.

"I'm glad to meet you, miss. Ms.?"

"I *was* married. Now I'm divorced. I went back to using my maiden name."

"I see. I usually just call all women *miz*. But if I'm going to help you, I guess everything is pertinent. Please have a seat. Can I get you some coffee? I make a pretty mean cup."

She found herself wanting coffee.

"Thank you. Heavy on the cream, sugar substitute."

"The station house has coffee," he said, "but I have a special Colombian brew I prefer and since I spend so much time here, I make my own."

She liked this man and wondered at the sadness that seemed to linger in his eyes. Was he married? Without meaning to, she looked and saw no wedding ring. What did it matter? After what she had gone through with Trey, it would be a long time before she'd want an in-depth relationship with another man.

In the kitchenette preparing to serve the coffee, Jon Ryson reflected that he was attracted to this woman. He liked her style.

Her ivory fishnet dress was worn over an indigo blue linen sheath. Simple. Smart. Her plain, wide-banded indigo sandals displayed well-tended feet. That neck was swanlike.

Jon chuckled. Damn! His inner camera had recorded her for posterity—*his* posterity.

As he handed her the coffee, his hand touched hers and her heart leapt. What in hell was wrong with her? she wondered. Then it came to her. She was reaching out in fear as she had reached out to him in her dream.

The lieutenant had a heavy jet-black moustache and his smooth black hair was cut close. His clear, black-olive eyes continued to sum her up, liking what he saw.

Jon Ryson rocked himself a bit. "So we meet again, Ms. Worth," he said smoothly, wondering at the fear etched on her face. He thought something was really bothering her and he wanted to help.

"I don't understand. We've never met before."

Jon Ryson chuckled. "How soon we forget. At Morrison's gas pump day before yesterday. You were rushing to get gas and get away, I think. You bumped into me. I steadied you."

The memory came flooding back. She nodded. "I remember now. I was going in to work late and I'd gotten another one of the cruise missiles—psychologically that is—that I've been getting lately."

"Cruise missiles?"

Francesca dug into her tote bag and brought out the envelopes, giving them to him. He opened each one and looked at it, then spread them out on his desk. When he had looked at the last clipping, he studied the envelopes and drew a deep breath.

"Who do you think is doing this? I see the dates go back to April of this year and they're mailed from different cities. Did anything specific happen then?"

She shook her head. "Not that I know of. My ex-husband and I have been divorced a year this month. I think he's the one doing this."

"It usually works that way. Was there bad blood between you two?"

"Yes," she said bitterly. "He wanted to knock me around before the divorce. I wasn't about to stand for that."

"Bully for you."

"Thank you. My ex-husband is Trey Hudson, who owns an automobile dealership here in Minden."

"I know him. Not well, but I know him."

"I'm not surprised. Trey makes it his business to know whoever matters."

Jon Ryson sat with his eyes half closed. He wanted to help this woman, wanted to erase the pain on her face. The thought of someone beating her made his blood boil.

"I'm sorry about what you've been through. Has your ex-husband tried to contact you since your divorce?"

"He calls once in a while. He called a couple of days ago. He's always the soul of civility."

"He wants you back."

It was a flat statement. Jon studied the lovely woman sitting across from him. The silken walnut skin and the thick dark brown hair was swept back from her brow and drawn into a french twist of straw curls. Maybe she wasn't conventionally beautiful with her dark brown eyes and straight-across black eyebrows, but he knew she was beautiful to him. Unlike a lot of men he knew, he liked the big sisters and if they had it all together, so much the better.

Finally she answered him, reluctantly it seemed. "He says he wants me back. With Trey, it's hard to know. There were other women, even when we were married."

"That's always a bad scene. And just let me interpose a question here. Is there anyone else you can think of who might be doing this? You're very much in the public eye with your radio show. . . ."

She looked up quickly.

"I listen to WKRX," he said, "and I like your show. And congratulations on your award as female variety-show broadcaster of the year."

"Thank you. I'm glad you like my show. I put so much into it."

"And it pays off—richly. Is there anyone who might be envious of your success? Could some creep be jealous that he can't have you for himself?"

Francesca didn't have to think about that first question. "I replaced a man named Rush Mason a couple of years ago. His show was losing listeners. He was drinking too much."

"So the manager canned him. Did Mason say anything to you about it?"

Francesca laughed shortly. "Yes. He accused me of being my boss's girlfriend, said I had undermined him. I had an afternoon homemaker show before I was switched."

"So now you've got *Morning in Minden,*" Jon said. "You've done great things with that show. It's educational now as well as entertaining. Has Mason bothered you lately? I mean in person?"

"No. He works with Trey now. He comes from an old, wealthy family from Diamond Point Island in the Caribbean. They could probably *buy* him a radio station, but he's hotly competitive. He prefers the States and he prefers this area."

"I see. So it *could* be him even after a couple of years."

"I guess it's possible, but I've felt it just seems the kind of thing Trey would do."

"Have you asked Trey if he's behind this?"

"Oh yes." Her voice became shallow. "When I got the first clipping, I asked him and he vehemently denied it. 'I'm not going to deny I want you back,' he said, 'but I'm moving on anyway.'

"Lieutenant, you'd have to understand Trey. Do you know anything about multiple personality disorder?"

"A little. He's multiple?"

"Yes. He has two other personalities that he's told me about. Most of the time he's just Trey is all I can tell. He's dedicated and works like mad sometimes, like a man possessed. He told me that's his real self. And sometimes he's a playboy and wants to party all the time."

"That could be hell on a business."

"He's always had someone else there to back him up. Rush Mason has a business administration degree; he's just more interested in communications. He has a degree in that, too."

"Well-educated guy."

"Yes, he just doesn't seem like the type to me who'd do something like this."

"You never can tell." Lieutenant Ryson's hands formed a pyramid. If he had a woman like this woman, he thought, he wouldn't want to let her go either. She looked strong and vulnerable at once, tender, and capable of giving a man what he needed.

"This is all that's happened then, and I don't mean that in a negative way. What brings you in here now, today?"

"I'll tell you in just a minute. Lieutenant, Trey told me he had a personality he was afraid of, that it sometimes did evil things."

"Did you ever see evidence of this?"

She nodded. "I think so. When he struck me, he seemed like a different person."

She brought herself up short. She was delaying telling him about the dream. Would it sound foolish when she told him?

She cleared her throat. "I had a dream last night, a nightmare." And she told him about the dream, leaving out that the man who rescued her had looked like him.

His face was grave. "That would do it." He examined the clippings again. No captions. No identification of the newspapers or magazines that had published the stories. Just pictures of women who had been murdered and the headlines of the stories related to them.

"At first I wasn't too frightened," she said. "I just thought Trey was doing it to scare me. That perhaps I knew something or he thought I knew something he didn't want me to know.

"Lieutenant, strange men came to our house when we were together. They didn't look like the salt of the earth. A lot of Caribbean island men he didn't introduce me to. Something was going on with him and I couldn't figure out what it was."

Jon Ryson ran his tongue over his dry bottom lip. He hadn't been interested in a woman since Stacy Lambreth had walked out on him four months before they were to be married. He already had had a basic distrust of women, gained from Melanie, his mother, who had left her family for another man. He shrugged. He wouldn't make that mistake again. But the haunted, highly attractive woman sitting across from him was bringing him out of his shell.

Suddenly he said, "The problem is he's walking a thin line. He isn't threatening you, except obliquely."

"I know. It's what I expect of Trey. He's nothing if not cunning. So do I just wait, getting more nervous by the day?"

It was a bitter question. Jon looked at her, tapping his pen on the desk.

"Tell you what. I could keep an eye on your place if you'll tell me where you live."

"That should help. Part of the trouble is I live out on Addison Road in a cul-de-sac. I got the house in the divorce because I was buying it when we married. Trey spent a small fortune redoing it. It's isolated."

"Just what you don't need right now."

"Yes." His warm sympathy was making her feel better.

He thought about asking her to have dinner with him and pushed that thought aside for the moment. She was a winner and he could fall for her.

"Then there's really nothing you can do." Her voice sounded bereft.

He raised a hand. "Hold on. I'm going to write this up and I will make it my business to swing by at odd hours. I'll also get a couple of other officers to do the same, and I want you to keep me posted on what's going on with you. Will you?"

He gathered the envelopes she had given him. "I'd like to keep these, study them. I think you ought to check in with me by phone daily. Come by when you can. I have a real hatred of men who prey on women. Some of them have led lives as children you wouldn't believe. Their screws aren't tight. The abuse has rattled their brains."

She nodded. "Once in a while, Trey would talk about the beatings his father and mother gave him. A friend took a picture of him when he was thirteen and his father had beaten him. It was a real horror."

"We come across that all the time, and in families you'd least expect of it."

She was tensing again. "I asked him why he'd kept the photo. He said it was so he could remind himself to pay his debt to society, in his own way."

"Your ex sounds like he's got a beef at the world, and when a child is brutally handled, that's usually the way it goes. I feel for the men and women these people become, but I also feel for the people they later make pay for their parents' mistreatment of them."

"Thank you so much, Lieutenant," Francesca said, beginning to get up. "I'll do as you suggest and keep in touch."

They both rose. "One other thing," he said. "I'd like to come by and check your house, give you tips to make it more secure. Would late this afternoon be all right?"

She was beginning to feel downright relaxed. "Yes, I get home around four. Trey spent a lot of money on a first-rate security system, but there may be failings you'd see. He always seemed to be looking over his shoulder."

Then on impulse she asked him, "Can you come at seven and have dinner with me? I make a mean crab-shrimp gumbo over brown rice."

Jon Ryson smiled widely. "Lady," he said, "you've got a dinner guest."

Jon walked with Francesca to the front door and came back to his office. He switched on his new, sleek black radio and listened to the early morning sounds of WKRX radio as some first-class gospel music came through. One of his favorites, "Talk About a Child That Do Love Jesus," was playing. For a moment he hummed along with a deep-voiced contralto lead singer.

Sergeant Keith Beaumont, his best friend, came in.

"The woman who was just here," Keith said, "I talked with her last May or so. Last spring anyway. She told me about some clippings she'd begun getting in the mail. Murdered women. Some creep's doing. Has anything further happened?"

"Yeah, she's gotten more of them. One every three to six weeks. Nothing has changed about them, except—" He paused.

"Except."

"Well, the last one to come looks a lot like her, is about the same age, even has a similar expression. I didn't mention it to her in case she's in denial. She's frightened enough as it is. Yeah, and she had a nightmare last night."

Keith whistled low. "That's enough to scare the hell out of her. Any idea who's doing it?"

"She thinks it's her ex, but there's also a guy she replaced at the radio station."

"WKRX? *Morning in Minden?* I knew her face was familiar. The station runs a weekly ad in the daily paper. She's, ah—easy on the eyes. Coca-Cola bottle. That kind of thing."

Jonathan laughed. "It's too early in the morning for you to be leching."

"As if," Keith scoffed, "you haven't lit up like the sun since she came in."

When Keith left, Jon leaned back with his hands clasped behind his head. He let his head fill with visions of Francesca, but even that didn't ease the ache in his heart when he thought of his brother, Kevin.

Kevin had been a rising star in Minden's police department, laughingly declaring to their chief that one day he wanted his job. His young brother had been on fire with the joy of living. Now he was dead. A little over a year ago someone had ruthlessly snuffed out his life. Shot him. That deed had taken two lives because his father's heart attack and death had followed soon after.

Going through papers left in Kevin's desk, he had come across a white sheet of paper with doodlings of arrows and the words: *Caribbean Caper?*

It had been a question to Kevin, and it was a question to him.

Wayne Kellem, the police chief, knocked and came in.

"How's it going?" he asked.

"Okay. Chief, we've got a problem."

"Does it have anything to do with Francesca Worth?"

"You know the lady?"

"Yeah, I've met her a couple of times at parties. She's invited me to be on her show. I just haven't gotten around to it."

"Yes. She's got troubles."

Jon proceeded to fill Chief Kellem in. As Jon talked, the chief paced the floor, then sat down.

When Jon had finished, the chief was silent for a while.

"Trey Hudson or Rush Mason. It could be either man," the chief said, "but if I had my druthers, I wouldn't want to be stalked by either one. They're both pure poison."

Jon told him about Francesca's dream and the chief pursed his lips before commenting. "It's beginning to get to her. *Inner* stress maims and kills us quicker than anything on the outside."

He shot a sharp glance at Jon and nearly closed his eyes.

"Jon, I've been meaning to talk with you about stress and what it does to you. You and Kevin were so close. Your father was a busy man with his shoe store and your mother wasn't there. Kevin was five years younger and you did your share of parenting him."

The chief got up and paced again in front of Jon's desk. He put his hands behind his back.

"What I'm trying to say is you haven't grieved the deaths of your brother and father, not nearly enough, but it hits you at times. I see it coming down on you. I wish you'd do what I've suggested before, take some time off. Go away or just stay here in Minden. Let yourself grieve your loss."

Jon let his chief's words wash over him, sink in, before he spoke.

"I guess you're right. At first, I was afraid I couldn't take it. Dad couldn't. Kevin was special. You know that.

There was something about my brother that lifted us all."

"Yes. Kevin raced along the top of the hill. He was a winner, but he moved too fast for safety sometimes. He was a cop at heart, and he hated criminals. That may have been his downfall."

Jon's head jerked up. "What do you mean?"

"As lawmen, we've got to look at both sides of the fence. Usually, not always, things that have happened to us from the day we are born help to shape our lives. In the case of criminals, that's usually something bad. Kevin never learned to give over, but he was learning. I just failed to teach him fast enough."

"Don't beat up on yourself, Chief. I failed him too. I was in love, in pursuit of a dream and a dream woman. Maybe if I'd had more time to keep mentoring him . . ."

"Now *you're* beating on yourself. Kevin was on to something," the chief said. "He told me it was something big and he'd talk to me about it the next week. You said he told you the same thing. That stolen-car ring we still haven't broken was very much on his mind when he died. Take some time off, Jon.

"Why don't you help Ms. Worth deal with her stalking problems? If you can help her, you'll help yourself. She's a nice woman." His face was wreathed in a smile. "Not to mention a good-looking, shapely woman. Venus, eat your heart out."

Jon laughed. The chief's appreciation of feminine pulchritude was well known at the station house, but he was faithful to his wife who had given him six children.

"I'd be glad to do whatever I can to help her," Jon said, "but we're dealing with one of the smart ones. He's not really doing anything we can get our teeth into. He's playing mind games, maybe trying to drive her mad. She's really bothered."

The chief got up. "Give it your best shot. And you'll think about what I've said?"

"About my taking time off to grieve?"

"Yes."

"I will consider, and I may take you up on the offer. I've been playing the stock market, and I'm getting pretty rich." He laughed.

The chief looked delighted. "No kidding. I've always said I was going to quit and be a day trader, but too many are falling by the wayside."

"I only invest what I can afford and it's paid off for me."

"Good." The chief glanced at his watch. "I've got a bunch of kids coming over from the high school to question me on crime and our communities. Rich subject for kids that age."

"Kids are pretty keen these days."

Two

"Good morning my precious friends! Welcome to *Morning in Minden.*"

Now that she was on the air, Francesca came to life as if nothing was wrong. Her listeners supported her as she supported them. They brought out everything that was good in one another.

"This is Francesca Worth bringing you the best in our fair city. . . ."

Then for a brief moment, her voice caught in her throat and she felt a moment of pure panic. In his glass-enclosed booth, the sound engineer, Max Goodloe, looked concerned.

"Pull it together, Worth!" she muttered to herself, and her order worked like magic. Her silken voice caught itself and came clear.

"Today, we have a lot on our plate. We continue our quest for this year's Minden's Woman of the Year, and we value your nominations, so please get them in." She paused. "Holly tells me she's got an exquisite lemon-lime cheesecake on tap that's easy to make.

"*And* we've got the Burbridge Boys to sing a song or two in their inimitable style."

Relaxing as she remembered Jon Ryson's thrilling presence this morning, she drew a very deep breath, then introduced Mark Walters, who began the newscast.

They were on the air for four hours, Monday through Friday, and this was the first time in three years that she had known fear like this.

Not even during her breakup with Trey had she been anything less than in control. She certainly was not an easily frightened woman.

Max came out of his booth to stand beside Francesca. *Is everything all right, Toots?* he wrote on a slip of paper.

Francesca nodded and gave him the A-okay sign.

He touched her hand as the commercials came on. "You're sure?"

"I'm sure. Thanks for your concern, Max. I'll manage this, with your help."

Max went slowly back into his booth and closed the door, frowning. He'd never seen Francesca like this. But she was as good as her word, and in a few minutes, she seemed her old, ebullient self again. Max gave her the A-okay sign.

Morning in Minden was one of Minden's most listened-to radio programs. Lou Seaman, the station manager, credited Francesca with pulling their ratings to a fantastic height.

Holly Crane, another broadcaster and Francesca's best friend, sat at her long table, which was laden with good-looking food. She had pushed most of it aside, leaving only the utensils and food necessary to whip up her lemon-lime cheesecake. She grinned at Francesca, but her face bore a quizzical look. She wrote something on a Post-it slip, came over and gave it to Francesca.

Is everything okay? she had written.

Francesca nodded and gave her friend her best smile. Holly, spiffed up in a dark rust, white-braid-trimmed dress that flattered her ample figure, paused at the edge of the table and looked back. She hadn't had a chance to talk with Francesca this morning, but she wasn't fooling Holly—something was wrong.

To Francesca, it seemed as if she took a long time to talk about the "Minden Woman of the Year" selection, but she thanked heaven her voice was even. After a half hour, Max gave her the A-okay sign again. Trouble was, the Post-it slip Holly had handed her had reminded her of the large Post-it slips on the news and magazine clippings. *Why am I so bothered now?* she wondered, and thought it must be the dream.

Francesca smiled as a group of young men in their late teens and early twenties came into the studio next to her. They waved, smiling, and she waved back. They were five in number, Minden natives, and pushing to get to the top of the music world.

Their music was eclectic. They did rap, rhythm and blues, and pop. They wrote wonderful tunes; their voices were superb. Trey had once talked of backing them, but he wanted them to go more toward gangsta rap and they weren't willing.

"Plenty of clean, loving stuff out there, man," Otis Burbridge, the lead singer, had told him. "We like the good stuff."

Trey had shrugged. "Stay poor," he had told them. "It's your funeral."

Francesca was glad that they were making it their way.

The tape of the Burbridge Boys' latest release came on and before they could finish their first song, the station lines lit up and the switchboard was inundated with calls and requests.

Lou Seaman, the station manager, came out on a commercial break, beaming.

"Well, old girl," he told Francesca, "you've done it again."

Lou was one of the handsome bald men. Immaculately attired and humorous, he backed her on everything. As he walked away, Holly came to her again.

"You want to talk, you've got a listener."

Francesca pressed her hand. "A little later I'll want to. Thank you for being there for me."

"You've been washed in my tears many times," Holly said. "It's the least I can do."

Genuinely smiling this time, Francesca snapped on her microphone. "Thanks for all your support for the Burbridge Boys," she told her audience. "You know they're the two Burbridge brothers, Otis and John, a Burbridge cousin, Carlton, then Rick Means and Paul Lassiter. All glorious. And you'll love knowing they're going to do *two* extra numbers for us.

"We'll put aside telling you next week's schedule this morning. Check with us tomorrow. And now our marvels will do one of their newest releases in person, 'If This Be Love.' Enjoy!"

The phones that had quieted down lit up again with congratulations. The group had just begun to release singles and they were working on another album.

The staff of WKRX applauded loudly as the Burbridge Boys finished and gave autographs to the station staff and a few guests. Several young women stood in the hallway waiting for the group to come out. Francesca shook her head. There must have been seven of them and two were teenyboppers.

Rich, the older security guard, threw up his hands, laughing. "What could I do? They were going to do themselves in if I hadn't let them in to see their idols. Besides, I remember what it was like when I worshiped Lena Horne."

Lou shook his head as he came to Rich. "You're too soft for this job, man." But he laughed. Lou walked over to the young women. "You ought to be in school— you can stay this time," he told them, "but be very quiet, and afterward, to school with you."

Happily the girls agreed and pressed against the walls

of the studio out in the hall. The Burbridge Boys grinned at them delightedly.

Driving home that afternoon in her four-year-old black Lexus, Francesca felt both restless and anxious. Thinking about Jon Ryson, her heart skipped a beat and she reined her emotions in.

"I've had enough trouble from a man to last me a lifetime," she muttered to herself.

Pulling into the garage that adjoined the house, she went in through the kitchen, nervously glancing around her.

"Cut it out!" she commanded herself sharply. She wasn't going to be scared breathless by her ex-husband. She would just be cautious. He wasn't going to get her down. She had always been a strong woman, and she was going to keep on being that way.

Mrs. Addison, her part-time housekeeper, was off that day. She could have used her help in making the gumbo. Getting out of her clothes, she changed into a periwinkle blue, small-flowered caftan and walked barefoot into the kitchen. The blue tile of the kitchen floor was cool beneath her feet. And she delighted in the quiet around her as she pulled utensils and food from the cabinets and the refrigerator.

Being in the kitchen reminded her of what had happened that morning at the police station, causing her to shudder, an involuntary thrill coursing through her.

Unwrapping a loaf of sliced French bread, she spread minced garlic butter over the slices and set the bread in an aluminum container to warm on top of the stove. She hoped the good lieutenant appreciated her efforts, because she was too tired to be doing all this.

She puttered around while the meal was cooking, putting the blossoms of fresh red and white carnations into fingerbowls, getting out her best crystal and china, and the beautiful curve-handled silverware that her house-keeper had polished the day before.

When everything was ready, she lay down for a quick nap, but she couldn't sleep. She was thinking of the day Trey had been suddenly called to his office and had left his safe door open. She had warily looked inside at the envelopes, papers and stacks of money.

After a moment, she had picked up a small manila envelope and looked inside. A gold pocket watch gleamed softly. Beautiful. Engraved ivy leaves spread over the cover and the initial "K" was etched in script in the center.

She had wanted to examine it more closely, but hadn't dared. Trey would be furious at himself for leaving the safe open and at her for looking in. He didn't share his business with her.

These days, she hated even thinking of her ex-husband. Jon Ryson's face came before her. She smiled and fell asleep.

It seemed only moments before she awoke to the sound of her door chimes.

Groggily jumping up, she glanced at the radial dial on the clock radio by her bed. Six-fifty! That would be Jon Ryson, due at seven.

She was a mess, but she didn't want to keep him waiting. She couldn't find her slippers, so she went to the door barefoot.

Flustered, she opened the door and there he was, all six-feet-three of him, absolutely fit and garbed in a navy suit that set off his splendid physique.

"I'm so sorry," she sputtered, "but I—"

A smile crinkled his dark walnut face. "You fell asleep." He handed her a sheaf of fern and blood-red roses and a box of chocolates.

"Thank you. They're beautiful. And I love Rhea's candies. I'm a mess. Would you prefer listening to some music or watching TV? I have a truly good collection of music. The old masters. Rock. Rap. Pop. Rhythm and blues."

"I need to listen to a newscast. We had some trouble on the east side late this afternoon."

"I'll get you the local news on the radio."

She switched on her ivory radio and listened to it purr as they were told the news would be given in the next half hour.

"Have a seat. It's going to take me a few minutes."

But his look at her was amused, and he didn't sit down. As he stood there, his face grew grave and his black olive eyes on her were unfathomable.

"You look beautiful," he said. "Rumpled. Sleepy. Tired. Bothered."

"Don't," she said. "Please don't mock me."

He stepped closer to her. The soft, natural scent of her filled his nostrils. It was a scent he had noticed that morning.

"I'd never mock you," he said solemnly. "Like this, you're real, and it moves me."

His index finger lifted her chin and with the other hand he cradled her head and kissed her long and hard, his tongue probing her mouth.

Oh my God! she thought, crazily. She wanted this man with a fever that shook her to the core. His body was lean and hard against hers, telling her how much he wanted her. The kiss seemed to go on forever before she pushed him away.

"No," she said, shaking. "Please."

Reluctantly he released her. "I'm not sorry," he said. "I'm not pressuring you. I wanted to kiss you this morning. I trust myself."

She pulled out of his arms and stood apart from him,

a little angry. Trey had seemed passionate in the beginning.

For a moment she wrung her hands, then stood stiffly. "I'm not ready for this," she said. "I'll be going it alone for a long time. I don't need a man in my life right now. It would just complicate things."

He nodded. "I know the feeling, lady. I've been hurt, too. Badly. But when I met you this morning I began to think there might be a chance to get over it. . . ."

She shook her head. "I just can't get involved now. Like I said, it will be a long time before I can, if ever. You're a nice man, Jon. If I wanted anyone, it could well be you."

"Okay," he said. "Why get dressed and ready to entertain me in high style, when I like you just the way you are? I'll listen to the news."

Going to her bedroom, she showered quickly, spritzed on light jasmine and slipped into a mid-calf-length, deep rose, crocheted dress over a deep rose slip. Sliding her feet into high-heeled transparent, acrylic sling-back shoes, she patted and rearranged her hair, brushed on rose lipstick and went out.

That kiss had been full of flames and wonder, she thought as she walked back into the living room and stood looking at Jon from the doorway.

Sensing her presence, he turned, looked at her and whistled long and low. Running his tongue over his bottom lip, he told her, "You tell me to back off and you proceed to make that impossible. You look even more beautiful. No, not more, just beautiful in a different way."

"Thank you. I'm going to see about serving you what tastes to me like a good meal."

"I would have been glad to take you out to dinner."

"I like to cook, and it's my treat for your kindness this morning."

His face got somber. "I've gone over those clippings
a few times, and I want to keep them a while if you
don't mind."

"Be my guest. They were like an evil cloud over this
house."

"Which by the way is a beautiful house. I like the
huge Grecian urns, the way you've got your plants and
the furniture arranged. I'm a fern man myself. And
there's nothing I like better than pandanus wood furniture. I spent some time in the South Pacific, and I
missed that particular beauty when I left."

"I did it all with help from a decorator. It's hard to
believe I was happy here once."

Francesca glanced around her at the deep beige
plush furniture with its touches of aquamarine, scarlet
and jade green pillows. If Jon liked it, then all the work
had been worthwhile.

When he had listened to the news spots he needed
to hear, Francesca turned off the radio and Jon walked
over to the grand piano that sat near the windows. Sitting down, he idly tapped a few keys, played "Chopsticks," then exercised his fingers and played a section
of Schumann's "Arabesque, Opus 18."

By the time he finished playing the light, sparkling
tune, Francesca was at his side in a frilly organdie apron.

"You play well," she said.

"Thank you. I look lessons for a long time. I should
play even better."

"Don't sell yourself short."

"Glad you liked that. How about this?"

He launched into a mean boogie and she laughed.
"Good Lord, is there no end to your talents?"

He stopped playing, wanting to pull her down on the
piano bench beside him.

"I wanted to be a jazz musician once. Teddy Wilson,

one of the old ones, was my idol. I have all of his records I could find."

"Interesting. I like him too, and I have a number of his singles. Seventy-eights and thirty-three-and-a-third records with artists like Wilson have become valuable."

"Yes."

Why was he looking at her so strangely?

"Let me know what you're missing in Teddy Wilson's department and maybe I have it."

"You're sweet," he said and her skin warmed.

He stood up. In heels, she was nearly as tall as he was.

Did he imagine, he wondered, that she withdrew?

She turned. "I'd better get back and finish our dinner."

He was hungry, he thought, but not only for food. He watched her retreating form. In fantasy his hands spanned that waist and his tongue caressed that silken skin.

Three

Dinner of crab and shrimp gumbo over brown rice
and a luscious, crisp garden salad finished, Francesca
scraped the plates and set the china in the dishwasher.

"I'll help you," Jon offered.

"No. You rest. Would you like more wine?"

"I would. You make great gumbo. It was one of my
mother's favorite dishes."

"Your mother's dead then?"

He shook his head. "Slip of the tongue. She's still
very much alive and into everything. I'm sure you've
met her."

His voice was cool, his body had stiffened.

"Melanie Ryson? The dynamo who's done so much
to help kids in trouble in Minden?"

"One and the same."

"I didn't make the connection. We've talked. I inter-
viewed her after her son was killed. That would be your
brother."

The look of pain on his face was palpable.

"Yes," he said tersely.

"I'm sorry if you'd rather not talk about it."

Jon drew a deep breath and sat up straighter. This
woman was getting to him, and he didn't even know
her. Steady, boy, he told himself. Once he had opened
his heart to a woman, his fiancée at one time—Stacy

Lambreth—and she had stomped on it. He was adamant about finding someone else to fill his empty heart. But he just intended to take it slow.

He enjoyed watching Francesca as she moved about her kitchen. Her movements were graceful, balanced. She had hips, he thought, that just wouldn't wait, under that narrow waistline and the high breasts. A walnut-tinted treasure. He grinned to himself. She had to let him through.

"Now for dessert," she said. "I hope you like praline cake and plain old vanilla ice cream."

"Love them both."

As he sat there, she stood opposite him at the table, talking. "The cake recipe is passed down from my great-grandmother, a New Orleans native. The vanilla-bean recipe I unearthed on my own."

"What a coincidence. My mother grew up in New Orleans and migrated here as a girl."

There was that coolness in his voice again. She chanced the question.

"Are you close to your mother?"

He looked down, sighing. After a minute, he said, "No. Once we were very close. Something happened. . . ."

"I'm sorry."

"Don't be. Some things can't be helped. She left our family when I was ten and my brother was five. My father raised us, but he was a shattered man. He withdrew into himself. I practically raised Kevin, and a ten-year-old boy can't be expected to do much of a job of parenting. But I did the best I could."

Francesca came from around the table and put a slender hand on his shoulder.

"I didn't mean to open old wounds," she said.

He smiled grimly. "I'm afraid the wounds have never

closed. Funny thing, talking to you helps. You're a savvy listener. Thank you."

"You're welcome. I'll listen any time."

"Be careful what you offer me. I might take you up on that. Your description of dessert has piqued my appetite."

She moved away from him. "Okay. Coming up."

She set the sparkling crystal cake plate on the dining room table, revealing a three-layer yellow cake with nuts, candied fruit and currants, topped by cream-cheese icing with crumbled praline candies.

"My mother used to make this often—before she left. Don't tell me *you* made this?"

"I did. I like to cook when I have time. I found the recipe in an old cookbook I was looking through."

He sat waiting for his ice cream and for her to sit down.

She put crystal dessert bowls and plates on the table and brought the ice cream from the refrigerator freezer.

"Go easy, moderate, or pile it on?"

Jon laughed and she reflected that she hadn't heard him laugh so merrily until now.

"Hell, pile it on. I won't lie to you. I haven't had a meal like this in ages. It all smells so scrumptious."

When she was seated, they smiled at each other, listening to classical music on the CD player.

"Would you like me to get the news again?"

"No, but thank you. I heard what I was looking for. There was a shooting on the East End. The wounds weren't life threatening."

A chill went through her. He looked at her stricken face, reached over and covered her hand with his.

"That was thoughtless of me," he said. "You're remembering your dream, aren't you?"

"It's all right. You're a cop. You live with that kind of thing."

"And you're not a cop, and it has no place in *your* life.

A woman like you—I'd make book you're doing every-thing right—ought to feel safe. I could skin the bastard who's doing this to you."

"Talking to you helps so much. This day would have been pure torment for me if you hadn't talked with me this morning."

"I'm going to do everything I can to help you—which I'm afraid isn't much when this creep is being so clever."

"I know." Because she was shivering and didn't want to dwell on thoughts about her stalker, she told him, "I'm thinking now. The Kevin Ryson who got killed, the police sergeant, was your brother. I was on vacation and out of the country when it happened."

"Yes." His voice was quiet, still. Then he opened up. "It was the worst time of my life. Kevin and I were so close. He worshiped me and I doted on him. As I told you, my father went into his shell when my mother left, but he loved my brother, and he couldn't take his death. He died three months later of a heart attack.

"I'm going to find the bastard who killed Kevin if it takes me the rest of my life." His eyes were hot and burning.

Francesca's eyes shone with tears. Her heart hurt for Jon Ryson.

"Tomorrow is the anniversary of his death. He was working on a stolen-car-ring case. The cars are being stolen and shipped to the Caribbean and sold there for fantastic prices. People in the States have connections to people there and we're not finding it easy to crack the case.

"Kevin loved doing this kind of thing, and he was good at it, but he sometimes got careless and over-reached himself. God, my brother was on the way to having a fantastic life for himself."

* * *

"Let me give you a grand tour," she told Jon later, after both had finished dessert. "I would wager," she said, "that we are both on the edge of no longer being able to eat like this without piling on the pounds. Already, I'm far from skinny. Men usually have a few more years in which to stuff themselves."

"I'm a meat-and-potatoes man," he said loyally. He hadn't meant to say it. "And I like the curves I'm seeing."

"Thank you. You're kind."

"Honest would be a better word."

"Okay."

As they walked about Francesca's beautiful two-story, four-bedroom home, with very large rooms and well-appointed decor, Jon was aware of tension in his hostess.

"How long have you and Hudson been divorced?"

"A little over a year."

"Around the time my brother was killed."

"About four months after."

"Was he abusive to you for long?"

"He only struck me hard that once. As I told you, that's when I filed for divorce." Jon's muscles knotted at the thought of her being struck by Hudson.

"He changed," she said abruptly. "Before we were married, he put up quite a front, but after, he was sullen, brooding. He got impossible to live with just several months before I filed. It was as if he had some devil inside him. He said his business wasn't going well, yet that I should quit my job and stay home, which was odd, considering. If the business wasn't doing well, then we needed the money I brought in."

"I wish you hadn't had to endure all that."

"I'm okay now, or I would be if my stalker would just let go. Oh, why do I say 'stalker' when I *know* it's Trey."

"These things are funny. It may turn out to be Rush Mason."

"You're right. Or they could have linked up."

"God forbid."

As they neared her bedroom, her breathing shallowed as quick visions swarmed her brain. She was in Jon's arms, and they made violent and passionate love. With the fire in her belly, she put more distance between them.

Jon's eyes narrowed. Was she feeling any of the overwhelming loving lust he was feeling?

At her bedroom door, she paused and didn't go in.

"I left it in such a mess," she said.

The bed was rumpled, and he wanted to rumple it more, but he didn't push her. She pulled the door to and took him to the black-leather-furnished family room with its oversize TV screen and pool table.

"Care for a game?" he asked.

"I don't shoot pool," she said, "but one day I'll learn. How about table tennis?"

"Not my favorite, but if you insist."

"No, I don't. Our conversation has been too somber to have a lot of energy left over for play. Come through here for the fitness room."

That room was small and well equipped.

"The punching bag was for Trey," she said dryly, "until he decided I made a better one."

"Did he beat you badly?"

She shook her head. "He struck me just that once. I was unconscious. I came to with him hovering over me. When he found out I wasn't in a desperate condition, he left and didn't come back until the next morning. I went to the hospital, had X rays made. There was no lasting damage."

He drew her close, and she rested her head on his shoulder.

"We console each other," she told him. "That's good."

"Are you going to stay here? It's a beautiful house. . . ."

"But with so many unhappy memories. No, I've decided to put it on the market. I'll take an apartment until I find something else. But I'm much too busy to do that now."

"I want you some place safe."

"That's where I want to be."

They examined the security system Trey had had installed and she explained the mechanism.

"Lord, there's so much heat-sensing lasers going on here, we could take care of the Hope Diamond."

"And all that doesn't keep some fool from mailing you photos of murdered women."

"Jon, I'm finally facing it. That last photo looks a lot like me."

"I noticed."

"I like to think I'm pretty safe for a while."

"He's creeping closer slowly."

"Yes. I'm glad I found you."

She felt the warmth and the strength of his sinewy body and her body answered his pleas, but her heart drew away.

"It will be a long time," she said, "before I can respond to you in a healthy way. My feelings have been crushed in the past year."

"I understand," he said. And he did understand that and something else. She was as deeply attracted as he was, and he was attracted to the core. She needed wooing, and he was prepared to woo her for as long as it took.

Four

The next morning, Francesca came groggily awake and climbed out of bed as the telephone rang. She picked up the receiver and lay back.

"Just checking," Jon said. "Thank you for a wonderful dinner."

"Thank *you* for sharing it with me."

"Are you busy tonight? Tomorrow night?"

Francesca came more fully awake. "I have a meeting with a community group tomorrow. What did you have in mind?"

"Another dinner in some romantic place. Dancing, if you'd like that. I pay my debts, and I am indebted to you."

"No, you're not. The debt is mine."

"Then, too, I'm concerned about you. I hate what you're going through."

Francesca's breath quickened. "I slept fine last night. No bad dreams. Jon, I'm not going to pieces over this. It didn't start yesterday, and I've managed to bear it." She hesitated. "I want to be fair with you. I don't want to get involved in a close relationship again right now."

"I know you don't, and I can't say I won't push you, but you're one cup of tea I'd like to drink often. Shouldn't I have kissed you the way I did?"

"What do you think?"

There was a brief pause. "I think it was in order and we both enjoyed it."

"The burned child and fire," she told him. "That's an altogether true saying."

"We can't live in a fireless world. We just have to learn to handle it."

This time it was Francesca who hesitated. "Let's just leave it like it is. We'll have dinner sometime soon, but I want to stop and catch my breath."

"Okay, I guess I have to accept that, but I warn you, I'll keep pushing."

"And I'll accept that." Then she remembered his talking about his brother and said, "You mentioned last night that today is the anniversary of your brother Kevin's death. I offer you my heartfelt sympathy."

"Thank you."

"How are you holding up?"

"Not too well. I woke up this morning somewhat depressed. Thinking about you helped. But Kevin's death came close to putting me under. It still hurts more than I thought it would after this span of time."

His voice caught and went ragged. "Then there was my father following so soon after. It leaves such a hole in my world."

"Jon, I will have dinner with you tonight if you want that. This is a special day. You helped me so much yesterday. I'd like to do the same for you."

"Thanks," he said huskily. "I'll look forward to that. Pick you up at seven?"

"Seven-thirty would be better. We're winding down a project, and things are apt to be hectic at the station."

"You've got it."

Lying back after that, Francesca sighed. Not even sympathy was going to make her to get much closer to Jon Ryson. He was danger, and she didn't intend to get hurt again.

* * *

The radio station was bustling when Francesca walked in. She glanced at her watch. Eight-thirty. One hour before she went on the air.

Holly came to her. "The light in your eyes tells me the dinner went well, but you look a little bothered, too."

"I'll fill you in on all the details over lunch. We had a very good time."

Lou buzzed and asked Francesca to come in.

"We've got a grand thing going, Francesca. I love the ideas you come up with."

"Thank you. We've gotten so much interest on this."

She looked at the poster behind him, asking people in the community to nominate Minden's Woman of the Year.

His eyes twinkled. "The thing is one lady has run way out front. E-mails, letters, slender manuscripts. It's like someone started an all-consuming conflagration. Do you know Melanie Ryson?"

Francesca looked up, surprised. "I've met her. She's a workhorse for children's rights here in Minden. She's a nice woman."

Jon's mother. A winner. She was going to enjoy telling her that she was Minden's Woman of the Year.

"Now I've got some news for you. You know I've been thinking about this for a long time, and this year we're going all out. I've been talking with our sales rep and he's been able to raise a lot of money from different advertisers.

"We're going to take our winner to an island in the Caribbean called Diamond Point. Ever hear of it?"

"I've been there. It's beautiful."

"My wife and I vacation there pretty often. Not to brag, but the prime minister is a friend. We were classmates at Howard. He went on to get a doctorate at Harvard. So they'll roll out the red carpet for our winner."

"What a wonderful piece of news. Good thing I never underestimate you, Lou. It's such a pleasure working with you."

"Thanks. I know you're overloaded, but two men are coming in this morning from Diamond Point. Matt Wolpers, an aide to Tom Barton, the prime minister, and Cam Mason, a wealthy businessman and a cousin of Rush's. I'll want you to plan to have dinner with us."

Francesca drew a quick breath. She would have to cancel her dinner with Jon, and he needed someone.

"Of course," she said, "but I'm going to have to leave early. I have something ultra special that requires my attention."

"Sure. I trust your judgment. You've never let me down. My wife and Holly will take up the slack. You take off early."

Holly was elated that Melanie Ryson had won the award.

"She's such a doll. Imagine her being Lieutenant Ryson's mother."

"Yes," Francesca said, "except that they're not simpatico. His face shuts down when he speaks of his mother, and I wonder why."

"The vicissitudes of being parent and child."

"I'd guess. I'm going to have to leave that dinner with the people from Diamond Point early. You'll fill in for me?"

"You know I will. Lou's so excited. He's like a kid on his way to the circus."

Francesca sat at her desk, sorting the stack of award nominations. *What's the story with you and your mom, Jon? How did you hurt each other? Women have run out on families before, but you said she tried to come back. And that was a long time ago.*

At ten-thirty, with Holly on the air, Francesca called Melanie Ryson, identified herself and began.

"Mrs. Ryson, I'm delighted to tell you that you've been chosen our woman of the year."

The soft, sweet voice gasped with surprise.

"Give me a moment. I've got to sit down." Her breathing was swift with excitement. "Do I deserve this?"

Francesca chuckled. "Well, a lot of people think you do. You're an icon in this community. And they've documented the wonderful work you've done with our children."

"Yes, our children," Melanie Ryson said. "One of my slogans: 'Take care of our children's present and they will take care of our future.' "

"A very useful sentiment. May I come to visit you briefly this afternoon?"

"You name the time and I'll be here. You've got our address? We're located on the corner in a white clapboard building."

"Yes."

"We're on the second floor. It's Hope House."

"Yes, I know. I'd like to come around one-thirty and I won't stay long. Can you go on the air one morning this week?"

"Oh, I'd be delighted. And thank you so much."

Francesca hung up and looked at her long, tapering hands on the phone. The wide band of flesh on the finger that had once held her engagement and wedding rings was darkening now to match the surrounding skin. The rings had become a noose. She thought about the clippings heralding death. *Damn you, Trey,* she thought bitterly, *if it is you, and I believe it is. Why are you doing this to me?*

* * *

It was raining, he thought. Goddamnit, it always rained when he had something planned. He was going out with his buddy and business associate, Rush Mason. They would pick up a couple of new fillies and be out until the wee hours.

Trey Hudson grinned and his eyes narrowed. He put out his hand toward his intercom to summon Rush, but decided to wait. He glanced around at the sleek and spacious office of his automobile dealership. Not bad for ten years in business.

He could and had for some time been able to afford the good things in life. Francesca had been a fool to leave him—no, to put *him* out. He still burned when he thought about that. She was an uppity chick who needed a couple of cuffs now and then to keep her straight.

Running his hand over his coarse, close-cropped, reddish-brown hair, he got up and walked into his private bathroom. Looking in the mirror, he thought there was no doubt about it, with his smooth copper skin and gray eyes, he was a handsome man. Stacy Lambreth, his new woman, often told him how handsome he was. He liked a woman who catered to his ego. He didn't feel that Francesca ever had.

Francesca. The name was bile on his tongue. He went back into his office and stood near the fax machine. It was a private machine because he got frequent secret messages from his *other* business, the better part of his automobile dealership.

Trey rubbed his chin and felt the slight, manly stubble. He needed to shave twice daily.

It wasn't easy keeping up a pretense of civility with his ex-wife. Did she believe he felt friendly? His mind was alert these days, winnowing ways to pay her back for dumping him. He didn't take kindly to rejection. He'd gotten enough of that in his childhood as one of seven brats who seldom had enough to eat. But that wasn't nearly as bad as the constant beatings dealt out by his father and mother. Trey had been the oldest and considered himself the worst treated. His father had seemed to get angrier with each birth, finally drinking himself to death.

His thoughts were burdensome, and he steered away. Stacy Lambreth was a far cry from Francesca. He had no intention of getting married again any time soon, but when he did, it could well be to Stacy. But he saw other women. There were too many women around to settle for one.

"Money," he said to himself. "How sweet it is." And the thought slid into his mind that having money was not nearly as sweet as getting vengeance, and revenge was something he didn't intend to leave to the Lord.

He wondered what was going on in Francesca's life. Was she seeing anyone? In his own way, he loved her, more than he had ever loved anybody, but she'd never understood that he desperately needed to be in control.

He had several ways mapped out to strike back at her. He called her from time to time, even after she'd asked him not to call. He'd pleaded what was true, that he missed her. The proud tilt of her head, that smooth walnut skin and the Coke-bottle figure just wouldn't leave his mind. He was still hooked, and she damn well was going to have to let him back into her life sometime.

He couldn't remember when murder where his ex-wife was concerned had first crossed his mind. He shrugged, thinking it was very shortly after she had filed for divorce. His throat still closed with anger when he thought about it. He could hire a hit man, but that wouldn't do. This was something delicious he wanted to accomplish himself. He had warned her early that she belonged to him or to no one.

She had looked at him in that level way of hers and told him, "I won't be bullied, Trey. Not by you. Not by anyone."

But this wasn't bullying, he felt. This was *justice*.

Every day now he considered the possibilities. He was pretty sure that when the time came to carry out his final plan, his friend and associate Rush would help him.

He looked up as a short, heavy-set man with coarse black hair knocked quickly and came in.

"Speak of the devil," Trey said. "Or in this case, *think* of the devil."

"I haven't quite got my horns yet, but they're coming out soon."

Rush grinned at his buddy and sat down.

"Rush," Trey said. "How far would you go for me?"

Rush thought a moment. "Well, I've never turned you down yet. I set up the Diamond Point deal for you, didn't I? And I'm setting up the rest of the Caribbean islands for what we're into. I've gotten heavily involved in overthrowing a government. Why are you asking, buddy?"

"Just wondering. Would you go the limit?"

"Killing?" Rush asked immediately. He looked amused.

"Yeah, if it came to that."

"I'd sure as hell *consider* it. You've been good to and for me."

Trey nodded. "Not that you ever needed me with the money your family has and you have."

Rush looked suddenly pained as he drew a ragged breath. "I hate the bastards. Don't mention them to me if you can help it."

"I know the feeling. Wasn't there even one you could stand?"

Rush nodded. "An uncle who died young. You're right, Trey. My small family is rich, powerful, and *cold*. Love was in short supply in my world. I was expected to measure up and I got my kicks from disappointing them by measuring up in a different way. They were bastards to me."

"I'm sorry."

"What for? From what you've told me, your lot was even worse. You were piss poor *and* criminally treated."

"I keep thinking that when, not if, our new deal goes down, there's no one in the world we'll need. We'll be even with the world and on top of it."

Trey rubbed his hands together and felt warm all the way through.

"You ever whack anybody?" The question came from Rush.

Trey felt the hairs rise at the back of his neck. "What the hell do you need to know that for?"

"I don't need to know. Just curious. As far as I'm concerned, we're blood brothers. We've swapped blood, remember? I've got no secrets from you." He paused a moment. Actually he *did* have a few secrets from his buddy, but it had to be that way.

Trey shrugged. "I'll tell you one day, and I'll tell you something else right now. Whacking *has* crossed my mind a couple of times."

Rush stood and looked across the desk at his friend. Trey and he were the devil's own, he reflected, and they belonged together. Trey had a new woman, but he still bled for his ex-wife. That wasn't smart. Francesca Worth was a witch. She'd taken the only job he'd ever liked, his radio broadcast show, away from him, and he was going to make her pay big time.

Five

When she reached Hope House, the agency that Melanie Ryson headed, Francesca stood outside admiring the neat, white two-story building. In the ten years since she'd founded the organization, Melanie had done wonders.

It wasn't Melanie whom Francesca thought of now, but her son, Jon. She was shocked and angered to find her toes sharply tingling as she thought of him. She didn't need this intrusion in her life. She had enough troubles. She took a few steps, looking down.

"Whoa!" a rich bass voice said in front of her. "Were you going to just walk right over me?"

Francesca looked up and burst out laughing. "Dad, I never saw you." She embraced her father, Garrett Worth. "I was so busy admiring Hope House. What are you doing in this neck of the woods?"

Garrett stood looking at his beloved daughter, whom he was so proud of. "You know what a really good pancake means to me. I was tired of making my own, so I came over for some of Kenny's."

Kenny Worth, a distant cousin, ran a small pancake house two doors down from Hope House. "Turnabout is fair play," he said. "What is my good-looking daughter doing here?"

Francesca glanced at her watch. "I'm interviewing Mrs. Ryson. She's our woman of the year."

"That ought to make her happy. She's a good woman."

Francesca's eyes twinkled. "Why don't you ask her out to dinner sometime?"

Garrett shook his head. "I've got enough trouble without adding woman trouble to it. I haven't seen you in a few days. Is that ex-husband of yours giving you more grief?"

Francesca hesitated. She hadn't told her dad about the news and magazine clippings she'd been receiving. No need to worry him. He'd go to Trey, demand an answer, and Trey would lie. She shrugged.

"He's the same old Trey, but I wouldn't say he's causing me trouble. He's even pretending to be friendly."

"Just watch out for him. He's a slick one."

Francesca's glance went over her father. Grizzled and ruddy skinned, with light brown eyes, he was a tall, stoop-shouldered man who had recently retired from the post office as a mail carrier, a job he loved. Now he spent his time teaching young men carpentry, hunting and fishing.

"Don't worry, Fran," he said. "One day you'll find someone good enough for you. God knows Trey isn't fit to wipe your shoes."

Francesca patted his cheek. "Dad, you're the one who worries. I'll be over soon or you come to see me. I always love seeing you. I'm running late, so I've got to go. I'm going to call you and give you a recipe for sourdough pancakes. They'll blow your taste buds."

"You don't say! Well, I'll be waiting."

She felt sad walking away from him. It had been many years since her mother died and her father had never married again. He blamed himself for her death. He had let their health insurance lapse in order to have money to build their house and her mother had died of liver cancer. There had not been sufficient money to treat her. He had never forgiven himself.

On the second floor of the scrupulously clean building, Francesca was greeted by Melanie Ryson, whose handshake was warm and firm.

"Ms. Worth, I'm so happy to meet you again. I've seen you around, but we haven't talked much."

"I know."

"And thank you for the help you gave us in our last fund-raiser and for your very generous check."

"I'd double that if I could."

Melanie introduced Francesca to two other women in the office, a social worker and a secretary, saying of the secretary, "She's more associate than secretary. They're both my right hand."

Melanie then led her to a small, gaily decorated office with many photos of children on the walls.

"First, let me congratulate you on being our Minden's Woman of the Year."

"There are others who deserve it more."

"I don't think so. You've done wonders. At a later time, I'll show you the glowing letters we got about you."

"People are kind."

Francesca smiled. "No. You really have done wonders for the children."

A look of pure pain crossed Melanie's face as she said huskily, "Please have a seat. It's too bad I couldn't help my own son." Her voice was tinged with bitterness.

"I was terribly sorry about your son Kevin's death. I think in time the police will find out who did it. They're ruthless when it comes to cop-killing."

"Yes. Do you know my other son, Jon?"

Francesca felt her heart skip a beat and she looked

down to hide the dancing in her eyes. "I've met him recently," she said. "You raised a very nice man."

Melanie shook her head. "I'm afraid I can't claim that honor. I left my family for reasons that weren't nearly good enough. Perhaps I'm trying to make up for the hurt I've caused my loved ones by helping others less fortunate."

"That works well sometimes." Francesca put her recorder on the edge of the desk. "Please tell me about yourself. Your hopes and your dreams, your life. I'll winnow it all out later."

"My hopes and my dreams," Melanie said slowly. "Before we begin, I want to tell you again how much I enjoy your show. It's a real winner. I'm glad you're there. We listen to you daily."

"And I'm glad *you're* here."

"Thank you." Melanie drew a deep breath. "I'm ready when you are."

As the questions and answers progressed, Francesca glanced at the lovely, molasses-colored woman with the clear brown eyes and smooth, rich skin. Melanie wore her Indian-black hair parted down the middle and drawn into two long plaits. The plaits were doubled and largely encased in dark brown leather. She made a fascinating picture.

Looking at the ample bosom and the wide hips, Francesca thought about her own mother. She vowed that she would somehow bring Jon and his mother together. They needed each other. Then she told herself sharply she didn't want to get too deeply involved in Jon Ryson's life. She planned to be alone for a very long time.

"I will tell you anything you wish about myself," Melanie said, "but I can't talk about leaving my family, or Kevin's death. Both hurt too much. Of course, you'll need to mention Kevin, but not my leaving them. I'm still too ashamed of that."

Francesca looked at the woman with sympathetic eyes.

"You know we all have to forgive ourselves. Life is hardly possible without forgiveness."

"I wish you could tell Jon that. But then how can he forgive me when I can't forgive myself?"

Francesca reached over and touched the worn hand of the older woman.

"In time," she said, "good things happen, too."

"Believing in God, I have to believe in that. I couldn't go on if I didn't."

So Francesca spoke little of Kevin and of Melanie's leaving her family. They talked instead of Melanie's childhood and her maturation years. And most of all, they talked of what she wanted for Hope House.

"I see this as an oasis in a desert of near misery that sometimes exists in this small city. It's a lovely city. Make no mistake about it, but there are many, many have-nots and they need help beyond what the city can give them.

"There are actually children starving here, children being neglected and abused, beaten. We work closely with city officials, with the police department. I like to think that we've saved many an errant youth from trouble. . . ."

"You're a beacon in the storm," Francesca told her. "I can't tell you how much I admire you, how much we all admire you."

Melanie made a dour face. "Except my son," and her voice cracked a little.

"I'm sure he loves you."

"I don't doubt that, even as I love him, but I know for a fact he doesn't *like* me and I guess I deserve that."

Francesca longed to help the older woman. "I always think of what my father says! 'Prepare your-

self for tomorrow's miracles, and work hard to
bring them about.' "

"I like that. I know your father. He's a nice man."

Francesca's smile was wide. "I ran into him on the
way here. He thinks you're a good woman."

Melanie blushed. "He's been very helpful around
here from time to time. He takes some of the boys hunting and fishing. As you know, he's an excellent carpenter
and does work for us. See my beautiful bookshelves?"

"Yes, they have his touch."

The interview lasted for more than two hours, with
Melanie growing more and more relaxed. Melanie
promised she'd come to the station that week to do the
broadcast and receive the award, and to give Holly a
favorite recipe.

As they stood up, Melanie and Francesca shook
hands. Then Melanie took one of Francesca's in both
of hers, saying, "I can't tell you how much I've enjoyed
meeting you."

"The pleasure is all mine. Rest, because you have
splendid days ahead of you."

At Caleb's Inn, everything was in readiness for
WKRX's dinner party in a private dining room. Dressed
in a long-sleeved, form-fitting, navy silk jersey and long
cream-colored pearls with a diamond clip on the side,
Francesca felt happy.

"My, don't we look spiffy?" Holly said. "You came
early and got with Cal to put it all together."

"Uh-huh," Francesca answered, surveying the white
damask-covered tables with the engraved silver napkin
rings. Caleb's set a great table. There was real china and
crystal, specially requested by her. Caleb had graciously
gone out of his way to accommodate her.

"The publicity I get from you means a lot to me," he'd told her.

And she'd replied, "It's always a pleasure to work with you."

Caleb Waring was a powerfully built, charming olive-skinned man. An ex-football great, he had by hard work and sharp thinking turned his restaurant into a show-place. People came from far away to dine with him. D.C. socialites adored him. But he gave his best to Minden, too.

"How'd your interview with Mrs. Ryson go?" Holly asked when Caleb walked away.

"Really well. I've convinced Lou to pull out all the stops for her, but he surprised me. He already had that in mind. Prepare, my girl, to be without me for ten days. I'm taking Melanie Ryson to Diamond Point in the Caribbean."

Holly rolled her eyes, smoothing her smart lavender-crepe dress. "You don't have to tell me where Diamond Point is. I spent a few of the happiest days of my life there. It's beautiful."

As they talked, Lou and two superbly dressed men came up to them.

"As usual, my dear, you've set the ball rolling," Lou said, "and I'll include you in that, Holly. Let me introduce you both to Matthew Wolpers, aide to Diamond Point's prime minister, Thomas Barton, and Cameron Mason, export-import businessmen extraordinaire."

Both men's handclasps were firm and confident.

Matt Wolpers was a tall, slender, light-brown man with a neatly trimmed beard and a suave manner.

"Would you prefer island music?" Lou asked.

Matt Wolpers answered, "No, I like listening to American music. I think you refer to some of it as pop music."

On special nights, Caleb's featured an excellent small band from D.C.

"I like the American music of the eighties," Matt Wolpers offered. "I hear it too seldom because I'm so busy, but I have a large collection."

Lou looked around. "Well, there's Lieutenant Ryson right on time," Lou said, and he stood beaming, waiting for Jon to reach them.

Francesca's breath caught at Jon's presence.

Lou looked at her sharply. "Matt Wolpers wants to talk with him and thought dinner would be a good idea."

Francesca couldn't still the flutter of her heart as Jon came to her, his smile warm and wide. She looked forward to seeing him alone later.

"Hello, Lieutenant Ryson," she said softly and introduced him around. Behind his back, Holly gave her a thumbs-up sign, not caring that the others saw her.

They were seated, with shrimp cocktail appetizers on ice and dry white wine on the table, the lights turned low and the music from the small band superb.

Jon sat between Francesca and Matt Wolpers, across from Cam Mason. So, Francesca thought, Mr. Mason was Rush Mason's cousin. Rush, whom she'd replaced at the station and who acted as if he hated her. The cousin was so different. A slight, brown man with black hair and a sardonic, sophisticated smile, he was immediately attentive to a sparkling Holly.

As they began their main course, Francesca heard Matt Wolpers ask Jon, "Have you thought about my proposition? Do you think you'd like working with me at Diamond Point? It's the chance, as they say, of a lifetime."

Jon appeared grave as Francesca turned to look at him. "Yes, I have thought about it," he said, "and as you say it's the opportunity of a lifetime. But I'm afraid at the moment, my life has to be here."

Alarm in his voice, Matt Wolpers said, "I had counted on being able to persuade you. I know you haven't had enough time to think it over. As you've probably guessed, money is no object. When we talked earlier today, I thought you might be leaning toward accepting my proposal, even at this early time."

Jon thought a moment. "I wanted to give it a fair appraisal. I still do. My life is pretty much set here, but if I reconsider, I'll keep in touch with you."

Did he look around at her when he said his life was set here? Francesca wondered. *Don't set your life around me, Jon,* she thought. *I have no time, no urge for a man just now, or maybe ever.* Then she smiled to herself. *How nervy of me. We just met.* But it was strange that it seemed to her as though they had known each other a very long time.

The dinner of beef Wellington, cheese-and-sour-cream-laden russet potatoes, artichoke hearts and tiny green peas with pearl onions was delectable. A large garden salad added its own green and red zest.

They ate in near silence, savoring the food, and when Matt Wolpers would have started up again with his pitch, Jon turned to Francesca. "Would you like to dance?"

Surprised, Francesca stammered, "Yes, I would."

They rose and he guided her out onto the highly polished dance floor, and she went into his arms. She realized then that in the brief time she'd known him, she had imagined dancing with him, being with him, kissing him again.

And she cried out inside, *No! Stop this! I am in enough trouble now. Once I thought Trey was all I wanted. I will not make that mistake again.*

It seemed they came together naturally, and she was too close to him as the sensuous music flowed around them. *But I will not let it happen again,* she thought. *I will train my heart to do a better job of protecting me.*

"I'm sorry I had to have dinner here and couldn't see you tonight. Lou asked you to go with them to that jazz club?"

"Yes."

"How are you holding up?"

"Kevin's death's anniversary is always a bad scene for me."

"I'm so sorry. I want to see you soon."

He held her away from him and looked her over, smiling slightly.

"I'll be calling you. The perfume you're wearing is wonderful."

"Thank you. It's French lavender. Actually it's bath oil. It helps me to relax and rests my spirit."

"That's not the effect it's having on me."

Did he have to push so hard? She didn't comment further.

"Why are you so afraid of me?"

"I'm not afraid of you. I'm wary. There's a difference."

"No, you're afraid. Is it what you're going through with Hudson or somebody that's making you afraid? You're a woman with a lust for life. I hate seeing you so subdued. You should be flying."

"It's best that I keep my feet on the ground and soar metaphorically and spiritually only," she said evenly.

"Usually that's one of my maxims, but when *you* say it, it's a cop-out. You know what I mean. I want the best for you."

"And I thank you. It was so helpful talking with you in your office."

"But not in your home."

"Don't twist my words. You know what I mean. At my

house, things were different. You move so fast. Isn't there someone in your life?"

He didn't answer for a moment as the band swept into a waltz and he led her expertly.

"Except you? Oh, there *was* very much someone in my life. She jilted me for bigger fish."

Because she saw the pain flash across his face, she told him, "You're big enough fish for anyone."

He held her away from him, looking at her intently. "You're quite a woman, Francesca Worth. No wonder I'm so taken with you."

Touching her, he mused that she had some special quality for him. Stacy Lambreth, the woman who had jilted him, could be spiteful, mean, then just as suddenly she'd change and be warm and loving. Francesca was deep and even and wonderful.

Francesca was talking and he came back to himself. "I'm sorry you were jilted. Stacy Lambreth isn't smart. I know her."

"I'm sure she'll make herself known to you in your position."

Stacy Lambreth. She was mildly acquainted with her. Masses of light brown hair, a heart-shaped face, golden eyes and pale skin, she was something to behold.

"I know her, but not too well. She's beautiful."

He held her closer and murmured in her ear, "I thought so, too, until I met you."

His words struck her to her core, but she hid it by laughing merrily. "You shameless flatterer." Then she changed the subject. "Why does Matt Wolpers want you to come to Diamond Point?"

He expelled a harsh breath. "They want me to head up the prime minister's private security group. An attempt was made on his life recently. There's some political upheaval going on. They need someone they can trust. Wolpers and I talked a long while this afternoon."

"Would you consider going? Might you change your mind?"

"Would you care?"

"Unfair question."

Holding her closer as they danced, Jon wanted more. He wanted to see her eyes blaze with desire for him, wanted to drink in the lovely fragrance she carried. He wanted—

Jon chuckled to himself. He had little enough to chuckle about these days, and his future was going to be filled with the search for Kevin's killer.

The music ended, and they headed back to the table and Jon seated her, then sat down himself.

Matt Wolpers remarked as they sat down, "You two dance well together."

"Thank you," Francesca said, blushing. Jon looked pleased.

Holly and Cam Mason had been on the dance floor, too. Now they returned. The table was full again.

"You know the trouble we've had with a major car-theft ring on Diamond Point, don't you?" Wolpers asked Lou.

"I've heard about it," Lou answered. "Think your government can handle it?"

"The ring is growing by leaps and bounds. Everybody wants American products. The traffic in stolen cars is far greater from America than from Europe. In the past year, it has almost tripled."

Lou whistled, and Wolpers continued.

"Frankly, we're becoming overrun. Our prime minister, Dr. Thomas Barton, is furious; he hates governmental crookedness and someone in his government is in league with the stolen-car traffickers."

Lou was seated next to Jon. He mulled over the information and asked, "Might that have something to do with the attempt on Dr. Barton's life?"

Wolpers's mouth looked pinched. "I think we can bet our fortunes it has *everything* to do with it."

Dessert was served, which consisted of a rich, wild plum and black walnut bread pudding with a whipped-cream topping, laced with brandy. Their waiter lit the pudding and the ghostly blue flames outlined their faces.

"Fabulous," Francesca told the waiter. He thanked her and bowed his pleasure.

Holly and Cam Mason were deep in conversation. Francesca said a small prayer for her friend's happiness. It had been a couple of years since Holly had been interested in someone. And, Francesca thought with a bit of mirth, Cam Mason came from a wealthy family. Was he as pleasant as he seemed?

"I'll want to talk with you a couple of times before I leave," Wolpers told Jon. "May I call you?"

"Yes, of course." Jon took a card from his jacket breast pocket and wrote his home phone number on the back. Wolpers took the proffered paper and tucked it in his jacket pocket. "I appreciate this. I don't mind telling you I am deeply concerned. We have one of the most beautiful islands in the world and up until now it has been one of the most secure."

"I have a good man who could help you if I can't," Jon said.

"Then I will want to talk with you about him and with him personally."

"I can arrange that."

Jon turned to Francesca. "Would you like to dance again?"

"Oh, I'd love to," she told him, "but I've had a hard day and have an even harder one tomorrow broadcasting your mother's being named our woman of the year. Has she told you?"

"Not yet. I suppose she hasn't had time. She's a busy lady."

"She seemed pleased," Francesca said, "and we're so pleased to have her win."

There it was again, that sense of strain when he spoke of his mother. What had happened between them? Melanie had said she left her family, but didn't go into details.

Lou leaned back. "As a matter of fact," he said, "my two guests want to visit a jazz club in D.C., so I guess we'd better be going."

The waiter brought the check and Caleb came to their table.

"I trust the evening went well," Caleb said.

"Great meal, great atmosphere and the best of service," Lou told him, sipping the delicious brandy brought with the dessert. "It couldn't have been better."

Caleb thanked him. Lou always left a big tip, but this was not Caleb's main concern. The best of service was what he sought to give.

"Caleb, would it be asking too much if I wanted the recipe for the wild plum pudding?" Holly asked.

Caleb smiled. "For you," he said, "it would not be asking too much. I will fax it to you tomorrow."

Six

As Francesca drove home, she felt more relaxed than she had in days. She had had a good time. Jon Ryson had presence. He was solid and oh, so attractive. Why hadn't she met him years ago?

Inside the living room, she closed the door behind her and breathed a sigh of relief. No one had followed her. No one ever had that she knew of. It was just that after the clippings of dead women had begun coming to her, she was always on guard for the whole hateful scenario. She walked over to the security panel nook and set the dials for night security. Then she remembered that Trey knew this system like the back of his hand.

It was going to be expensive, but she was going to have the system changed.

The house seemed so still, so empty, and she had no wish to go to bed. The evening had sparked life into her. She hadn't danced in a long time with anyone who mattered.

Pausing by an end table, she picked up a large photograph of her mother. Katherine Aldama Worth had been a strikingly beautiful woman. Very dark skin, brown almond-shaped eyes, an oval face, thick black lashes and bountiful, coarse black hair were all hers in full. But it was the grace and the simple elegance of her that Francesca as a child had always found fascinating.

"I wish I could have had you with me longer," she said softly.

Setting the photo down, she turned as the phone rang.

"I just want to gossip and sign off on a wonderful evening," Holly said. "Are you in bed? If you were sleeping, I'm sorry."

"I'm not in bed. I'm not even undressed. I'm wandering around in this mausoleum. And I don't have to ask you if you enjoyed the evening."

Holly giggled. "Cam Mason is quite a guy, but he's married. You weren't doing so badly with the lieutenant."

"He's nice."

"Oh," Holly said, laughing, "I'd say you found the lieutenant more than just nice."

Francesca's face was grave. "I didn't get a chance to talk with you today, but I went by his office yesterday before I went to work. I discussed those damnable clippings with him."

Holly waited a moment. "And?"

"Nothing can be done at the moment until Trey or whoever it is shows his hand. These clippings come from all over. Trey isn't likely to do anything that will land him in jail."

"Do you think he'd hurt you?"

"Again, you mean? He knocked me unconscious, which is why I got the divorce, or one of the reasons. I think you mean, would he kill me? I don't know. Trey's got a split personality and he's got one *bad* side he's told me about. He doesn't know what's coming up in him next."

"You're lucky he didn't keep it a secret."

"He was trying to gain my sympathy by telling me."

She paused. "Then I could see a glimmer of it for my-self. Let's not talk about Trey so late at night. I'd like to get at least a few hours' sleep. For all I know he's had my phone tapped since he's been gone. Subject change, girlfriend, please."

They talked then about the stolen-car trouble on Dia-mond Point and the suave graciousness of the two men from there.

"Don't I envy your going to Diamond Point with Melanie," Holly said, feigning a pout in her voice. "That is one gorgeous place."

"I'll be sure to bring back many photos and videos."

"Not good enough. You seemed different tonight, Francesca. More like your old self for a while, but then you seemed to get sad again. And it isn't as if you don't have plenty to be sad about."

"Yes."

"I'm going to say good night. I pray for you. It makes me feel even closer to you. Good night, love."

Placing the phone in its cradle, Francesca went to her bedroom and undressed. It was so good to have good friends. Slipping into a thin, blue-nylon-tricot nightgown, she looked at herself in the mirror. She looked frightened and more than a little angry. She kept hearing small noises. Her heart thumped against her ribs a couple of times.

She snapped on the clock radio by her bed and night music from WKRX drifted in. Tom Kaye was a very good disc jockey with a huge following. Now he played a med-ley of soft love songs.

Putting out her hand to shut off the radio, Francesca decided she would leave it on. She didn't expect to sleep and she didn't want to take one of the sleeping pills her doctor had prescribed. But after a little while, she drifted off, dancing in the clouds with Lieutenant Jon Ryson.

No, she reflected in her sleep. This wasn't going to do. She had to stay down to earth and alone. But a tenderer, needier part of her took over and she danced on, unmindful of anything else.

Seven

The rest of September, then October passed without Francesca getting more newspaper and magazine clippings. She was beginning to relax, beginning to feel that the clippings were aberrations. Frankly, she thought, it seemed now more the type of thing the childish Rush Mason would do. But feeling a sense of unease creep through her, she knew that she could rule nothing out when it came to Trey. And the men were friends.

These days she thought of Jon more than ever, refusing to see him as frequently as he wanted her to, holding herself away from him, still flushed with memory of their first kiss. There had been other kisses, but they were gentler.

She let the phone ring a few times before picking it up.

"Am I interrupting something?" Jon's smooth voice was music to her ears.

"No. I'm just sitting here pondering my present and my future. Welcome back."

"Thank you. Just don't live in the past."

"No. The close-in past would be too difficult. How are you?"

"Well. I got back from Chicago this afternoon."

They had talked while he was in Chicago and he hadn't been certain when he'd return.

"I'm happy you're back. I missed you."

"That makes *me* happy. Has anything else happened? Any more hate mail?"

"Nothing. There's peace now in my life, the way it used to be years ago."

"Good. Listen, I picked up some really amazing barbecued ribs from Caleb's. Hush puppies. Baked beans. The whole works. Would you share this largesse with me tonight? I'll pick you up."

"I don't know," she began slowly.

"You won't be alone with me. I plan to invite Keith and your friend, Holly."

She felt flustered. "I wasn't going to say no, even if we were alone. I trust you."

"Good. You should. I missed you."

"I missed talking with you."

Jon tapped the side of the phone with his fingertips. She could be so evasive, but whatever she was, he wanted her.

"Pick you up in a half hour."

"I'll be waiting."

She got up and went out to the kitchen.

"I've got a dinner invitation for tonight," she told Mrs. Addison, her part-time housekeeper. "Would you just put my food in the freezer? I'm sorry. Why don't you take off?"

"Gladly—to both suggestions," the older woman said. "I can get some church work done."

Mrs. Addison hesitated a moment before she asked, "Is it that nice lieutenant who's been by to see you?"

"Yes. You like him, too?"

"Oh yes, I think he's the best."

Francesca smiled and patted Mrs. Addison's shoulder.

"He thinks you're a sweetie just as I do."

Francesca showered, and then dressed in soft yellow cashmere pajamas with a long, soft, yellow scarf of silk polka-dot print around her waist. She was pleased to note that her face didn't look so haunted, and she was gaining back a bit of the weight she'd lost in the past few months.

Jon's apartment proved a pleasant surprise. Large, multishaped rooms, two bedrooms, it was a bachelor pad to cherish. Black banana-leather sofas, a bright blue-and-white-striped chair and a big, black leather recliner adorned the living room. Soft blue vertical blinds filled the window space. The floors were polished to a high gloss, and covered with beige berber scatter rugs.

Once he and Francesca were inside, he bowed low. "Welcome to my humble home." He lifted her hand and kissed it. "You'll notice," he said, "that I didn't kiss you when I picked you up. Don't you wonder why?"

She smiled faintly. "There's nothing here anymore for loving and cherishing, Jon. I've told you that. I'm sorry."

"There's plenty left," he said staunchly. "You've got to put the past behind you and move on." He drew a deep breath. "I didn't kiss you because I was too hungry for you. I'd have gobbled you right up. Now I've had a few minutes to get used to you again. . . ."

He stopped and took her face in his hands. His mouth gently sought and held hers. She placed a hand on each side of his face and the old flames she had first felt with him enveloped her. Pulling away, she knew a moment of panic.

He let her go without protest. He could wait. She was worth waiting for.

His knocker sounded and he went to the door to let Keith Beaumont and Holly in. Holly had been off that day, so she and Francesca hugged. Then Keith and Francesca shook hands.

"Oh, this is wonderful!" Holly went over to the big bay windows and ran her hands lightly over the keys of the black baby grand piano. She sat down and tapped out "Chopsticks."

When she had finished, they all applauded.

"Nice piano," Francesca told him, smiling. "I would have complimented you on it, but . . ."

"I've kept you too busy to say much, haven't I?"

"Play the song for us that you played for me," Francesca said. "I think you said it was 'Arabesque' by Schumann."

She turned to Keith and Holly. "He played a number of songs for me at my house and I warn you, he plays a mean boogie."

Jon laughed. "After we eat. Help me with the food," he said to Francesca.

Jon's kitchen was stainless steel and pine paneled. A large tray of pork ribs, other trays of hush puppies, corn pudding with cheese topping, and baked beans lined the big yellow stove top.

"How can I best help you?" she asked.

"Look in the fridge, take out that pan of rolls, and the salad. I'm going to put this on the table with the trays. Easier all around that way."

As Francesca set about doing what he asked, she told him, "You really didn't need me. You've got everything under control."

"I beg to differ. I needed you, all right." Then he didn't say any more. He wasn't going to make her run scared if it killed him.

"What are we drinking?" she asked.

"Beer. Heineken. Lager beer. Lite beer. Choose your poison."

"I only like beer with barbecue. It just seems to belong."

"Uh-huh."

"And dessert?"

"I hadn't planned anything special. I keep a ton of first-rate ice cream in the freezer and I've got a cherry cheesecake. Or we could go to Caleb's for some of the black walnut, wild plum pudding you liked so much. Ever get the recipe?"

"Oh yes. Caleb faxed it to Holly the next day."

"Then I'll insist you make it for me sometime."

"You're a pushy soul." But she laughed merrily, liking his pushiness in spite of herself.

"How do you think the world got built?"

"I guess you're right. About dessert, I never have room left for any after I've eaten ribs. Oh, they smell so good! They're the one dish I'm greedy for."

His eyes twinkled, then narrowed. With a mock leer, he told her, "That's not what I'm greedy for."

Eating dinner, they were all in high spirits. Holly and Keith seemed to be hitting it off. Jon had loaded songs by Luther Vandross and Nancy Wilson into the CD player and the wondrous voices of first one CD, then the other soothed their ears.

Midway through the meal, Francesca looked at Jon and smiled.

"What are you thinking?" he asked.

Somberly she answered, "That I wish my life could always be as perfect as it seems right now."

Jon shook his head. "Your life isn't perfect. Right now you don't let yourself love."

"Except for that one small thing." She wasn't going to let him get her into an emotional corner. "I'll settle for what I have."

His look at her was fond, indulgent, as if he waited, knowing that she had to succumb at some point. What he didn't know, she thought now, was the depths of her terror of being hurt again.

After the ribs and the delicious side dishes, no one

wanted dessert. They lingered, chatting about WKRX, about Minden, about national issues and the world they lived in.

Holly leaned back, looking at Keith. "Why don't we clear the table and wash dishes?"

"Willing," he answered.

Getting up, Jon patted his stomach. "Food never tasted so good," he said to Francesca. "Let me finish showing you around."

He took her hand and led her to his small study, and a game room with a pool table and a large dart board. He pointed out a dissembled table tennis set. "Do you like any of the three?" he asked.

She nodded. "All three, although I'm a dunce when it comes to pool and I'm not the greatest ping-pong player.

In his bedroom with the king-size maple bed and triple dresser, he paused and looked at their reflections in the mirror.

"The two of us," he said gently. "You a study in walnut browns, me in *black* walnut, black eyes, black moustache, a man foolish with wanting."

She liked what she saw.

"Tall, dark and handsome," she told him. "Jon, I wish I'd met you first."

He took her in his arms and held her close to him, but he pressed her no further. This time it was she who came closer to him, trembling with a fear that she didn't understand.

"What is it?" he asked.

"I wish I knew."

Then the frightened spell passed, and she smiled as he looked at his big bed with its dark blue cover. She could almost read his mind. He wanted her on that bed, beneath and over him.

"Let's get out of here," he said.

Back in the living room, he sat at the piano and they listened to the merry laughter of Keith and Holly in the kitchen.

"They seem to be hitting it off quickly," Francesca said.

Jon thought a moment. "She'll have to be careful," he said. "Keith is gun shy. His divorce took him for just about everything he had, including his self-esteem. He gets so close, but never closer. I've watched him. I wouldn't want your friend to get hurt."

"Thank you for telling me. I'll warn her. You told me you'd been scorched by love. By Stacy. Why aren't you bitter?"

"I *am* bitter—about other things. As for Stacy, she always seemed to be too rich for my blood, no matter how much I loved her."

Back in the living room, they found Keith and Holly engrossed in deep conversation. Francesca took a chair near the piano. "Play for us," she told Jon.

He sat down, announced a medley of Duke Ellington tunes, and began to play. He was really good, Francesca thought. She got up and went to the piano.

"Why have you never done anything with all this talent?" she asked him.

He grinned. "I have. I entertain myself." He was silent for a moment, then paused in his playing. "My right hand was hurt when I was fifteen. Kevin and I were playing with cinder blocks. One nearly crushed my wrist."

"Oh God, I'm sorry."

"It got well enough to do most things, and I can still play, but I could never do the amount of practice that stellar playing demands."

He went into "Take the A Train," and she marveled at his skill. His music lifted her heart, making her close her eyes. With her head back, she tapped her foot to the music.

"Hey, that's *on*, buddy," Keith called out.

"Thanks."

Finishing those tunes, he went into Gershwin's *Rhapsody in Blue* and they all clapped in anticipation. He felt really good, better than he had since Kevin died. And he spelled it all *Francesca*.

When Jon had finished playing, he and Francesca played darts in the rec room. She found herself nervous and trembling. After they had practiced a couple of rounds, he turned to her.

"What about a game?"

"What do I get if I win?"

He laughed. "The question is what do *I* get if you lose?"

She liked the tender look on his face.

He stroked his face and jostled the dart in his other hand. "You have to agree first that if I win, I'll have my choice of rewards."

She chuckled. "What if you want everything I have?"

It was his turn to chuckle. "I only want you, not your possessions."

Francesca looked down, then back at him and she could not stop the blazing attraction she felt. "Okay, maybe I'm being a fool, but I mostly trust you. I agree to whatever wild stipulation you set up. What *do* you set up?"

He took her hand and squeezed it lightly. "Just this. That I see you every night for a week. If you're tired, I'll settle for fifteen minutes, but I want to see you often—badly."

Francesca laughed merrily. "You're a lover. A dyed-in-the-wool lover, Ryson. And you look so businesslike."

Her voice caught then in her throat as she told him, "You're so many things, Jon. And so far I like all of them."

Later at Caleb's, the four found it crowded. As they walked in, Francesca saw her father sitting across from Melanie Ryson. They both looked a trifle embarrassed, but it was plain that they were enjoying themselves.

Garrett stood up. "Fran," he said. "My baby girl." He kissed her. "You know Melanie."

Francesca nodded and introduced him to Jon and Keith. He acknowledged the introductions and complimented the women on how well all three looked. Jon kissed his mother's cheek perfunctorily. She patted his face.

"So you're the wonderful man Fran has talked so much about," Garrett said, grinning.

"Dad!" Francesca winced, then laughed. "You're telling tales out of school."

"I just want you to be happy, and you've been happier these past few months."

"Thanks for telling on her," Jon said. "Every little bit helps."

"Would you like to join us?" Garrett asked.

Francesca shook her head. "No point in our spoiling a good thing."

The four—Jon and Francesca, Keith and Holly—were soon seated with steaming café lattes set before them.

"The end of a perfect evening," Francesca said, sipping the fragrant thick brew. The other three agreed.

"We need to do this again," Holly said. Keith looked down as if that were a situation he was unwilling to face.

Jon looked delighted. "I'm game for us to get together any time."

* * *

At home, Jon saw her in and checked around, saying, "When are you going to change security systems?"

She shrugged. "Maybe the hassling is over," she said. "Maybe it's neither Rush nor Trey, and the clown has been arrested for something else."

He looked worried. "I wouldn't bank on that. Like you, I hope for the best, but I'm prepared to face something worse." Then he said grimly, "It only takes one time."

Francesca shuddered. He saw it and took her in his arms.

"I don't mean to frighten you unnecessarily, honey," he crooned to her. "I just want you safe. I wish you weren't allergic to dogs."

He decided not to stay long, saying, "I don't trust myself if I stay."

"I appreciate that. And I love the way you understand how I'm feeling about not wanting to go too fast."

"Okay, but the world isn't going to last forever." He sat on the arm of the sofa.

"You've got a high-profile job. You've told me about the clown you replaced at WKRX and his hatred. Your ex-husband is no prize." He got up and took her in his arms again. "If anything happened to you, I couldn't take it. I'd be a maniac. I want you to be careful."

Francesca breathed in a very deep breath before she answered him. She felt more threatened by what she was beginning to feel for him than by all the Treys and Rushes in the world.

Francesca started when the phone rang as she was undressing for bed.

"Girlfriend," Holly bubbled. "It looks like you've hit the mother lode."

"What about you?"

Holly sighed. "I'm not so lucky. It seems my wished-for man has had his heart crushed once too often. He told me upfront not to expect much from him. He's still hurting."

"You're a good nursemaid."

"I'm not sure I can convince him of that. He told me he wants no commitment with a woman for a long time. You know, how you are since Trey."

"That's different. Trey or somebody is being an absolute bastard with those clippings."

"But you haven't gotten one for more than two months."

"That's right and I've got my fingers crossed. Maybe the culprit was hit by a car or fell out of an airplane."

"Then that rules out Trey. I forgot to tell you I saw him with his latest love."

"Stacy Lambreth?"

"The same. She's a gorgeous woman to be such a witch. I've met her often and he spoke, but she turned her head."

"Count your blessings."

"I will."

"Listen, love, I'm sorry about Keith's heartbreak. Just give him a long line and pray he'll come around."

"I'm praying twenty-four hours a day, seven days a week."

"That's my girl."

"Meanwhile, *you* latch on to Jon. He's a living doll."

"I've said it a hundred times. He's a nice man, but I'm not ready for any man again."

"I understand. Now that this stalking-by-mail business has simmered down, you might feel better and warm up more to Jon."

Francesca shook her head. "It isn't a matter of warming up. If I got any hotter for the man, I'd have flames shooting out the top of my head. I've been running scared but, thank God, everything seems to be getting better."

Eight

Stacy Lambreth's long, light brown hair streamed in the wind that whipped over Trey's black Cadillac convertible. Brushing her hair out of her eyes, she looked at him and touched his thigh.

"You're awfully quiet. Once I get you inside, I'll liven you up."

He patted her hand. "I'm not coming in, babe."

"Of course, you are. We have plans. Remember? Don't you remember the new book you bought me on one thousand things for lovers to do?"

Trey laughed mirthlessly. "Too much on my mind, but give me a rain check."

Stacy pouted as he knew she would. In the few months he'd gone around with her, they'd done their share of quarreling—and making up. He felt they both liked it that way.

"What is it you have to do that's more important than you and me?" she asked petulantly.

He could never tell her in a million years. Francesca was the only other person he had told, other than the shrink who had treated him when he'd had his breakdown at nineteen. The other part of his personality that he called "Warlock" was real, and he never knew when Warlock would take over.

The shrink had said that he had atypical multiple-personality disorder. It was Warlock who stole the show. Warlock, his third and strongest personality. He came back to himself. He usually had a little while before Warlock showed his muscle.

Stacy slid over to him and hooked her arm in his.

"The car isn't driving itself, you know," Trey said.

"Sorry." She pulled away. "You know how much I want you."

"No more than I want you."

He brushed a hand across his brow. Thank God, they were nearing Stacy's apartment complex. The real, centered Trey liked women all the time. Warlock hated them. Trey crossed his fingers on the wheel. So far, he had some control of Warlock most of the time, but the devilish other was growing stronger as the shrink had said he probably would.

"Trey, are we serious about each other? Sometimes we seem to be. Then again I feel you don't even like me."

"I like you all right. I've just got a lot on my mind."

"Are we still going to Diamond Point in February?"

"That's a long ways away."

"I know, but I'm anxious to go. It's Rush's home and he's promised to show me around."

"I can show you around."

She threw her head back, letting the November late-afternoon sun stream over her arresting face. "I'm glad you're rich. I hope I'm not a gold digger, but I do like what money buys."

Stacy was a catalog model who worked in both D.C. and New York. She angled her sylphlike body to better see Trey. What was wrong with him today? she wondered.

He patted her hand again. "Anything my money buys for you, you're welcome. Just hang on. We're going to make it together."

"I'm glad. I was a bit worried. You seem so preoccupied these days."

They had pulled into the grounds of her apartment complex. He parked and didn't offer to open the door for her. She lingered.

"I said I wasn't coming in."

"I know and I'm sorry. Will I see you tomorrow? I have an evening shoot. I wish you'd come to see me strut my stuff."

"I've seen you. You're something else." He wished she'd get the hell out. He didn't know what was coming over him.

Gritting his teeth, he leaned over and opened the door.

"Out you go," he said. "I'm in a hurry."

"You seemed so relaxed when we started out."

"Well, I'm not relaxed anymore. Go, Stacy!" He smiled broadly to take the edge off his command.

She gathered her purse, tote bag and packages. They had been shopping for her.

She got out, closed the door, walked over and stood on the steps of the apartment building, watching him turn around and zoom out of the complex. She didn't think he saw her as he sped out the gate. Where was he going?

Trey wondered too, where he was going, but some part of him knew. It was dusk and he was headed to Francesca's house, the house *he* had rebuilt for her. They had had three good years together—no, two, because since she'd provoked him into striking her, their life together had been over.

His hands were tense on the wheel. He liked owning a highly successful automobile dealership. It gave him a feeling of strength. Power. But he grinned as he put the top up. This was a new car Francesca wouldn't recognize, and he didn't want her to recognize him.

Power, he thought now as he parked a half block away from the cul-de-sac in front of her house, a house he'd spent a lot of money on. A few lights were on in the house. Power. It had always been Warlock, he thought now, who held the power. Before the evil genie had come to him, he had felt weak and helpless. Warlock was a composite of his brutal father and the boys who had mercilessly teased him when he'd come to school with black eyes, bruises and ragged clothes. "Slave boy," they'd called him.

Then at ten, an ally had come into his body and his psyche to protect him from his father's blows and the boys' teasing. Slowly, and with rough assurance, he had felt Warlock's presence. Had felt it when he beat one of the school bullies to a pulp. Everyone had respected him then.

Next was his father. When he was thirteen, he had taken his last beating. He had stopped crying long before when his father beat him. One summer day, his father had come at him with a length of barbed wire and he had sucker punched him.

His father had doubled over in agony. "You—" he had gasped, cursing him.

Trey had felt powerful beyond belief. "Hit me again," he had told his father, "and I swear I'll kill you."

His father had never hit him again and had died when Trey was eighteen. He was shocked to find he missed his father, but by then Warlock had been father, friend, warrior, protector.

Warlock had a mind of his own. He liked wringing chickens' necks, torturing and killing small animals. They lived in the country and he loved hearing the animals scream as they were slaughtered.

It had been Warlock who helped him see that power and killing were intertwined. Killing was not just power, it was *magic*. Pure golden magic. How much did

Francesca know about him? That day more than a year ago when he'd left his safe open and rushed out, what had she seen?

Of course, he'd questioned her adroitly and she said she hadn't been back upstairs. She wasn't a devious person, so maybe she had seen nothing. Still—

Was he going to have to work his magic on her? She was the only other person who could have known. He'd certainly never told Rush, and he told Rush almost everything.

As a long beam of light from an automobile shone a block away, he slid down in his seat, picked up his leather cap from the dashboard and put it low on his forehead.

The car passed him slowly and pulled into the driveway of Francesca's house.

Francesca and Jon sat in companionable silence before she turned to him. "Not many cars come this way," she said.

"Do you want me to go back and check him out? If it is a him."

"No. I can't keep jumping at every noise. Nothing's happened for quite a while. Maybe the siege is over. Like I said—"

Jon chuckled. "Maybe he took a trip on a plane and fell out, like you said. You're relaxing somewhat."

"It's about time."

They sat in the car in the driveway a little while longer.

"Have you got a busy day tomorrow?" he asked.

"Definitely. As a matter of fact, I'm taping Melanie again. She wants to talk about the new plans they've got for school dropouts. Advertise it."

"Melanie's always got something going."

"Something absolutely worthwhile."

"Yeah. I got a call from Wolpers today."

"Diamond Point's prime minister's aide."

"Yeah. They're really sweetening the pot. Listen, I think I'll go over with you and Melanie when your station sends you both in February. They'll wait for me."

"Then you're really considering going?" She felt her stomach go hollow with alarm.

"Sort of. What do you think? I'll see you through what you're going through. And maybe it's over."

"I certainly hope it is. Jon—"

"Don't tell me again that I'm a nice man. I couldn't take it. I want to be your roughneck, raunchy lover in spades."

She sighed. "I wish things were different."

"So do I. Let's get out," he said, "and go in. I want to take you in my arms and press the length of my body against yours. I want to feel those glorious curves and kiss you until your knees turn to jelly and you're half fainting."

His hand cupped her chin.

"I want to make love to you, Fran. I'm not going to force myself on you, but if there is anything I can do to get you to let me in, I'll do it. I warn you, when I want something, I don't always play fair."

Francesca pulled away from his hand and smiled. "Okay, you're *not* a nice man, but dear God, you're a wonderful man."

She turned on the interior car light to get a box of aspirin she had left in the dashboard cubbyhole.

What the hell were they sitting in the car so long for? Trey grumbled. He turned on the ignition and with his lights off, backed into a driveway a block away and turned around.

So she was seeing Ryson, was she? This was going to prove to be a damned dangerous game for her to play.

Rush Mason strolled slowly from his office down the hall from Trey's office to the water cooler. Looking around, he liked what he saw. Trey's automobile dealership, which Rush's inheritance had enabled him to expand, left him pretty much where he wanted to be for the moment. His future was another matter.

Plate-glass windows caught the sunlight and reflected it back. Rush took out a cigarette, lit it from a small gold lighter in his jacket pocket, and took a few drags.

He drank water from the fountain, then took a paper cup and filled it. He lifted the cup in the air. "Here's to me, to Trey and everything we're going to have."

This time of the afternoon, things were beginning to cool down. It was a Friday, and it had been hectic. He wasn't Trey's partner yet, not in business, but he was his buddy, his *brother*, emotionally speaking. Was there anything the two men wouldn't do for each other? Rush didn't think so.

His pale brown face reddening, he thought about his family on Diamond Point in the Caribbean. The old patriarch, Arthur Mason, had left them all rich from his large coffee plantation and his investments. They were all so upstanding. His father, Boris, had threatened to disown Rush because he'd been so wild.

When Rush was an older child, he'd stopped wanting his parents' love. They were both successful, cold, proud people who were socially busy and had no time for the boy. No, they'd never hit him, not even once, but he and Trey often argued now about what hurt the most, emotional or physical blows. His parents had simply ignored his existence most of the time.

His parents' love had been focused on their only

other child—Laura, his sister—a lovely girl two years his junior. Rush was an attractive youth, but felt he didn't match his sister's beauty. His heart would squeeze dry as he watched the love flow between his parents and his sister. Then he'd overheard his parents quarreling when he was eleven.

"I think I've done damned well," his father had said. "Not many men would have taken the boy in when he's not my son. My best friend was his father, if you haven't forgotten. That hurt."

"I would have forgiven you," his mother had cried. "Why can't you forgive me?"

His father had been silent a moment. "Men are different, Kay. You *loved* Bert. You married me for my name."

His father had come out of the room, his face flaming as the boy tried to blend into the wall. He had caught Rush by the scruff of his neck and turned him around.

"How much did you hear?" he demanded.

"Some," the boy had answered.

"Then you know why the sight of you sets me off?"

"I'm—I'm sorry," Rush had stammered.

His father had clapped him on the back. "Don't be. It's hardly your fault, but you're a reminder I hate being reminded of."

His father had never alluded to that time again. Instead, he had grown more distant as he lavished even more love on Laura.

Laura was destined to be a stunning debutante when her turn came, and Rush bore it stoically with his heart breaking. At thirteen, he had made few friends for himself; he was mostly a loner. But the friends he made were wild, leading a contraband life. Stealing. Plundering. Pillaging. When he was seventeen, his father had let him go to jail for vandalism—defacing a church front—just to teach him a lesson.

"Make an example of him," his father had told the police. "By God, I won't have him destroying my family's name."

And while he had languished in jail, cuffed around by older prisoners while the jailer looked the other way, his sister had been introduced to Diamond Point society.

Rush didn't change, but went his willful way. When he was eighteen, his father had offered him a very large sum of money to go away, since he didn't want to attend college. Rush had jumped at the chance.

He had made the best of his time in the United States and Canada for ten years. He had changed his mind and had gone to good colleges, finally earning a degree in business administration at Columbia, and another in communications at Howard University. His manner smoothed out and he made a better class of friends, but they all were basically hurt and angry.

Then he had come to Minden, Maryland, and fallen in love with the town when he won a spot on WKRX's morning show.

At twenty-one, he'd come into his inheritance from his grandfather. A year later, his father had died and surprisingly had left him another tidy sum of money.

Largely an isolate socially, he'd run a good show and had a large following. Rhythm and blues. Rap. Some rock. Some gangsta rap. His time at WKRX had been a high point of his life. Here, cocaine was his friend, and the music he played, the fans who adored him put him on top of a world that had rejected him. He was still putting it together when Lou Seaman, the manager, wanted to change the station's format to a more conservative tone.

Francesca Worth had begun working there two years before that. Her show was mostly for homemakers and in the afternoon hours, but she caught on quickly and gained a large fan base. She was so damned much like

Laura, he'd thought from the beginning. Proud. Straightforward. He was losing everything again. Lou called him in early one morning and told him he was thinking about replacing Rush's morning show with a revised version of Francesca's.

Lou had gone on to say somberly, "I'm aware of your cocaine habit, Rush, and your drinking. Frankly, I think you'd be happier elsewhere. You've done well enough here for someone else to take a chance on you."

Rage filled him then the way it had exploded in him when he was a child.

Once again, he felt the impulse to kill, but who? Lou? Francesca Worth?

As his mind had sped along, Rush had taken a stance in front of the open door of his office looking out the plate-glass windows at the brilliant sunshine. Now he began remembering again. Lou had seen his rage when he fired him and had not flinched. As he had gone out the door, Francesca had come down the hall, bubbling with warmth and energy.

He had never liked her, but he had tried to be civil. "Well," he greeted her with a twisted grin, "I guess sleeping with the boss pays off after all."

Francesca stopped in her tracks, and it was all he could do to keep from throttling her. The morning's cocaine hit was wearing off. He glared at her.

"What on earth are you talking about?"

"Go to it," he snarled. "Sometimes I wish I had a skirt I could pull up."

"You're mad," she said. "Don't speak to me like that."

He got a little closer. She stood her ground. "What's wrong, Rush?" she asked gently.

The blood left him then and he was afraid of what he might do. "As if you didn't know."

Lou came out into the hall. "Trouble?" he asked.

"I'm not sure," Francesca answered.

Lou placed a fatherly hand on Rush's arm. "Go home, Mason," he said. "Get some rest and some sleep. You've got two weeks here. Come back in and talk to me again if you wish, but don't abuse Francesca. I won't have it."

Rush fled then, icy with rage. Even his eyeballs were cold. Another father had driven him out. Another father had loved Laura but not him.

Trey had rescued him. The drugs hadn't depleted his fortune, because he'd sold more drugs.

He couldn't look for another spot at a radio station. The rage inside him wouldn't let him parlay easy banter into another success. He began to formulate a plan that was about getting even.

Six months after Lou had let him go, he had become close friends with Trey, who needed money to expand his business. Now it was Trey and him. Trey was a few years older than he was, not really old enough to be his father, but a father figure all the same. Trey always knew where he was going. Trey told him nearly everything. He had long wanted to talk with Trey about wanting to kill Francesca. Trey was plenty mad at her for putting him out. For divorcing him. Would he be willing to be a party to snuffing out her life?

Nine

The week was over. Monday morning, coming awake, Francesca yawned and stretched slowly. She kept her bedroom warm for sleeping, with a small breeze coming in through the partly open window.

She had seen Jon every night in the past week, as penalty to having lost another dart game at his house. He wanted what he'd wanted the first time she'd lost. She smiled now, thinking about their week. They had gone dining and dancing at Caleb's. He had taken her to D.C. to Planet Hollywood and to Baltimore to the Baltimore Aquarium's fantastic restaurant. He had insisted on paying for everything.

They had played more darts at his house, alone, and the last time she'd won. His penalty had been that he'd go slow and understand that she was battle weary emotionally from her relationship with Trey.

Under the warm, beige, down comforter, she felt happier than she had felt in ages. Jon had gravely told her, "I won't push you more than I can help. I want to make you know that no pain lasts forever."

Then he'd looked thoughtful. "Except I'm a fine one to talk. Kevin's death leaves an emptiness in me that I can't seem to fill. I guess the truth is that I should take some time off. The chief keeps pushing me to do that."

"I'm sorry about Kevin," she had told him again as

she had so many times. They had been sitting on the sofa in his apartment. He'd nuzzled his face in the hollow of her throat and held her close while she had stroked the back of his head and his long, rippling-muscle back. Then she'd pulled away.

He'd pulled her back to him. "You're good for me," he'd said, "and I think I'm good for you."

She couldn't deny that what he said was true, but it would be a long time, she thought, before she would be involved in a relationship with a lover.

That resolved, she threw back the covers and sat with her legs over the edge of the bed. She stroked first one, then the other arm as Jon so often stroked them. "Walnut and black walnut," he said from time to time, musing over their skin colors. "Aren't we a great pair?

"But we could be any colors under the sun and it would be the same. I'm going to prove to you that even *nature* meant for us to be together."

"I won the dart game last time," she'd challenged him, "and remember you promised to go slow."

"With you," he'd come back, a hundred miles an hour would seem slow compared to the speed I'd like."

When the phone rang, she picked it up and didn't answer for a moment or so.

"Hello." Jon's rich baritone came singing along the line. "Cat got your tongue?"

She laughed. "I'm practicing being psychic. I concentrated and thought it was you."

"Are you up and about?"

"I'm just getting up. I slept like a baby."

"Good. I tossed a bit thinking about you. If you're just getting up, does that mean you're the way babies so often are—bare?"

"Oh, you. No, it doesn't. I've got on a rose tricot, long-sleeved nightgown. It's pretty though."

"No long-sleeved nightgown is pretty. When we're *married,* I'm going to outlaw them as contraband."

Francesca held her breath. What was he saying? "We're not going to be married, Jon," she said levelly. "Please be realistic. I've taken you into my confidence. You know how I've been savaged by my past marriage. You said you understood."

"Hey!" Jon said. "I'm sorry." But he wasn't sorry. She was what he wanted most of his life, and he wasn't giving up on her. He thought now he would stop pushing, but he'd made that vow a hundred times in the months he'd known her.

"Am I forgiven?"

"Yes. Our week is up. It was wonderful. I'll play you a game of darts anytime."

"Even if I win?"

"Even if you win. Would you like some news about your ex?"

"Only if it's bad enough."

Jon laughed. "I'm not talking out of school. He's deep into, or heads—I'm convinced that he heads—a stolen-car ring that's sending cars into the Caribbean and collecting big time on them."

"Trey's always had big dreams, but his auto dealership has always done well. Why would he need to get illegally involved?"

Jon sighed. "Sometimes, honey, it's just for the hell of it. The thrill. The danger. Then a successful car-theft ring would net him a whole lot more than a legal dealership. In his case, he's got them both. Greed happens."

"You're right. Trey likes to be on the bleeding side of the cutting edge."

The grandfather clock chimed seven o'clock and

Francesca started. "I've got to be into work early," she said. "I'm planning a Christmas pageant with your mother."

"Well, good luck. I'll talk with you later, Fran."

Before she could get up, the phone rang again. It was her father.

"You've been a busy woman."

"I have a feeling you know all about my being out with Jon Ryson every night this week."

"Now how would I know if my daughter is too busy to confide in me?"

"We've both—you and I—always just known about each other. You've been a great father to me and I want you to know it."

"And you've been an even greater daughter. I took your advice and I've been stepping out a bit myself."

"With Melanie?"

"Who else? She's good company. I haven't laughed so much in ages. She likes my fried chicken and potato salad."

"She's got good taste. Are you getting serious?"

"Not this soon. But then we don't have forever the way you youngsters do. Oh, what the hell. Melanie told me she'll never marry again and it's something she doesn't even want to talk about."

"She's operating on a guilty conscience."

"Then you know what's going on with her."

"A little. Dad, let me talk with you later. I've really got work coming out of my ears for today."

Hanging up, she stood, held her arms high above her head and stretched. She was happy for her father. He deserved a good woman's love.

She would only be able to meditate for fifteen minutes, and she'd eat a health bar covered with rich dark chocolate. Then, too, Holly always had something good cooking at WKRX.

* * *

A brisk shower and rubdown with a thirsty, terry bath towel brought her further awake. Looking in the big, full-length bathroom mirror, she liked her reflection. She was healthy and robust and her skin was as sleek as a seal's. She grinned—a *walnut*-colored seal.

Going to her closet, she chose a taupe faille coatdress, gold herringbone jewelry and brown lizard slingbacks. She pursed her lips and half closed her eyes as she slipped into the deliciously lacy taupe underwear she loved.

Okay, don't, you haven't got the time, she told herself, thinking of the fact that she liked to fantasize about Jon holding her close and taking off those same deliciously lacy pieces. She blushed and sharp thrills ran the length of her body.

By seven-thirty, when everything was done and she was fully dressed, she got her coat from the hall closet and set the alarm panel for daylight. Pausing in the hallway, she thought about how her house had taken on Jon's persona. Good. After Trey, the house needed somebody nice to come into its bosom.

Opening the heavy oak door, she paused as a gold-foil-covered box that had been propped against the door plopped over onto the floor. A box with Rhea Smith's *Floral Shoppe* emblem on it. From Jon? It could be from Wolpers and Cam Mason, the visitors from Diamond Point. They had sent Holly and her flowers because they wanted to keep in touch for the trip Francesca would take in February honoring Jon's mother as Minden's Woman of the Year.

Smiling to herself, she thought about her efforts to sharpen her psychic powers. The box probably held chocolates as well as flowers. Rhea had designed a box that was widely used in Minden by men to please the women they cared about.

She put her purse and tote bag on the marble table near the door, lifted the box and walked back to the kitchen. She didn't really have the time, she thought, but perhaps she'd take the flowers to the radio station with her.

The box was heavy, maybe it was the two-pound size of specially made chocolates Rhea was noted for. Putting the box on the table, she slipped the ribbons off and lifted the top. A scream froze in her throat and the room spun crazily as she fought to breathe. Dear God!

With her hand over her mouth, she ran to the bathroom and gave up the health bar and orange juice she had just consumed. Then she knelt against the doorjamb, praying not to faint.

She told herself she had to go back and look at the monstrosity in that florist's box. Who on earth would be twisted enough to degrade a box meant to hold loving offerings by putting in the burden it held?

When she had first seen what lay inside, she had quickly put the top back on.

Call Jon? No, she would handle this; *then* she'd call him. Now, gingerly lifting the box cover, she was face-to-face not with flowers and chocolates but with a large, dead wild rabbit.

She could not stop herself from touching the dead animal. She loved pets and wildlife. The flesh was still warm. In a daze, she stroked the pelt.

"Oh dear God," she whispered. "What is the meaning of this?"

Thoughts and memories swarmed her brain. The clippings of the dead women, the last one so closely resembling her. Then the clippings had stopped coming and everything had quieted down—or so she had thought.

She had been a fool. Happy—or happier—than she had been with Jon, she had forgotten the malevolence of the only two men she knew who would have done this: Trey or Rush.

Half whimpering, she put the back of her hand to her mouth and looked around, forcing courage she really didn't own at that moment. She felt an evil presence in the room as if someone else were actually there.

The storm door was not wired for security, just the heavy oak door, but no matter. *Had* Trey found some way to circumvent the expensive security this house offered? The system he had had put in. Someone had put that florist's box between the storm door and the oak door. Who?

But more than anything, it was the warmth of the animal's body that frightened her. It had only recently been killed. There was no note.

"You son of a bitch," she cried aloud. "I'm not going to let you scare me to death like this! Back off, Trey. Back *off!*"

Then she thought, what if it was Rush? It came to her that the two men worked together. They were close. Most likely, it was *both* men.

Slowly she walked to the sink and ran water into a glass that she had used a little while before. That glass of water seemed to symbolize the before and after of her life this morning. She had come awake a happy woman. Now she felt as if the gates of hell were yawning before her.

Sitting on the phone bench, she called Jon. He had said he was going in early. Keith Beaumont picked up Jon's line.

"Beaumont here. How may I help you?"

With her throat so dry she could barely talk, she asked for Jon.

"How are you, Francesca? Gee, I'm sorry, but Jon had

to stop by a school this morning. He should be back in an hour. Are you all right?"

"No. I'll call him on his wireless." Her voice sounded weak.

"Francesca, can I help?"

"Thank you for asking, Keith. I'm not sure anyone can help me right now."

"Good lord? What's wrong? Can you tell me anything?"

"Only that something ugly has happened. No one's been hurt or badly injured—*yet*, but—" The words choked her.

"You call Jon and I'll call him," he said grimly. "You hang on and I'll get help for you. Are you able to call Jon on his wireless?"

"Yes," she whispered. "I'm not hurt. Not physically anyway."

Putting the phone in its cradle, she stood up on shaky legs and went back to the table where the dead rabbit lay in its ludicrous gold-foil-covered, white-plastic-lined coffin.

She sat at the table. Licking her dry lips, she couldn't take her eyes off the carcass. Would she die like this, temporarily entombed in the equivalent of a fancy florist's box?

Sharply, she reminded herself that she couldn't just stop functioning. She had to call the station. She got Holly and told her what had happened.

"Oh, sweetheart," Holly said. "Oh, good Lord. I'll tell Lou and I'll get someone to cover for me. I'm coming over."

"No!" Francesca told her. "I wasn't injured. This is just a terrible shock. We're a radio station. You know entertainment. The show must go on. I'm calling Jon. He'll be here very soon."

But *would* he be there soon? Why hadn't she yet called

him on his wireless? She thought she knew the reason for that. She wanted to pull herself together. Jon was going to be furious. And she hated the thought of getting him involved in this danger.

She was breathing a little more easily or she was numbed—she wasn't sure which—when Jon's voice came on his wireless phone.

"Hello." There was no threat in that voice, and she clung to him.

"Jon," she said softly, and her voice refused to function again.

"Yes, love." He had begun to use that term with her from time to time.

"Something has happened." She was sliding away from the reality that lay before her.

His voice was warmly probing. "What is it, Fran?"

Somehow she managed to tell him what had happened and before she could finish, he told her, "You hang on. I'll be there as quick as speed can take me. Where are you calling from? I mean what room?'

"I'm in the kitchen."

"Looking at the poor critter, I'll bet. Go to another room, Fran. You're going to get further shell-shocked if you keep looking at the carcass. Will you do that? I'll be there right away."

"Yes, I'll do that." She could not help but plead, "Please hurry."

As she hung up the phone, she kept her hand on the warm receiver as if that gave her a link to Jon. At first, she could not do as he asked and move away from the table. It was as if the still-warm, lifeless body held a key to her future. As if its fate mirrored her own.

Ten

Time seemed to drag as Francesca made herself leave the table and wait in her living room. She hovered near the door and quickly answered when Jon rang the chimes. Once inside, he took her in his arms and held her close.

"Baby, tell me just what happened."

Breathlessly, she told him again, only then realizing that she still had on her coat. Gently, he helped her take it off and put it onto the sofa.

They went into the kitchen then and for a long time Jon looked at the dead rabbit. He felt a chill of fear sweep over him, because he knew very well that all too often dead humans followed the killing of an animal.

"Son of a bitch," he said softly, his brow furrowing. He touched the animal. "Rigor mortis hasn't set in yet."

"I think they killed it just before putting it in the door."

He followed his train of thought. "You were leaving earlier than usual. The blood's been washed off, but now there is some blood on the plastic bottom. Did you hear anything?"

"No. Nothing. My mind was on getting in to work early and beginning to tape the Christmas pageant songs." For a moment, she flushed. Her mind had also been very much on Jon.

He carried an investigator's kit. Now he took out a pair of thin plastic gloves and slipped them on. Then he pulled his wireless phone from his coat pocket and dialed a number. Dimly, Francesca heard him ask for someone to come to do fingerprints and transport the rabbit to the medical examiner at the city morgue.

"Did you have a chance to get something to eat?" he asked. "I don't want you to faint."

"I had orange juice. A dried-fruit bar. What about you?"

"I was up very early. I did a full breakfast. I know you're in a state of shock, but it might help you to talk to me."

She didn't tell him she had lost her breakfast.

"I feel better since you're here."

"I'm glad to hear you say that. You're so damned independent. It helps to have someone around at times like this. Fran, you would have called me if you had gotten another letter?"

"Yes, of course. I haven't gotten another one. This is far worse."

"Yes. I notice the florist box is from Rhea Smith's. I'll be questioning her about orders she's sent out lately."

The numbness Francesca felt wasn't letting up. She took deep drags of breath, then went to the kitchen door and opened it, letting the cold air come in.

"What is it?" he asked.

"I'm beginning to panic. When Trey and I got into bad trouble, I started having panic attacks. My therapist told me that one of the best ways to handle it was to take deep breaths of fresh air."

"Good advice." He came to her and held her again, massaging her back.

"You won't feel better for a while. Just keep trying to relax. It'll come."

He went up the hallway to answer her door chimes. In a moment, the fingerprint technician who worked with Jon came in with another man in a police uniform. A small, earnest man, the technician smiled and shook hands with Francesca.

"Ma'am, I'm sorry you had to have something like this happen," he said.

"Yeah," the policeman, a beefy, brown-haired man, said. "The world's getting crazier by the day."

The technician dusted the box for fingerprints, then went to the front door and dusted the door, the knobs, and the sill.

All the while, Jon had been jotting notes on a pad he had taken from his inner coat pocket.

After a short while, the technician and the policeman left, taking the florist box with the dead rabbit inside with them.

Jon turned to Francesca. "You've got sleeping tablets. I want to be sure you sleep tonight."

"Yes, of course."

"Take an aspirin now, and I want you to rest awhile. I'm going to stay with you. I'll call the chief."

He got a glass from the cabinet and filled it with water. Setting in on the counter, he took a small cellophane package from his coat pocket, opened it and handed her two aspirin.

"I have to go in," she said. "I'm feeling better. A couple of cups of strong coffee will see me through. Remember, we're beginning to tape the Christmas songs."

"You've already called the station?"

"I did. I said I'd be in later."

He came to her, took her hand in his and kissed the palm. He hurt for her.

"I keep wondering if this is the beginning of an acceleration of this whole monstrosity," she said, her voice ragged. "I haven't been afraid. Not a whole lot. I don't frighten easily, but I'm scared now."

Jon tipped up her chin and looked deeply into her eyes. "You're restless. You keep moving around. You're in psychic pain. I'm going to move in a few of my things and stay with you for at least a few nights."

She looked at him quickly. "I'll be all right. You don't need to do that. Holly will be glad to stay, if I feel I need somebody."

Still looking at her intently, he touched the side of her face. "Holly's not me. I care about you, Fran, a whole lot. know you don't want all I have to offer right now. . . ."

"I appreciate everything you try to do, and I'm sorry I can't respond." But she *was* responding, she thought, flustered.

"Where there's life, there's always hope. You know Jordan and Raine Clymer. He's one of the best security people around. I trained with them a while back, so I'm pretty savvy about this kind of thing."

She nodded dully. "I've worked with Raine on several community projects. They're good people."

"They are. You're going to have to go to the police station with me to give a statement."

She saw him through a haze of angry tears. The numbness was wearing off. "Does this kind of thing happen often to other people?"

"Sometimes it does and . . ."

"And worse?"

"And worse. But I won't let anything happen to you, and I'm plenty experienced in keeping people safe."

"I'm glad you're around. I can't begin to tell you what this is doing to me. I've always been so strong."

"You are strong. I think you'll prove to be one of the strongest women I've known, but everyone needs support from time to time. And you're still hurting from your hellish divorce."

She stepped away from him and folded her arms over her chest, then rubbed the sleeves of the faille material of her dress.

"I'm so edgy," she said plaintively. "I've kept looking for another clipping to come in the mail, but I *have* been relaxing more. . . ."

"You and I both had hoped all this was over."

"But we were wrong, weren't we? Oh, Jon, is this the beginning of a more dangerous phase? Children who torture animals often go on to torture and kill people." She sat down slowly.

"Don't focus on that, although God knows it's true."

"I haven't told my father about this. I didn't want him to worry."

"It's always better to let other people know what's going on. You're usually safer that way."

"I'll tell him today. He's going to worry."

"And be mad the way I am. He needs to know."

Standing, Francesca rocked a bit. She felt so close to Jon, yet she didn't want a too-close relationship with any man just now. Broken hearts took time to mend and Trey had shattered hers.

"Jon?"

"Yes, love?"

"People are going to talk if you move in. Gossip."

"Let them. We're people, too, you and I. Even if I'd just met you, which I didn't, I'd want to move in, protect you, take care of you."

"I could move in with Dad."

"Not a good idea. You tell me he suffers with arthritis and doesn't always get around well. You need someone strong."

Against her will, her mind added: *I need* you. But she fought the feeling. She was never again going to bare her heart to anyone. Jon didn't say it because he didn't want to frighten her, but he thought it all the same. He was coming to love her and he would kill or die to keep her safe.

Later that morning, Jon drove along Minden's downtown Maine Avenue. He was on his way to Rhea Smith's florist shop. He felt she might be able to give him some answers.

He had taken Francesca to work and told her he would pick her up; she was in no condition to drive. She had protested, "Of course, I thank you, but I'm not as shaky as you think I am. I can take it, Jon."

"Can you? Someone is furiously rattling your cage, if not worse. I intend to help you take it. I meant what I said about staking out a spare room in your house for at least a little while."

To his surprise she had not demurred this time, only nodded and said, "Okay." She had given him the keys and told him how to change the security system once he was in.

There were several parking spaces in front of Rhea Smith's Florist Shoppe. Jon parked and got out. Rhea greeted him at the door.

A middle-aged woman with twinkling eyes and a merry smile, Rhea was a gregarious widow who knew and seemed to like almost everyone. Her shop was homey, tasteful.

"Good morning, Lieutenant Ryson!"

"Good morning, Mrs. Smith."

"I've got some beautiful orchid plants from South America. Today's dark red roses are gorgeous."

"I think I want something special, but I'd appreciate it if you'd answer a few questions for me first."

"I'll be pleased to help you in any way I can."

She asked one of the women in the shop to take over and led Jon back to her small office. Closing the door, Rhea extended a hand inviting Jon to be seated in side-by-side chairs.

He wasted no time. "I need to know if . . ." He broke off for a moment. "You know Trey Hudson, the automobile dealer?"

"Yes. From time to time he has been one of my best customers. Since he and his wife divorced, he doesn't come around so much anymore. I haven't seen him in months. He ordered flowers and candy then. They went to Stacey. You'll want a customer list."

Jon stroked his chin. "Yes and thank you. I'll stop back this afternoon."

Rhea nodded. "You're free to stop back by," she said, "but I can pull it up for you in a jiffy."

"I'd appreciate it."

After a few minutes she found a brief list and printed it out. Then she looked it over, startled.

"It seems he ordered three large boxes of flowers with the detachable candy box. One went to Stacy's address and two to his." She handed the list to Jon.

"You know, Lieutenant, I was out a couple of days getting some badly needed rest and my husband, Carl, took over. He mentioned that Trey had been in, but not the size of the order."

Jon smiled grimly. "This may be *very* helpful."

"Do you want to talk to my husband?"

Jon shook his head. "Not at the moment, perhaps later. I'm grateful for your help."

He sat musing. One box for Stacy and two for Trey. Was the extra box for the rabbit?

"Could I pour you some coffee? Tea? Chocolate? They're all right there on the sideboard."

"Thank you. I'll take coffee—cream and sugar."

"I have skim milk paste if you're watching your waistline like most of us are these days."

"Thanks. I'd like that."

Jon's eyes fell on a long, gold-foil-covered box that Rhea had designed to hold both flowers and the fancy chocolates she made. It was just like the box from the morning.

As she handed him the mug of coffee, he realized he had expected her to say that Trey had bought flowers recently. Dead end.

"So, once Hudson was a very good customer. What did he usually order?"

Rhea laughed. "Never red roses. He ordered birds of paradise and sometimes expensive orchids. Trey is something of a character and he has a volatile temper. He often said he thought love was for fools. Simple attraction was all he needed. I think he loved his wife. After they broke up, he always seemed sad to me. He also told me that a woman for him was for keeps, that when a woman belonged to him, she was his for life."

"Oh?" He and Francesca had often talked about Trey. She hadn't mentioned this.

Rhea continued. "He's an odd man. He talked to me a lot, and he didn't like being interrupted. He told me that a man could and should find at least one woman he could *control*. I kind of laughed up my sleeve because I know Francesca Worth well enough to know he was never going to control her."

Jon smiled inwardly. He finished drinking his coffee, got up and set the mug on the golden oak sideboard. "Thanks so much for your help."

"You've only asked me a couple of questions. Sorry I couldn't be of more help."

"What you've told me has been very helpful. I want to compliment you on designing that beautiful box for flowers and candy and I want to pick up a sheaf of red roses this afternoon around three. I'd like two pounds of your best chocolates, but don't put them in your beautiful box. I have my reasons."

"Of course. Many people don't want the fancy wrappings. I can give you a plain white glossy box for the chocolates. Oh, and, Lieutenant?"

"Yes, ma'am?"

"I'll tell you who *has* been in." She hesitated. "I need good customers and I don't like telling tales out of school, but I trust you and I don't think you'd ask if you didn't need to know. Do you know a man named Rush Mason? I think he's second in command at Hudson's car dealership."

"I know him."

"Well, he's been by recently. He always insists I wait on him. Says he deals only with top people. He's been coming in since he had a show at WKRX. He sends flowers to several women. He said he greatly admires my boxes and last week he asked for an empty box, which I gave him."

"Thank you. That's useful information. You've been a big help."

"You're welcome. Mr. Hudson has a new woman in his life who seems special, but he doesn't send her flowers, at least not from me. He brought her in once to look around. He told me in her hearing that she preferred jewelry and stocks and bonds to flowers.

" 'My expensive doll,' he said. 'And I do mean expensive. But the emphasis is on *my*. I'll pay any amount of money to keep that true.' "

Rhea's caramel-colored face then reddened, and she began to stammer, "Oh, good Lord, Lieutenant, I'd forgotten that you and his new girlfriend were once an item."

"You keep up with what's going on. Don't worry about it. Not everything was meant to last."

"She had the best possible in you."

"Thank you," he responded, reflecting that one day soon he hoped to have the best in Francesca.

Eleven

Francesca, Lou and Rush Mason sat at a conference table at WKRX.

"Sorry I couldn't see you in my office, Rush," Lou said. "My newsman is using it to sort some items. As you've probably noticed, we're humming this morning."

"I noticed," Rush said. "What's the occasion?"

"Well, one of the occasions is our Woman of the Year Award," Francesca answered. "Tomorrow we'll talk with our honoree about her coming trip to Diamond Point. Audiences in Minden seem really interested. Then, we're pushing the Burbridge group."

Rush was silent, seeming as comfortable as if he were with two friends.

"What brings you by?" Lou asked.

Rush cleared his throat and for a second, his eyes on Francesca were hostile. Francesca thought: *Did you do this awful thing to me this morning? Did you take an innocent animal, kill it and put it at my door?* She didn't want to look at Rush.

Rush looked from Francesca to Lou. "I want you to know I have no hard feelings toward either one of you, although it was pretty cold the way you let me go."

"That was awhile back," Lou said gravely. "Look, Mason, you're a talented guy and you had a good program. I just wanted the station to move in a different direction.

As part owner, I had that choice. There're other stations."

"I know that, but I'm satisfied now with where I am, and that's why I'm here. Usually Fred Keyes handles our advertising account with you, but I wanted to talk this over personally, with you and Francesca. I want our spots moved from her show. I don't think it's a fit."

"They're not paying off?" Lou asked, looking surprised.

"We're not sure, Trey and I. People come in to Hudson Automobiles to buy cars and they talk about the male disc jockeys and your news guy and gal. They never mention Francesca."

"I see." Lou thought a moment. "That shouldn't be a problem. Francesca has quite a following. I'll take your spots off her show."

"Not a problem," Francesca said, looking at Rush. "Sorry I didn't get results."

Francesca sat frowning a bit. What was going on here? All Rush had had to do was pick up the phone himself or let his ad man talk with Lou. He didn't need to come in. Did he come to see what state Francesca was in? To see if he had shaken her the way he wanted to? Did he and Trey work together? She did her level best to relax and be calm.

For a long time no one spoke; then Lou looked at his watch. "I've got an appointment across town, so I've got to be moving on. Look, Rush, we're your servants, Francesca and I, but it's not a problem that she didn't get results. Tom and I will write up some new copy and—"

Rush held up his hand. "The copy for the other spots has been just fine, Lou. It's all the same and it's been good. This is just a personal thing Trey and I hit on. No hard feelings, Ms. Worth?"

"None," she said flatly. Francesca thought that she

would be glad to get rid of the spots for Trey and Rush on her show. Each time she read part of the copy, she got a strange feeling, as if both men were in the room with her. Now, with what had happened this morning, she wondered how she'd continue to go on with the ads. Rush was setting her free.

"Short visit," Lou commented. "Walk out with me?" Lou nodded at Rush.

Rush shook his head. "I want a few words with Francesca. I want to make sure she's not hurt. You see, Lou, I want to prove that I no longer bear any ill feelings toward you and Francesca for what you did to me."

Lou's mouth opened a little, but he thought it best to hold his tongue. Francesca sat with her eyes half closed, wondering what in the hell Rush was up to.

"Sure," Lou said. "Is that all right with you, Fran?"

"Yes, it's fine."

Lou left them sitting there, but he stuck his head back in the door when he'd gotten his briefcase.

"May has my number where I can be reached this morning," he told Francesca. He didn't like the idea of leaving her alone with Rush. In most circumstances, Fran could take care of herself, but Rush was no ordinary circumstance.

The man was something of a devil. When he'd worked at the station, Lou had found him sadistic. All that brilliance wasted on someone like Rush. Lou shrugged. Of all the times to have an appointment, he thought. What, really, was Rush's reason for coming in this morning? He hadn't called to make an appointment. What was going on?

In the conference room, Francesca thought that she wasn't going to be cornered by Rush Mason. She cleared her throat, unsmiling.

"What is it you want to say to me?" she asked evenly.

"What I said, that I don't want you to feel bad because

I'm—we're, Trey and I—pulling our ads from your show."

"Don't worry," she told him. "It's okay," and she couldn't help telling him, "I've got my choice of ads these days."

She thought she saw a flicker of anger cross his face.

"I could have been on top the way you are," he said after a moment.

"You *are* on top, Rush. Being an associate and part owner of an automobile dealership, a successful one, is no small feat. And as Lou said, there are other stations."

"I've fallen in love with Minden. It's where I want to be."

He was studying her. Stalking her with his eyes. "Trey sends his regards."

"Oh?" Her voice sounded panicky.

Suddenly, he grinned, slid a bit down in his chair. "So what's going on in your world these days that's exciting, Francesca?"

Holly stuck her head in the door. "Sorry. I didn't know anyone was in here." Her eyes sought Francesca, whose glance gave her reassurance.

"We'll be out in a very short while," Francesca told her.

When Holly had closed the door, Rush grinned again. "Do I get my question answered?"

She decided to play it straight. "There's a whole lot going on in my world," she said, "but I don't think any of it would interest you."

He continued to visually stalk her, and she was determined not to let it bother her, but it did.

Finally, he said, "I'd ask for a cup of coffee, but I have an idea you'd be happier with me out of here. How's your affair with Lou going? Too bad *I'm* not a woman."

Her chest tight, Francesca said, "I want you to stop

this foolishness. I think you know very well that my relationship with Lou is one of friendship."

Plainly, he was enjoying his little game.

Francesca stood. "I'm afraid I'm going to have to cut our meeting short. As Lou said, I'm sorry my spots weren't paying off for you, but I'm happy the DJ and the news spots *are* paying off."

She sounded weary, uptight to herself. The grin hadn't left his face since Lou had departed. It was as if, she thought involuntarily, *she* were a rabbit and he had her in his crosshairs.

Later that morning, Jon sat in Rush's office.

"Nice place you've got here," Jon complimented him.

"I like it, thank you. Are you sure you don't want to see Trey?"

Jon looked at him levelly. "No, you're the one I want to see. Why do you ask if I want to see Trey?"

"It's his woman you're on to."

Jon felt the start of heat in his body. "She's his *ex*-wife."

"I don't think Trey sees it that way."

"Nevertheless . . . I wonder if you'd answer a few questions for me?" He forced a coolness in his manner he certainly didn't feel.

"Maybe. It depends on what the questions are. Am I under suspicion of some murder?" He grinned.

"Well, I hope not. My questions may not make sense to you. Bear with me."

"Get your ball rolling."

"Are you a great one for sending flowers?"

"Often enough. What's your point?"

"Do you order those flowers from Mrs. Smith?"

"Sure. Rhea with the fancy boxes she designed. Smart woman."

"Have you ordered any flowers lately?"

"What the hell's your point, Lieutenant?"

"I'd be grateful if you'd just answer the question."

Rush leaned back with his arms behind his head, thinking. A grin played about his mouth.

"I guess I've sent more flowers in the past several months than I've sent in a year before that. I'm running across a lot of good-looking babes and their interest in me rivals mine in them. Does that answer your question?"

"Yes, and thank you."

"Would you like coffee?"

"Thank you. No. You've been very helpful. Nice operation you've got here. . . ."

"Me and Trey. It's his of course. I come in second."

"You're very good friends."

"The best. I'm going to ask you again what you want to do with that smidgen of info I gave you."

Jon smiled. "I'm just checking out a lot of angles that have to do with something I'm working on."

"Nothing bad I hope."

Jon caught a flash of something he couldn't quite decipher in Rush's eyes before he shuttered them.

"It depends on how you look at it. Certainly nothing good."

"Well, that's what we pay you cops for, weeding out the bad guys."

Jon agreed and thought that it was getting to the point where there was sometimes a thin line between the good and the bad, and all too often they were the same person.

Rush began to get up. "I hate to boot you out, Ryson, but I've got a rough morning. One of my salesmen is out. She'd die if she knew I was calling her a salesman. She prefers the term *salesperson*."

Rush was sneering now, and he laughed at his own criticism.

Jon stood reluctantly. He wanted more time to psych Mason out, *be* his alter ego. The man was a jerk—that much was plain.

Suddenly, Rush sat back down. "On the other hand, I want to help you in any way I can. Finished?"

It was a hundred-and-eighty-degree turn and Jon thought that he'd take it.

"Thank you. I appreciate it. You were a well-known disc jockey a few years back. Ms. Worth replaced you."

Rush tensed, his eyes got narrow. "You're damned right she replaced me. Woman are the schemers of this world."

Jon smiled ruefully. "Machiavelli was a man and he's generally thought to be the greatest schemer the world has known."

Rush shrugged. Jon sat thinking that the hostility reflected on Rush's face when he'd mentioned Francesca had been remarkable. The man was doing well. Why didn't he get over it?

"That notwithstanding," Rush said. "I stand by what I said. Look, Ryson, I want to talk with you, but"—he glanced at his watch—"as I said, time is running short and we're busy."

Jon dug in. "Please answer one more question. Do you sometimes save boxes the flowers come in? I mean get them back from the person you sent flowers to?"

Rush thought a long moment. "Yes, I do on occasion. I admire Rhea's designs. Why?"

"Just curious."

Rush looked nervous now. Jon could see gears switching in his brain.

"As a matter of fact, I gave an empty box of Rhea's to a woman who cleaned for me."

"Oh?"

"Yes. She went back to Diamond Point, my old island, last week."

"Thank you for your time," Jon said, getting up.

"Don't mention it." Rush got up too.

Jon left thinking that the fury and the hostility on Rush's face had been all too apparent. Was he the one who had put the rabbit at Francesca's door? And, if so, why after all this time?

After Jon left, Rush sat down in his chair with a heaviness he hadn't felt before. Why was Ryson snooping around? Francesca had recently gotten the Female Broadcasters of the Year Award, and it rankled the hell out of him. It was him and Laura all over again, just when Francesca's taking his job had begun to hurt a little less.

He had seen Jon and Francesca together several times. What did Ryson hope to learn from him? Sure, he bought flowers from Rhea Smith, lately a lot of flowers. He had women coming out of his ears.

Funny the detective should ask about the florist boxes. He had put one of them to good use, and he chortled thinking about it. Trey was a fool to moon over one woman. Too many fillies to waste your time on one. He, Rush, played the field.

Rush thought that he hadn't been able to stop the powerful surge of anger that had swept over him at the mention of Francesca's name. Was the detective baiting him?

He got up slowly, feeling ten years older. Somehow he was going to have to keep his anger in check. Maybe it hadn't been too smart a move going in to WKRX this morning, but he had been struck with a need to interact with Francesca, to see if he could see her armor cracking, because he intended to hurt her the way she had hurt him.

Twelve

By seven o'clock that night, Jon had moved a few of his things in. Now he had gone out to pick up a few sundries from the drugstore.

Mrs. Addison and Francesca talked in the living room.

"I'm glad you wanted me to stay and chat with him for a while," Mrs. Addison said. "He has come to be a favorite of mine. I hope you two take it all the way."

"Matchmaker," Francesca said quickly.

"And a good one too. I've got two granddaughters who wouldn't be married if I hadn't meddled. Now they've got two kids each. I say marriage is a great life."

"You're a romantic at heart."

"Those flowers and the candy he sends you say that Lieutenant Ryson is a romantic."

Francesca's skin warmed and glowed for a moment, and she hugged herself. It wasn't so much to see Jon again that she had wanted Mrs. Addison to stay. She didn't want to be alone. It had been pleasant having someone there when she'd come in. With someone else's presence, she wasn't haunted by the dead rabbit.

Oh, wasn't she? she thought grimly. Her mind kept going back to that morning, the way the tongue seeks out and probes a sore tooth.

Francesca went to the door when the chimes

sounded. Jon smiled as she let him in and kissed her cheek. He walked over to the older woman.

"Hello again, Mrs. Addison."

"Hello, Lieutenant."

"Call me Jon. I haven't seen you often enough."

"Well, I usually get off early, as you know, but this bad thing happened this morning and . . ."

"Don't worry," Jon said. "I'm here now. I'll take care of you both. How much has Francesca told you?"

"She told me the whole story, going back to the clippings. I didn't dream this was going on."

Jon nodded. "Tomorrow I'm checking with a very good friend to set up a new security system. You'll both be safer then. I'm talking to postal inspectors in the cities where the clippings were mailed."

"That's good." Mrs. Addison stood up. "I'd better be going." She nodded to Francesca. "I'm leaving you in capable hands."

"We'll run you home," Jon told her.

Later, as they came back to her house, Francesca reexperienced the sense of fear as she and Jon went in. Jon helped her out of her coat, which she hung in the hall coat closet. Then she went back to the kitchen without thinking why. She was simply drawn there.

Her glance fell on the table where the rabbit had lain in the box that same morning. Jon followed her.

"You're going back to this morning," he said softly. "Please try not to dwell on this. Somehow we'll get to the bottom of it."

She turned to him. "I know you'll try," she said, "because you're that kind of man."

She told him then about Rush's visit to the station and he listened carefully.

When she had finished, he said. "I paid a little visit

to Rush Mason this morning. Trey wasn't there. I wanted to see where Mason was coming from." He told Francesca what Rhea Smith had told him about giving Rush a box like the one that had held the rabbit, and what Rush had told him about giving that box to his cleaning woman, who had left the country.

Francesca was thoughtful when he'd finished. She sighed long and deeply as Jon stroked her hands.

Finally, Jon said, "It's almost impossible to know which one did this because either is capable. One thing for sure is they're both hellishly angry men. I know this for myself where Rush is concerned, and from you with Trey."

"Every day when I get my mail, I keep looking for another envelope with a clipping."

"That's natural. From what you tell me about Trey, this could turn out to be a war of nerves. If he merely wants to hurt you, he could do it by driving you out of your mind, or trying to. You're a radio personality and you've got to be on top of things. If you fall apart, he's won. The same would hold true for Mason."

"I'm not going to fall apart."

"That's my girl. Not if I can help you stay on an even keel."

Francesca glanced at Jon's soft, brown, brushed-wool sweater and his brown slacks and loafers, then at her own more formal garb.

She stood up "Excuse me while I get into something homier."

A wide smile creased Jon's face. "Don't you mean 'get into something more comfortable'?"

Francesca bent and touched his cheek. "You're a card, Ryson. A card after my own heart."

In her bedroom, she looked around. She had moved downstairs when she and Trey broke up. The upstairs master bedroom and the other two bedrooms were empty. Quickly putting on an aquamarine jumpsuit with a long, leopard-print silk scarf she tied at the waist, she went back out to the living room where Jon lounged.

"Are you hungry?" she asked.

"A bit. What about you?"

"Not really, although I've hardly eaten all day. A superb new pizza place has opened downtown and they deliver."

"I've tried them. They're good. Pepperoni, black olives and double cheese is what I'd like. Would you like me to order?"

"No. I'll do it. How about getting a big one? I take what you mentioned, along with mushrooms, green peppers, and onions. Couldn't we just combine the two? I don't like leftover pizza . . . and I can't eat a whole one."

"Sure."

"I've got plenty of things on hand to drink, but I prefer sangria with pizza."

"I haven't tried it, but I'm willing."

She ordered and they sat, waiting. Several times, Jon looked over at the piano.

"I'm thinking," she said, "that I'm downstairs. You have a choice of three bedrooms upstairs."

He smiled narrowly. "Do you have a master bedroom?"

"Of course. Why do you ask? It's upstairs."

"I don't want that one."

Francesca thought about his statement a moment, then rocked a bit with laughter. "Let me guess. It's the bedroom I shared with Trey."

"Your mind clicks, lady. I'd like to wipe out everything you've known with Trey, at least all the pain. I'm going to have to sleep down here. We can move your things tomorrow night."

As he looked at her, she placed her hand on his smooth, close-cropped black hair.

"You're nervous and upset," he said. "It's natural."

"Yes. It's early. Why don't we drop over to see my dad?"

"You're not too exhausted?"

"No. As you said, I'm nervous. I want to get out of the house after we eat the pizza."

"Sure. I'll drive you over. Hadn't you better call and see if he's there?"

"I'll take my chances. I want a brief ride anyway. Get some air."

Jon thought of her standing in the open kitchen door that morning, trying to breathe deeply. She was scared and his heart went out to her.

The order arrived. Jon got the delivery and insisted on serving the large slices of delectable pizza and sangria.

Eating from trays, they sat on the sofa and listened to jazz from WKRX. Tom's mellifluous voice spoke to them between tapes.

Listening to the music, lulled by Jon's presence, Francesca steadied herself as she thought. Trey was making her hate her own home. He had chosen the leather-and-mahogany tables that graced one corner of the living room.

"What's wrong?" Jon asked.

"Nothing. Just a vagrant thought."

"One thing I'm pretty sure of, Fran, as upset as you are over what happened this morning, you're very nervous, too, about my staying with you.

"And it isn't just the gossip. You're hurt and you're running from me. I want you to know I'm not going to crowd you. Perhaps one day you'll come to me. I can and I will wait until you do."

He was so sterling, she thought, and there was so much she wanted to say to him.

"Thank you so much," was all she could manage.

* * *

The lights were on in Garrett Worth's house. Francesca looked lovingly at the white-frame, dark-blue-shuttered house she'd grown up in and pleasant memories filled her mind. How very different those times were from now. Garrett answered the door before they could finish knocking.

"Well, what a great surprise! How about a hug for your old father?"

Francesca looked at him mischievously. "You're not that old. You're still chasing the fairer sex."

Garrett blushed. "Ah, you keep up with everything."

He shook hands with Jon. Each time he saw him, he felt more impressed. He wanted his daughter to have another chance at happiness.

"Can I get you a snack, something to drink?"

"Oh, good Lord, no," Francesca said. "We're full to the gills with pizza and sangria. I didn't know I was coming over here or I would have ordered you one."

Garrett shook his head. "I made the sourdough pancakes from the recipe you gave me, along with some blackberry syrup. They were scrumptious. I had Canadian bacon. No, I'm the one who's full to the gills."

Francesca turned to her dad, who sat in a nearby chair as they sat on the sofa.

"Dad, we won't be long. I have something to tell you."

Garrett's heart slowed. She looked so troubled. She had always been a sturdy, with-it, and not easily frightened woman. He waited.

Francesca told him slowly, leaving out nothing—the clippings that had come over the past few months, and what had happened that same morning.

She took Jon's hand. "He's going to stay with me a while," she said. "I thought about moving in with you, but your arthritis acts up sometimes and I don't want to be a burden."

"Then, too, I know a lot of the finer points of protection, as a cop," Jon added.

Garrett sat looking from one to the other. "I'm glad you're there for her, but can you give her enough protection? A cop's job is long, hard. Will you have the energy left over?"

"I've decided to take some time off that's long overdue. The chief has often suggested it. I have some serious grief work to do, and it can fit in nicely with this."

"Grief work?" Garrett asked.

"Yes. My brother, a fellow cop, was murdered a little over a year ago. I've run away from it, taking all the overtime I can get and it isn't working. I can stay with Francesca, protect her and see this through, too."

"I remember your brother's death. I was really sorry; sometimes I wonder if we're not tipping over the edge."

They were silent a moment before Francesca said evenly, "We have separate bedrooms. I'm moving back upstairs and Jon will stay in my room."

Garrett smiled. "No need to explain yourself to me, Fran. You're a grown woman and you'd never run your life in any way that wasn't exemplary."

"Thank you. I'm always thanking the Lord for making you my parent."

"I'm the lucky one."

They watched a television sitcom. Garrett wanted to ask them how serious they were, but what his daughter had just told him prevented that line of inquiry. Hadn't Trey Hudson caused her enough pain? But then, she had said she wasn't sure it wasn't Rush. He hadn't liked Rush Mason either on the few occasions he'd run across him.

When the sitcom was over, Garrett asked, "This comes as such a shock. What do you want me to do?"

Jon pondered his question a moment. "Just be there for her as you've always been, Mr. Worth. This is so damnably ingenious. I think, I *hope* someone is just trying to frighten Fran. They can make her lose it, or move away. That may be all they want."

"But it may be even more evil," Garrett offered.

"Yes. This dead rabbit thing is a step beyond the clippings. Trey calls from time to time as if he's checking on her for something, and today Rush came by the station. I'm thinking that could be to see how Francesca was taking what happened this morning."

"Would he want her to know if he did it?"

"Rush and Trey are both strange characters. It's hard to say which one is the strongest. I think they'd actually be delighted to pull something off that can't be traced to them, even if they know they are suspects."

Garrett lightly scratched the side of his face. "God knows Trey Hudson is strange enough. No telling what he'll do. When he hit my daughter and she told me, I wanted to go for him."

"That's why I waited so long to tell you. I didn't want you beaten up. Trey wouldn't do it himself, you know. He'd hire someone. That's his style."

"At first, he seemed like a nice enough fellow. Not in your class, Jon, but nice enough. I saw the change though, and it didn't take me long. He'd raise his voice at Francesca, put her down sometimes. I was happy when she filed for divorce."

"Having had a father like you," Jon said, "a woman might make a bad choice, but she would come away from it."

"Thank you. My daughter means everything to me."

"That's the way I feel about you," Francesca said.

Garrett smiled a bit. "I'm hoping you'll soon find someone else to add to that magic circle."

Francesca and Jon stood to leave and Garrett brought

their coats. At the door, he hugged Francesca and shook Jon's hand. Then he hugged Francesca again and held her.

"You take care and watch around you," Garrett told her. He turned to Jon. "And I know I don't have to tell you to take care of her. There'll be gossip, but that's not nearly so important as having her safe. Then, too, Minden is a mite more sophisticated than many small towns because it's close to D.C. I'm depending on you, son."

The last word had slipped out and Garrett glanced at Jon to see how he was taking it. "I hope you don't mind my calling you 'son'?"

Jon looked at the older man gravely. "I'm honored," he said.

Thirteen

Entering the front door of her house with Jon after visiting her father, Francesca could not suppress a shudder.

"Easy." Jon put his arm around her.

"I'm glad you're here." Her voice sounded fragile. "Would you like me to fix you a drink?"

Jon shook his head. "I've had my limit for the day. I'm going to unpack some of my things."

Francesca sat down at the piano and played "Chopsticks." Jon came to stand by her.

"As you know," she said, "that's about the limit of my repertoire. Would you like to play?"

"Not right now." He shrugged, still standing there. It was the weirdest thing, he thought. He wanted to keep comforting her, didn't want to leave her side.

"Okay. I'm going to get ready to turn in. We're interviewing your mother and discussing our trip to Diamond Point in February. I want to be fresh, but that's hardly possible."

Jon's face set. She looked so haunted sitting there. He touched her shoulder, and she smiled up at him.

"I think you're taking it well," he said. "And don't worry about how you're taking it. What happened this morning was a hell of a thing."

From the minute he had come at her call that morning, he had thought about paying Trey Hudson a visit, and he intended to—soon. Cops had to tread carefully these days; a man like Hudson would sue for millions if he felt tightly pursued without reason.

Jon left the room and Francesca played a nursery rhyme tune, then went to her new bedroom. Looking around at the upstairs bedroom, which was done in shades of rose, she reflected that Jon was in the downstairs bedroom where she had slept since her divorce. Did he have everything he needed?

She got a stack of towels from the upstairs bathroom, which was adjacent to the master bedroom, and took them to Jon.

Knocking, she found him putting articles away.

"I thought you might need more towels. The shower down here is wonderful."

"Thanks. You're thoughtful. Sweet and thoughtful."

A big smile tugged at the corner of his mouth. She put a couple of bath sheets at the foot of the bed and opened the linen closet, which was well stocked with towels. Had she been looking for excuses to come down here?

She imagined his big, sinewy body under his garments and felt faint with longing, even as he imagined her lovely body under and over him. They looked at each other, and for a moment neither could breathe.

"Good night," she said softly. "I hope you rest well, and if you need anything, call me." She indicated an intercom system that connected the entire house.

His face got serious. "You're nervous," he said. "I'm sorry."

"It's okay. You're here with me."

He came to her and put a hand on each of her shoulders.

"Don't try to keep yourself from being frightened. You have every right to be. But I want you to know this.

I'm going to do everything I can to protect you, and that's considerable. I've called Jordan Clymer, the security man who's handled security for some very big names. He's coming out tomorrow night and we'll talk. . . ."

"Thank you." Her eyes were still wide with fear.

Fury filled him at the thought of someone harming her. He touched the soft, corkscrew curls and smoothed back her hair.

He didn't tell her how malevolent Rush Mason's face had gotten when Jon had spoken of Francesca.

And he didn't tell her that he planned to pay a visit to Trey Hudson at his home. He'd always found that people revealed themselves more deeply at home than in impersonal offices.

After she left, Jon finished putting away his things and took a long shower. The hard force of the water stung his body and invigorated him. He picked up one of the bath sheets she had put on the foot of his bed instead of using the towels that were already in the bathroom.

Drying off, he looked at the queen-size bed covered with ruggedly masculine shades of very dark blue. He thought she had changed the bedding for him and he was touched.

She had slept in this bed, he reflected as he put on his pajamas and slipped beneath the covers. He still smelled the lavender she had worn and the lushness of her body was still with him as he closed his eyes and drifted off to sleep.

Upstairs, Francesca took a leisurely bath scented with lavender oil, so good for relaxation. Drying off, she studied her body's generous outlines in the bathroom mirror. He was attracted, no doubt about that. How did *she* feel?

She didn't deal with that question until she lay between the pale blue, Egyptian cotton sheets. She breathed deeply. She was more drawn to Jon than she had ever been to a man, but her life had been shattered and she needed time, a lot of time, to put the pieces back together again.

She was drifting off to sleep when the powerful vision came of the piteous creature lying lifeless in the florist box that morning. Then it was lying beside her on the bed. Warm, soft and very dead. Merciless fear chilled her every pore. She screamed involuntarily.

Jon fought free of his covers and raced upstairs. He had helped her move upstairs, so he knew where she would be sleeping, and he pushed the door open to find her sitting up in bed in semidarkness. A dim light came from the open window. He snapped the light on at the door. Her eyes were huge.

"I'm sorry," she said in the steadiest voice she could manage.

He sat on the edge of the bed and drew her to him. Her nylon tricot, periwinkle blue gown felt good beneath his hands; her skin felt even better.

"You had a nightmare."

"Yes." She told him about the hallucination.

"Damn whoever did this!" he exploded, stroking her back and arms. Walnut sweetheart. Walnut love. Those were his thoughts, but he thought, too, of malice and danger. He couldn't wait for a new day when he could talk with Hudson face-to-face and see what he could learn.

Holding her, he thought of something. "You need

sleep," he said, "and you need it badly. Did you take a sleeping tablet?"

"No. I drank valerian herb tea. It always helps me to sleep. Go back to bed, Jon. I'll be all right."

"No. I'm going to sleep up here—for tonight anyway. I'll feel better when Clymer has checked your security system and changed it. That's day after tomorrow. I'll sleep up here tonight and tomorrow night."

"I don't want to deprive you of sleep."

"You won't be. Do you have a footstool or hassock around?"

"In the master bedroom, there's a hassock. What do you need it for?"

"Something I have in mind. I'll be right back."

She told him the exact location of that bedroom and he went out into the hall. She didn't have to tell him; he remembered it all too well from when she had given him a tour of the house.

Pausing at the door, he felt his mouth go drier. *This was the room she had shared with Hudson.* Switching on the light, he saw the big, plush brown hassock, walked over and picked it up.

Back in the room with Francesca, he saw she had slipped into a blue, perriwinkle quilted robe and was sitting on the edge of the bed. He set the hassock down by the bed.

"What are you going to do?"

"Did you ever hear of reflexology?"

"The foot massage that's supposed to date back to ancient Egypt?"

"One and the same. Know much about it?"

Francesca knew a little, but wanted to know more.

"It's based on the theory that the feet and hands all have certain spots that correspond to inner organs. Massage these—it's called *pinpointing* and *walking*—and you can heal inner maladies. I know a doctor who swears by it. He claims to have avoided operating on a woman for ovarian cysts by using this method. And, oh Lord, does it ever relax you."

Sitting on the hassock, he took one of Francesca's soft feet into his hands and began.

"Ryson, tell me, how did you ever learn this?"

For a moment, his brow clouded. "Kevin dated a woman who was a master at it. She studied in Canada. I was interested. She taught us both."

"Is it something you can do for yourself? It sounds expensive."

"It is fairly expensive and yes, you can do your own. That's not as satisfactory, but it helps a lot. How does that feel?"

"Wonderful! Would you like to show me how sometime?"

"Sure."

For a short while, he massaged the other foot and when he massaged the lower part of her calves, she purred with pleasure. With the first calf, she had been too tense, too afraid that she couldn't control her passion for him.

When he began to massage the top part of her other foot, she asked, "What does this part correspond to?"

"The whole top part of the foot corresponds to the lymph glands. There. Feel better?"

He breathed as best he could. Her lovely silken walnut flesh was doing him in, and he had to cool it. The important thing was to protect her.

Not knowing she would do so, Francesca half closed her eyes and leaned forward. Her mouth touched his and flames of desire licked around them both.

Passion leaped in him like a wild deer as he stroked her calf.

Her heart pounded crazily and a dizzying surge of wanting him nearly overwhelmed her.

She was going to be calm if it killed her.

She leaned back and said, "Take the bedroom next to me. And sleep late. I hate having bothered you. I need to be out early."

He stood, aware then that he wore only his pajamas. He wanted to get out before he embarrassed himself.

In his room, aware of Francesca only a wall away from him, Jon tossed at first, then fell into deep sleep. His dreams were riotously, wickedly wild and they were about her. But he dreamed of Kevin, too. They were studying reflexology again, together. And they were laughing. Happy. Now Francesca was in trouble and he meant to protect her the way he had not been able to protect his brother.

He sighed deeply and slept on.

Francesca lay back under the covers and pulled the comforter up around her chin. Her window was open a little and a breeze swept the warm room. Her flesh still tingled with the memory of Jon's hands on her feet and legs. He was very good at this form of massage and it had felt wonderful. For a few minutes, she was able to put aside the hellish hallucination of the rabbit lying on her bed tonight. But she knew she must let the mental picture come as it would. Her sadness was deeper than her fear. She simply was not particularly afraid of Rush. Perhaps she should be.

She *was* afraid of Trey because she had felt his anger more than once. Her mind's eye went to the master bedroom she and Trey had shared. He'd kept a large, heavy, gray-steel safe in that room, the old-fashioned kind, and one day . . . She closed her eyes tightly seeing a slightly open safe. She wasn't going to think of the safe, because it seemed that that had been the beginning of the end for them.

Like Jon, she didn't expect to sleep. Smoothing the bed beside her, she fully realized her emptiness. She was not a woman meant to be alone, but perhaps she would never be able to be comfortably close to a lover again.

Turning to the side that faced the room where Jon slept, she stroked the covers lightly before sleep overcame her.

The next morning, Francesca was in the kitchen early. She glanced around nervously at first, then began to prepare fresh orange juice and coffee, waffles and Canadian bacon and eggs with baby shrimp. The best way to handle what had happened yesterday morning was to stare it in the face. She didn't intend to be intimidated.

When everything was done, she leaned against the kitchen sink and looked out the window on a beautiful day with the sun peeping over a few lazy clouds. WKRX was playing soft rock. Ron Emerson's rich, smooth bass voice soothed her. His program would segue into hers, but she had a lot to do before her program this morning.

She jumped as Jon said behind her, "Good morning, and how did you sleep?"

She flushed as she turned. "Surprisingly well. Jon, I can't thank you enough."

"Don't try. It's something I want to do."

"You're that kind of man. I hope you like waffles and the rest of what I've made."

A grin lit his eyes. "I'd eat mud pies if you made them."

"You're a romantic. How did *you* sleep?"

"With some people I can't help being a romantic. I slept well. I was worn out. I'll take you to work and I'm going in, but the chief knows I'll be off for a few months.

It's something he's been urging me to do." He frowned. "We can make this work, Fran. We just have to keep our heads like the adults we are. You mean too much to me for it not to work."

They ate in the glass-enclosed breakfast nook next to the kitchen and as the Belgian waffle iron sizzled, Jon took her hand. "I've got to give it to you. You've got guts."

"Sometimes. My mother died early. My father couldn't do it all by himself. Someone had to help him."

"You're very close to your father, aren't you?"

"Very. Like you, he's one of a kind."

"You say I'm a romantic. Well, I say *you* are. I know you're running scared and things are happening to make it worse. But you keep paying me compliments like the one you just paid me and I keep wanting to kiss you when you do."

Francesca smiled. "Okay. I'll stop the heartfelt compliments. I'll just think them to myself. Eat your breakfast, Ryson, and stop looking at me like that."

"Like what?"

"Like you're a big tomcat and I'm a delicious pigeon."

"Oh, you noticed. Guilty as charged."

"Eat up and let's get going. I've got to be in early, you'll remember."

He saw a shadow cross her face, and she shuddered slightly.

"What is it?"

"I guess I was thinking about how I was going in early yesterday, too. We're so busy these days. Maybe I'm afraid to open the front door."

"I'll open it for you. I'm going to be with you, Fran. All the way."

Fourteen

"A cheery good morning to the world's greatest listeners!"

At nine-thirty, Francesca was already on a roll. Today she was ebullient—so different from the day before.

"Later this morning, we have that lovely lady, Mrs. Melanie Ryson, executive director of Hope House. When we selected—or when *you* selected—Minden's Woman of the Year, we did it right.

"Today, Melanie will tell us about her plans for the year for Hope House, and her personal plans to take advantage of the many things we're doing for her throughout the year. Not the least of these is the trip we're sending her on to Diamond Point in the Caribbean. I get to accompany her, and I tell you I plan to enjoy every moment.

"We'll be going during the carnival season, and we'll be there as it culminates in one wonderful, special day. Take a minute and stop by the station to see our exhibit on Diamond Point. They want you to visit them, and everyone, including their prime minister, Thomas Barton, extends a gracious welcome.

"Two men from Diamond Point—Matt Wolpers and Cam Mason—have visited here and will be back next spring. Call our toll-free number if you'd like literature on the island."

Lou came to her side during a long commercial break. Holly had waved as she came in.

"How's it going, kid?" Lou asked.

"Better. Lou, I want you to know Jon Ryson is going to stay with me until at least some of this blows over."

Lou's face lit up. "That's great. I think you two make quite a team."

"It's not like that. I'm scared and he's a helpful man. . . ."

The engineer's assistant signaled that she was going back on the air and Francesca adjusted her headset.

For the next half hour, Francesca read Minden's local news, and gave the schedules for various organizations. Spot news was given every hour. Then Holly went on with her homemaker segment. Today, she would tell her listeners how to clean quickly and effectively.

Free of the cumbersome headset for a while, Francesca walked about the studio.

Lou came to her side and patted her on the back. "You've rallied in a hurry," he said, "but I think we can thank the good lieutenant for that."

"Lou," she said suddenly, "how dangerous do you think Rush Mason is?"

Lou thought a moment. "What I have to say about Mason isn't fit for your ears, Fran. I don't care if he's got a good bit of the world's goods, he's a loser. He hates himself, and you know the saying: 'We must fear he who hates himself for *we* will be the victims of his revenge.' "

Francesca nodded. "I'm pretty sure either Rush or Trey is behind all this, and I know what Trey is capable of."

Just talking about it had shallowed her breath.

One of two security guards pushed open the door and came in with Rhea Smith, who held a potted white cattleya orchid plant. The guard carried a splendid bird of paradise.

"Hello, Rhea," Francesca said. "Who's the lucky recipient?"

"Pat yourself on the back," Rhea said. "The orchid is for you. They're coming in from Matt Wolpers and Cam Mason. Aren't they both gorgeous? The bird of paradise is for Holly."

Ron Emerson came up to admire the flowers. He handed Francesca a long sheet. "Be a doll and check my playlist for me," he said. "Take special care on the gospel segment. We're really going strong there."

Francesca nodded.

Max and Rhea chatted a moment before she turned to Francesca. "If you twist my arm, I'll take a raspberry Danish."

"Come with me."

"Bring me one back," Ron called. "Strawberry Danish, and a fresh cup of coffee, cream and sugar."

Francesca shook her head. "Some people like being waited on."

Ron grinned and raised his eyebrows. "Privilege of being a young, single black man and an endangered species."

"Nothing wrong with you a little ego boost won't cure," Francesca came back. Rhea smiled at the easy banter between the two.

Melanie Ryson came early. A longer newsbreak was being broadcast by Max, and Francesca went to the older woman and hugged her. Then she walked with her to the small lounge where they sat down.

"You look really good," Francesca told her, admiring her steel-gray coatdress and silver jewelry.

"I may, but you definitely do." Melanie was in top

form and beaming. "That dark rose is your color and the creamy pearl jewelry really sets it off. You could have been a model, my dear."

"I'm a little hefty, don't you think?"

Melanie's eyes twinkled. "What I think is you're beautiful. Just the wife I want for my son. Plus-size models are becoming popular. And Francesca, I'm sorry about this trouble you're having."

"Jon told you."

"No. My son doesn't confide in me. I hope you don't mind that your father told me. He's coming in a few minutes to give me moral support."

"It looks to me like something is beginning to perk between you two."

Melanie suddenly looked sad. "I had my chance for a great life some time ago and I ruined it. My life now isn't too bad, but I miss the friendship of my boy, my late son, and my late husband." She paused. "I'm glad Jon is staying with you."

"Thank you. You did a wonderful job of raising him."

"While I was there, I did, but I failed them all—and myself."

"You have to forgive yourself," Francesca said quietly.

"Perhaps I can one day."

They went out then to find Francesca's father sitting on a couch in the studio. He got up and came over to them, kissing Francesca's cheek.

"Dad. I'm so glad you came by."

Garrett Worth smiled. "I thought the lady could use an audience of one. As quiet as it's kept, she's bashful."

A youthful glow settled on Melanie's face. "Oh, you, telling my secrets."

Francesca noted the easy air of camaraderie between Melanie and her father and was happy for them, but theirs would be no smooth road. Both had been hurt and were wary. They had hurt others and never forgiven themselves.

"How're you doing today?" her father asked.

"Better," she said quickly. *Much* better."

"I'm glad you finally decided to do as I suggested."

Jon sat across the desk from Police Chief Wayne Kellem. His best friend, Sergeant Keith Beaumont, sat in a nearby chair.

"I pretty much have to now," Jon said. "A woman I admire needs help and I intend to provide it."

"Any idea how long you'll be off?" Keith's eyes on his friend were warmly sympathetic.

"Several months anyway. It all depends on how the deal goes down."

"The fancy stalking, you mean," Keith Beaumont offered, his head cocked at an angle.

"Yes. I intend to do a lot of investigating into my brother's death while I'm on leave. I'll have a chance to get to know more about Hudson and Mason. I know my informant thinks a kid on the East End shot Kevin when he caught him red-handed with a big stash of drugs he was trying to sell, but other things have long made me wonder.

"We have reason to believe Hudson is into stolen cars that he ships to the Caribbean area mostly. It's Mason's stomping ground, although he left there as a youth. He goes back all the time."

"Does Hudson go to the Caribbean, too?" the chief asked.

"He does. Mason came up on an island called Diamond Point. His family is wealthy, well known. His father is dead, but his mother and sister live there. I understand they're not too close."

The chief nodded. "Tell me a bit more about this

stolen-car ring. We've talked about this before, but I'm going to put a man on it full time."

Jon cleared his throat. "The deal, so far as I can find out, is to have a large band of men from here and other countries steal SUV's, vans and other larger vehicles. They give them phony registration papers and change the vehicle identification numbers. We're dealing with professionals here. They pay someone a hefty fee to take the cars to one of the islands, where they sell for two to four times their going price here."

"Everybody wants a piece of the USA." Keith stroked his chin.

"It happens in Europe, but it's not as extensive. The guy I have on tap has a healthy regard for his life. He tells me that one day he'll tell me some stuff that will blow my mind. One day soon."

"Oh?" The chief looked at Jon closely.

"Yeah. Right now he's telling me things and saying he's fantasizing, telling me to regard it as a dream."

"Things about the stolen-car ring?"

"The same. And Hudson. Mason as well."

"You trust this informant?" Keith asked.

"I do. I'd like to get him away from Minden. He's twenty-four and has a damned good mind. He can do better. I'd like to see him finish college. He's got a year of community college under his belt and he did well there."

"What happened?" the chief asked.

"In a brief word, *drugs*. He got hooked, stayed hooked a while, then went into rehab at Minden's drug center. But he's still in touch with the homeys he did drugs with."

"Maybe we could help him if he'll help us," Chief Kellem suggested.

"I'm sure he'll do what he can, but we all know it can be damned dangerous."

"I'd guess they use the cars to more easily traffic in drugs in the Caribbean."

"Partly, Chief," Jon said, "but the cars sell to the wealthy all over the islands, too. And with drug running so prevalent, there're a lot of wealthy takers.

"I'd guess, though, that the main use for these cars is drug trafficking. I've been talking to a policeman in New Orleans who did extensive undercover work in the Caribbean for his agency. He spent a lot of time on Diamond Point.

"According to him, these vehicles are souped up to fantastic speeds, they're fitted with guns and they're leaving the police departments on the islands in their dust."

"Sounds like a good place for police corruption to start, too," Keith said.

Jon nodded. "Diamond Point is having some political trouble. The present prime minister is very popular, but one attempt has been made on his life."

"Which is why he wants you," Chief Kellem said gravely.

"Yeah. He has word that knowledgeable thugs and well-educated thugs are planning to take over Diamond Point, use it as a base for their entire Caribbean operations. This is in the fledgling stage. It won't happen now, but it could in the future."

"How far up in this operation do you think Hudson and Mason are?" The chief leaned forward.

"It's anybody's guess. Mason has maintained connections with people on the island, not all of them savory. He's estranged from his family. He's well educated and smart. I'm surprised he's played second fiddle to Hudson this long. He's got brains, but he's immature."

Chief Kellem got up. "I've got a meeting across town. You'll be around for another couple of days. I told you I'm assigning Keith as your replacement. I know you want to protect Ms. Worth, but while you're off, I want to see you protect your own mind, too. Grieve, man. It's necessary. Kevin would tell you the same."

The chief left and Jon stood. Keith sat still for a moment, his hands in his lap. He got up slowly and hugged Jon.

"All the best, man," he said softly, slapping Jon on the back. "I'm going to miss having you here."

Keith looked so sad that Jon's heart went out to him.

"It's not like you can't see me whenever you wish," he said. "Come by often. We'll have you and Holly over. Go out. I'll be guarding Fran closely for a little while, but from what I can determine, this thing heats up, then cools down. Stops. It could be a war of nerves."

"I wouldn't bank on that. Stalkers are crazy these days, and where an ex-wife or an ex-husband is concerned, there's no limit."

"Well, there had sure as hell better be a limit. How much can Francesca take?"

The two men were silent for a moment. Jon wondered how Francesca was doing. She said she was feeling a lot better this morning than yesterday.

Suddenly, Jon made up his mind about something. "You know, I'm going to pay Hudson a little visit."

"At his dealership?"

"No. I called to say I was coming by, but Mason said he's home until the afternoon."

"Something special in mind?"

"Yeah. I want to talk with him on his home turf. What people listen to, their furnishings, their music—it all tells you a hell of a whole lot about them, and I want to know much more about Hudson."

Keith looked rueful. "He may not want to talk to you."

"I'll take a bet that he *will* want to talk. He's a gambler, Keith. He goes to Atlantic City and Las Vegas all the time."

"Hey, you've been doing some spade work on this guy."

"On him *and* Mason. I'm going to find out what makes him tick; then I'm going to stop his clock."

A policeman came in with a report in his hand. Medical examiner's office," he said. "I worked on this case. Looks like the little bunny died from chloroform, but its throat was also cut."

Jon and Keith looked at each other. Jon took the paper and put it in the middle of Chief Kellem's desk, weighted it and turned back to Keith as the policeman left.

"Chloroform, a cut throat," Jon said. "Some no-good bastard's got nothing better to do than kill wild rabbits and scare women half to death. We're living in a sorry world, Keith."

Keith nodded. "And it didn't just get that way."

Fifteen

Dressed in black tights and a black T-shirt, Trey Hudson faced the huge man standing before him.

"Give it your best shot, I dare you," he chortled.

The six-and-a-half-foot, ginger-brown man narrowed his eyes and took Trey in. "I sure hope you know what you're asking for."

He moved closer to Trey, muscles bulging. His breath coming faster, Trey stood his ground until the man reached him, reached out and began to wrestle him. Trey grunted as the big man twisted him around and put him in a chokehold.

Gasping for breath, outweighed by one hundred, taut pounds, Trey jumped up, the top of his head hitting his tormentor's chin hard, throwing the other man off-balance. With a deft move, Trey grabbed the giant's arm and slung him forward, making him hit the floor with a thud.

Trey leaned back and laughed long and hard. "See? I don't care how big you are, you need to learn karate. Get up, Jersey. I won't tell anybody I could have beat the hell out of you."

The big man got up slowly, rubbing the side of his head.

"Jeez, bossman, maybe you're right." His breath was coming fast.

Trey looked at his houseman, driver and general helper.

"You're sure you didn't just let that happen?" Trey asked.

"Uh-uh. I ain't looking for no lumps like that."

"Okay. You consider karate or ju-jitsu, get me a beer and we'll call it even."

Jersey Jakes left the room and Trey sank onto a leather-covered exercise bench. Winded, he was finished for the day. Getting the best of anything always made him feel good. Getting the best of a bigger man satisfied his very soul.

He looked around his lavish exercise room, filled will all the latest fitness equipment.

Jersey brought the beer and a glass back on a small silver tray.

"I won't be needing the glass."

"Sure thing. Bossman, I thought I'd take the dogs out in the country for a run."

Trey stiffened. "Don't you think it's up to me to decide when my dogs go out?"

Jersey quickly retreated. "Sure thing. I don't mean to be overstepping my bounds. Just thought I'd mention it."

Trey grunted and said nothing as Jersey shifted from foot to foot, looking very much like a bull elephant. Trey laughed deep in his throat.

"You got anything special you want me to do today?" Jersey asked.

"If I did, don't you think I'd tell you?" His voice had the edge of a snarl. Then suddenly he relaxed.

"Sorry, Jersey. I'm on edge these days. You keep standing by me, no matter what, and I'll make it up to you."

The big man laughed. "You already made it up to me. You pay me enough."

Trey put his head to one side. "And if things go my way, I'll pay you plenty more. But one thing, Jersey. You've got to be loyal to me and me alone. I'll hurt you if you're not loyal."

"Sure thing. I'd need hurtin' if I wasn't. You got a friend, bossman."

Trey looked at his man and laughed aloud again. "I'm not too sure I need a friend. I need a faithful servant. Are you on for that?"

"Yessir. I'm on for that. I'm your man."

Trey lowered his head thinking about Jersey Jakes, who still stood before him. Jersey was a few cards short of a full deck, but he followed orders and didn't question those orders too closely. He worshiped Trey. His shaved head gleamed and his two-hundred-and-seventy-five pounds didn't seem to contain an ounce of fat.

Trey fought with Jersey for fun and because, with his knowledge of karate, he could and did take him every time. An even six feet, Trey kept himself fit. He was building bigger and better muscles every day.

"Look," Trey said, "take an hour or so off and enjoy the house. Just don't go away. I'll be at the office all this afternoon. It's nine-thirty now. Rest an hour or so."

Jersey left and Trey walked from the fitness room to his den. Passing the ornate staircase, he thought about the plush bedrooms upstairs. Maybe he needed a nap. Even though he'd just gotten up a couple of hours ago.

In his den, he poured himself a scotch on the rocks and sat down in the swivel chair behind his desk, sipping it slowly. Funny thing about Jersey, how the big fellow loved him. At twenty-two, Jersey longed for the father he'd never known. Trey fit the bill well. He filled in as father figure, too, for Rush. Yeah, he was a better man than his father would ever be.

Sipping the scotch, he thought he hadn't been proud of himself the way he had snarled at Jersey. And maybe he'd taken him down harder than he'd needed to. Without being aware that he did so, he clenched his teeth. He was in full possession of himself at that moment, but Warlock had had his sway for a while as he went after Jersey.

Warlock. He felt that Warlock was the real reason he was still alive at thirty-eight, instead of being killed by his father when he was younger.

After the multiple personality was firmly established in Trey's life, he had only to look at his father to make the man shiver. "You *evil,* young'un. You got a devil in you, boy!"

Whatever it takes, Pa, Trey now whispered to himself. But more and more Warlock seemed to be asserting his own presence, quite apart from what Trey wanted or when he wanted it. Had he really intended to strike Francesca? He decided she needed it. She had been getting too big for her britches.

He'd torn it there though. She had never forgiven him the blows that had left her unconscious. She had filed for divorce and won, citing assault and battery and irreconcilable differences. He'd fought it because once divorced, she could testify against him, if she knew anything.

He'd begun to knock her about because he was scared. What had she seen the day he'd left his safe open? Cops had uncovered a small-time drug outfit operating at his business, and had moved in to arrest two salesmen. Trey wasn't involved, but Rush was on the fringes. It had taken the best lawyers to keep Rush out of jail, and Rush had been grateful that Trey had stood by him.

Trey drained half of his scotch in one gulp and the liquor burned its way down his gullet and into his stomach. The goddamn thoughts had been nibbling at his brain all night and they still plagued him.

Francesca. He wasn't getting over her the way he'd

thought he would. Stacy, with all her glamorous jazz and glory, did very little to assuage the grief he felt at losing Francesca. He was pretty sure she'd loved him in the beginning. She sure hadn't in the end. He had plans for his ex-wife. Did she even suspect that her time was running out?

Thinking about Francesca made him think of Dr. Anderson in San Francisco, who'd warned that he needed treatment to integrate his most powerful multiple. But that had been long ago and he'd stopped going to his three-times-weekly sessions after two years. It had been too expensive and he'd wanted to use the money for other things.

He had two multiples and his own basic personality. He had never bothered to name the party-loving multiple, and then there was Warlock.

The real reason Trey had stopped going was he didn't *want* to integrate Warlock into his powerless self. Warlock could lick anyone and anything. "What I'm afraid of," Dr. Anderson had often said in the two years he'd worked with him, "is that you're creating a monster inside yourself that you'll be afraid of one day—with reason."

Warlock wasn't just physically powerful, he was brilliant. Together, he and Warlock had been able to accomplish a great deal: His automobile agency was booming. The Caribbean Caper, which was what he and Rush called their stolen-car ring, was thriving. In a few years he was going to be way up in the millions. And every dollar took him further and further away from his hellish beginnings.

He didn't want to think of what Dr. Anderson had told him. "Multiples come into play when a person's pain is beyond endurance. The psyche splits into others to help handle the trauma. I've seen worse cases, Trey. Therapy can help you integrate and get over this."

But Trey hadn't stayed and had never gone to another therapist. Instead, Warlock had become his mentor, his friend, his guard, his god. He would never give him up.

He thought of his father often because Warlock had taken the fear away, but he still had trouble with his memories of his mother. A large, dominant woman with black eyes and long, black hair she wore in a big knot at the back of her head, she had shredded his heart.

"You're no good," she often yelled at him. "You're just like your sorry pa." And when he'd begun to prove her right in their little Louisiana town by stealing and beating up drunks, she'd put him out for good. Put him out and even his father had protested.

"Now where in hell's he goin' t'go? He don't know how to do nothing. He ain't little more'n a child. Don't do it, woman."

But his mother ruled the roost and she'd locked her door against Trey. Maybe that's why he'd felt so helpless when he'd lost the house in his divorce from Francesca. Warlock couldn't get him over his pain at his mother's throwing him out, and Warlock couldn't help his pain at losing Francesca. No, Warlock couldn't help with either woman. But Warlock sure knew how to *hurt.*

Warlock lay beside him every night, guarding him. Warlock whispered to him in dreams, in fantasies, fashioning fancy ways to destroy the bitch. Ways that could never be traced back to him. *Do it slowly,* Warlock had begun to whisper. *Take your time. Wear her down.*

Dr. Anderson had been his savior. He had believed in Trey, had thought he had good stuff in him. But in the end Trey couldn't let himself trust—not anyone.

He'd rambled over the country and finally settled in Washington, D.C., where he commuted to the University of Maryland and picked up a degree in business administration. He worked in a used-car dealership and he had begun to believe in himself more.

He'd made friends with his boss and five years later, he'd made his mark in the scrap-iron business and he'd set up his own used-car agency in Minden, Maryland. Again, he did well, and he opened a general automobile agency.

He'd gone all the way back to San Francisco to see Dr. Anderson when he wanted to marry Francesca. He'd come a long way from the sorry young guy the doctor had set on a fairly even keel.

"What are you afraid of now?" the doctor had asked.

He hadn't hesitated. "I guess that she'll leave me. Put me out. Mistreat me in some way."

"You'd have to go along with that, wouldn't you?"

"Yeah, I guess. I'm afraid mostly she'll put me out, like my mother did."

"That's what she'd be selling. Why would you be buying? Let yourself up. If she did put you out, you could find another woman.

"I want to posit that you're afraid of your own multiples, Warlock in particular. I'm afraid he might kill somebody one day and take you down with him. Warlock is a mighty menace to you. I've told you before I'd like to see you integrate him. He's powerful and that's good. But he doesn't always know his own power or how to use it. You loved your father, blows or not, and I think he probably loved you.

"Someone has loved you, Trey. You've got a lot in you that's good. Put it to the best use. If you don't want to work with me, find someone else. I'll recommend someone in D.C. Would you, perhaps, like a woman therapist?"

"No! No women."

The doctor had looked grave. "You're marrying a woman."

"Oh hell, you know the difference. She'll be my wife."

"And a separate individual for you to love and cherish. You're afraid she'll dump you one day and you'll lose it and hurt or kill yourself and/or her."

"You're crazy, Doc. The only one I'd kill is someone who's trying to kill me."

"A part of you would see her as trying to kill you."

Trey had leaned back in the soft chair. Then he suddenly came forward. "I gotta go, Doc. I'll think about what you said."

He had left then, twenty-five minutes into a forty-five-minute session, and he'd never gone back to Dr. Anderson or to another therapist. He and Warlock had done just fine—until now.

He had begun to know fear again when he'd had a glimpse of Francesca and the cop. It had been unexpected and boiling anger—rooted in pain—had nearly stopped his breath. She had looked quietly happy, secure. When was *he* going to feel secure?

The night he had first seen the two of them, he dreamed that she lay at his feet, lifeless. Warlock had killed her and Warlock gloated while Trey grieved. It had been too late then.

Out on the highway, Jon drove at a moderate speed. His destination—Trey Hudson's house—was close at hand. No, Trey Hudson's *estate*. He drove slowly past the showy house, turned around and came back. It was one mile out from Minden.

Why had he changed his mind? He had intended to visit Hudson sometime, but the urge to talk with the man now was overpowering. The clippings that had come to Francesca in the mail were bad enough, but the rabbit caper was far more threatening. Was it Trey?

Tomorrow he would oversee the installation of a new security system for Fran. Tonight, Jordan Clymer was coming over to explain much of the system, leaving him with charts and an explanation of equipment for him to study.

Jon parked on the side of the road. He got out and stood for a moment, admiring the big house. Not his choice, but nice, he thought. It was built of dark beige brick, a roof that nearly matched in color, and black shutters that added a somber note to the house. The five-acre yard was impeccably landscaped and massive evergreens added grandeur.

The sour note was a tall, chain-link fence that stretched back midway from the sides of the house. A sign with blazing red letters said BEWARE! VICIOUS GUARD DOGS! And yes, Jon could see two huge beasts, pit bulls, their long bodies stretched out against the fence, snarling for blood.

He fingered his shoulder holster under his coat. Hudson probably fed the dogs gunpowder for breakfast. "Sorry pals," he said to the dogs. "You'll have to settle for dog chow this morning."

It was a breezy, cold day. He walked up the sidewalk at a quicker pace and rang the doorbell. After a moment, a big man, taller than Jon's own six feet three, came to the door and opened it.

"Yes," the man said. "What's your business here?"

Friendly bastard, Jon thought. "I'd like to speak with Mr. Hudson, if I may."

Jersey stared at Jon long and hard. He didn't like it when men were only a few inches shorter than he was. "Name?"

"Lieutenant Jonathan Ryson of Minden's Police Department."

Jersey's head jerked up. "You don't say. Well, I'll find out if the boss wants to see you. Just stay here."

"Thank you."

When Jersey closed the massive golden oak door, Jon

stood thinking it was a good thing he had carefully thought over a cover conversation to hold with Hudson. He had talked about it with Chief Kellem and Keith and they had added ideas. Later, he had done the same thing for Rush Mason. He thought his visit with Rush had gone very well.

Jersey came back, opened the door and looked at Jon with a face of stone.

Trey came from his study into the living-room. Walking over to Jon swiftly, he offered his hand, which Jon took. Trey's handshake was firm, his hands surprisingly hard.

"Well, Lieutenant, what brings you to my humble abode?"

"You've got a beautiful place here."

"Thank you. I'm competing with the place I renovated for my ex-wife, whom I believe you know quite well."

Jon kept his cool. There was an edge of malicious anger in Hudson's voice. Francesca's house didn't compare with this one, as nice as it was, but it was warm, homelike. This was a padded mausoleum.

Trey rubbed his hands together. "I was in my study going over some figures. I'll take you back there, and maybe you'll tell me why you're here."

"Sorry I didn't answer you." He reflected that Hudson had nearly knocked the wind out of his sails bringing up Francesca so soon into the conversation.

After the men were seated, Jon spoke up.

"Actually," Jon said, "we're specially contacting the movers and the shakers in Minden, along with other folks. We're beginning a policing movement, and we'd like ideas from the community."

"I'd guess you've noticed I'm *outside* Minden."

"That's true, but your business makes you one of the

important people in the area. We're not just limited to Minden."

Trey looked at him, frowning. "I'm not much of a joiner. Chamber of Commerce, Jaycees, that sort of thing is about all I belong to."

"Sure, but you might want to consider this: There could be a good business cycle coming in from the people you'll be associated with."

"Hell," Trey said, leaning back in his chair, "if business got any better, I couldn't handle it."

"That's always good, when things are going well."

Trey raised his head and chortled. "Things couldn't be better. Excuse me a minute." He snapped on a curved, ivory radio and Francesca's lovely voice spilled into the room, this time reading Langston Hughes's poetry. Trey fiddled with the dials, changed the station, then came back to Francesca's voice.

While Trey toyed with the radio, Jon looked around. The deep, smooth, black-leather chairs reminded him of his own apartment. The richness of the cedar-paneled room left him in the dust by comparison.

Jon's breath caught in his throat at the sight of one of Rhea Smith the florist's larger boxes, one exactly like the one the dead rabbit had been in. Trey saw him looking and grinned.

"Care for some candy?" he drawled.

Jon shook his head "You like sending presents?"

Trey shrugged. "They're cheaper than diamonds if you're talking about the flowers and candy that came in the box."

"Did you order those recently?"

"Recently enough. If you're digging for information, Lieutenant, you're going to have to do it another day. I can talk a bit more, but don't go off on any tangents."

So the subject was closed, Jon thought with narrowed eyes. He had found something interesting. So Trey had ordered three boxes of candy and flowers. One had been sent to Stacy and two to his home. At any rate, Trey looked irritated, uncomfortable. Jon decided not to press it further.

Trey got up, asking, "You heard about this new radio?"

"No. I can't say I have."

"It's got the latest in electronic engineering. Listen to the quality of that sound."

"It's good."

"Yeah. We'll get back to the community-policing bit, Ryson. I've seen you out with my ex-wife."

"We're friends."

"The best of luck with her. She isn't all she seems from the outside."

Bile rose in Jon's throat. *Don't criticize her, you son of a bitch,* he thought.

"Guess you'll learn in time if you stay with her. You planning to stay?"

Jon started to say that he and Francesca were only friends, but he wasn't going to lie. It was none of Hudson's business.

"I guess she's told you I roughed her up a bit."

"We haven't talked all that much about her past."

Trey threw his head back, laughing. "You're an expert liar, Ryson. I'm dead certain she's whined on your shoulder. Just remember when it comes your turn that I told you Francesca is not what she seems to be."

Jon smiled thinly and didn't respond at first. Then, "May I tell you a bit about how we'd like you as a citizen and businessman to fit into our plans?"

"You sure can." Trey pressed a buzzer by his chair and in a few minutes Jersey came hulking in.

"What're you drinking, Ryson?" Trey asked.

"Nothing, thanks. I don't drink when I'm on duty."

Trey raised his eyebrows. "But I'll bet you make up

for it when you're off. I never met a truly sober cop yet.
You're a smooth operator. You really ought to talk with
Rush Mason. He's more into the social stuff than I am.
Come to think about it, Rush told me you *did* talk to
him—about florist's boxes. What was that all about?"

Only then did Trey become mindful that Jersey was
still standing there. He looked up at the big man. "Well,
Jersey, make yourself useful. Do me a piña colada and
go heavy on the rum."

"Yessir." Jersey went out and Trey turned again to
Jon. "What about the florist's boxes? Why did you need
to know?"

"Just checking out some information," Jon said
mildly. He watched Trey carefully. There was something
strange about the man. Something odd. Francesca had
said he had multiple personality disorder, and he
thought he saw shadowy differences flickering in and
out of Trey's presence.

For moments, Trey would be calm and controlled;
then he seemed much livelier, more animated. Then a
sinister presence seemed to come in. A powerful presence that seemed dangerous in the extreme. Then it
was gone.

Finally, Trey spoke again. "I'm not really up to discussing your community policing this morning, Ryson, but
you're welcome to come back and discuss it another
time—soon. Let me take you on a cook's tour of my
house."

Disappointed, Jon decided to take advantage of the
offer. Jersey came in with a tray and handed Trey the
piña colada from it. Trey smacked his lips. "You don't
know what you're missing."

"I'll take your word for it."

With his drink in hand, Trey told Jersey, "Hit me with
another one."

Sipping his drink, Trey and Jon walked from room

to room of the house. Downstairs, each room was more opulently furnished than the last. The kitchen was a chef's paradise. The gleam of mahogany furniture complemented the double-arched living room. A master decorator had been at work here.

Trey's den, where they had talked, was surrounded by windows from which they could see the dogs racing and rolling, using their razor-sharp teeth on each other.

"Like my dogs?"

"They're something else."

"They could rip you apart in minutes. I had them specially bred in Hong Kong. You like dogs, Lieutenant Ryson?" He sounded almost respectful.

"Yeah. I've owned a few."

"Those dogs are my army and my arsenal. Know what I call them? Killer I and Killer II."

"I see."

"Let me take you upstairs." They climbed the staircase with its ornate golden metal and one by one Trey showed Jon five lavish bedrooms and baths.

Trey paused at the end of the hall and motioned him into a long room that went across the side of the house. Looking out a window, Jon saw that they were again overlooking the backyard and the fierce dogs. The other part of the room faced the front.

"Now this," Trey said, "is my pièce de résistance. My electronic room."

It was a comfortable large room with a huge TV screen, a movie screen, state-of-the-art CD player, and stereo equipment. Trey slid open a door at the end of the room.

"My security panels," he said. "Only a palace would have finer."

Jon was relieved to be moving about. He had begun to feel that Trey unexpectedly had him in his psychic crosshairs. He thought again about the way Trey's presence shifted. Who was he being now?

Jersey came up with another piña colada on a tray.

"I guess I've had enough for me," Trey growled. "Why don't you drink it?"

"Sure, boss. Thank you."

When Jersey had gone, Trey turned to Jon. "If you're going to get a servant, get one like old Jersey. He'd do anything I asked him to. *Anything.*"

Jon made no comment, but looked at him narrowly.

The tour took more than an hour while Trey talked about his business and his residence.

"I'm looking for an even bigger house," Trey said. "Maybe you and Francesca would like to buy this one." He laughed harshly. "But then I don't guess you could afford it on your paycheck."

Jon felt easy inside. If it came with Hudson's private hell, he wouldn't have his wealth for all the world.

Back in the living room with the cedar panels and dark jade walls, Trey turned to Jon. "Lieutenant Jonathan Ryson, huh? Know what I think? As a liar, you're a man after my own heart. I think you came here to study my case, size me up. You want to know all about me so you won't make the same mistakes I made.

"But you know something, I'm going to make you guess. What I had with Francesca was mine, and it's going to stay mine. I'm not spilling my guts to you."

Jon thought about the fact that Francesca had said that one of Hudson's multiples was called Warlock. And damned if the man facing him didn't seem like something out of a deep, dark forest. Then he saw another presence seem to take over and Hudson appeared clear again.

"Well, I've got to start getting ready to go in. Come to see me again, Ryson. Hell, you *and* Francesca are welcome. And you can talk with me about community policing and your plans."

Jon thanked him and left. Heading down the long walk to his car, he mentally chewed on the visit. What in the hell was going on with Hudson? How long before the more dangerous personality took over and wreaked unchecked havoc?

Driving away, he thought about the dogs again. Trained in a foreign country. Even Hudson was foreign to this and any other country.

Jon thought of Francesca and felt he had failed her somehow. Maybe he hadn't thought this through long enough. But no, there had been nothing wrong with his plan. A psychiatrist friend of his had once told him that people with multiple personalities were often brilliant in at least one aspect of their lives. And they had attenuated feelings. They'd had to develop these qualities in their childhood to escape certain injury and often death.

After Jon had left, Trey went into his den and cut off the radio. He looked sad, and watching him, Jersey wanted to help, but he didn't dare say anything. Trey brightened when the telephone rang.

"Hey, Trey," Rush said. "I've got an idea. A friend of mine from New Orleans is giving a big bash this coming February during Mardi Gras season. I know you don't give a damn about Carnival Day, but he's inviting people from all over the world to this soirée. We've got to go."

Trey slid down in his chair. "Listen, Rush," he said. "Our plans are already made for early February. We're both going to spend the first ten days of February on your old stomping grounds—Diamond Point."

Sixteen

At home that same night, Jon briefed Francesca on his visit with Trey.

"Was Jersey with him when you were married?" he asked.

Francesca shook her head. "No, Jersey is new. He wrote Trey from prison, I understand, and wanted to be connected to him. He told him how much he admired him. Trey likes flattery.

"I was shocked after the divorce when he brought Jersey by here one night to introduce him to me. Then, too, he wanted to look at the security system he'd had installed, wanted Jersey to see it. He was putting one in in the house he had bought. . . ."

"It's quite a house."

"Yes, I've never been inside. He's invited me several times."

"Chummy—after all the trouble he's caused."

"Yes. Well, when he was coming by, the clippings hadn't started. At some point, I told him I thought it best that he not come by again. He was angry, but took it well. As you know, he still calls from time to time."

He told her about seeing the florist's box on Trey's sideboard and his conversation with Rhea Smith. Her head jerked up with fear.

Slowly she said, "I hope it's Rush doing this. I'm a

little less afraid of him. Are we ever going to know? And if we do, people get away with so much these days. Trey has the best lawyers available."

She was so scared in spite of her brave front, and Jon's heart hurt for her.

As they sat on the sofa, Jon patted Francesca's hand nearest him, then put the back of his hand to her cheek. "Do you remember how much time elapsed between his visits and when you began to get the clippings?"

"Several months, I'd say. I didn't sit still for him to come by too many times."

He leaned back and closed his eyes, letting her scent of lavender softly soothe his nostrils. She turned him on in every possible way and he was fighting it, and *losing*.

She wore a cream-colored hostess gown of silk crepe with a long gold rope knotted at her breasts.

She fingered the rope nervously. "The Clymers should be getting here soon," she said.

"Jordan's nothing if not prompt."

As if summoned, the door chimes sounded and both Jon and Francesca went to the door.

The Clymers happily hugged them both.

"My girl," Raine Clymer said. "You're the picture of glamour."

Francesca smiled ruefully. "I'm afraid I love dressing up."

Raine's own pale blue velour jumpsuit and her silver jewelry set off her lovely brown skin. The men laughed at the fact that they had both chosen brown slacks, beige jackets and natural-color sports shirts.

"How are your children?" Francesca asked as they sat in a circle of plush chairs.

Laughing, Raine reached in her tote bag and brought out a pad of Polaroid photos.

Francesca felt her heart catch as she looked at the

pictures of eleven-year-old Kym and three-year-old Kyle. Both children were bursting with life and happiness.

She handed the photos to Jon, who looked at them with longing. *One day*, he thought, *it will be us showing photos like this.*

"Would you two like a snack? Or heavier food?" Francesca asked.

"No, we stopped by Caleb's, and he insisted we try his Chinese-style roast duck."

"Enough said," Jon commented. "You may not need food for another couple of days. Caleb is generous to a fault with his serving sizes."

Instantly, there was a warm scene of camaraderie between the two couples. Francesca had met them before, but neither couple had visited. They decided on sangria and Francesca served it in her best Waterford crystal wineglasses, which Raine and Jordan admired.

"I'm ready to get started whenever you are," Jordan said after a short while, "but I do want to ask you about something. You may regard it as too personal."

"Shoot," Jon said. "If I do, I'll be upfront about it."

Jordan sat, pulling his thoughts together. "I'm not sure if you know that Matt Wolpers is a pretty good friend of mine."

Jon looked surprised. "No, I wasn't aware of it."

"He told me how impressed he is with you, and how much he wanted you on Diamond Point to head up or at least have a major role in Dr. Tom Barton's security setup."

"He's talked with me about it."

"And?"

Francesca looked at Jon, hardly breathing, thinking, certainly she couldn't expect him to stay when she wasn't truly available to him. She thought he would stay through her present ordeal, but after that—

Jon returned Francesca's look.

"I'll tell you this," Jon finally said, "I'm giving it deep thought. They're willing to pay a king's ransom with all sorts of perks. And they're willing to wait at least a while for me to make up my mind."

"It's the chance of a lifetime," Jordan said. "If I didn't have my own establishment, I'd jump at it. But then, we *do* fall in love with places, same as with people. Minden's a great place."

Again, Jon looked at Francesca before he said, "Like I said, I'm thinking deeply about it."

"I think Diamond Point is a fabulous island," Raine said. "We were there last October and one year sometime soon we're going back for the carnival."

Francesca brightened, thinking about her upcoming trip to Diamond Point with Jon's mother. Before she could mention it, Raine said, "While I was at home with the flu, I had a chance to listen to your show more and I notice you're accompanying Mrs. Ryson there to the next carnival."

"We're there for ten days."

"Lucky you."

Jon cleared his throat. "I told you I wanted to talk with you about why I need this security system changed so quickly."

"Yes," Jordan said. "Should we talk alone?"

"No, it isn't necessary. This concerns Francesca." His mouth drew down into a straight line as he thought— *and what concerns Francesca concerns me.*

He told them then about the clippings and about the dead rabbit. As he talked, Francesca relived each clipping that had come to her, each photo of a murdered woman. And the rabbit. She wasn't far enough away from that for it not to nearly stop her breath.

"My God!" Jordan said. Raine sat frowning. She remembered all too well her own troubles with a husband who had pretended amnesia and deserted the army in

Spain, only to come back and kidnap Kym, the child who was Jordan's, but whom her first husband had partially raised.

"I'm so sorry," Raine offered.

"Thank you," Francesca said.

"Have you any idea who might be doing this?" Jordan asked.

Jon and Francesca told him about Trey and Rush. He nodded.

"Either one would be a prime suspect."

The four of them walked through the house. Jordan inspected and studied the major security-control board located in the fitness room, lightly checked the wiring and the response systems.

"This was top notch when it was installed—about three years ago?"

"Yes," Francesca said. "My ex-husband kept wanting it updated. It took awhile before it was finished."

Putting on their coats, they went outside into the cold November air. Jordan kept making notes in a small notebook.

"No dogs?"

"I'm allergic to dogs. I wish I weren't," Francesca answered. Jon thought of Trey's two gigantic and murderous pit bulls.

They checked the garage and the back of the house.

"Ever had any break-ins?" Jordan asked.

"No. Not one. I've always felt safe with this system," Francesca said.

"Yet someone left a package between your storm and front doors."

"All too true." Francesca felt the beginning of cold sweat as they stood there.

Out in the deep backyard, coming back toward the house, Francesca looked at the lights shining in a house in which she had been happy, and her heart felt heavy.

A dog howled in the distance, stopped, and the night was tranquil again.

Back inside, with a fresh round of sangria, Jordan talked with them about security.

"This was a great system," he said, "a few years back, but we have incredible systems now. They're expensive, bur some are fully satisfactory and not prohibitive.

"What do you know about infrared that can see through and photograph figures through brick walls? Ultrasensory equipment that would have gone off when someone opened your storm door?"

"To be honest," Francesca said, "I left it all to my ex. I guess it sounds a bit silly now, but I don't bother people and always thought they wouldn't bother me—until Trey."

"That's understandable," Jordan said. "I know you know the whole setup, Jon."

"Yeah, I do. We're a small police department here in Minden, but I trained in D.C. We went to Quantico fairly often for additional training. I began specializing in security. I know you're one of the best, Jordy. Word gets around."

"And Diamond Point brass wouldn't want you so badly if you weren't one of the best."

Jordan put his notebook in his shirt pocket. "I think we'd better shuffle off. I've got a couple of early morning meetings with clients." He smiled at his wife.

"I'm staying here with Fran until at least some of this blows over," Jon told them. "And I'm going on a leave of absence."

"Good idea," Jordan said. "Keep your chin up, Francesca. Don't hesitate—either one of you—to call me for whatever reason. I'll make it my business to come out on a moment's notice. I'm not slated to go out of town for at least several weeks."

He moved toward Francesca and touched her shoulder. "I wish you all the best, and I think this is a damned shame. I put the security system in your ex-husband's new house. I'm sure he remembers everything about security in this house. When I come back tomorrow, I'll throw in a few curves that will throw him for a loop."

"We're grateful for your help," Francesca told him.

After the Clymers had left, Francesca sat in a corner of the sofa. Jon went over and squatted in front of her.

"One way or another, we're going to stop this bastard in his tracks," Jon growled.

Francesca reached out and stroked Jon's hair.

"Dad never liked Trey. He told me he thought I shouldn't marry him," she said. "If only I could have been as wise."

Jon got up and sat on the sofa beside her. He reached out and lifted her chin with his forefinger.

"Do you want me to make you a cup of valerian tea?"

"I'd love it, but I want to try the kava kava. Let me fix it."

"Nope. I intend to earn my keep."

"Jon," she asked softly, "are you really thinking hard about moving to Diamond Point? Taking that job?"

He squeezed her hand, his blood running fast as his glance lightly swept her full figure. He wanted to crush her to him, kiss her until she trembled.

"I don't want you having bad dreams tonight and from now on," he said.

His lips barely grazed the corner of her mouth as he told her, "I'll be here for you, Walnut Dream, for as long as you need me."

Seventeen

Christmas Eve! At WKRX, Francesca reflected on how soon this day had come. Jon was still living at her house, still ensconced in her downstairs bedroom.

After three weeks with her, he had just decided to move back to his apartment when another obituary clipping had come in the mail and she had been frightened. The other six clippings had had the yellow Post-It note on them with the note: *Just thought you'd like to know.* The new clipping was a *photo* of her and an obituary of someone else. This time the yellow slip read: *Could this be you?* Her blood had run cold as Jon swore softly.

He had stayed on for support, and because she needed him.

Now Lou came to her, and touched her shoulder. "How's it going, Fran?"

"I'm okay for now." No sense in upsetting everybody else. She hadn't told her father about the latest clipping. In the beginning, the clippings had come three to six weeks apart. If the culprit was reverting to his beginning ways, she possibly had at least another two weeks before she'd get another one.

She glanced at her watch. Jon had brought her in early again. They were very busy with the Christmas programs. Ron Emerson would fill in for her, broadcasting

Christmas music. Holly was late. As Francesca thought about her best friend, Holly came through the door and to Francesca.

"Can you spare a moment before going on?" Holly asked, nearly out of breath.

"Sure."

"Change of plans. Listen, I know we were to have dinner with you and Jon tomorrow, but Keith has asked me to go with him to New Jersey. His father was taken ill yesterday and his only sibling is a sister who's in the army and stationed in England."

Francesca looked at her shrewdly. "Things must be taking a turn toward romance if he wants you to go with him."

Holly looked wistful. "I wish. No, we've just become really good friends now. I want to be there for him."

Jeannie, their office assistant, came up bearing a big florist's box with a poinsettia and two pounds of Rhea Smith's chocolates.

"For you," she told Francesca. Then she turned to Holly. "Yours is next."

The women oohed and aahed over the gorgeous rose poinsettia and the candy in the exquisite packaging.

"Rhea sent these earlier," Jeannie said, "along with an extra gift package for the station. She's such a love. I was here practically at daybreak because I wanted to get the schedules and playlists for next week put together."

Smiling, Francesca looked at the scripted card. "Cam Mason and Wolpers," she said softly. "I'm really looking forward to seeing those guys again."

Holly nodded, studying her. Francesca looked strained this morning. "Anything wrong, love?"

"I'll be all right," Francesca answered. "I'm just a little tired."

Jeannie brought Holly's package and put it on her desk. Ken Curtis, their chief ad executive, came over to them, his usually merry, dark brown face serious. "I know you're close to broadcast time," he said, "and I'll talk with you about this later, but I'm puzzled."

"What about?" Francesca asked.

"Well, a while back Rush Mason's ad man had me change his spots from your show to Tom Kaye and others' shows. The ads aren't pulling the way they were on your show, yet he's not switching back. . . . Okay, it's time for you to go on. I'll talk with you later."

The electronic boards lit up and Fran slipped her headset on.

"Good morning and a wonderful Christmas Eve to the world's greatest listeners," she said in her lyrical voice, sending a world of good will and all the help she knew how to give.

Looking at the laminated playlist, she saw that there were several of her favorite spirituals on tap. The first song was the Burbridge Boys' rendition of "O Holy Night" from their surprisingly popular album of Christmas songs. Bless their hearts, she thought, they really had it going for themselves.

During a long commercial break, Lou came back. Rubbing his hands together, he told her, "You've really put us on the map. Who would have ever thought your type of class would play so well?"

Francesca blushed. "Thank you."

He stood there thinking she looked bothered as she sipped a bottle of lemon Crystal Light.

"In six weeks, you'll be going to Diamond Point. I know Wolpers and Mason will be delighted with your visit. They tell me your show is helping to send tourists their way."

"I'm glad."

"I have to say I'm concerned though, Fran. What if it *is* Mason who's doing you all this dirt? What's to keep him from following you to his home territory?"

"He hasn't lived there in a long time, I understand. Jon's going with me."

"Hey! That's wonderful! I'm crazy about the idea of you two."

Francesca looked at him gravely. "Don't get too happy. After what I'm going through now, I don't want to get involved again anytime soon."

He touched her hand. "I know and I'm sorry. I've told you before. Anything I can do to help, I will."

"Thanks, Lou." Francesca scanned her schedule. Jeannie and Max were signaling to her to go back on the air.

Late that afternoon, shopping at Kennington Department Store in downtown Minden, Francesca and Jon selected last-minute items for Christmas Day. Piped Christmas music filled the air and a lanky brown Santa Claus traversed the length of the store, then settled in to bring joy to the children.

As she looked back over her shoulder at a perfume display, the edge of her shoulder struck someone and she felt Jon's arm pulling her away.

"Well, hell-o-o-o." Trey, Stacy and Rush stood in front of them, carelessly blocking much of the aisle.

For a moment, Francesca began to move on, but Trey reached out and grasped her arm. "Caught the early segment of your show today," he said. "Seems to me like your show has an edge to it now. You're more down to earth. Life brought you down, love?"

Francesca loosed Trey's fingers from her arm. He frowned, his eyes narrowing.

Rush said nothing, merely glowered at her. Stacy, resplendent in black that set off her light brown eyes and hair, looked from one to the other of them.

"Merry Christmas, you two," Stacy said. And then she

said to Trey, "Darling, hadn't we better be moving on? I've got a lot of shopping to do."

Trey frowned deeply. "You go ahead and shop, Stacy. I'll catch up with you—or I won't. Right now I'm talking to my *ex-wife.*"

By then, Francesca and Jon realized that Stacy and Trey had been drinking heavily. And probably Rush, though he seemed steadier than the other two. Jon kept his cool.

"Actually," Jon cut in smoothly, "we're in a bit of a rush. Merry Christmas to all."

Jon steered Francesca away, but not fast enough to keep her from hearing Trey mutter, "Son of a bitch."

"Oh, Trey, sweetie," Stacy cooed to Trey. "You've got me. You don't need anybody else. *We* don't need anybody else."

Then Rush said in a loud voice, "You're selfish, Stacy. That's your trouble. You're selfish."

As they reached the revolving doors of the department store, Jon led Francesca to the regular doors. "I don't want to lose you even for a minute," he said.

Outside, clouds covered the skies. When they had come in, there had been stars.

Francesca turned to Jon. "Do we have rain forecast?"

"They've had the forecast wrong all week," he answered. "It sure feels like rain."

They did not speak of Trey, Stacy or Rush, but each one had bitter, virulent or frightened thoughts about what part each one played in the evil tableaux that had partially become Francesca's life.

At home, they found Mrs. Addison bustling about, preparing the part of the holiday feast that could be done ahead of time.

"My, you two look happy," she said as they came into the kitchen. And to Francesca, "How did your day go?"

"Not bad," Francesca told her. Then she remembered she had left the special white poinsettia for Mrs. Addison in the car. Jon remembered at the same time and went to get it.

Francesca opened the refrigerator where the big turkey sat in all its trussed splendor in a heavy stainless-steel pan, waiting to be baked. They no longer stuffed the bird, but baked the corn-bread stuffing separately.

"It's getting late for you to be here," Francesca said. "I can finish up."

"It's early and I have little else to do. I told you I'm going to my son's house for dinner, so I don't have that to do. I'm going to church tonight." She put her head to one side. "Are you all right?"

"Yes. I'm okay. A little tired I guess."

"Well, none of that awful mail has come. That's surely a good thing."

"You're right. Thank you for caring."

She kissed the older woman's cheek. "Jon and I have a present for you I think you'll like."

Francesca went to the Christmas tree in the living room and picked up a brightly colored, beautifully wrapped package. She brought it back to Mrs. Addison, who beamed. "May I open it now? I've got a child's enthusiasm for gifts, although this is so pretty I hate to unwrap it."

With the package unwrapped, she reached into the box and took out a large, cream-colored, fringed, pure cashmere shawl and held it up.

"Oh Lord," she said. "I've wanted one of these for so long. They're so *expensive.*" Tears came to her eyes as she hugged Francesca.

Jon came in the back door from the garage, carrying the white poinsettia. He put it on the table.

"I see you got your gift," he said, and Mrs. Addison came to him, giving him a big hug.

"Lieutenant," she said, "you're a wonderful man."

"I thought you were going to call me Jon."

"Jon," she said softly. "I forgot. I don't mind telling you I'm glad you're here."

"Me, too," Jon said, grinning.

In a little while, Mrs. Addison had finished her tasks and bundled up as she prepared to leave.

"I've wished for snow," she told them, "and all I get is rain. Cold rain."

"Aren't you the lady who always tells me to count my blessings?" Francesca patted Mrs. Addison's shoulder.

"Oh, mind you, I'm not complaining. I'll have grand-children coming out of my pores tomorrow. I'm a happy woman."

"And you should be," Jon said heartily.

As Mrs. Addison went out the door to the three-car garage, Francesca told her, "Take care and Merry Christmas."

"Merry Christmas to you both, and I'll be thinking about you."

When Mrs. Addison had left, Francesca turned to Jon. "What did I ever do to deserve her?"

"What did I ever do to deserve *you?*"

"You've done everything right. Jon, I want you to know how much I wish things could be different. Can you understand the way I feel inside?"

"About the torment you're suffering?"

"Yes, and being afraid of love turning to hate."

"I don't think Trey hates you. I think he still loves you. They're flip sides of the same coin."

"I don't want his love. It's too twisted. And it didn't just get that way."

They stood near the stove, and Jon put his arms

around her. "You know, don't you, that I'd bear all this for you if I could?"

"Yes, and thank you."

He nuzzled her neck for the briefest of moments, then pulled away. It was the Christmas season, a time of love and giving. And what he wanted to give her was himself.

Eighteen

Francesca went upstairs and changed to a navy, silk-jersey jumpsuit with flared legs. The silken fabric made her skin glow. She put a hint of lavender behind her ears and at the pulse point of her throat. When she walked back in, Jon gave her his best wolf whistle. "I wish we were close enough for me to kiss you savagely. But I won't." She smiled, flushed, and they settled down in the living room to listen to Christmas music.

With the big Christmas tree decked with exquisite crystal ornaments and angel hair, with a crystal angel adorning the top, each felt the happiness of the season, yet sadness also permeated their spirits.

They sat on the sofa a little distance apart. "I guess in times of trouble we think of past happier times," Francesca finally said.

"That's true. What are you thinking about?"

"The way I always opened half my presents on Christmas Eve, the rest very early Christmas morning. I guess I was a *can't wait* child."

Jon laughed. "Kevin and I went into ours before daybreak. . . ."

His voice had gone hoarse.

"You miss him so much, don't you?"

"Yes. Last Christmas was hell. You help me more than I could ever tell you."

"I'm glad," she said softly, then pulled him closer. "Put your head in my lap and stretch out. I want to be there for you."

Jon did as she suggested and she stroked his face and shoulders.

"Remember the first night when you did the reflexology on my feet?"

"How could I forget it? I was a tense hombre for a couple of days."

"You've got great control, Jon. I like that. More control than anyone I've ever known."

He reached up and stroked her throat. "I've got an idea."

"What is it?"

"I'd like to bring back happier moments for you. Let's open our presents tonight."

Francesca's face lit up. "I'd love to, but not just this minute. I've got a few more things to do in the kitchen. I like the tension of waiting—with things for you."

Lying with his head in her lap, feeling her soft flesh juxtaposed against his rock hardness, Jon reflected that she could come to mean more to him than life itself. But he had to play it cool.

Only then did they speak of Trey.

Shifting slightly, Francesca got nervous just thinking about their encounter with Trey and Rush.

She laughed ruefully. "Rush Mason hates me, and it isn't a matter of there being another side of the coin."

"I'd have to agree with you. Whatever else is wrong with Mason, he's a spoiled brat. I've got the feeling he was brought up with everything but love."

"He gave me no real trouble until I won the Female Broadcaster of the Year Award. He could have been well on the way to one for himself in another place. Instead, he hangs around here—with a wonderful job, mind you—and broods."

"And broods and broods. There's no accounting for the paths a sick mind takes."

"I think there's something pathologically wrong with him."

"That's the idea I got when I paid him that visit."

"He's shuddery at least. Looking at him tonight, I thought it could be him sending the clippings, leaving the dead rabbit. And the one clipping since then."

Jon nodded.

"But that one was more awful than the others. A photo of my head attached to another woman's obituary. Jon, does it end only with my death or some terrible injury?"

She hadn't known she would say it, and he heard the anguish in her voice, saw that she involuntarily wrung her slender hands.

He sat up and pulled her close to him, smoothing her hair, comforting her.

"I won't let anything happen to you," he said, "and you can depend on that."

Nervous, she got up then. She was getting closer to Jon than her fear would let her. She needed to move away.

"I'm going to get some devil's food cake and eggnog."

Jon read her perfectly. He couldn't help coming closer. Everything in him reached out to her, but he was going to wait until she was ready.

"Okay, you do that," he said.

In the kitchen, standing near the cake box on a table by the refrigerator, Francesca closed her eyes. *You're going to lose something too precious to lose. He isn't going to wait forever,* the right side of her brain warned her.

But the left side of her brain cautioned: *The burned child. You know the rest.*

And she did know the rest, felt it screaming in her veins.

Once the cake and the eggnog were on a silver tray, Francesca peeked through the open door to the break-fast nook. Ten two-liter Coke bottles were lined against the far wall, each filled with choice black loam and with one rose cutting in it.

Come spring, each cutting would go into another rose garden she had planned to be located just under the downstairs bedroom where Jon now slept. She'd come back and examine them later. Going to the win-dow, she raised one of the blinds. It had stopped rain-ing, but it was heavily overcast.

She wanted to be out in that cold rain, breathing deeply. That would stop the anxiety. Stop it on the sur-face anyway. A terrible thought came to her mind: Would she see another Christmas?

Don't get maudlin, my girl, she told herself. But it was flying in the face of reality not to acknowledge that she was in danger.

They ate the delectable food slowly and she got Jon another cup of eggnog.

"I guess your father and my mother are painting New Orleans red." Jon's face was grave. "Life hasn't been too kind to Melanie since . . ."

Francesca waited for the end of his sentence; it was not forthcoming. Jon shrugged.

"Why don't we open our presents?" he said quietly.

Francesca got up and got the presents from under the tree, admiring its splendor. She wished Christmas would last a month; but truthfully, she did celebrate it all month.

She had had Jon's large gift wrapped in midnight-blue, shiny paper, tied with ribbons ending in plastic cherries and mistletoe.

Jon took the package and grinned. "Mistletoe," he said. "You're asking for it again."

Francesca's face went hot. For a long moment, she felt mixed up with desperately wanting what she was afraid to reach for. Did Jon guess the depths of her tension? Of what she felt for him? She wanted him in her arms, wanted to be in his, and yes, she wanted him deep inside her.

She had wondered about her gift since he had left it under the tree three nights before. Now she sat down and slowly began to unwrap the gold foil package with its fancy white-and-gold chiffon bow and gold bells.

Jon held up his present and caught her to him.

"You must have read my mind," he said. "Baby, I *love* this."

He held up a superbly tailored, camel-colored, cashmere sports coat with brown leather and ivory buttons. He got up, slipping the coat on over his gray wool turtleneck.

Francesca found herself holding back. Why was being with him tonight so much harder than it had been? They had both been proud of their control.

He reached for her to pull her up and to him, but she continued to hold back. "No, let me unwrap your present," she said. He looked hurt, and she bit her lip. Deftly, she unwrapped the rectangular box and opened it. She gasped when she saw the navy leather jewelry box and snapped it open to reveal a pendant on a navy glove-leather bed.

Holding the pendant up with shaking fingers, she gloried in its beauty. A large sapphire, held in place by gleaming waves of gold, caught the light and reflected it. Eight small diamonds glittered, set at various outer points, adding to the luster of the sapphire and the gold.

She closed her eyes against the onslaught of emotions

and, watching her, Jon wondered what she was thinking. Why had she rebuffed him when he'd wanted to draw her close? You didn't give a man such an exquisite present unless you cared for him. Or maybe she was merely grateful. He drew back, stung.

"Jon," she said in a hushed voice. "It's *so* beautiful."

"I'm glad you like it."

"I love it." She got up and gave him a brief kiss on the cheek. He started to pull her to him, but decided not to. He was getting sensitive, tender where she was concerned. And he'd had enough rejection from Stacy to last him a lifetime. Not to mention Melanie.

He took the pendant and fastened it around her lovely, silken, walnut throat, reveling in the way her eyes and skin reflected the warmth of the stone.

"You don't need to look in a mirror," he said. "My eyes tell you how you look. You're beautiful."

There. He was gallant in spite of her pushing him away. Reaching back, she unfastened the pendant and put it back in its case, leaving the case open to display the jewel. Her breath was coming too fast.

She had to get away, but she needed to be close to him. She got up and left the room, going to the fitness room where many of the security panels were. She disengaged one of the smaller panels. Jon would be furious.

When she went back out, she touched Jon's hair as she passed the sofa.

"I'll be back in a jiffy," she said. "I forgot something."

She fled the room, feeling like a frightened deer. The clippings and the rabbit had scared her, but not like this. Was she going to have to ask him to leave?

Going out to the kitchen, she snatched up a raincoat from a peg in the back hall closet, got a flashlight from the back hall table and went outside. Standing on the back steps, she began to breathe deeply and immediately became less anxious. Then she remembered leaving her leather notepad that she had been using to sketch her plans for a rose garden under her window. In her mind's eye, she could see the coming roses, smell their fragrance.

In actuality, the smell of rain was in the air and dark clouds covered the heavens. Gingerly, she rounded the corner of the house. The notepad was no more than twenty feet from the kitchen door. She picked it up and turned to go back inside. My God, but she felt *free*, she thought. Untrammeled. Secure. *Nobody* was going to make her a prisoner.

The cloudburst came as she was about ten feet from the kitchen door. She felt it soak her and for a moment blind panic struck. Could she drown?

Staggering to the door, she opened it and half fell inside, where driving rain caught Jon as he pulled her in. He pushed the door shut and held her thoroughly wet body against his own.

"Let me dry off first," she stammered. "I'm getting you wet."

He was furious. "What in the hell were you doing out there, Fran?"

She tried to explain that she had been retrieving her planning pad, but she wasn't going to lie to him. The night's rain had already ruined it. No, she was running away—from him.

Feeling like a half-drowned animal, she went into his arms and he held her tightly, fear and anger raging inside him.

"Why didn't the alarm go off?"

"I disengaged it."

For a moment he was struck dumb. "Why, Fran? Why would you jeopardize your life like that?"

"Oh God," she whispered. "I don't know. I just don't

know." Now she was lying to him when he meant the world to her.

In her bathroom, he blotted her dry with a big bath sheet and continued to hold her. He toweled her wet hair. Then he let her go and dried himself.

"That was a hell of a cloudburst," he said quietly. "I'm glad it wasn't worse."

"Thank you," she said softly. "Thank you for everything."

"You'd better get into some dry clothes and I'd better do the same."

Letting go of her, he went to the fitness room and re-engaged the panel she had cut off. Then he quickly went back to Francesca.

He didn't want to let her out of his sight. She looked so precious and he wanted her so much it was unbearable. She didn't want to leave him, and she valiantly fought her feelings.

The embers of a fire long in building caught and the flames of desire flashed around them. Pressed against him, she felt the hardness of his body and the rock-hard proof of how he wanted her. They moved to the bedroom he now occupied and they undressed each other hastily, breath catching in their throats.

"I came out to check on you when you didn't come back," he said. "I don't want anything to happen to you."

She stroked the back of his head. Then she drew his mouth to hers and he savagely kissed her so hard her mouth hurt. She clung to him as if she were drowning. Her melting softness filled him with glory and his solid muscular hardness filled her with feelings of security.

The patter of rain against the windowpanes soothed them both. They were in this world, but not quite of it. Each felt the other's passion as his or her own.

"My darling," he said huskily, "don't ever do anything like that again. Fran, I couldn't take it if anything happened to you."

The gorgeous, deep curves of her body thrilled him. As they lay on the bed, he began to traverse her body with ardent, swift kisses. Then his hands were in her damp hair and he held her away from him to suckle her swollen, brown breasts.

She was falling away from earth into a cloudburst of her own. As flames of desire licked her mind no less than her body, she felt one moment of despair. She was lost in this dream, in this man. And how would she find her way back?

He slipped on the thin latex shield. Then suddenly it didn't matter. She let herself be swept away, let the smooth strokes and the hardness of him inside her take her over, spin her away.

In the hot, tight sheath of her body, Jon felt closer to heaven than he'd ever been. But there was danger here, for now he could never let her go. Thrusting rhythmically, he thought of oceanic tidal waves sweeping majestically onto shore, sweeping everything before them.

Crying out beneath him, she brought his mouth down to hers and their tongues intertwined into a sweet tangle of love and cherishing and intense satisfaction.

Hard rain drove against the windowpanes and it sealed them in with each other. A jagged streak of lightning lit up the windows in the room. He slowed and propped himself on his elbows to keep his entire weight off her. Arched above her, he blew warm streams of air onto her face and body.

Her arms went around his neck, pulling him down onto her.

"I don't want to hurt you," he said, panting.

"You won't. You never would. Jon?"

"Yes, sweetheart."

"Never mind. We can talk later. I want you so badly. I felt as if I'd die if I didn't have you inside me."

"I'm here and I love it, and I love you, but I don't have to tell you that."

"I love you, too," she said hesitantly. She wanted to tell him how afraid she was, but for these moments she knew no fear. He was taking her in love and passion. Where would it end? For the moment, she was unable to care for anything save this moment and this man.

Time spun effortlessly as he stayed inside her, probing her depths expertly, her nectared sheath surrounding him until he thought he'd go mad with joy.

As a burst of thunder shook the house, he turned her over and she arched above him, her curves fitting his body's lines. The sheath of her tightened onto him like a fist. His mouth found hers and again his kisses hurt.

This was like nothing she had experienced before. Her mouth granted him easy access, and they explored their passion together. It felt to Francesca that they would go into each other—meld. And that was right.

If he hurt her later, she would have known this wonder. And that, too, would be right, for at that moment the precious, urgent tremors shook her entire body and she was lost in a radiant burst of love, as she held him with all her strength.

Holding her, Jon knew that this would be a stellar experience for the rest of his life. There would be more. He had to have more. More of her lovely face, her large, soft, firm breasts. More of the wide hips with their gentle curves.

He could spend the rest of the night outlining the glory that was this woman. Glorious body. Glorious spirit. Glorious warmth.

She drew him in as a magnet draws filings and now

he was lost inside her, inside their private world. And nothing in him wanted to be found.

Feeling the climactic tremors of her body, Jon felt himself drawn into her lushness, the splendor that was her body and her spirit. His loins trembled on a long brink, then exploded in savage ecstasy that lasted a long, thrilling time.

They lay for a while, spent, silent. Then her fingers traced his eyebrows and moustache, and he raised up on his elbows again.

"I was afraid I was going to crush you."

"I'm a big woman."

"And I love the whole package of you."

She laughed shakily. "Jon, men often aren't, but you're sweet."

"I want to be sweet for you. Do I satisfy you?"

"Oh Lord, yes. In all my life I've never known anything this beautiful."

"Neither have I. Experiences like this are meant to last a lifetime."

When he said it, it took her breath away. Quite bitterly, she thought, *damn the fear that holds me away from him*. But she hadn't been afraid when he was inside her, when they were spinning gloriously out of control.

"Fran."

"Yes, my love?"

"You're still afraid, aren't you?"

"Yes. I won't lie."

He rolled over beside her. "I'm going to switch the light on. Do you mind?"

"No."

"I want to look at you." He leaned over and flicked the lamp switch, bringing the room into brighter focus.

"Fran, we've got to talk more about this; I'm scared, too. I've been hurt. Not as badly as Hudson hurt you, but I knew a more basic hurt—from Melanie. Stacy hurt me, but I think we hurt each other. Now, since I've known you, I'm determined to put my past traumas aside. I want to be with you."

He chuckled. "I used to tell my father after Melanie left that I was going to have a forever love. This was what I wanted, not fame or fortune."

"That's beautiful." And she hurt with knowing that she could not give him that love.

Rain still drummed against the house and the wind howled.

Still naked, they propped themselves onto thick pillows.

"Do you believe in destiny?" she asked.

"Yes, sometimes. Why do you ask?"

"I dreamed about you the night before I came into your office."

"You told me about the dream, but not that the man turned out to be me."

"I know. I couldn't. We met before that time at the gas pump. We met at a party, but I was still married. I didn't run across you again, but I was evidently impressed. And it stayed in the back of my mind. You seemed like a man a woman would be secure with."

"I hope I am—I know I want to be—for you."

They lay there, each caught up in tenderness and spent desire. Francesca yawned.

"Getting bored?" he teased.

"Sleepy. Aren't you? The sex manuals all say men are apt to be tired and sleepy after making love."

"Forget about the sex manuals. Try reality. I'm not sleepy, and given half a chance, I'll prove it."

Francesca laughed delightedly.

"Okay," he said. "It's late. I'll let you go for the moment, but expect an early morning awakening."

They snuggled down close to each other, and Jon switched off the lamp on the night table.

Drifting off to sleep, Francesca murmured, "What is there about rain that makes us so romantic?"

"I don't need rain with you."

"I'm glad, because I don't think I need it either."

It was near morning when the nightmare struck. She had not had another one since the dead rabbit was put at her door. She walked in a forest again, as she had in the dream she'd had with Jon in it. The beginning of Jon and her.

She walked along in a happy springtime. The trees were beautiful, wet with recent rain and struck through with sunlight. Suddenly, Trey was on the path facing her. This time, he held no gun, but his brutal fists were raised to strike her down. She knew he would kill her, and he wanted her to know.

Jon heard her scream and came awake. He drew her to him, shook her gently, calling, "Fran, wake up!"

She came awake gasping for breath. It took a moment to get her bearings. These dreams, that hallucination when she had "seen" the rabbit were all so real. "I had a nightmare. I'm sorry I woke you up."

"Don't be. Tell me about the dream." He switched on the light by their bedside.

She told him, shuddering all the time.

He stroked her gently, murmuring endearments. "I'm sorry," he said, "sorry you have to go through this at all."

Her eyes stung, and Francesca got up to get allergy drops from the bathroom.

Back in bed, he caught her hand and kissed it. "Merry Christmas, sweetheart!"

He kissed her gently on the lips.

"Merry Christmas, Jon," she whispered.

His tender eyes drew her, and she felt alive with wanting him. The nightmare fear subsided, and she kissed the corner of his mouth, pressing her tongue into the dampness.

"Don't ask for what you don't want," he teased her.

"What if I want what I'm asking for?"

"In that case . . ." His eyes crinkled shut with laughter, and he drew her to him, planting wet kisses over her with the tip of his tongue.

"That tickles," she said, laughing.

"That's not the effect I'm aiming for."

Her hands played out wide arcs onto his body. "What *are* you aiming for?"

"Something more precious than gold. You."

"Do you know something?" she murmured. "You're a lover. An extraordinary lover."

"That's what I want to be for you."

He drew her close, and her arms went around his body. She was rich with his kisses, charged by his love.

This time he slipped on the thin sheath, and they made love lazily, in slow motion, and each felt the other's soul-deep need.

Francesca craved what she was getting from Jon with a need that shocked her. *Can I let this happen?* she asked herself. He spoke of wanting a forever love. *I want that, too. But life disappoints us sometimes and if he leaves me, I'll be hurt beyond bearing it.*

Jon stroked the pulse in the curve of her throat and wondered at the passion surging through him. A forever love. It hadn't lasted for his father and mother. It hadn't lasted with Stacy. Could love ever last for him?

Nineteen

Jon and Francesca decided to have Christmas dinner at four. Both were relaxed and exhilarated. The glow of their lovemaking still lay on them. Both had slept much of the morning.

Her father and Melanie had called that morning saying that they were having a great time. Then Francesca and Jon talked with Keith and Holly. Keith's father was better. He and Holly would return sooner than expected.

Now as various pots simmered on the stove, Francesca prepared a big garden salad and Jon candied the sweet potatoes. They listened to the holiday music Ron Kaye spun on WKRX. A vocal version of "O Holy Night" came on and Francesca sat down to listen to it.

"I get goose pimples when singers sing various phrases of that song," Francesca said.

"Yes. It's beautiful."

"We're taking Ron his dinner when we're finished eating. He wants it brought over later," Francesca commented.

"I guess he's a pretty lonesome guy since his wife checked out."

"I think so, but he's taking it well. I invited him over, but he's licking his wounds and wants to be alone."

Crossing the room to the stove, they bumped into

each other, and Jon held her for a moment. He kissed the tip of her nose. "Merry Christmas, sweetheart," he said.

They served dinner in the dining room, with the table set with an ecru tablecloth under heavy ecru lace, Waterford crystal and Wedgwood deep cream china with broad gold borders. The silver gleamed from Mrs. Addison's polishing the day before, and the centerpiece was partly fashioned from the orchids that had come from Matt Wolpers and Cam Mason. Francesca touched a white orchid.

"This reminds me that early February will find us on Diamond Point. Are you looking forward to it?"

"Certainly. A beautiful island with a beautiful woman. You bet your life I'm looking forward to it."

Francesca sounded wistful. "I know what a boon it would be for your career if you took a top policeman's spot in the prime minister's security. . . ."

"I'm mulling it over. That's all."

"Serious consideration?"

"Going there will help me make up my mind. They've had little more trouble since the last easily put down attempt on Tom Barton's life."

Francesca looked at the finished table and liked what she saw. It was a first Christmas for Jon and her.

Dressed for dinner, Francesca wore one of several indigo-blue dresses she owned. This one was silk faille with a boat neckline that showed off her lovely shoulders and back. She wore the gold, diamond and sapphire necklace Jon had given her and its meaning and loveliness filled her heart.

Seated at the table, she looked at Jon, resplendent in his tan cashmere coat and dark brown gabardine pants, his pale cream shirt and brown-beige-and-gray-patterned silk rep tie.

"Do you want to say the blessing?" he asked.

"No, you do it. I'll add my silent thanks."

He recited a long blessing that ended with the words, "Lord, we are forever grateful for the bountiful gifts you've sent us. Amen."

Francesca sat with her hands in her lap. "I'm starved," she said. "How about you? It was smart of us to skip lunch."

"Ravenous. I was about to begin nibbling on your fingers."

"You're a living nut."

"Call me what you will, but I'll get around to that."

Jon stood up, turned on the carving knife and began to carve the turkey.

While he worked, she served their plates with the beautifully done and colorful foods, giving him an extra portion of the cornbread-and-sausage dressing. He had opened the wine in the kitchen. Both had decided they wanted homemade blackberry wine. Her father made it every year, and it had been her favorite since she began drinking alcoholic beverages.

The wine had quickly become a favorite with Jon.

On the radio, Ron Emerson announced in one of a few interruptions in programming that the forthcoming segment of his show was being dedicated to Francesca and Jon. They looked at each other and laughed.

"What a sweetie," she said.

"I'm your only sweetie," Jon teased her.

She felt her heart turn over. It was such a lighthearted remark, she thought, but it moved her. Since the night before and this morning, she was going to have to watch her step. They had traveled on the crest of an incredible wave of passion unlike anything she had ever known. But she was still shaken with fear.

Dinner was leisurely, ending in the wild plum pudding Holly had gotten the recipe for from Caleb. Francesca flambéed it after turning off the lights, and the aroma filled the room. Early winter darkness was setting in.

They ate the plum pudding slowly, savoring every bite. But they savored even more the closeness they felt. Jon told himself that whatever the future brought, he wanted this woman.

Francesca wanted to be able to want him without fear, but she knew that even in giving herself to him, a craven part of herself had held back, whimpering from past hurt.

When they had finished, Francesca proposed that they play hooky from the dishes for a while.

"A woman after my own heart," Jon said. "I'll do them later."

"You'll do no such thing. The dishwasher deserves a break. I'm trying to make this a special day for you."

They sat on the sofa by the window, and he took her hands in his and nibbled her fingers. "I warned you," he said.

"You're really something, you know."

"You're even more."

Snapping his fingers, he excused himself, got up and went to his bedroom. He came back out holding a black-leather box much like the one her necklace had come in. He sat down and opened the box, revealing a man's antique gold pocket watch with engraved ivy leaves on its cover.

Francesca nearly fainted with shock. It was a long moment before she could get her breath. That watch was familiar, and her head began to swim with the memory.

"What's wrong, Fran?" He saw the alarm on her face.

"I've seen that watch before," she said, drawing back.

Puzzled, he looked at her. "I never let it out of my sight. I keep it in a safe at home and only wear it on special occasions. I went to my apartment and got it yesterday because I wanted to show it to you. Things happened between us that made me forget." He shook his head. "No. You couldn't have seen it."

"But I *did*," she insisted. "It was the same day Trey knocked me unconscious."

For a moment, she clenched her teeth. How to talk about something she had so doggedly held in?

"You don't have to talk about this now. I want you to enjoy your Christmas."

She closed her eyes. "I think it's *time* I talked about it."

He took her hand, and pressed it.

"Trey was upstairs in the master bedroom. I was down here. A call came for him, and I answered the phone. It was Rush telling him to come quickly. Cops were swarming the place because one of the salesmen was being arrested for selling drugs. I didn't hang up the phone, you see. I couldn't. I needed to know what was going on."

"Yeah."

"After Trey drove away, I went upstairs. For the first time since we'd been married his safe was slightly open. He'd always told me never to look inside his safe, and I didn't.

"But I looked this time. I took care to see how far he had left the door open so I could close it back the way he'd left it. A small, open manila envelope faced me. I pulled it out and looked at the gold watch it held.

"The watch was exquisite. I could never forget it."

"Was there a 'C' engraved on the back of it?"

"Yes."

"Kevin," Jon said, nearly choking. "Dad gave us both watches when we graduated from college. Kevin wanted his nickname initial—'Cookieman' for the cookies he was so fond of. But dear God, maybe it wasn't . . . Other people have the initial 'C.' "

Francesca felt chills go up and down her spine. "I closed the safe door exactly as I'd found it and went back downstairs. Trey came back an hour or so later in the worst mood I'd ever seen him in.

"He asked me if I'd looked in his safe, and I said no, I hadn't. He didn't believe me. I'm not a good liar. 'Well, if you have,' he said, 'you're going to pay for it.' "

Francesca could not stop the visions that flashed before her of that time. She was back in the room with Trey. Jon reached for her, and she shook her head.

"No, I've got to tell you the whole story."

"Okay." Jon's eyes had filled with tears.

"Somehow I managed to pull it together. I put on quite an act. I had run into Trey's temper before, but not like this. I felt my life depended on my acting.

"He caught me by my shoulders and almost shook the breath out of me. I could see Warlock in his face, and I was scared, but I toughed it out. 'In all our time together,' I told him, 'have you ever known me to do anything you asked me not to do?'

"That seemed to slow him down, but for only a minute. Then the rage was back. He pushed me from him, shouting that I was lying and he'd kill me. I was paralyzed when he hit me, and I lost consciousness."

Jon stroked her hands. "Dear God, I'm sorry."

But Francesca was feeling Trey's blow more than Jon's compassion. She had needed to relive those vicious moments. Now she was going to, and her life was coming clearer.

"I got up and called a cab. I went to the hospital. My temple and the left side of my face were badly bruised. I had a black eye. I couldn't believe what was happening.

"He didn't come home until the next morning. I told Lou, and he told me to take a few days off. When Trey came back, he acted as if nothing had happened."

"Would his other personalities be responsible for that?"

She shook her head. "He told me his therapist had told him that he was largely atypically multiple, which means he changes personalities, but if he tries hard enough, he can be aware when it happens. He *likes* being Warlock. He told me many times he does."

"Yet he's managed to build a thriving business, so he's got to be *Trey* most of the time."

"Yes. He's greedier for money and success than he is for revenge on a father who beat him senseless again and again."

Quite bitterly she said, "I guess I've always known it. Trey will kill someone one day, if he hasn't already."

"My brother," Jon said grimly. "Kevin told me he was psyching out a stolen-car ring and he was pretty proud of himself. He said he thought Hudson was at least involved, if not the mastermind of the outfit.

"Unlike me, Kevin kept his watch with him all the time. If Trey had that watch, then Trey may have killed him, or may know who did."

She touched his face. "Jon, I'm so sorry. I wish I had known before. Couldn't you arrest him now?"

"Nope. It doesn't work like that. The watch was specially made by a company in New York, the same one that made your necklace. I can't prove that someone else didn't get one made just like it. It would be good circumstantial evidence, but that isn't enough.

"Things have got to add up these days for criminals

to get what's coming to them. That's right—they should
have to add up. But I've got a hunch. . . . We've worked
hard on it, but all we're coming up against is dead leads.
This may help."

"I'm glad."

Jon's face was taut with hurt and anger.

"Watch out, Hudson," he said softly. "I'm going to
be on your hide as tight as the husk on wild rice."

Diamond Point—
The Caribbean

Twenty

"Bonbini! which is our word for welcome!" Matt Wolpers flashed a wide smile at Francesca, Jon and Melanie as he shook hands with each of them.

His private boat had been used to get them from Aruba where their plane had landed.

"Thank you," all three said.

Francesca threw her head back, reveling in the soft trade winds. "Is the air always this delightful?" she asked. "Or is it seldom this way?"

Cam Mason, who had come with Wolpers, filled them in. "It is almost always this way. We may not have the lushness of some of the islands in the Caribbean. We are dry—arid—here, but we make up for it in other ways. Hurricanes pass us by."

"What a marvelous place," Melanie said.

Matt Wolpers smiled. "Thank you, 'Minden's Woman of the Year.' We like it. But wait until you get to our private paradise of Diamond Point. You will love it there as we do. And we plan to show you the best of times."

On Diamond Point, across the way from Aruba on its leeward side, the island of Diamond Point shone like a small jewel. Its sandy white beaches curved invitingly. Cacti of every type and size sat in prickly glory. Palm trees, divi-divi trees and kwihi trees abounded. It was an island of large and small brightly colored cottages, with only two hotels and the prime minister's white mansion. There were a number of lovely restaurants and many jewelry shops.

Jon watched silently as he, Francesca and Melanie rode in a Jeep over the island.

They had gone to the cottage assigned them, which belonged to Cam Mason. There they had changed into comfortable cotton clothes.

At the beginning, Matt Wolpers had urged them, "When I bring you back to your cottage, I would suggest that you give your bodies time to acclimate to the change in climate. Rest, sleep and begin to watch our splendid carnival and that of Aruba tomorrow night."

"That would be wise," Cam Mason agreed.

Abruptly, at Matt's suggestion, the driver pointed the big Jeep in the direction of a very high hill.

"I want you to see something of beautiful significance to us," Matt said.

They rode for a while in silence, their faces wreathed in smiles at the plants and birds around them. Hundreds of green and yellow giant parakeets flitted around them, so tame they lighted on the passing Jeep and rode a short while with them, then flew away, calling to their mates.

"How charming," Melanie said.

"You have all visited before," Matt said.

Melanie shook her head. "They have. I haven't."

"Then we promise you the best we have to offer," Matt said.

Cam laughed. "We are intent on giving every visitor the best. And you shall have even better."

Melanie laughed. "It's plain I'm going to enjoy this."

At the top of the hill, they got out and the driver retrieved several pairs of binoculars from a large leather case. He gave a pair to each of the visitors, who took them and looked through the powerful lenses.

"There is a knack to this," Matt told them. "Look carefully and you can see the whole of the island from tip to tip. You must come here at night also when our lights and the lights of Aruba can be seen in the distance."

A flamboyant plant with red blossoms grew not far from several kwihi shade trees. Giant red and white mushrooms grew nearby. The group drank in the beauty of the place. Many species of brightly colored birds flew down to the ocean and back up again.

Sailboats and scuba divers in bright colors dotted the turquoise Caribbean.

Coming down from the top of the hill, the driver went to the side of the island where the land was scrubbier, and goats wandered, alert and bleating. The whole section was bleak. There were scattered large, drab buildings that seemed unoccupied and added to the bleakness. The coast here was jagged and rocky.

"Warehouses," Cam said. "Our people are entrepreneurs. They rent from the island and store their wares here." But even here the colorfully flowered cacti flourished. "My cousin, Rush, owns a car barn here."

Francesca looked at the stretch of island before her and felt sad. It was, she thought, as if the other sides of the island had drained the beauty from this side. A coolness came into her blood and lingered there, though the day was very warm.

"Now this." Francesca and Jon had wandered a bit away from the others, and Cam summoned them as he put on gloves and told them, "This is a Bushi cactus. Tell me if you like this."

Cutting a piece of the plant's fruit in half, he peeled it, cut it up and put the pieces on a paper towel, offering some to each of them.

Francesca found the taste very like strawberries.

"Delectable," she said, and the others tried it and agreed.

"Later I will show you more fruits and nuts you will love. Caribbean cherries, grapes, and cashews grow both wild and cultivated. We are blessed."

Yes, they were blessed, Francesca thought. This time around she had already seen parts of the island she had not seen before. But she was tired from the hustle and bustle of their trip, and she wanted to rest as Matt had suggested they do.

Looking out at the bleak landscape with its sparse hints of color, she felt another shudder move her and wondered at the cooling of her blood.

Back at their cottage, they drank tamarind juice and ate bagels and cream cheese on their patio. "We once lived here in this cottage," Cam said. "Then I moved up in the world, as you can do if you go along with our plan." He looked at Jon and smiled. Jon returned the smile, but didn't answer.

Francesca looked down at her shapely feet in their natural, wide-strapped sandals, and Jon's eyes lingered on her in her blue sundress with big, white pearl buttons going up one side. His own polo shirt was the same shade as her dress. Melanie had chosen beige cotton.

When they had finished their tamarind juice and bagels, Cam and Matt gave them a tour of the house. The rooms inside the bright yellow, red-roofed cottage were large and well appointed.

"The furniture is beautiful. What wood is it?" Francesca asked.

"It is the wood of the Kwihi tree, aged for several years and polished to a luster it never loses. Yes, we like it very much."

The rooms were filled with throw and floor pillows, and the large side porch had wonderfully woven rattan furniture.

Then the two men took them on a tour of Cam's big orchid greenhouse. He laughed. "My cousin, Rush, called this an orchid *maze* when I built it years ago."

Francesca drew breath quickly at the mention of Rush's name. Jon looked at her sharply.

"Oh yes," Cam said, sighing. "As boys we were close friends. Now . . ." He shrugged.

Stretched out before them was an orchid wonderland. So many orchids of every color and shape. "It is a full-time job for the people who care for them," Cam said. The group looked at the winding corridors of the orchid greenhouse.

"We ship them all over the world," he said, pointing out the several people working in the greenhouse. "We think we have the best."

Guiding them down to the end of the long orchid greenhouse, Cam took them into a room with satiny cream walls halfway up to the ceiling and transparent, wide, breast-high windows. At a double-glass door covered with ecru ninon curtains, one could see the turquoise Caribbean and its pristine white sands.

A wide blue couch of glove leather lined one wall. Orchid plants were set about and a fountain flowed from a corner of the ceiling.

"Oh, this is wonderful." This time Melanie came alive.

"Thank you," Cam said. "My idea. At night, a watchman patrols to keep out thieves and young lovers who might wish to tarry here."

Matt Wolpers grinned. "He built his own honeymoon niche."

Cam shrugged. "Please feel free to visit here anytime. It is guarded and so, safe."

Jon laughed. "Does it get any better than this?"

Matt looked at him keenly. "I hope you will come back on your own honeymoon. I think now I can divine the reason you resist accepting our offer."

Three nights later, after dinner was served inside their cottage dining room, Jon went to meet and talk with the prime minister. Melanie got into her nightclothes, but Francesca felt restless and did not undress. She felt no sign of the coolness inside her now. It had disappeared with their leaving what she now called the bleak side of the island.

Carved chocolates and cashew nuts in glass dishes were in every room, and orchids were everywhere about the cottage. Francesca felt more relaxed than she had in many months. She felt as if she had left her fears behind her to rest on this peaceful island.

There was a gorgeous moon, and she enjoyed its glow as she stood at the window.

A knock sounded, and at Francesca's bidding, Melanie came in, tightening the belt of her dark rose robe.

"It's beautiful here, isn't it?" Melanie seemed nervous.

"So very," Francesca responded. "And to think you're going to be in the middle of all this magic come Carnival Day."

"I keep pinching myself."

Hesitatingly, Francesca said, "Is something bothering you?"

"Yes. May I sit down?"

"Of course. My house, my room, is your house and your room."

Melanie's smile didn't reach her eyes, which looked sad.

"You're the kind of woman I want for my son," she said, "but I don't feel I have the right to play a part in his life."

"Why can't you forgive yourself?"

"You don't know the whole story."

"I wish I did."

Sighing, speaking just above a whisper, Melanie said, "I ran away with another man. I dumped my family for another man, a man I thought I loved more than life itself. . . ."

Melanie's eyes filled with tears. Francesca got up and went to her with a box of tissues. "Melanie, everything ends sometime. Life itself ends. So, stop being so hard on yourself. That was long ago."

"My husband died without forgiving me. Kevin died without forgiving me. Jon hates me."

"No. He doesn't. He's mixed up. You've got to keep being open to him. Give him a chance. Ask his forgiveness."

Melanie shook her head. "I keep wanting to, but I can't. I get to the brink, and the words just won't come.

"My husband was a good man, but he couldn't show his feelings. I felt I was dying inside. He never wanted to go anywhere, do anything. We were young, and I felt life was passing me by. He worked his fingers to the bone, but he seldom told me he loved me."

"This happens so often."

"I met Jeb, a musician in a rhythm and blues band. And he was everything I wanted my husband to be. I was a fool, but he talked me into having an affair. We planned to run away. I was to meet him in Memphis, and we were going to be married when my divorce became final.

"He left me a letter with his aunt, who we were going to stay awhile with. The letter said he couldn't go through with it. He couldn't stand being tied down. He said I was still married, and I should go back to my husband and forget him.

"The letter was full of endearments and compliments, like the man, but it was empty like the man. I had thrown away gold and run after dross.

"His aunt told me to forget him. I was not the first married woman he'd brought home. 'He's my nephew, and I love him,' she said, 'but I think he hates women. He's hurt so many.'"

Melanie's tears flowed freely now. Francesca kneeled in front of her chair and put her arms around Melanie.

"Let it all come out," she said gently. "And tomorrow or tonight, tell Jon how you feel. Please."

Melanie thought a long while. "I'll try, but I don't think I can stand it if he turns me away. He's all I have left."

"No. You have yourself left. You're a wonderful woman, and I don't want you to forget it. Try it and try again. Make him know how much you love him."

"The hurt I caused him is the reason he's never married, but he loves you."

"And I'm glad, but I have my own problems now. I don't know if I can ever marry again."

"Francesca, be good to my son. I see how he looks at you."

"And *you* be good to him by asking his forgiveness. I care deeply for Jon. If I weren't so mixed up, I would love him."

Melanie smiled wanly. "One day we'll both get it straightened out."

"I'll do my best if you'll do the same."

"I promise," Melanie said, and her smile was a little brighter.

They decided to cut out the lights and sit at the windows. Carnival music and ringing laughter filled the air.

Steel bands were strutting their stuff and socarengue music vied with calypso tunes.

"Sock-a-ren-gay music," Francesca said, spelling it out for Melanie. "Isn't it lovely?"

"The whole island is incredible."

The night was lit with thousands of lights that vied with the starlit sky. There was a waxing moon. Francesca started as the telephone rang.

She picked up the phone to her father's pleasant voice. "You ladies must be having a great time. I've tried several times to get Melanie. I miss you two. The town is dry without you."

"We miss you, too. I'm not going to waste your money talking to me. Melanie's right here."

"No time wasted as long as I'm talking to my baby girl."

Francesca laughed. "Dad, you're a wonder, and I love you very much."

"I love you, too, Fran."

Francesca carried the phone to where Melanie sat. "I'm going out in the hallway to look around," she whispered. "Don't hurry."

Melanie nodded and patted her hand, her voice gone dulcet as she talked with Garrett.

Outside in the courtyard, Francesca reflected on how much better her world seemed in this moment. The orchid greenhouse lay before her with its night lights. At the front of the building she could see the tall form of the watchman pausing and pacing in front of the complex. How long had it been since she felt secure? She felt secure here.

She also felt very close to the carnival merrymakers and the music. Calypso was one of her favorite types of music, but she found the socarengue—a blend of soca and merengue music—running close.

She tried the door of the orchid greenhouse, and it opened. She was about to step inside when Melanie called to her. She went back in, and snapped on the light. Melanie seemed transformed.

"Hey, you look happy," Francesca said, and Melanie gave her a little hug, smiled and yawned.

"I think I'm going to call it a night," Melanie said. "I've had my share of happiness today and, for that matter, for several months."

"Never underestimate my father," Francesca said, grinning.

In a cozy inner room of the prime minister's mansion, Jon, Prime Minister Thomas Barton, Matt Wolpers, and Cam Mason were seated in a circle, each sipping his beverage of choice. After a few minutes, a tall, distinguished, partially baldheaded man with ruddy skin and brown hair came in. Matt Wolpers introduced him as Arne Milton, Diamond Point's chief of police. Jon found his handshake firm, as the prime minister's had been.

Matt Wolpers cleared his throat. "In such a delightful season, it's unfortunate we have to deal with criminal matters, other than a few revelers getting rowdy."

"But we still have a wonderful island," the prime minister said, "and we will deal with this new malfeasance."

"I'm on the brink of new information," Cam said, "about the car-theft ring. I have two new informants who seem knowledgeable. I'm arranging for them to speak with the chief, but they tell me it will not be possible until after the carnival."

"I suppose that's understandable," the prime minister said. "We're a joy-loving people. Pleasure before business." He looked in Jon's direction. "I hope you're considering our proposal, Lieutenant Ryson. We can use a man of your immense talents. You come so highly recommended."

The prime minister then sighed. "The last coup attempt was weak and so . . . ineffective. Who knows but what next time . . ."

"Put that thought out of your mind, sir," Matt Wolpers told him. "We will leave nothing undone to protect you. You have brought our island into the twentieth and now the twenty-first century."

"He's right," the police chief said.

The prime minister coughed softly. "We have not given Lieutenant Ryson a chance to tell me if he will accept our offer."

"Thank you for the offer. There are reasons I may not be able to accept, at least not right away."

Cam sat by the prime minister's side. He reached out and patted Cam's hand. "I am indeed fortunate to have men like you, Cam, and like Matt and the chief."

They were silent a minute as carnival sounds carried from outside. "You will be reveling with the others shortly, I presume," the prime minister said. "As for me, I'm going to turn in early and revel all the harder the rest of the week."

A tiredness settled on the prime minister's features. "Tell me about this car-theft ring. How does it operate? I have made and I intend to keep this a clean, law-abiding island, in many ways a small replica of Aruba. We cannot do this if we let lawlessness hold sway."

Matt Wolpers spoke up. "You are right, sir, and we will all move heaven and earth to keep Diamond Point the way it is now.

"As for the car-theft ring, it seems someone here is illegally processing the stolen cars after they are shipped in by freighter. False passports for some drivers, false freight papers that begin at the point where the cars are stolen. It seems a carefully worked-out scheme. Since Aruba and some Caribbean islands have cracked down on smuggling and other contraband, we can expect Diamond Point with its very small police contingent to be a crack in the armor. . . ."

"Are these cars coming mainly from the United States?" the prime minister asked.

Matt Wolpers nodded. "Mostly, but some are from Europe. U.S. and European customs departments are good, but they are far from perfect. It is up to us to do a sterling job on cracking this ring."

Cam Mason looked glum as his eyes settled on Jon. "You see how valuable you will be to us."

"Money will be no object," the prime minister said, "although I hesitate to speak of money to a man of your bearing. You will work directly with Chief Milton. The island will be yours if you can help us. If you *will* help us."

Jon thought a long moment. "As pleased as I am," he said forthrightly, "to have you make this offer, there are personal matters that presently prevent my saying yes. Believe me, I would not hesitate if this were not true."

For a moment, the chief was silent and he looked crestfallen. "Of course, there are other good men," he said slowly, "but I am a firm believer in my own psychic abilities. I have met no man who strikes me as you do. I believe this group of us sitting here could work together and solve our problem."

He sighed. "But I will not crowd you. A man's personal life is sacred to me, and I will not ask you to go against it. What I do ask is that you find a way if you possibly can to work with us. Will you do this?"

"I will, sir," Jon replied. "And if I cannot see my way clear to taking your job offer, I will still be at your dis-

posal to help you. Part of your problem may start in my
city of Minden, Maryland."

"Oh?" the prime minister looked alert.

"Yes. We think someone from this island who now
lives in the United States may be a part of the stolen-car
ring that is shipping its cars here and providing them
with false shipping papers, serial numbers, and registration papers. Matt Wolpers told you how it works.

"There are many things I can do for you back home.
I can give you a definite promise that, although I am
presently on leave, I will work with you. We are now
investigating such a car-theft ring."

Cam looked thoughtful. "As you know, I have a first
cousin who lives in Minden. He is part owner of an
automobile dealership. As a child, he was a wonderful
little boy to me. As a man, I am sorry to say, he has
taken a deviant road in many ways. He inherited money,
and has made more. But I would say he likes the thrill
of the underworld; he finds satisfaction there."

Words from a page found in his brother Kevin's desk
drawer swam to Jon's mind: *Caribbean Caper.* What did
it mean? And why did he think of it now? Jon sighed
and sent the thought to his creative mind.

Twenty-one

After Melanie had left the room, Francesca turned down her bed and undid the last button of her sundress. She couldn't relax for the life of her. When Jon came in, she intended to talk with him for a while.

She knew he was interested in taking the position offered him on Diamond Point. Only she stood in his way. She hugged herself. Why had she married Trey, a loser in spite of his wealth? Was he going to haunt her for the rest of her life?

Picking up the phone, she called Melanie, told her that she was going for a walk in the orchid greenhouse and asked if she'd like to come along. Melanie demurred, saying that the day had left her worn out.

Francesca wrote a quick note, went into Jon's adjoining room and placed it on his pillow. She walked down the short hallway and onto the short flagstone path that led to the orchid greenhouse.

Opening the door with its quaint brass knob, she went in, closing the door behind her. A gorgeous array of varicolored orchids lay before her and in one very large corner birds of paradise grew. Ferns hung from the ceiling, and thick ivy climbed poles.

It was so peaceful here. She closed her eyes to let the scene wash over her, then slowly walked halfway into the giant room. As in the cottage, carnival sounds of

music, laughter and singing had taken over the night.
Through the high windows, she could see the waxing
moon.

"How exquisite," she said as she paused before several lavender-to-purple hybrid orchids, and glancing at
the green orchids just beyond her.

She glanced at her watch, smiling, as she thought she
could move her bed out and spend the rest of her time
here.

"You're an earth woman," Jon had told her. "You
belong to the universe really; it's what makes you so
special."

My darling Jon was the thought that caressed her
mind. She never wanted to stand between him and his
dreams, never wanted to be the cause of his not getting
what his heart desired.

Looking closely at the blossoms she passed, she
turned right and walked ahead to the room that Matt
Wolpers had teased Cam about, saying it was his honeymoon suite. In the moonlight streaming in through
the high windows, its loveliness was enhanced, and she
sat for a few minutes on the blue leather couch.

Getting up and going to the big, glass double doors,
she pulled the door curtain aside and gazed at the
moon for long moments.

Sighing, she thought she had better go back. Jon had
said he didn't expect to be too long at the prime minister's.

As she walked slowly back down the corridor, she cut
to her left to study a magnificent group of full-grown
white cattleya orchids. Moving, she stubbed her sandal-clad foot on a table leg.

"Rats!" she said aloud and laughed. Usually graceful,
she could be a klutz. She bent to rub her toe and hairs
prickled on the back of her neck. Someone else was in
here!

Maybe, she thought, it was a worker who checked on the plants. But no, Cam had said all his workers partied on the last few nights before Carnival Day, which was only four days away.

Listening carefully, she stood. There had been the sound of low laughter; she was sure of it. She had laughed a moment before, but it was not her laughter. A man's laughter?

A low whistle sounded to her right, and she jerked her head around to trace the sound.

"Hello!" she called. "Is anybody else here?"

Nobody answered.

Okay, she thought, she wasn't going to be a frightened ninny about it. This was Diamond Point, not Minden, not Washington, D.C. She pulled herself together and started toward the door she had entered through earlier.

Eons of time seemed to pass as she moved along the corridor on shaky legs. *Just remember,* she told herself. *Trey isn't here.* But in one of his more communicative moods when they'd worked together, Rush had told her he visited Diamond Point often.

"Steady, girl!" she told herself. She was wet with perspiration in the cool building by the time she reached the door, only to find it locked! She stood there, frantically twisting the knob. Were the doors locked after a certain hour?

"I won't panic," she told herself. The door had been unlocked when she came in. It *had* to be open. Cam had told them that the double doors in what he'd laughingly called the "honeymoon suite" were often locked, and she saw no other doors save the front entrance, which was where the guard walked, occasionally going around the building outside and inside.

She turned and moving on icy feet, she began to walk what seemed miles to the front door and the guard.

"Damn it!" she whispered. Someone giggled wildly, and it was a sound from hell.

"Why are you doing this?" she exploded. "Stop it!"

And the sound stopped. The orchid greenhouse was the peaceful place she had come into.

But no, it hadn't stopped. There was a prolonged, low, wavering whistle. Eerie! She was a target in the open corridor. She stepped aside to one of the orchid niches and squatted there. Silence again. She shook her head to clear the cobwebs from her brain.

How long did she cower there? No, she wasn't the cowering type, she thought, then grimly corrected that: She'd never been the cowering type *before*. Something ancient in her blood warned her that she was in danger the way she had never known danger.

Her eyes hurt with unshed tears and her very eyeballs felt cold. Her scalp squeezed dry as rivulets of sweat ran down her back and legs. She had to get to the front door and the guard.

She would make it. She had to. Girding herself, she forced herself back to the corridor and the danger it presented. She couldn't stay in one spot all night, waiting for God knows what.

The orchid greenhouse spread out ahead and beyond her, its beautiful lushness and long poles of ivy belying the danger that had invaded it.

"Oh God," Francesca whispered, "please help me to move, to just get to the front door."

Her courage came flooding back and her gait steadied. The former sounds were silent. Finally, after what seemed an impossible span of time, she was within a few yards of the front door and the guard. She nearly jumped to the welcoming brass knob, only to find that door, too, was locked!

She beat on the door with furious fists, but the guard

didn't come. She opened her mouth to scream, but no sound came.

"If this is a dream, please God, let me wake up!" It was a nightmare, that's what it was. Her immobility, her frozen limbs were what in her childhood people had told her was a *witch riding*.

That was it! She had only to push herself over the edge of the bed and she would wake up, be safe. Tears flooded her face at this new knowledge. But it proved false.

It was no nightmare. She was in Cam Mason's orchid greenhouse and someone was stalking her. It was carnival time. People came from all over the world for the festivities. Trey and Rush could come. Rush still owned property here.

Moving slowly at last, she hid among hanging fern and tall poles of ivy until she could find her voice, which had betrayed her. Awkwardly, her foot twisted against a table leg and she went down, striking her head against a table edge.

Someone knelt beside her, breathed evil breath on her face and body. Stroked her body, rubbing hateful hands across her breasts. Something broke inside her then, and she began to fight a demonic fight. Better to go out like this than to just cravenly give in.

Slumped there, she found her voice and began screaming—in fear, in anger. In savage hope that did not intend to give up.

In the dimmed lights with her vision blurry, she could see that the hateful figure was clad in a skull-and-cross-bones mask with a black jersey jumper imprinted with a human skeleton. Shuddering, she bumped the figure's chin with her head and a man's wild laughter rang out.

"You little bitch! I'll get you for that."

He punched her then, and her senses reeled with the

blow. He expertly kept his private parts from her reach as he grasped her hair in one hand and banged her head against a table edge with the other. She scratched at his hands and face with all her might.

At last she found the full depths of her voice and—terrified that he would choke her—she began to scream, a full-bodied harridan-from-hell scream of fury that echoed crazily throughout the room.

She felt powerful then.

But his hands were on her throat as she'd thought they would be and in a moment it was darker than any night she'd ever known.

It seemed another dream that lights flooded the room and doors were opening.

"Fran!" She heard Jon's great shout and tried to respond, but she was so dizzy. She was determined not to pass out.

Jon and Cam Mason and the guard were around her then.

"There's the son of a bitch!" Jon shouted as a man's tall figure disappeared through a high window.

The guard went pounding off in hot pursuit.

Squatting beside her, Jon crooned, "Oh sweetheart. You're hurt."

Cam took out his cell phone. "I'm calling a doctor," he said grimly. "He's a friend. He'll be here shortly."

Francesca was lucky. She had bruises along one edge of her jaw, but the monster had not hit her with all his strength and his choking had just begun when her rescuers had come. There was a lump rising from where she'd struck her head.

Lying in her bed after the doctor left, with Melanie, Jon and Cam around her, she sat up.

"I'll be all right," she said.

Jon looked at her steadily. "Fran, I'd like to know what made you go out there. You're having trouble at home. I'm not surprised that it followed you here."

Francesca said solemnly, "I want this to stop. I pretended it had."

Cam sighed. "We've been having a bit of trouble with teenagers and some ruffians lately. They well may be the culprits. They live in the hills and come down at times to torment us. I'm going to make a call."

He dialed and spoke to someone for a few moments. They heard him say, "But do you know who it is?"

Hanging up, he told them, "The guard thinks it was one of the teenagers from the hills. He thinks he knows who it is. They're daredevils. Foolhardy."

Jon knelt by Francesca's bedside. He was angry with her for wandering out there, the way he had been angry the night of the cloudburst. Looking at her beloved figure, his heart squeezed dry with the thought of what might have happened to her.

"Promise me," he said, her hand in both of his, "you'll take no more chances like this. Please, sweetheart." He kissed her fingertips.

"I promise, love," she said softly. "Jon, I love you so."

Twenty-two

The next morning, Francesca came awake to the sounds of twittering birds outside her window. She moved and pain shot through her shoulder.

"I'm glad you're awake, honey," Jon said.

He lay beside her, fully clothed, looking tired and sleepy. The past night's scene flooded her mind.

"You haven't gotten any sleep," she told him, sitting up to stroke his cheek.

"Sure I have. It was a late night for both of us—late and *harrowing*." He sat up and drew her to him. "How do you feel?"

She thought a moment before she answered. "Sore, some pain in my shoulder. I'm going to stand up and walk around. That should tell the tale."

"Okay."

She swung her legs over the side of the bed and looked at the wide bruise on her left calf. She grimaced with disgust at the thought of the beast groping her the night before.

"Fran?"

"Yes."

"How do you feel now?" he asked as she stood.

"I'll be okay. I want to move around a lot today."

"We're going to have to be very careful."

The doctor friend of Cam Mason had checked her

out the night before, looking angry and disturbed. "Damn it," he'd said to them, "there was a time when something like this would never have happened on Diamond Point. The damned *Hill Warriors*, as they so grandly call themselves, are trying to turn this island inside out." Then he added grimly, "But we'll stop them, I swear. We'll get our island back."

"I've heard about them," Jon had told the doctor. "Good luck. I have a feeling you're going to be hearing more about them, rather than less."

Francesca thanked her lucky stars that the doctor had told them there were no sprains or fractures. The muscles in her left shoulder were pulled.

"This morning, you're having accupressure and a salt glow," Jon announced.

"Yes. It's what the doctor ordered. I want *you* to get a massage, too. You need one."

"I will, later. I'm walking over to talk with Cam and the police chief this morning. There's going to be a guard outside. He'll be one that Cam knows better. I hate to leave you alone, love, even for a little while. But what I'm looking for may put an end to this madness."

The maid knocked, came in and set up a table, then came back with fresh tamarind juice, grapes, a shrimp omelette and flaky blueberry pastries.

After washing up, they sat down to eat in near silence.

"Fran," Jon said, "I don't want you to take any more chances until we find out who's behind last night's attack."

She nodded. "You heard what Cam said. It could be one of the youths who've taken to the hills."

"And it could be Rush—or Trey."

"Would they expose themselves to the danger of being caught? If what you're thinking about the car-theft ring is true, they're in enough trouble already."

"I don't know. I keep thinking that Rush is especially

culpable. Diamond Point is his home, and if we *had* caught him lurking about, it's his cousin's house. He could plead that he was looking around. He and Trey are men who've never grown up."

Francesca leaned across the table and pressed Jon's hand.

"Thank God I wasn't badly hurt, or worse."

He gazed at her steadily, then stopped eating and stroked her hand. Anger rose in his chest when he looked at the bruise on her jaw. He was a strong man, accustomed to protecting his own. And, he intended to protect this woman, but things were not going according to plan. Francesca followed his gaze and told him, "It's all right. I can cover the bruise with makeup."

"How much do you hurt?"

"A fair amount. I'm glad the doctor ordered a massage for me. I can use it."

Melanie knocked and came in, her face all tender concern.

"I hate whoever did this to you. I couldn't sleep last night thinking about it. Do they know any more about it?"

"I don't think so. You were here last night when Cam said it could well be one of the island roughnecks."

"Yes." Melanie stroked Francesca's back as tears of sympathy trickled down her face. She had cried the night before.

Now Melanie said, "I keep thinking about what you've been going through in Minden. Now this . . ."

"I'll be all right," she reassured Melanie. "Cam says they've had some trouble lately at the greenhouse. That may be a part of it."

But something deep inside her shuddered. There had been something familiar about that form and that sadistic laughter.

* * *

Cam Mason and the police chief greeted Jon with excitement at the police station.

"We've got two excellent footprints from below the window where the perpetrator jumped out."

"Well, that is good news." Jon felt his spirits lift.

"We were fortunate that the plants outside the green-house were watered so thoroughly. Otherwise, Diamond Point's soil is arid and footprints might just fly into the trade winds."

"They'll have to be sent away to a lab, of course," Jon offered.

"Yes, to London," the chief said. "We're still not out of the woods. Now, if it *is* Rush, we can get a pair of his boots or shoes as the case may be." His face went grave. "Of course Rush belongs to the island's elite and, frankly, the law favors him. It shouldn't, but it does."

The police chief looked thoughtful. "After the carnival, there are a couple of thugs I want to bring in on suspicion of mischief. We'll get their footprints. Then we have our informants who are so useful to us. We have the ones who call themselves the Hill Warriors infiltrated. . . ."

Cam laughed ruefully. "And *they*, no doubt, have us infiltrated." Cam shifted uneasily. "Another thing you should know is that one of the entrance doors to the greenhouse has been kept locked since we've had some theft and vandalism. The double doors to the room I showed you are locked at all times.

"Only the back door is open. I had a latch put on the outside of the door to help us lock any intruders inside. Someone latched that lock in place once Francesca was inside.

"When you and I came to the door and it opened a bit, I realized immediately what had happened and unlatched it. In the turmoil of rescuing Francesca, I forgot to tell you this."

Jon nodded. He had been too upset about Fran's safety to ask about seeing Cam reach up and unlatch that lock. He, in fact, had been crazy with desire to get to her as quickly as possible.

The chief and Cam stood. "I told the new guard to pay special attention to the cottage," Cam said, "so Francesca will be safe. Unfortunately, last night was a slip up. We are not accustomed to crime and sometimes we fight it badly."

The chief of police nodded as Jon stood. "We are taking you on a visit to the warehouses, what we call the *nether* side of Diamond Point."

The masseuse came to Francesca's room shortly after Melanie left. A slight woman whose build belied her strength, she and a man brought in a steel-framed massage table, sheets and pads.

The man left and the woman turned to Francesca.

"I am Helena," the woman said, smiling, "and I promise you one of the best massages you will ever have."

"I could use just that."

"Could we talk a moment?"

"Of course."

The two sat down in chairs. Helena brushed back a few strands of dark blond hair from her slender face, and began speaking.

"It is so important that you relax. Saying a mantra will help you. Do you meditate?"

"Yes."

"Good. Then you already have your mantra. Think of beautiful scenes. Trees. Plants. Flowers. Sunsets." She smiled again, half closing her eyes. "From here, you can see the ocean and I have positioned the table so that you will face it still. That is beauty enough.

"I am going to use accupressure with you. I find it an excellent way to relax those who have been under severe trauma, as you underwent last night. Believe me, it is *wonderful*. I will do this each day you are here. You will feel the difference in your very bones."

"I thank you in advance."

"Bonbini," the woman said, "our word for welcome means more than a simple greeting. We must see that you enjoy your visit here, and we will leave no stone unturned to assure you pleasure. Then you will come back. I cannot tell you how sorry I am about last night's events."

Francesca thanked her and climbed onto the table.

The night before, after going to bed, she had fought against reliving any of what had happened in the orchid greenhouse. She had been horribly tense, furious. In sleep, she had tossed, taken out again by the sleeping tablets the doctor had given her.

So deep had been her sleep that she hadn't known Jon was in the bed beside her. Now, she didn't have that defense. She cooperated with Helena and relaxed. With the now calm Caribbean foaming at its shoreline, visions came flooding back of the night before. The skull-and-crossbones mask, the skeletal costume. Figuratively speaking, she had fought death and won, but what if she had continued being unable to scream? What if Jon and Cam hadn't come back? What if . . . ?

A strangled sob rose in Francesca's throat. The clippings were one thing. The dead rabbit was still another. Now this new monstrosity. Hysterical laughter bubbled in her throat. She and Jon had thought she'd be safe here on Diamond Point. Trey and Rush were an ocean away and probably laughing at what they had perpetrated on her. Who was the perpetrator here?

Was it just a random Hill Warrior youth as Cam thought? Or was the answer much more frightening?

With the rest of her body covered, Helena's expert hands and highly skilled fingers kneaded and probed a section of Francesca's aching flesh. Soft island calypso music played on a radio. Soft trade winds swept across the room. The air conditioner was turned off, the windows were open and the perfume of frangipani bushes—transplanted from other, lusher islands—wafted in.

After a few minutes, she grew more relaxed, although she fought it at first. She wanted to ask questions, but she was drifting off. She roused herself to ask, "What is the oil you're using? It smells wonderful."

"Monoi oil. I import it from Tahiti, or rather from a smaller island there—Lyric Island. Have you heard of it?"

"Yes. We're going there next summer."

"Good. I loved it. Now, don't fight me. Be with me as you and I work to bring you peace and comfort."

Helena began a chant in her soprano voice and Francesca listened quietly.

"That's lovely," Francesca said.

Helena didn't answer. On her stomach, Francesca couldn't see Helena's face, but could imagine the deep, caring look.

By the time Helena had reached her thighs, Francesca couldn't believe the peace that swept through her, the comfort.

"You have magic hands," Francesca murmured. Helena continued chanting and massaging with the expert thrusts along her hips, her thighs, then her calves.

For a while Helena didn't respond to her comment about magic; then she said, "Now we will turn you over. And you don't know what magic is until you've had another couple of accupressure sessions."

* * *

On the westward side of Diamond Point, giant waves crashed like the sound of thunder against boulders that lay farther out. Chief Milton, Jon and Cam Mason walked into the warehouse where a man, Winthrop Hall, greeted them effusively. Jon noted the reddish-brown skin, squat build and closed countenance. The eyes were black, gimlet and piercing. This was not a man you'd want to cross.

"What can I help you gentlemen with? And how are you, Mr. Mason?"

"We're checking," the police chief said. "It's the carnival season, and in the past few years we've had a bit of trouble. Have you had any vandalism? Thefts?"

The man thought a moment. "No. I'm lucky I guess. Would you like me to show you around?" He nodded at Jon.

"Sure. I'd like that."

The man led them through the cavernous car barn, which presently housed twenty or more cars ranging from brand new to well-cared-for older models.

Two men worked on several of the older models.

"How's business these days?" Cam asked.

"I'm doing okay."

"New shipments coming in with no hassle?" the police chief asked.

"What do you mean?"

"Hassles. Trouble. Are shipments coming in on time?"

"They are at that."

They walked slowly and Jon took in everything. It was hot and they perspired freely.

"Beautiful cars," Jon said, "even the old ones. What do they go for?"

"Whatever I can get. The sky's the limit."

At least he was frank, Jon thought. He cleared his throat. "How many stay here and how many go on to other islands?"

"That's hard to say. Aruba people buy a lot of them."

Jon pursed his lips. There was a world of profit in the stolen-car racket. Few expenses. Sky-high prices. It was a sweet racket, he thought.

As the four men strolled back toward the front of the building, Cam turned to Winthrop Hall. "How well do you know Trey Hudson and my cousin, Rush Mason?"

For a moment Hall couldn't seem to get his breath; then he steadied himself. "I run this end of the business for them. Rush and I go way back. We both like cars. Then he got interested in broadcasting. We all get along."

Hall then gave Cam a searching look. "Why do you ask?"

"Do you know if he's back for the carnival?" Cam asked.

"I haven't seen him. He'll be around if he's here." He sounded evasive now.

"Maybe I will, too," Cam murmured.

They reached the front part of the warehouse with its small, cluttered office. Winthrop Hall looked a bit unsettled. His glance settled on Cam. "I'd like to talk with you sometime. It's private."

"Easily arranged," Cam said. "Call my secretary and set up an appointment."

Hall hunched his shoulders. "It might be better if we talked here. I'd be more comfortable and I could better demonstrate some of the things we've talked about in the past."

"Just call me and set up a time."

Hall took out a pad and pencil from his shirt pocket and jotted down the number Cam gave him.

Then Hall said, "Lieutenant Ryson, I'd like you to

visit my showroom in town. Maybe we can even sell you
a car."

Jon smiled widely. Winthrop Hall was a smooth operator, he thought.

Hall and his three visitors talked about the island,
about the carnival and how it had changed over the
years to be a major tourist attraction.

Finally, Hall scratched his face and looked livelier. He
nodded to Cam. "Expect a call from me. I may have
information you'd like to know."

A short distance from the warehouse, Jon, Cam and
Milton lingered by a Kwihi tree that grew near a big
jutting rock ledge. Cacti abounded and Jon marveled
at several that stood a prickly six-and-a-half-feet high.

"Great island you've got here," Jon complimented
the two men.

The police chief grunted. "Thank you. If we could
get rid of cultivated thugs like Hall, we'd be even better
off."

"What's the skinny on him?" Jon asked.

"Hall?"

"Yes."

"We know damned well he's in the stolen-car business
up to his ears. But his cars come in clean," Milton said.
"All the registration, sales, and serial changes are made
back in the United States. What Hall does is distribute
the cars to this and other Caribbean islands.

"We get cars from Europe, too, and the same thing
applies. Hall has ties to Rush Mason and Trey Hudson.
That's another reason you'd be invaluable to us, Lieutenant. You know what's going on in the States and
we're determined to put a stop to the stolen-car racket.
At some point, betrayals are going to happen and bodies
will start falling.

"Our prime minister wants a clean island. He's a God-fearing man, and he wants the best for all of us. We don't figure the best men are like Hudson, Mason and Hall."

Cam's eyes on Jon seemed to plead with him. "You've been here such a short time. How are you leaning?"

"I'm mulling it over," Jon said reluctantly. "I have some very important things to clear up at home."

Jon told them then about the trouble Francesca had had in Minden. Both men looked startled.

"My God," Cam finally said. "No wonder you don't feel free to take us up on our offer. Couldn't Francesca come here with you? Oh, I know she's a star, but we could find her an important job here."

"She loves her job and she loves her father, who lives in Minden. She doesn't want to leave either."

Cam looked a bit crestfallen. "Matt Wolpers and the prime minister keep asking me if you're leaning toward us, but now I understand what you're up against."

"I can't tell you how much I appreciate your offer," Jon told him, "but you can see the drawbacks."

Cam nodded. "Again, I can't tell you how sorry I am that something like what happened last night should happen to Francesca. I'm glad she is feeling better, although not enough time has passed to know for sure.

"This afternoon we have dinner with my wife and Matt and his wife. Do you think that is too soon for Francesca to recuperate?"

"No." Jon laughed. "She is determined to be there."

"Meanwhile," Cam said, nodding to the police chief, "we're going to find out if my cousin has seen fit to visit us this carnival season, and what he's up to."

Riding back to the cottage, Jon felt increasing anxiety. Last night he had come home to find someone attacking his love. Though, now one of the most trusted policemen patrolled the area, Jon didn't breathe easily until he was in Francesca's arms again.

He couldn't believe what he was seeing. She looked radiant describing the accupressure session.

"I missed you," she said huskily.

He touched her bruised face.

"And I missed you. You look beautiful." Her walnut skin glowed, complemented by the pale blue caftan she wore.

"Now that you're here I feel A-OK. If you'll just kiss me."

Taking her in his arms, he sucked the honey from her lips and felt her body melt against his. He held her fiercely, as if he'd never let her go.

Francesca was still thrilling to Jon's kisses when the doorbell rang, then a knock sounded. Jon answered to find Cam Mason and the guard who had been on duty the night before standing there.

Jon invited them in.

"I will be only a short while," Cam said. "My guard, whom I had such trust in, would like to apologize to the lady. Waldo?"

The big, cinnamon-colored man with brown dreadlocks twisted his cap in his hand. "Ma'am, I am truly sorry," he said in very good English. "The truth is I went a small distance away from my post to meet a friend"—he hesitated—"a woman. It seems I lost my head and did not hear you when you screamed, or notice anyone going into the greenhouse."

Francesca nodded. She saw how young the man was, not more than twenty or so.

"Can you find it in your heart to forgive me?"

Francesca said gravely, "Yes, I forgive you, but you caused me quite a fright, not to mention some pain. I'm sorry for that."

"I will go on my knees to you if you wish me to."

Cam looked thoughtful. "He has always been one of my best men. He was very poor and lived in the hills. Since he has been with me, he has done well."

"Thank you, sir," the guard said to Cam. Then to Jon, "Can you forgive me, sir? I can see what the lady means to you. I will flog myself in my mind a thousand times. It will make me a better man."

Francesca smiled. "Don't flog yourself. Forgive yourself as I forgive you. It's the carnival season; let's enjoy it."

Only then did Jon speak. "If it helps you to do your duty in a more efficient manner next time, then I forgive you."

"He asked me to bring him here to apologize," Cam said. "Now we must go. I will see you this afternoon around four at Caribbean Gold. I promise you a feast of major magnitude. It is yet another place that tells you that *Bonbini* is more than just a word to us Diamond Pointers."

After the two men left, Jon paced the floor. "I want to swear," he said. "I want to ram my fists through concrete walls. I won't have you hurt, my love. I mean it."

"I wear well," Francesca said. "I can't believe how much better I feel. Oh, the accupressure helped so much, but . . ."

"Yes?"

Francesca put her hands on Jon's chest. "Your being here is what matters."

Words without number crowded Jon's mind. He wanted to declare his love and ask her to be his own. He wanted to cherish her, keep her with him forever. But in spite of her bravado, or her true courage—he was not certain which—he had grown accustomed to seeing the fear that lay just beneath the surface. He held his peace, taking her hands in his.

Gently he said, looking at his watch, "We'd all better

start getting ready for the scrumptious dinner we've been promised."

"Yes, we'd better." She hesitated. "Jon, I want to go back to the orchid greenhouse. That special room is so beautiful." Then in a voice so hushed Jon wasn't sure he heard her: "I want us to make love there. It will be so memorable."

Jon caught her close, feeling the soft outlines of her voluptuous body meld into his hardness. He made small, massaging motions across her shoulders and down her back. He kissed her bruised jaw with gentle kisses.

She felt the thrill in her very bones as his hardness let her know how much he wanted her.

"Your wish, my queen," he said, "is my command."

Twenty-three

Francesca felt her heart lift even more when Jon, Melanie and she reached the Caribbean Gold restaurant. Set on the Caribbean, it was a very large building of limestone and imported spruce logs. The sides were made mostly of logs and glass, with a glassed-in front and back. Outside was a sidewalk café on the side of the building.

Large potted palms and orchid plants were beautifully arranged throughout. One mirrored wall was lined with exquisite shells.

Cam Mason and his wife, Alicia, Matt Wolpers and his wife, Katherine, and a pregnant Laura Mason Waring, Rush's sister, greeted the three as they came into the cool restaurant.

Alicia and Katherine were charming, attractive women who complemented their spouses. They were immediately friendly to the trio. Laura hugged Francesca.

"I have wanted to meet you for so long. I know you and my brother once worked at the same radio station, but he left to go into automobile sales." She looked sad for a moment. "Do you know if he is coming home this carnival?"

"I rarely run into him," Francesca said truthfully, "so I can't tell you. Does he come back often?"

The elfin Laura shrugged. "He doesn't write. He comes back several times a year, and he doesn't call when he comes." She hunched her thin shoulders. "I'm afraid sibling rivalry describes us well."

"It happens sometimes," Francesca comforted her.

Suddenly Laura smiled. "I visited Minden once. I didn't call and unfortunately Rush was away. . . ." Her voice drifted off and her face bore the sad look again.

Seated at the table, which was covered with rich ivory damask, set with sparkling crystal and Spode chinaware, the group began their feast with shrimp, coconut and pineapple served in a coconut-shell bowl with the coconut meat left inside.

Francesca was seated between Matt Wolpers and Jon. Matt said, "I haven't gotten a chance to see as much of you three as I'd like to. Carnival season is workaholic season for me."

His wife laughed. "Every season is workaholic season for my husband. He only needs the slightest excuse." She took his arm and held it fondly for a moment. They smiled at each other companionably.

Cam and his wife were seated across from Francesca. From time to time, Alicia smiled at her, and for some reason, Francesca felt she had known her a long while.

"We have a toast to offer to our charming Woman of the Year," Matt said, raising his glass as the others swiftly followed.

"To Mrs. Melanie Ryson! We salute you!"

Beautifully dressed in butterscotch linen with a high neckline and cut-in shoulders, Melanie looked every inch the queen.

"Thank you so much," Melanie murmured, looking down to hide her tears.

Quickly, Francesca looked at Jon. His face was pleasant, impassive. He looked proud enough, but somehow unfathomable. He loved his mother, Francesca felt sure, but the two of them were too full of pride to come together in a shared love.

Francesca felt Jon blamed his mother for a youthful passion she could not control. It was a different time, a different place. She was going to have to help Jon realize that.

Their wine was sparkling chianti at first; then the wine steward switched them to a delicious, all-purpose, fruity French wine.

Dinner was, indeed, the feast they had been promised. Roast pig with a red apple in its mouth, orange-glazed roast duck, and shrimp, prawns and crab in garlic sauce, as part of a seafood platter. Wild rice. Lightly cooked and buttered vegetables were side dishes, and one of the most beautiful salad bowls Francesca had ever seen graced the table.

"Caleb would love this," Melanie said, "not that his restaurant pales beside anyone's."

Francesca caught Melanie's eye and smiled. "Are you enjoying yourself? Enjoying your visit?"

"I've rarely had a more wonderful time," Melanie said. "When my boys were small, my husband took us to New Orleans a couple of times. I enjoyed myself then the way I'm enjoying myself now. Oh, yes."

Her eyes sought her son's, but he glanced away, smiling. Then he looked back at her. "You deserve all this, Mom," he said evenly, but his voice was cool, overly controlled.

For a moment Francesca was exasperated with him until she thought: *I have to forgive him for not forgiving his mother.*

Three strolling guitarists moved gracefully through the restaurant, playing socarengue, calypso, European and American tunes.

"They're very good," Francesca said to Matt Wolpers.

"Yes, they are." He looked across at his friend, Cam,

who looked bothered. "What's on your mind?" he asked him.

Cam expelled a harsh breath. "Nothing much," he said. "Great dinner we're having. I'm enjoying myself." His words belied his expression, Francesca thought.

Jon lightly rubbed his leg against Francesca's and when she looked at him, he grinned. She thought he looked so handsome in his cream sharkskin suit and pale blue shirt. He was thinking about what she had said about wanting to make love to him in the orchid greenhouse. He'd never been more in favor of anything. His heart swelled with pride at how beautiful she looked in aquamarine linen that coolly flattered her silken walnut skin. A rich, pearl-shell necklace threaded through an aquamarine velvet rope graced her throat. Natural leather sandals displayed her coral pedicure.

As she had said, makeup covered the bruise, but he still ached with anger at her injury. No apology on earth could make up for that. He looked at Francesca's long, graceful hands and the thought came unbidden: His rings would look good on her finger. She'd do them full justice.

Matt leaned around to look at Francesca. "Cam told me about what happened last night. I'm really sorry. I've been over on Aruba much of the day, or I'd have called."

"Thank you. It could have happened anywhere. I was lucky. Jon and Cam were coming home."

"I can't remember anything like that happening more than a few times on this island. It happens more on larger islands."

"It's all right," she said. "Believe me, I'll be more careful next time. Jon had warned me to watch it. Cam had told me. I guess I'm just a hardheaded woman."

"You're a wonderful woman, Francesca Worth. That's what you are," Matt said.

Cam cleared his throat. "Dessert is being temporarily held up. Now if we are finished with the main course, I have a small presentation to make—to Mrs. Melanie Ryson."

Melanie looked surprised; her eyes lit up. "The dinner is presentation enough," she said huskily.

"We don't agree." Cam stood. "You deserve it all."

Cam's wife reached into her tote bag and brought out a fairly large box wrapped in embossed gold paper. The paper bore the insignia of one of the island's most famous shops.

Melanie took the package and exclaimed, "Thank you!"

"Open it," Matt demanded. "I want to see what good taste my friends have."

Melanie swiftly undid the wrapping and opened the white satin box. She gasped with delight when she saw the exquisite handmade, burgundy leather bag. She held it up.

"It is so beautiful," she said. "How can I thank you?"

"That's easy," Cam's wife said. "By coming back to Diamond Point soon."

Melanie laughed. "You can count on that."

The group finished their delectable dinner and lingered as the waiter cleared the table. The strolling guitarists slid into a socarengue song as they interacted with the diners. Pausing by the table where Jon and Francesca sat, they switched to a popular American love song as the men bowed low.

The maitre d' came to them, saying to Cam, "Sir, you will be having dessert on the terrace—with champagne, our finest, as the Americans say it, *on the house.*"

Cam thanked the man and patted his stomach.

"Greed is not good," he said. "In a few hours I will pay dearly for this repast."

Out on the terrace with the soft trade winds and the ocean roaring ahead of them, Francesca felt happy. She wanted to believe that what had happened the night before in the orchid greenhouse was an aberration—nothing more. Certainly Cam seemed to believe it had been one of the youthful islanders. Yes, that had to be it. Mesmerized for a moment, she idly watched a foaming wave crest onto the shore, then looked up into the eyes of first Trey, then Rush.

Laura gave an exclamation of delighted surprise, got up and went to Rush, trying to hug him as he stood unresponsively.

"When did you two get in?" Jon asked.

"Late this morning," Trey answered, his glance challenging Jon's. "Don't worry. We won't be crashing your party for long. Rush needed to say hello to his cousin Cam. I wanted to pay my respects to my ex-wife, who looks gorgeous." He bowed. Rush sent him a surly look.

Francesca looked at Trey evenly. Why was he here? He had been down to the carnival before, she chided herself. She didn't have to be the reason he was here. Something else needed to happen before suspicion fell on him about what happened last night. She couldn't help touching the bruise on her face, expertly covered by makeup.

Laura was bubbling over. "Rush," she said, "as you can see, you're going to be an uncle, and oh, you were once a great radio personality like Francesca. When my baby gets here and gets a little bigger, the Diamond Point station has offered me an island show. You have to help me set it up and . . ."

Rush stared at his sister with open hatred. "Don't pretend to what isn't true," he said in a harsh voice. "I'm your brother in name only, and I don't indulge myself in appearances. Your baby and your job are your business. I don't give a damn about either one."

The elfin woman recoiled from the blow as if she'd been physically struck.

"Rush, please," she said softly, still gazing at him.

Rush turned and walked back to a nearby table where Stacy and Jersey sat. Stacy had watched closely all the while.

Laura came back to her seat and stood there. Bending awkwardly, picking up her purse from the floor beside her chair, she said in a small voice, "Please excuse me. I have to go to the powder room."

They all nodded.

Trey grinned. "What has my friend Rush wrought here? He's not a very smooth operator. I apologize for him. How are you, babe?" he said to Francesca who stood. Furious that he was on Diamond Point, she didn't intend to let him ruin her visit.

"I'm going to see about Laura," she said to her table-mates. "That was a pretty cruel thing to do," she said to Trey, who crossed his arms and stroked his chin. Trey had grown a goatee and a pointed beard and Francesca thought it made him look more like a polished devil.

"Hey, don't blame me. I'm sworn to be good this trip."

In the ivory-and-gold powder room, she found Laura standing in front of the mirror, dry eyed, her face pinched, hardly breathing. Francesca took her in her arms, felt her slight body's violent trembling.

"It doesn't matter," Francesca said. "It's all right. Some people are cruel. We have to learn to live with that."

"Why does he hate me so?"

Francesca looked grave. "Let's sit down."

They sat on a blue, padded window seat. Behind the opaque glass, they could still hear the ocean roaring.

"Your brother told me once that you were born when he was seven. He said he already felt there wasn't nearly enough love to go around. You took what little there was. . . ."

"Yes, I took his hope of ever being loved. He's told me that many times. I'm sorry. I always adored him, looked up to him, but he never wanted my love. He doesn't write. He doesn't call. He doesn't visit when he comes home. My mother is aging rapidly, and I think she's sorry for the way she and my father treated Rush. She'd like to be forgiven, but he doesn't forgive even my birth." She put her hands to her face.

"I should leave him alone," Laura said, "the way he wants me to. But he's my only brother, my only sibling. I love him. Can you understand that?"

"Yes."

"My parents thought he was bad as he grew up, that he was headed for trouble. Before my father died, he told me that he wasn't Rush's father, that my mother had cheated on him with his best friend." She laughed shakily.

"Yet it was Rush he blamed. Can you believe that?"

"I'm afraid I can believe anything. You're a lovely woman, Laura, and I wish you all success with your coming baby and the radio show I'm sure will be great."

"I'm going to ask you for pointers."

"And you've got my promise to give them to you if I can."

Looking at Francesca steadily, Laura's voice was warm again. "My brother hates you, too, doesn't he?"

"I think so."

"I ran into him at this very restaurant after he lost his job at the Minden radio station. He was drunk and furious. I shouldn't say this, but you need to know. He swore he'd pay you back. Rush has money my father and grandfather left him. He wouldn't hesitate to hurt you. He can afford nefarious things neither one of us knows about."

"Thank you for telling me," Francesca said slowly.

"I would have told you earlier, but I chose not to believe him. He was *talking* to me, where he hadn't before, and I was happy. I wanted to believe he wouldn't harm you. Has he tried to?"

"I'm not sure. I'm still trying to find out."

Laura seemed to feel better. The two women went back outside and were seated. Trey had gone back to his table.

Jon looked at her and smiled, his eyes narrowing. "Hudson left a message for you."

"With you?"

"That's his style. He wants you to know that he wants only the best for you, and he hopes you enjoy your visit."

Cam rocked in his chair. "You know," he finally said, "Hudson said they got in this morning. I'm pretty damned certain I saw him on Aruba early yesterday morning."

"Well, honey," Cam's wife said, "maybe he means he came onto *this* island today."

"Perhaps." Francesca mulled it over. "With Trey, you never can tell."

The blueberry-strawberry-pineapple crêpes were excellent with their smooth, rich vanilla cream sauce. The champagne was a rare vintage year.

Matt raised his glass. "I propose a toast to all three of our American guests. May they come to visit us often."

With glasses raised, the spirit of camaraderie linked the tablemates again. Even Laura seemed much better.

As they sat in desultory conversation, a Barica Heel, a small bird with a bright yellow breast, lit on the table, unafraid of the humans who sat there. The bird looked at them for a quizzical moment, then dipped its beak into the open sugar bowl.

"If I didn't see it, I wouldn't believe it," Melanie exclaimed.

"Ah," Matt Wolpers said, "we have here the 'sugar thief.' It is easy to see why we call them that."

"How pretty it is." Francesca reached into her tote bag for her camera, retrieved and focused it just as the bird flew away, unhurried, unconcerned.

But for Francesca the bloom had been taken off the rose. Jon smiled at her, and she smiled back wondering how much longer she could bear the subtle and now not-so-subtle torment Trey and Rush had brought into her life.

Twenty-four

By the next carnival night, Francesca had had two accupressure sessions, and her body felt an ease she had seldom known. That day, both Jon and Melanie had had Swedish massages and sang its praises. Helena, the masseuse, beamed at their compliments.

"You must continue this when you are back home," Helena told Francesca. "If people only knew the joy that sessions release, they would move heaven and earth to have them."

Francesca had smiled. "I certainly will."

Now Jon, Francesca and Melanie were with Matt Wolpers and Cam Mason and their wives mingling with the carnival crowds.

The night sky was midnight blue. Steel bands were everywhere. Guitars. Drums. Wondrous drums of African origin with their heartbeat rhythms that soothed the soul and lifted the spirits.

Matt Wolpers grinned at them. "I want you to listen for a song, a socarengue song. I had the artist write it for you today. It's lively. Very good."

No sooner had he spoken than a roly-poly man, and his small steel band, came to stand in front of them, bowed low and began to sing a welcoming calypso in good English. Francesca found herself moving with the rhythm. The band leader's eyes on Francesca were flirtatious.

Jon looked at her and smiled. "He's asking for trouble."

"You have all of me you need."

"Never!"

"You're not the jealous type."

"That was before I met you."

The bandleader bowed again. The band was silent for a few moments before he said, "Now the song for two special ladies and the gentleman who is with them. I love America. I visit there as you visit here." He waved his baton as the music surged from the group. *"Bonbini!"* he sang out.

It was a good song. Smooth. Melodious. Cam told them, "You can see now what I mean about the difference between calypso and the socarengue. The calypso is all about words. The socarengue is about rhythm, melody."

"I love them both," Francesca said. "And I love the song you had commissioned for us. Can we get it recorded?"

"We can," Matt said. "We will."

Looking at Jon, Cam said, "I mean to make you know that we want you here. We *need* you here."

Francesca's eyes sought Jon, who only smiled. "If it ever proves to be possible," he said, thinking about the attack on Francesca in the orchid greenhouse.

"It's a beautiful song, that socarengue tune for us," Melanie said. "I'm having such a wonderful time."

"Francesca? Jon?" Matt Wolpers asked. "Are you two having a good time, in spite of what happened in the greenhouse?" He looked anxious and so did Cam.

"It could have happened anywhere," Francesca answered. "And yes, I am having a wonderful time."

"That goes for me as well," Jon answered.

The steel band played the tune again, waved good-bye and moved away as a coterie of drummers moved toward them, their music softly rolling.

The brilliance of thousands of lights tried to outdo the stars, but failed. The stars were watching, twinkling competitively. A nearly full moon hung in the sky. A blue moon.

The ocean's roar was subdued tonight. Jump-ups were in the streets, strutting their stuff.

"Oh, look at that jump-up!" Melanie exclaimed. "Look at his fantastic movements." She pointed out a man dressed in a feathered, yellow-and-red suit, who jumped up and spun around at incredible speeds.

Near the other side of them a man and a woman danced in tangolike rhythm to a tune that was not like the tango at all. They made their own music. This was carnival season, the anything-goes season.

When all this was over, the quiet season would begin. Forty days of hallowing the spirit, then glorious Easter.

"You know," Francesca told Jon, "I've been to Mardi Gras in New Orleans and found it wonderful, but the joy in the air here seems to me to surpass even that."

"I think you're right," Jon said.

Many people were in costume, but most were not.

"If you like the costumes," Matt's wife said, "you'll enjoy Carnival Day. Some of the people spend the whole year on their costumes. They're truly fabulous."

Lost in the reveling, Francesca jumped as she felt someone's hard breath on the back of her neck. Jon was on one side of her, Cam and his wife were on the other. She turned quickly to see a skull-and-crossbones death mask blending downward into a black-and-white skeleton-printed costume.

Suddenly she couldn't get her breath. In what now seemed mere cacophony, she thought she heard the weird laughter, high pitched and derisive, she had heard in the orchid greenhouse. Her body went stiff and cold rivulets of sweat drenched her.

Jon caught her as she swayed. *No*, she thought, *I'm not going to faint. I've seen these costumes on Halloween. Many times.* "What is it?" Jon demanded. "Why are you trembling so?"

She tried to explain to him what had happened, but she was also trying to right herself. Had the man laughed that weird, high laughter? Or had she imagined it?

"Did you hear someone laugh?" she asked the group. "Did you hear strange laughter?"

"No," Jon said. "Is that what you heard? Like the laughter in the greenhouse?"

Her throat had gone dry and her eyes hurt. "I thought I heard it," she said in a weak voice, then brought herself up. "It must have been my imagination."

"My God," Cam said.

"It didn't have to be your imagination," Jon said. "You could have heard it."

By then a man had pushed through their line and stood in front of them. He had unzipped his mask and stood before them in his skeletal black-and-white costume holding up his death masked head. An attractive, middle-aged man, tall and spare, he looked concerned.

"I was going to move on," he said, "but I came back. I saw a look of fear on the lady's face, and it bothered me. My mission is to bring joy, not sorrow. Why were you afraid?"

Jon answered for her, studying the man. "She is in a state of nerves because of something that has happened. It'll be all right. Thank you for being kind enough to explain."

"You are welcome. A beautiful woman should never have to be afraid."

By then a tall, slender woman and two pre-adolescent

children—a girl and a boy—come up to the man. When they saw him without his mask, they took theirs off and grinned friendly greetings.

"I am Mario," the man said, "and this is Louisa, my wife, and my two children Harry and Belle. You are visitors, because if you lived here you would know that carnival is a time when there is nothing to fear. The devil and death are on vacation these blessed days."

Cam took over and made further introductions.

"Ah, we will entertain you," the man said. "We do beautiful jump-ups."

He took his wife in his arms and they danced merrily; then the children joined in. So, it was all right, Francesca thought. This was certainly not the man in the orchid greenhouse.

Had she imagined the laughter?

Back at the cottage that night, they talked of the small family in the skull-and-bones costumes.

"You were frightened and the lights were so brilliant he could see it in your eyes. I'm sorry you have to go through this," Melanie said.

"Yes, I'm sorry, too," Francesca told her. "But it makes me feel better to know that someone isn't always after me."

"They'll come through me first," Jon said grimly.

Melanie went to her room shortly after saying she wanted to call Francesca's father.

Alone, Jon and Francesca sat on her bed. The loving pull toward each other was there, but Francesca still felt cold. What was going to happen next? she wondered. Even if this night and the costumes were an aberration, the man the night before in the orchid greenhouse with the same type of costume had been all too real. She could still see that mask, hear that laughter and, finally, the fingers pressing into her throat.

"Perhaps I'd better sleep in here," Jon said.

Francesca shook her head. "I want to be alone to gather my thoughts. Besides, I want to sleep late, and I'll get no sleep if you're here." She gave him a slow, impish smile.

Jon's voice was husky as his gaze roved her face and body. "You're very right," he said. "Anyway, sleep well and I'm nearby. Cam's taking us to see a special beach and the shipwreck diving area."

"Oh yes, I'd forgotten. Do we dive?"

Jon frowned. "I don't think so, Fran. Too many things could happen. We know now that Trey and Rush are on this island, and Rush is all too familiar with it. Cam thinks he saw Rush a couple of days back, yet Rush says he only got in yesterday morning. Why would he lie? Or was Cam wrong?"

"I hate this," Francesca burst out. What he was saying heightened her tension, cooled her blood even more.

"I want you to stay," she said. "Stay here with me."

"You know I will."

They talked a short while. Francesca undressed in the bathroom, and in the mirror her face looked strained, her skin pale with stress. In bed, Jon kissed her brow and touched her face.

"Sleeping with me is going to be hard for you, isn't it?" she asked him. "Believe me, it won't be easy for me either."

By then they were under the covers with the lights out. "There will be other times," he said. "Tonight I want you to sleep and not worry about anything."

As she drifted off to sleep, the phone rang and she picked up the receiver. It was her station manager, Lou.

"How's it going, Fran?"

"Well enough," Francesca said. "Melanie—the three

of us—we're having a wonderful time." Her voice closed on the half-truth.

"Well, everything's fine here. Holly is filling in well."

"I know. I talk with her daily. She said you were away for a couple of days."

"Yes, attending that broadcasting convention in Minneapolis."

She wasn't sure she should tell him. "Lou, Trey and Rush are here."

"Oh? Well, Rush is from there, so he probably goes back every year. They give you any trouble—that you can prove?"

"What do you think?" she said bitterly. "Do they ever do anything that anyone can prove?"

"Fran, I'm sorry to see you go through this."

Francesca could have wept. How many people had said how sorry they were? But it helped her to bear it.

"Well," Lou finally said, "continue to have a good time. I'll be delighted to have you back, and don't forget to bring me a great souvenir."

"Anything special you'd like?"

He thought a moment. "Yeah, a couple of those polished coconut shells and a bird of paradise."

"You've got it."

Jon lay with his arms behind his head. Moonlight streamed through the open window and soft breezes fanned their faces. Trade winds were nearly always mild on Diamond Point.

Jon touched his finger to his mouth, then to hers.

"Good night," he whispered.

Sleep came swiftly to Francesca. At first she dreamed of Garrett and Melanie, who were getting married in a country church on Diamond Point. She was the maid of honor and Jon was best man.

The scene segued to a carnival scene like the one she had been in that night. A man came up behind her, breathed down the back of her neck and laughed—weird, crazy laughter.

Where there had been crowds surrounding her, everyone fell away. Everyone except her and the man behind her, and that man wore a costume like the man tonight. She was paralyzed with terror as she prepared to fight the way she had fought in the greenhouse.

She turned. The man ripped off his mask with one hand. Trey held a gun as he had in the very first, frightening dream that had led her to Jon.

"No!" she screamed. "I won't let you kill me, Trey! I won't let you!"

She came awake, damp with cold perspiration, wrapped in Jon's arms, with him cuddling her. He held her face to the side of his and murmured reassuringly, "It's all right, sweetheart. It's all right!"

Twenty-five

By the time Cam Mason came to get them the next morning, Francesca was much calmer. Her accupressure session helped. She, Jon and Melanie had only tamarind juice and raisin-nut muffins for breakfast. Coffee with cream and a natural sweetener for Jon and Francesca. Red clover tea for Melanie.

Cam came promptly at eleven o'clock.

"Another sight-seeing dream," he ventured, "is what I promise you. Fran, you look a bit bothered. You're not letting what happened last night upset you. The man at the festival?"

"No. Thank you for asking. I had a bad dream. I guess I'm just jumpy."

She had told Melanie about the dream. Now the older woman's sympathetic eyes were on her.

"I have nightmares," Cam said thoughtfully, "more lately than usual." He shrugged. "I guess I'm the nervous type. I've got lots of goodies packed up for us in the way of food for our journey."

He pointed to one side of the backseat of his Jeep, which displayed thermos bottles of water, juice, coffee and tea. He uncovered a large picnic basket filled with delicious treats.

"My wife got up at daybreak," Cam said.

"Please thank her for us," Francesca told him. "It looks delectable."

"We'll explore much of the day," Cam said. "I'm like a happy child when it comes to entertaining my guests."

On the leeward side, out in the turquoise Caribbean in their glass-bottomed boat, they rode above the fantastic coral reefs with fish of every color and description darting in and out. Again and again, Melanie exclaimed at the fish, her face sparkling with delight.

"There is so much I wanted to show you," Cam said sadly. "Wreck diving that you would have loved. Reef diving. There are wonders beneath us you would have gloried in, but since the attack the other night, Jon doesn't feel it is wise, and I agree."

The six-pack boat rode the waves smoothly, its engine purring. Sailboats and divers were everywhere. To their left, a motorboat pulled up to them and they looked into the unwelcome faces of Trey, Rush, Stacy and Jersey. Only Trey waved. The wave was not returned.

"Hey, cousin," Rush called. "Imagine meeting you again."

"It's a small island," Cam said mildly.

"Yeah," Rush came back. "Not as big as Aruba where you imagine you see someone who wasn't there."

"I'm not so sure," Cam murmured too low for Rush to hear.

"How are you, Fran?" Trey asked, his voice oily with fake friendliness.

"I'm fine, thank you," Francesca answered.

Jon shot Trey a cold look.

"Are you enjoying the sights?" Trey asked him.

"We are," Jon answered.

"What sights are you planning to take in?" Trey's eyes had narrowed, his breath quickened.

"We haven't really decided," Cam answered. "We'll write the script as we go along."

Trey shot him a sharp glance, then lifted his hand in farewell. "I'm sure we'll meet again soon."

Rush grinned at Cam. "As you say, it's a small island."

They rode off laughing merrily. Stacy had been glum, and had said nothing.

Fifty or so yards ahead of them there was a sheer, high wall good for deep diving. Many people were diving.

"How I wish you could do this," Cam said. "There is a deep plunge for the divers. The fishes are beyond description. Each time I go down, I get a feeling of freedom I seldom know elsewhere."

"Don't forget, we'll be back," Jon told him, "under more favorable circumstances."

"I will look forward to that. Another activity you must get involved in next time is taking underwater pictures. They are fantastic."

"I would love that." Melanie's face was enraptured.

Cam smiled at Melanie. "The island is here for us as natives and for people who enjoy it as you do."

Like neighboring Aruba, Diamond Point had its countryside. Arid, desertlike, the layout was akin to the much larger island. Back in Cam's Jeep, they bumped along rocky, country roads. Goats trotted along and off the road, causing them to slow down, but Cam drove slowly anyway.

He stopped at a small, white church with its double doors open. A woman worshiped at the altar.

They all piled out.

"This church dates from the beginning of development of the island," Cam said as they looked around them.

Inside, the church was spotless. Furnishings and

benches of aged and polished Kwihi wood shone. Each of the four joined the woman at the altar and prayed. Shuddering, Francesca prayed for an end to her torment. Jon prayed for the strength of Samson to keep his beloved safe.

As they went outside, a man garbed in a short-sleeve black shirt with a white clerical collar came from a nearby white house.

"Greetings," he said softly. *"Bonbini!"*

All four acknowledged him. "I am so happy that you are here. Would you like to stay awhile?"

"We'd like that, Father," Cam said, "but we have much ground to cover."

"Ah," the pastor said, "that is life itself—much ground to cover. Well, come again and see me. I know you, Mr. Mason. Are the rest of you visitors?"

"We are," Jon answered, "and we admire your lovely church. It's so peaceful here."

"Yes," the pastor said, "I find it so. It is so easy to commune with God in a place like this."

A goat wandered up, and the pastor bent and stroked its head.

"Even the goats are peaceful here," the pastor said, his eyes twinkling. "Even the cacti seem less prickly." He held up his hand. "I have inside something you may like to take with you. Let me get them."

He came back with a small wooden tray on which lay four smooth white stones shot through with turquoise. Each was the size of a hen's egg. "I cut and polish them myself, enjoy them and sometimes give them to others."

He gave each of them a stone, warm with sunlight. Francesca felt her heart stir at the gift. "People say the stones have brought them luck," the pastor said. "May they bring you every blessing you could wish."

They thanked him and climbed back into the Jeep. Driving back toward the leeward side of the island, the roads were even rougher. Giant green and yellow parakeets eyed them in friendly fashion and from time to time lighted on the hood of the Jeep.

"Your visit would not be complete if I did not show you a country house, a *cucunu* house," Cam said. "The one I will show you is part of a plantation and is well preserved."

Driving along, they came to the beginning of endless rows of coconut palms. "Here copra and coconuts are processed for our use and for export," Cam explained.

Workers in the grove of coconuts greeted them, smiling. Francesca hunched her shoulders, thinking, *They are so happy. Will I ever be happy again?*

Jon gauged her mood and reached for her hand, pressing it. "How're you holding up, Fran?"

"Okay." She smiled to reassure him. "You're here. How could I not be okay?"

Her reply filled him with tenderness.

They pulled into the yard of a brilliant yellow house with a red tile roof and a white picket fence. A woman in a brightly colored apron came out.

"Bonbini!" she welcomed them.

Cam spoke with her in his Dutch-English patois. She answered in broken English.

"May we look around? We were admiring your house," he said.

"Of course. If you need food, drink, I get for you."

"You're very kind." Cam introduced them. The woman's name was Heleen. Gravely, she shook hands with each.

"You probably come to see a *cucunu* house. This one replaces such a house. We built a *cucunu* house for my parents. It was such great fun."

They understood her well as she talked about building the *cucunu* house in her childhood. How they erected a frame and all the children pitched mud at the house with great glee.

It hardly ever rained on Diamond Point so there was not that to worry about. With steel trowels, they had smoothed the mud and let it bake in the hot sun for weeks. When it was dry, they painted it in brilliant colors and put on a tiled roof.

"*Cucunu* house," the woman said. "It seems like a dream. But I tell you the figures you see on the walls are like you find on the old *cucunu* house. They ward off evil spirits.

"Once we had an enemy who wished to hurt us. He plotted to hurt us. My father got strange, new figures from an African man he knew, put them up and our enemy soon stopped bothering us."

Mildly hysterical laughter rose in Francesca's chest. "I need some of that magic," she murmured to Jon.

As they prepared to leave, the woman led them around the house and pointed out the figures she had said the African man had given her family. "Some say we are superstitious and ignorant to believe in magic," Heleen said softly. "How can we not believe in what works for us?"

They reached the leeward side of the island around two o'clock that afternoon. Now the road was as smooth as the transparent turquoise Caribbean waters spilling onto the white sand.

"I am taking you to a special beach," Cam said. "I think you'll like it."

He drove a short distance on and parked. This was a secluded spot. Beyond them, adults and children romped in the white sand.

Getting out of the Jeep, they sat in the shade of divi-divi trees and a large Kwihi tree. Out on the horizon, white sailboats were like toy boats in the distance. There were also some closer at hand. Down the beach from them, several other picnickers lounged about.

"Who's up for a swim?" Cam asked. "Then we can eat."

Francesca, Jon and Melanie, along with Cam, shed their outer garments to reveal swimsuits and trunks.

Francesca wore a sarong-wrapped, coral-and-white, matte jersey suit that took Jon's breath away. Her skin was like a brown version of the powdery white sand. Her deeply indented waistline and the curved hips shook him. She smiled when she saw the desire in his eyes; it reflected her own.

Melanie wore a pale yellow, one-piece suit with a skirt that displayed her still shapely legs.

"Ladies," Cam said gallantly, "you both are beautiful." Each woman accepted the compliment.

Jon said, "I agree," and Melanie's eyes lit up with her son's approval.

The water was warm, caressing their bodies with its surges past them onto the beach. After a few minutes of silent swimming, they began to cavort like children, splashing water on each other. This was such a glorious place to be, Francesca thought. Then she thought of the evil-fighting signs on the house they had just left. She thought, too, of the stones the pastor had given them. Would hers bless her? Keep her safe?

They floated on their backs and watched the brilliant, nearly cloudless blue sky, felt the hot sun on their closed eyes, faces. The silken waters supported and soothed their bodies, lifted them.

"We'd better go back and eat," Cam said. "I am starved."

On the beach, the men took the picnic hampers and

the thermos jugs out of the car. The women spread the cloths, took out blankets and towels and settled down to eat.

Francesca scooped up sand, exclaiming, "This is like white powder!"

"Yes," Cam said, grinning. "I can't think of another place like it."

Cam's wife had outdone herself. Stuffed crabs, crab cakes, fried and boiled shrimp, fried clams. Deviled chicken, from her own special recipe. Potato salad and wild rice. Island and other fruits. Tamarind juice and several other juices.

"She prepares a *feast* and that's no lie," Jon complimented Cam.

The women agreed; Cam looked delighted. "She is tied up with carnival plans or she would be here. She likes the three of you very much."

"Cam," Francesca said guardedly as they ate, savoring the delicious food, "what about Laura and Rush? Has he always been this angry at her?"

Cam nodded. "Ever since she was a child. My uncle adored Laura, and she was close to her mother. Laura was a good child, never any trouble, pretty, well liked. Smart. My uncle was unfair, of course. He often called Rush 'the devil's own' and in front of other people. That was wrong."

"Yes," Francesca said, "Rush must have been very hurt."

"But we grow up and we put our past hurts behind us or we cannot go on. Rush has never put his past behind him. While he has done well financially, there seems to be no love in his life. Oh, a gaggle of women who may or may not be after his money.

"You've told me how he acts and reacts to you. Where mortal happiness is concerned, I'm afraid my cousin is a loser."

* * *

Cam pointed out a row of grapes beyond the divi-divi trees. They went over and plucked bunches of the purple fruit, took them back and washed them.

Popping several in her mouth, Melanie asked, "Do they grow wild?"

"Wild, and we cultivate them," Cam said. "These are wild." He looked around them where the cherries grew wild, too. "There is one more interesting plant I want to show you." Walking along, he suddenly stopped.

"This is a Bushi plant. We call it our erotic plant, one of our trademarks."

The three smiled at the shape of the plant, balanced between a short, plump base and a long central part. He broke off several fruits and picked the outer rims from the white pillow in its center.

As the delicious strawberry flavor filled Francesca's mouth, she chewed and swallowed. "You picked some for us the first day," she said gently. "They are delicious."

"Ah, so I did," Cam said. "I suppose I wanted to make certain you tasted them."

"And we have," Jon said. "I would love to have them every day."

"That can be arranged."

When they were seated again, eating more grapes and more of the Bushi fruit, Francesca turned to Cam. "I keep wondering about sharks. I didn't dare mention them while we were swimming just in case one might feel I called him."

Cam laughed merrily. "Let me tell you the shark is one of the world's most maligned creatures. You stand more chance of being hit by lightning than of being bitten by a shark. They tend to strike when they are harassed in some fashion."

"Perhaps," Jon said, "but if I see one coming, the one thing I won't say is '*Bonbini*'!"

Cam Mason dropped off Francesca, Jon and Melanie at twilight.

"I hope you enjoyed your sojourn," Cam said.

"I think I speak for all of us when I say we had a wonderful time," Francesca assured him.

"Thank you for taking so much time with us," Jon added.

Cam smiled at Jon. "Of course, I have an ulterior motive. You three would fit in like natives on Diamond Point."

"I know I would love it here." Melanie was vividly enthusiastic.

"Score one for me." Cam grinned. "You're certain now you don't want to go to carnival activities tonight?"

"No," Francesca said quickly. "Day after tomorrow is Carnival Day. I want to be well rested for that."

"I think we all do." Jon drew a deep breath. "Although, I'm certainly glad the man in the skull-and-crossbones costume was kind enough to let us know who he was. I guess we're just tired. We had a great time, Cam, and thank you again."

Inside her room, Francesca lay on her bed and closed her eyes. She wanted a soothing bath, and she wanted to walk to the orchid greenhouse and lounge in the honeymoon suite with Jon. She needed to overcome the terror she had felt the night the carnival-garbed monster had choked her. She needed to throw off the horrible memories of the past months—the clippings, the dead rabbit.

Patting the side of her face, she went into the bathroom and began running water into the big, deep, salmon-colored sunken tub. Geraniums grew around a partial border of the tub. Putting in powdered oatmeal and Shalimar bath oil, she ran her hand back and forth in the water.

Walking into the bedroom, she began to undress, lightly stroking her body. This had been one of the more sensuous days in her life. Diamond Point countryside was unexpectedly gorgeous. Nature helped, but the natives made their own glory—planting and nurturing plants and flowers that were not indigenous to the island.

She could still imagine the giant parakeets' raucous calls to their mates. She lay naked on the bed for a little while, pictures of the erotically balanced Bushi plant and fruit dancing into her mind. Jon wanted to take the job here; she was partly certain of that. And no, she didn't want to live here, just to visit often.

In the tub, she slid down until only her head was above the delightfully soft water. She planned what she would wear when she asked Jon again to take her to the orchid greenhouse. A cream sundress with crossed straps in the back. No jewelry. Her heart held him gently and tenderly, yet she could not deny the fear of being deeply involved again.

But she had to try to make a niche for herself in someone else's life and let him into hers. Into Jon's life. No matter the fear, she had to try, because she didn't think she would find a man like him again.

In the orchid greenhouse, Francesca found her heart beating too fast. She and Jon had traversed the length of the building, inhaling the fresh odor of green plants. She had closed her eyes and followed his steps as he

led her. In her hand, she held the polished stone the
pastor had given her. Would its magic work for her?

Once in the honeymoon suite, Jon flipped a switch
and soft light filtered through the room. Cam had unlocked the door. Now Jon turned the doorknob, opening the door, then locking it behind them. The scent
of Shalimar that Francesca wore was driving him wild.

They stood in the middle of the room, which was
filled with orchids and birds of paradise. One plant with
small yellow flowers gave a deliciously fruity scent that
blended with Francesca's perfume. Strong light filtered
in from outside. Through the fan-shaped high window,
they could see the moon and the thickly clustered, star-
spangled, midnight-blue sky.

He took her in his arms, then pausing, took the stone
from her and placed it on a nearby table. He was sick
with longing.

"My very own darling," he whispered. Hugging her
around the waist, he lifted her a few inches off the floor.

"You're aching for a broken back." She laughed.

"You're worth it."

Slowly he slid the heavy cotton dress over her head.
She removed her lacy coral panties and bra and stood
naked before him.

"My mind is a camera where you're concerned," he
said. "I snap every part of you constantly."

She helped him shed his clothes, and they stood
pressed against each other, he relishing her softness and
she glorying in the rock hardness of his superb, muscular body. Thrills ran through her as he stroked her
back, smoothed the corkscrew curls back from her face
and probed the depths of her mouth with his tongue.

He placed her on the wide, blue-leather divan, then
arched over her. His kisses began with her scalp and
covered her body as flames of desire licked them both.

"Your breasts are so beautiful," he whispered, cupping first one, then the other, before bringing one to his mouth to be greedily suckled. He kissed the hollows of her throat, tongued her stomach and left no part untouched.

"Silken woman," he said in a low voice "Why don't I eat you alive right now? That way, I'd never lose you."

Francesca laughed as delicious shudders ran through her. "You're so wonderful," she told him.

He paused at a special place and kissed her fervently, his hot kisses and wildly exploring mouth making her feel she would go mad.

With stroking hands, she rolled him over onto the bed and arched above him, kissing him as if she could never stop. She teasingly tongued his nipples as he thrilled to her touch. He was hard and pulsing, and she wanted him more than anything on earth. Sadly, she thought, *Damn the fear that stands between us.*

His hands trembling with eager desire, he slipped on the protective shield. Rolling her over, he arched above her again and sliding his hand around her waist, the swollen magnificence of him slowly entered her in gentle, rhythmically smooth thrusts.

The glory that shot through her was like nothing she had ever known. Inside her, he lay deep in a special place. Love had created the honeymoon suite that enhanced their love and blessed it.

They moved together with richly orchestrated thrusts and responses. The hot, tight, nectared sheath of her made him shudder with delight. Thrusting, he was a master of his universe. She was an earth mother, altogether receptive of him.

Moaning, half-fainting, Francesca felt tears come to her eyes. There was a blue moon outside. Was this the cause of the madness she felt? She knew it was the man and what he engendered in her, not madness. She called his name and nipped him lightly on his muscular shoulder.

With breathtaking awe, he heard her cries beneath him—the cries of a beloved woman being taken in love.

What they felt *was* magic, she decided. Only the power of magic could make this so. No, not the cheap fly-by-night magic that was so common, but the magic wonder of the universe.

"Inside you," he murmured, "I feel like I'm one with the world. Sweetheart, I love you, no matter how you feel. I'll wait for you to come around."

He slowed himself to make the magic last as the raucous music of drums, steel bands and merry voices of carnival celebration filled the air.

Inside him, he felt erotic explosions, like the gorgeous geometric patterns of fireworks on the Fourth of July.

She was a tide sweeping in with shuddering waves, so deep into life it seemed she teetered on the edge of insanity.

They came together, with him feeling the hot earthquake of his loins spilling his seed into his beloved. And she was like a rushing tidal wave breasting a sandy shore.

They lay together side by side as she kissed him, running her tongue into the corners of his mouth as he stroked her hair.

"Fran," he said quietly, "I don't have a ring because I intended to wait to ask you, but I can't wait any longer. Will you be my wife?"

There, he had said it, he thought, and he hardly breathed with the anticipatory tension he felt.

She had known he would ask it one day; he hadn't hidden the way he felt about her. So many thoughts crowded her mind. So many words rushed unbidden to her lips. What about the hurt Melanie had given him?

Would she, Francesca, hurt him? So many unanswered questions.

"Yes," she told him quickly. "Oh, my darling, *yes.*"

He caught her close and hugged her tightly until she laughed and said, "I hope you know how to set broken ribs."

Laughing, he relaxed his hold. "Maybe I'm afraid you'll slip away."

Propping herself up on her elbow as Jon lay flat on his back, Francesca told him, "You know we've got problems. You're still angry with Melanie for leaving you, and I'm terrified to get involved again."

"I'd never hurt you. I think you know that."

She thought a moment. "Not intentionally, but things happen. People do things they can't help. Oh Lord, I wish I had a simpler personality to offer you. I'm running scared, Jon. You know how much I'm running scared."

"Yes, sweetheart, I *do* know you're frightened. But we're going to see this through together. I'm disappointed that this trouble has followed us here, but I think it means we can be almost certain that Trey and Rush are causing it.

"I'm thought to be a damned good cop, a good investigator, and I'm going to leave no stone unturned to get to the bottom of this."

Francesca reached behind her and got the white stone Jon had put on the table, covering it with both hands.

"I'm not all that superstitious," she said, "but I'm going to hold onto this as a talisman. The pastor is a nice man. We can use his blessings."

Jon sat up, cupped her face in his hands and kissed her lightly, teasingly.

"You've just made me the world's happiest man."

"You've done the same for me. Jon, I'm going to try to lick this terror. With you, I think I can."

He lifted her chin, kissed her again. "I would kill," he said, "to keep you safe."

He was only quiescent for a short while; then passion began to build in him again. Stroking her body in circular motions, he gloried in the feel of her, the electricity that went through them both.

"This is as good as it gets," he said, and she echoed, *"as good as it gets."*

They were silent then, their hands exploring each other, seeking out the in-view and the secret places. He drew on a latex sheath and breathless with yearning and rife with passion, they lay together before he swung himself over her and entered her body, which was still hungry for him. Even as his body was starved for hers. She crossed her legs above his back and pressed him deeper.

This time they tarried, lavishing small and deep kisses on each other, feverish hands stroking and touching willing flesh.

Inside her now, there was time to savor each part of their love, to know each other in the deepest biblical sense. To be with and of each other.

Pausing a long moment as he throbbed inside her, Jon murmured, "What they say is true. If God made anything better, He kept it for Himself."

The tall man scrunched down on the front seat of his old Honda, grim faced, yet giggling. The electronics equipment the guard had helped him put together had worked almost perfectly. He had listened carefully and it had paid off.

"You'll never marry that bitch," he grated. "Depend on me to see that you don't."

Fumbling, he switched on the player section of his

recorder, which sat on the seat beside him. Again and again, he pressed the fast-forward button, then the re-wind at the part where Jon asked Francesca to be his wife. The man was stuck in that time warp. He cut the machine off, leaned back.

"She'll never be *anyone's* wife," he spat. "Very, very soon, she isn't going to be around anymore."

In spite of her fear, Jon and Francesca went to one of Diamond Point's best jewelry stores to select her ring.

"I'll wait, you know," he told her. "I want to push you and I would, but I know what you're up against."

Trembling, but happy, they stood in the shop with the manager giving them every assistance. Francesca's eyes went wide when she saw the oval diamond. Jon pinpointed her gaze and picked it up.

"Do you like that one? It's beautiful," Jon said.

Mindful of his finances, she said softly, "Something smaller."

Jon laughed. "I'm a police lieutenant, but I'm also having a lot of luck in the stock market." He asked to talk with the manager away from Francesca. They went into a small room and when they emerged a few min-utes later, Jon was beaming.

"It's yours if you want it," he said. "I could never pass up a deal like this."

He kissed her then, lightly and teasingly. "Thank you," he said huskily, "for taking a chance on us."

Twenty-six

"Come in, man. What kind of news have you got for us?" Trey slapped the slender man on his back as he greeted him.

Winthrop Hall shrugged. "Some news, but it's probably not what you want to hear."

"Have a seat—of your choice," Trey said. "What are you drinking?"

"Nothing for me. When it's carnival season, I like to keep my wits about me."

"Well, *I* can drink *and* drive," Trey came back. "Not everybody can."

Rush and Jersey lounged on deep chairs, with drinks in their hands. Winthrop Hall spoke to them both, and they welcomed him.

"Anybody want to watch a show?" Trey asked.

None of them did. "Well," Trey said, "I see you're in your business mood, Win. Out with what you wanted to see me for. Do you need privacy?"

Hall shook his head. "We're all in this together, but I'm not the one who needs to remember that."

Trey opened his mouth to say something when a light knock sounded and an ebullient Stacy danced in. Dressed in a white, snug-fitting, low-cut sundress she was wolf bait and Rush whistled.

"Don't flirt with the master's meat," Trey said, giving him a grin.

Stacy frowned. "How are you, Winthrop? 'Master's meat,' indeed. I'm changing our course, Trey. I'm not going to be your sleep-with piece anymore."

For a moment Trey ignored her, talking to the three men. "To the table, guys." He pointed to a large table near the window.

The men got up, ambled to the table, leaving Stacy and Trey standing in the middle of the room.

"Don't you know it's not polite to spill our beans before company?" Trey's hard eyes on her belied his mild words.

"It's still Francesca with you, isn't it, Trey? When we stopped by their table in that restaurant, you noticed the engagement ring on her finger. I guess Rush did, too. I know I did. It's beautiful."

"That's enough, Stacy," Trey growled at her.

Her voice went up an octave. "Why don't you get smart, Trey?"

Forcing himself to be civil when he was on fire with anger at her, Trey pulled a wad of bills from his pocket.

"Go shopping, babe. Get yourself something real pretty and there's more where that came from."

"You gave me money yesterday. I don't need more."

"Sure, you do. You're a greedy woman, just like I'm a greedy man. Buy yourself a couple of black-lace nighties—for me."

Stacy hunched her thin shoulders. "I mean what I said at first. Francesca's moving on with her life, marrying someone she loves. Why can't you move on with yours?"

Trey could feel Warlock coming up, and he didn't want him there. Then with a sigh of relief, he reminded himself of what he had had to remember so many times: Warlock only came when Trey was threatened.

Stacy took his inattention as indifference and lashed out, "Get used to it, lover. Francesca doesn't want you anymore."

He slapped her then, leaving the print of his fingers on her fair-skinned cheek.

Rush got up, and came to them. "Trey, for God's sake, man. Pull yourself together. We've got company."

Trey swung toward his friend. "Stay out of this, Rush. I can run my own show."

Rush went back and sat down at the table. A crafty gleam came into Trey's eyes. He pulled Stacy to him and kissed her. Fighting turned her on; well, it turned him on, too. But he couldn't get rid of the others now. There were things he needed to know.

He patted Stacy's backside. "Be good to me, baby. I've got some hard-nosed business I need to take care of. You go shop, have a nice, long lunch. Bring me back some butter cookies, and when you get back, I'll show you what I'm made of."

"Okay," Stacy said reluctantly. "Okay, but remember what I said." She looked at him bashfully. "I'll take some more of your money if you're still willing to give it to me."

Trey laughed long and hard. "That's my girl. That's my woman." He reached into his pocket and drew out a money clip, giving her several large bills. She left the room, blowing Trey a kiss.

Trey came to the table, grumbling, "We need to do something about women. They're getting out of hand." None of the three men responded. It bothered him that what Stacy had said shook him so. So, the bitch was getting married. He'd known it would happen sometime, but hadn't expected it this soon.

As soon as Trey was seated, he noted that Winthrop Hall seemed angry.

"What's on your mind, Win?" Trey scratched his face lightly.

The man looked at Trey earnestly. "I'm going to come straight to the point. It seems like I'm getting less of the pie than I was getting. We've done a lot for each other. I want that to continue."

"Why sure," Trey said. "Why not? You're our man on this island."

Hall leaned forward. "I don't think you've forgotten I was to be the man who not only supervises the distribution of cars on *this* island, but in the whole Caribbean area. You've both said I was the one you trusted most."

Trey tugged at his soft shirt collar. "Well, you see it's like this, Win. More and more our legit business is running on greased wheels—beautifully—so I've got more time. This scheme is getting bigger and bigger, and Rush and I want to take over more and more of the hands-on part."

Hall shook his head. "I've gotten it from the grapevine that you've got not one, but two men on other islands you're going to farm out some of the business to. I've sweat blood, risked my butt in jail to set up Diamond Point for you as a safe haven. . . ."

"We know and we thank you," Rush said.

Winthrop Hall expelled a harsh breath. "That's not enough. The money isn't piling up for me the way it's got to be piling up for you."

"We can cut you in more," Trey assured him.

Hall hunched his shoulders. "I want a whole lot more. I've been doing some figuring, and I think I'm falling way short."

"We'll work it out," Trey said. "You're our man. Listen, Win. Why don't either Rush or I meet you in your office tomorrow and draw up specific plans for your getting a bigger piece of the pie?"

Hall smiled. "On Carnival Day? Man, you've got no sense of celebration."

"I celebrate every day I'm making plenty of money," Trey said. "We can meet around ten and talk a couple of hours and celebrate the rest of the day. Anyway, I'll let Rush come and talk with you. He's seen a lot of carnivals; he won't miss a few hours of this one. Now, how about a drink?"

Hall shook his head. "Like I said, I need a clear mind today. I've got a whole lot to do."

Trey's eyes were half closed on Hall. "We're tight for all time," he said. "You're our man."

Hall looked at him and his smile was tight. He knew when he was being screwed over. He'd come to this island one step ahead of Jamaica's law and he'd soon linked up with Rush Mason, then Trey. When had they begun tricking him? He wasn't sure when, but he was now certain that it was happening.

When Hall had gone and Jersey had left the room, Trey and Rush smiled at each other. "Well, that didn't take long," Trey said. "I think he's getting as much as he deserves."

"You told him we'd cut him a bigger slice of the pie."

"And maybe we will—in time."

"He's pretty upset."

"I'm depending on you to smooth his feathers. You've got a gift for that."

Jersey came back in. "You need me for anything right now, Mr. Hudson?"

Trey shook his head. "You're on your own. Take a walk on the beach. Find a woman. Hell, a couple. Need some money?"

Jersey laughed. "You're generous, boss. Like you did

Stacy, you gave me enough money yesterday. I won't be too long."

"Yeah, don't be too long," Trey told him. "I never know when I'm going to need you."

When Jersey had left, Rush stood up. "I'm going to go in another direction for a stroll on the beach. Jersey always goes toward the leeward side. I'm going to face the rocky shore. That's my mood today."

"Tell me, Rush, do you think Hall is going to give us trouble? We haven't monitored him closely. Now that we have so much money coming in, we've got to be more careful who works for us."

"Winthrop's hungry," Rush said slowly. "He's not going to rock our boat."

"We can easily cut him in deeper, but I no longer want him over the whole Caribbean deal. He's not smart enough to maneuver the whole thing and keep it hidden. The way we're expanding, we're going to have to buy and sell lawmen often. I don't think he's got the smarts for that."

"We're going to have to be careful. He's no fool."

"Neither are we, Rush." Trey chortled. "Neither are we."

When Trey was alone, he changed into shorts and a polo shirt. Going into the living room, he sat in a deep chair by the window. This morning he and Rush had run into Francesca and Jon having breakfast at a sidewalk café. They had walked over to speak and Trey had been knocked over by the brilliance of the ring on her finger. Hell, it was nearly as big as the one he had given her. She had sent it back after the divorce. That had hurt.

His head began a mild throbbing. Warlock always signaled his coming with a headache—a *bad* headache.

"Down boy," Trey muttered to Warlock. "I don't need you—*yet*."

He hated still having strong feelings for Francesca. He liked to keep his feelings and his mind free. He hadn't really wanted to get married, but he couldn't get her any other way.

Did he still love her? It wasn't a matter of love. His whole life was based on *control*. A man had to dominate and control a woman the way his father had dominated and controlled his mother. The way his mother had dominated and controlled her son.

If he could be sure Francesca hadn't seen the watch in his unlocked safe, he'd feel better. She had said she hadn't looked into the safe and sometimes he believed her. Sometimes he didn't.

He thought about it more clearly now. He had taken his safe with him, of course, when they'd split up. If she'd seen the watch, she hid the fact well. But then, Francesca was quiet, deep. You never knew what she was thinking.

Somehow he had to find out what she knew, but how? If she hadn't looked into the safe, he was home free. If she had—

Trey felt a pain in his chest so sharp it frightened him, but it quickly settled into a drawn-out ache. She was getting married. And Stacy was right, he *couldn't* take it. Seeing her with Ryson was almost more than he could stand. And having Stacy didn't help. Stacy was a beautiful fly-by-night broad, while Francesca had been his rock.

Warlock was with him now, and he felt his multiple inflame his mind. Rising on nimble feet, he thought he was not Trey, the man, but Warlock, the god!

It was simple, he thought dully and his head cleared with thinking it. The pain in his chest stopped. *Francesca*

*had belonged to him. Francesca was always going to belong to
him. In life or in death—whichever it took.*

Rush Mason walked a long way out to the rocky shore
where the warehouses were, but he stopped short of
going to Trey's warehouse.

Along the way, he had passed his parents' palatial
white-stucco, red-tiled-roofed house, with its masses of
well-tended evergreens and mixed cacti and flowers.

He could imagine his mother sitting in the double
parlor, nervously stroking her pearls, sternly setting up
plans for her social day. His sister, Laura, had a house
of her own now, a husband of her own, and would in
the near future have a baby of her own. Laura had had
it all from the day she was born. And he had been pretty
much left out. His mother had once loved him. Why
had she changed?

Once, when his parents were away and he had been
quarantined with measles, they had warned him to stay
away from the one-and-a-half-year-old Laura. But the
nursemaid who liked and indulged him, left him alone
with the infant while she went to another part of the
house.

Lifting the baby from her crib, he had held his baby
sister and kissed her all over her face and neck, again
and again. The nursemaid had come back and praised
him for taking such good care of his sister. "Yo' daddy
and mommy," she'd said, "they be too tough on you.
Nothin' gonna happen to little bebby if I leave her wit'
you. You like my own li'l boy."

The nursemaid's name had been Lily and after all
these years he felt warmth spread through him thinking
about her. Laura had caught his measles—a very mild
case—and had rallied quickly. He had been disappointed that she didn't die.

He looked over at the family cemetery on the grounds where his father was buried. Did his mother see him passing by? In his mind's eye, he saw her rigid figure, the beautifully coiffed salt-and-pepper hair, the pale skin and the cobalt-blue eyes.

His mother had never hugged and kissed him since childhood. She shuddered at his touch. Laura had garnered all the affection the family had to give. But as an older child, and now, he *dreamed* of earning the love of his mother even more than he had of his father. He still woke up crying the nights he dreamed she pushed him away as if he were a monster she could not abide.

Annoyed, he found himself slowing down. What the hell did he expect, that she'd see him passing, call his name and rush out to embrace him? He had come far without her love; he intended to go even farther and earn her love. She worshiped legitimate society. He would clean up his act. Trouble was, he liked being a bad guy. It was his revenge for not being loved.

"Trey," he said to himself. "What do you have in mind?" His friend Trey, who was so much more than a friend. One day he wanted to help Trey as Trey had helped him. Sure, Trey was dominating, controlling, just like Rush's parents, but the two men loved each other. Each provided a presence the other needed. Their lives meshed in total syncopated rhythm.

He shook his head, his mind lingering on Trey, then jumping to his father—his *dead* father. But before he could think about the elder Mason, his mind went back to his mother. Increasingly, he was determined to make her love him, be proud of him.

But first, he had to convince Trey to let him go. He wanted to be legit. Yeah, after all this time. There were other businesses he could go into. He had a good head on his shoulders. Trey would let him go. He believed that.

A memory that would not be denied boiled up inside him like a cauldron out of hell. The words were his father's, but his mother had said it, too: *You're no good, boy.* His father had added one day, "I'm glad I found out *why* you're no good."

What had led him to try to deflect that pain? He was ten and knew better. "I love you, Dad," he'd said.

Flint had come into his father's eyes. "The son of a bitch who was your father said he loved me, too," he'd said. "He slept with your mother behind my back."

Ragged laughter had grated in his father's throat. "I called her my ice maiden and told myself gently raised women just didn't care that much about sex. What a fool I was. My best friend lit her fire, all right, and it burned long enough to get you.

"I heard the rumors. Diamond Point is a gossip-ridden place, but I laughed. Not my Estelle."

He had looked at Rush then with rage and loathing that burned into a permanent memory. "As you grew older, I knew it wasn't just gossip. By the time you were six, you began to look like him. Now you're the spitting image of your bastard father, and every time I look at you, I want to wipe him from your face. God, forgive me. I can't stop hating you or him."

His father had turned then and walked away. They had never really talked again. He had been dead a long time, but the wounds he left didn't heal.

Rush thought he wouldn't see his mother this time. He would talk with Trey, and after a time, he would come back home. His mother's social activities were so many during the carnival season. But later, she would have time for him. He had to believe that.

A good feeling came over him. Trey would understand. Rush had a legacy to fulfill—not the man who'd been his father's friend and *was* his father, but Boris Mason, his mother's husband, who had despised him.

Twenty-seven

In the kitchenette of their cottage suite, Francesca rummaged about for the ingredients necessary to prepare a mini-breakfast for Jon. It was such a bright cheerful day, she thought, but then nearly all days in this part of the Caribbean were bright and cheerful.

Francesca smiled at the thought of Jon. He was really having a ball here. Pouring the last of the freshly squeezed orange juice, which she had mixed with cranberry juice, into two tall glasses and taking the fourth raisin bagel slice from the toaster oven, she placed the items onto plates on a large, clear plastic tray.

Cutting two orchids near the flowers, she floated the blossoms in a small bowl of water, and carrying the tray, rapped lightly on Jon's door.

Once in Jon's room, she put the tray down quickly on a bedside table.

"Good morning," she said softly, suddenly shy because he was coming out of the shower with a towel wrapped around his lean hips. She felt the blood rising to her head; her heart hammered. He was so beautiful.

"Good morning, yourself." Jon grinned and stood looking at her. "To what do I owe this honor?"

"Just being you."

"Great-looking breakfast. Great woman serving it. You look beautiful, Fran."

He came around the bed to her and took her in his arms. His smoothly rippling muscles wrapped her in his embrace, and he pressed her to him as if he would mingle with her.

He kissed her deeply, even as he pressed her. With the tip of her flickering tongue, she traced a short path back and forth under his ear. She felt the hard thrust of his maleness against her and went weak.

"You look so beautiful," he said, slackening his embrace and looking at her lush body.

"I'm not beautiful."

"You are to me. I love you in that color."

He was getting to her, and she sought to lighten the feeling. Did they have time? "I like you in that outfit," he said.

"Thank you. I'm just afraid that any minute now that towel is going to abandon you."

Jon laughed. "I do a mean wrap. It'll last. But if it doesn't, would you rescue me?"

"I would, you know."

"I do know."

Jon stood, holding her a little away from him, admiring the periwinkle-blue, sheer cotton, fitted gown she wore and the matching peignoir that was fitted in the front and sweeping in the back. Periwinkle embroidery outlined the bodice of the gown and the deep V-neck of the robe. Her breasts were warm, curved globes just inches from his mouth, which hungered for them.

He pulled her back to him and kissed her again, more deeply this time. Thrills ran the length of her body as he uncovered one breast, bent and sucked it gently. His big hands caressed her deeply curved hips through the sheer fabric.

"You're driving me up the wall," she murmured. "Have we got time?"

He sighed. "Not really. Cam is coming by, and we

have to talk. He's mapping some pretty crucial plans for us."

"I guess it's just as well. I feel famished for you. I'll be a long time getting this hunger filled. Ryson, when are we ever going to get it together?"

"I only know we *are* going to," he said gently. "I don't know when, but I know we will."

"I wish I had your faith."

"I'll lend you some of mine. Listen, I'm going to get my robe and pajama bottoms, and we'll have breakfast."

"Mini-breakfast. I'd like to go to that restaurant that specializes in omelettes for lunch. I'm starved for a ham-and-cheese-and-scallion omelette. Are you game?"

"I'm game for anything you want to do."

A few minutes later, barefoot and dressed in his tan-striped pajama bottoms and beige cotton robe, Jon sat with Francesca on the side of the bed. Suddenly, she leaned over and unfastened the belt of his robe and pulled it off his shoulders.

"Hey! What're you doing?"

"I was enjoying the beefcake show," she said. "If you have an appointment with Cam and nothing else can happen now, at least I can enjoy the view."

Swallowing a piece of his bagel, he leaned forward and blew a stream of air into the crevice of her breasts, making her tingle and draw in a sharp breath.

"Careful," she said slowly. "Today is my turn to seduce you."

Her eyes were limpid dark pools he wanted to look into endlessly. "Jon, do you know how precious the times we've made love are to me?"

"I can guess, love. I know how precious they are to me. In all my life I haven't known anything like the time I've spent with you."

They were silent then, enjoying the food. Their eyes locked and held, looking forward to a later hour when they could lose themselves in the magic they had discovered in each other.

Cam was prompt. Jon had hardly gotten dressed when he knocked. "I may be a bit early," Cam said, "but I think you'll like to hear what I have to tell you."

"Great. Would you like a bit of breakfast?"

Cam patted his stomach. "I ate a heavy breakfast, but I'll take a cup of coffee, heavy on the cream and sugar."

Jon poured the coffee in the kitchenette and poured himself another cup. Taking the two cups out, he put a decanter of brandy on the tray. "I like a shot of brandy in my coffee when I'm relaxing," he said. "How about you?"

"I'd like that very much."

They drank in silence as Cam seemed lost in thought, his eyes narrowed.

"You seem upset about something."

"Yes. My informants are telling me everything I need to know about my cousin Rush. I'm able to tie him now to specific times and people who handle the stolen cars for him. The ones who call themselves the Hill Warriors are very active in this.

"The only thing is Rush is covering his tracks pretty well. He chose Diamond Point as his headquarters because he knows people here. So many of us are poor that we'd sell our souls for money. Not to mention the ones who have and just want more."

"Those were good-looking cars we saw at his warehouse," Jon commented. "I'm sure they'll fetch a pretty price."

"You wouldn't believe how much. Someone other than our prime minister might turn a blind eye to it, but I've told you how honest he is. He loves this island

and wants it to be a moral place. He wants the best for our youth. Things like this don't help."

"So what are your plans?"

"Rush has been all over the place, more so than usual this time. As I said, he's well linked now to the Hill Warriors and is supplying them with money for their cause. They're true outlaws, and I think they feel their cause is justified. I think Rush has pipe dreams of being a very important man on this island one day."

"Prime minister?"

"I don't know. Maybe in his maddest dreams. My cousin is a hurt and bitter man. He has a scalding past. He hates me now where we were once close. But he wants something. This time he's making overtures to me. Then there's Win Hall, the man who runs Rush and Hudson's car dealership here. . . ."

"What about him?"

"He's fallen in step with me a few times lately, where he once had little to say. He asks me many questions about my work, about where the prime minister and I want the island to head. I'm getting vibrations that he's a troubled man."

"Have you known him long?"

"He came here from Jamaica five or so years ago. He's lived in the United States; that's where he met Trey and Rush. I'm going to keep talking to him. There was a book once, a popular book, about a man who had killed. He made friends with the detective on the case in order to throw him off. Winthrop Hall brings that book to mind. I don't think he's as ruthless as Rush and Hudson."

Jon began to say something when Cam looked up quickly. "Oh yes, I'm about to forget to tell you. You mentioned that a piece of paper was in your brother's papers with the words *Caribbean Caper* on it. . . ."

"Yes?" Jon held his breath.

"Winthrop Hall murmured those words to himself when he and I were talking lately. Then he asked me if I'd ever heard them. I said I hadn't. He wouldn't elaborate. His behavior is strange to me now. He wants Rush and me to meet this morning, he says to clear some things up. I suspect he and Rush simply want to know how much I know."

"And are you going?"

"Oh yes. Carnival morning is an odd time, but they've piqued my interest. Hall says it will not be a long meeting. Rush craves power to satisfy his inner anguish. He would do anything to please Trey whom he sees as the father he never had, although he's only a fair number of years older than Rush is."

A shudder passed the length of Jon's body and he wondered at it. "There's no chance they may turn on you?"

"None. They're too smart for that. Then I think Hall is growing away from them. He's asked me about becoming a policeman while owning a small business. It's done here."

"What did you tell him?"

"That I think he'd make a hell of a policeman. He's bright, sharp, savvy. Way too good for the type of chicanery I think he's involved in now. He seemed pleased at what I had to say."

Looking at Cam Mason through his detective's lenses, Jon liked the man very much, but thought he may well look at the world through glasses tinted a shade of rose that covered too much of the world's darkness.

Back in her room, Francesca felt relaxed and dreamy. Already the memory of the attack in the orchid greenhouse was fading. She was having such a good time.

And Jon—she hugged herself—that gentleman was beyond belief.

Yet fear was still rampant in her bones. She and Trey had started so hopefully. True, he had never wanted children, but she had once thought she could persuade him to father at least one child. Now gall rose in her throat when she thought about it.

As she sat musing, the odor of frangipani outside her window wafted in. A soft knock sounded and at her bidding, Melanie came in with two dresses over her arm.

She thrust them toward Francesca saying, "I feel like a foolish girl, but I'm undecided which dress to wear Carnival Day. Give me some advice."

Francesca looked at the dark blue-and-white print, then at the white waffle pique. Both dresses were lovely.

"I'd choose the white," Francesca told her. "You're one of those women with rich skin who can wear stark white. It drains most people. And those buttons are wonderful."

Melanie hugged her. "I knew I could count on you. I hear voices from Jon's room."

"Yes, Cam Mason is with him. Would you like to go with us later this morning to get a great omelette?"

"Oh, I'd love that. Have you talked with Holly and Lou today?"

"Both. I also called my father who's pining for you."

Melanie blushed. "That man. He's a love."

"I'll second that. Nothing wrong in his life that you couldn't set straight."

A look of anguish crossed Melanie's face. "I wish it could be."

"It can, Melanie. You have only to let it happen."

"I never want to hurt someone else, fail someone, the way I failed my husband and my boys."

"You have to forgive yourself. I'll tell you a little secret. I'd say Jon is feeling much closer to you now."

Francesca wasn't absolutely certain of what she had just said and she crossed her fingers.

"I can only hope that one day . . ." Melanie's vibrant voice drifted off.

Melanie started to leave; then she turned back. "Your bruises are much better." She touched Francesca's face tenderly. "You know, even if Jon never forgives me, and I did ask him once . . . He said perhaps one day, but not then. I've never gotten up the courage to ask him again."

"Only once, Melanie? You're a savvy woman, smart about everything. But you're stubborn, and Jon is your child."

Melanie nodded. "You're right, of course. Perhaps soon I will."

"That's my girl. He's proud of you, I do know that."

"Do you think he is?" Melanie's voice lilted now.

"I *know* he is." And Francesca felt on solid ground saying it.

As Melanie started out again, Francesca told her, "When you knocked, I thought it was Neena bringing me a packet of carnival photos and material. I'd like to look at them before I take my bath. Cam's wife said she'd send them early. Cam didn't come from home, or I'd guess he'd have brought them."

As the door closed softly behind Melanie, Francesca went into the bathroom and began drawing her bath. She hummed a socarengue melody as she moved about. "Jon," she murmured, loving the sound of his name. "Francesca Ryson," she said in a stronger tone, and wondered if it could ever be. He had asked her to marry him, and she had said yes.

Still, as deeply as she gave herself to him, as wonderful as they were together, she knew very well that she held back a part of herself that she wanted to be his for the taking. They had the stars and the moon. They could have the universe, if she could heal from the terrible hurt Trey had inflicted on her.

She was near the door when a light knock sounded. She opened it to find the maid, Neena, standing there, holding a large manila envelope.

"Ma'am, a man left this for you. He said you would know who sent it."

Francesca smiled at the winsome girl. "Yes, and thank you." She put the envelope on the table, walked into the bathroom and cut off the water. Sprinkling jasmine oil into the bath, she decided to look at the contents of the envelope, then bathe.

Sitting on the chaise longue near the window, she picked up the envelope and opened it with a letter opener in eager hands. Cam's wife hadn't sent many pictures, she thought.

Pulling out the photograph that was attached to a thick sheet of cardboard front and back, she removed the aluminum-foil-lined front cardboard and stifled the hysterical scream that rose in her throat.

The room spun as crazily around her as the orchid greenhouse had spun several nights back. Face up was an enlarged bust photo of her, like so many of her publicity shots. Superimposed on her photo was a picture of a filmy white wedding veil fastened with a tiara. In the photo, she wore a white satin bridal gown.

Looking at it, she gasped. This was the gown, the veil, and the tiara she had worn to marry Trey.

Francesca touched the dark red, still-wet blood that smeared the photo from the neck down and moaned deep in her throat. "Oh my God!" she choked. "What is the meaning of this?"

She was beyond fear now. Terror swept every portal of her being. Could she get up? Go through the living room to Jon's room? Was she as paralyzed as she felt she was?

She couldn't trust herself to stand. The intercom between her room and Jon's was near her. She leaned over and, choking, told him, "Please come here quickly."

Jon was there immediately. He saw the photograph, touched the blood and swore softly. Not since Kevin's death had he felt this towering outrage, this urge to pay back, to annihilate.

He put the photograph aside on the table and drew her to him.

Her finger, which had touched the blood on the photograph, touched his robe and she recoiled at the red print left on it. Getting up, he got a robe from her closet and helped her into it.

"Don't try to stand up," he told her. "You're shell shocked. I'm going to get Cam."

Francesca rallied after a few minutes, but hot tears scalded her eyes. The attack in the greenhouse may well have been an aberration. This was no aberration. This was a photograph of her, a bloody photograph. There was no mistaking that.

Like Jon, Cam was beside himself. He talked to her for a moment, then left the room.

Jon left the picture on the table, the edge of the manila envelope picking up bloodstains from the uncovered photograph. As Jon drew her to him again, she saw the glint of tears in his eyes.

"Don't cry," she said gently. "It's only a photograph. They haven't got me yet." She managed a smile.

"Sweetheart, don't," he told her. "You're scared and you've got every reason to be. Trey and Rush are here on Diamond Point, so we know they're likely to be behind this. The longer it goes on, the more I feel they're working in tandem. Twin devils."

His mouth was set in a grim line. "Believe me," he

said, "they will have to come through me to get to you. They'll get to you over my dead body."

Feeling his strong body against hers, Francesca wept and thought dully, *I got you into this. Your life was already painful enough. Oh, my darling, I'm sorry.* Then she spoke those words aloud to him.

"Hush!" Jon crushed her to him. "Don't you know by now that my life has no meaning without you?"

Cam came back in a short while and silently paced the floor in front of them.

He stopped and, sighing, sat on the edge of a chair. "I'm just trying to pull this together in my mind," he said. "Neena told me that a man in a carnival costume— a clown suit—brought the envelope.

"She said she teased him about walking about in a carnival costume during the day when it wasn't Carnival Day. He told her, 'Not everything strange happens on Carnival Day only. Please see that the lady gets this!' "

"A carnival costume," Jon said. "What was the size of the man?"

"She said he was tall, heavy, but in a clown's costume he may be smaller than he looks."

"Right."

Cam stroked his chin. "Good Lord, Jon. You don't know how sorry I am. That blood is unforgivable."

Jon breathed harshly. "I thought I had whoever this was psyched out. If there are two, I thought I had both of them psyched out. Now, I'm no longer certain. The blood—it may not be human blood."

"True, but it *may* be."

"It's a quantum leap from clippings, then a dead rabbit, to this. I don't like what I'm seeing here. I think I feel safer with Fran at home."

"I've been thinking," Cam said. "I believe Rush is in some kind of trouble. He doesn't look well, he's lost weight, and maybe he and Trey are at odds. He spoke of coming back here to live at least part-time, of setting up a major auto business here.

"His mother has no love for him. His sister loves him, but he hates her. My cousin is riding on the rails. His mother doesn't want him back here. He reminds her of a part of her life she wants to forget."

"The wedding dress," Francesca said suddenly. She had been so shocked she hadn't made a connection. "Jon proposed to me night before last. I accepted. How would anyone know that?"

"It may be a coincidence," Cam said softly.

The three of them looked at each other. "Unless the room was bugged," Jon said.

Francesca felt her heart race and thump painfully.

"If it is bugged, then I've got things to worry about," Cam said. "It means I've got some employees who can't be trusted. I have only a few people at this cottage and the orchid greenhouse. Neena, whom I trust. The two guards I use, I trusted, but with no real reason to do so. I've been checking them more carefully since that attack in the greenhouse.

"Francesca, I am so much sorrier about this than I can convey to you and Jon."

Jon nodded. Francesca told him, "I know you are, Cam. We've had a wonderful time in spite of everything."

Looking at her, at the courage and the grace, Jon wanted to bundle her up and take her far away from everyone and everything hurtful to her. Somewhere in some world in which there was no danger to her. He took her hand.

Somberly, Cam told them, "Please accept my congratulations. You two make a wonderful couple."

"Thank you," they both said.

"In the meantime," Cam said, "I will continue to check on the man in the clown suit. I will also check on my two guards. It will be easy because I have very good, well-paid informants. There is little that I cannot find out.

"Francesca is in excellent hands with you, and now I will get with our police chief and begin my search for answers. I will be in constant touch."

Cam took Francesca's hand. "Again, I will send my doctor to you. He will give you something to calm your nerves. And I will have answers to this monstrosity for you and Jon. You'll see."

After Cam left, Jon held Francesca, stroking her back. Then he got up and picked up the envelope and the bloodied photo.

"Do you have an accupressure session today?" he asked.

"This afternoon."

"You don't have to go anywhere, do anything except what you really want to do."

"I know, but I want to keep going. Jon, nothing and nobody is going to make a prisoner of me."

Jon smiled a little. "That's my girl. We won't get the omelettes today. Tomorrow perhaps."

Francesca shook her head. "I want to see that beautiful restaurant again. And I haven't gotten the pocketbook for Holly or the watch for my dad.

"I don't have the big appetite I had earlier, but I'm not going to wallow in this. I'm assuming now that Trey and/or Rush is behind this. I think they want to run me ragged, make me hurt myself in an accident, something like that."

Jon thought she spoke the truth, but it chilled him when he thought about what Francesca had told him about seeing his brother's watch in Trey's safe. Two bodies didn't hang you any higher than one.

"We'll get them dusted for fingerprints and get DNA samples."

"Thank you," she said. "I love you so much, and I'm more afraid of that than of the photographs."

Later that night, Cam came back. They talked in the living room. "I wanted to check on you," he said to Francesca, and to Jon, "I have some disturbing news."

With the wildly joyous sounds of the carnival in the town and steel bands vying with the rhythmic heartbeat drums in the background, Cam looked from one of his friends to the other. Finally, he cleared his throat.

"How are you holding up, Fran?"

"About as well as you could expect," Francesca said. "I'm still shocked, upset. The blood on the photo really got to me."

"I'll say again that I'm sorry. I am finding out much more."

"Oh?" Jon shifted in his chair.

Cam looked sad. "I have found betrayal," he said. "Men I trusted I now find are in the employ of my cousin and Hudson. My guards are not loyal to me, but to them. Only God knows where this leads.

"Francesca, the guard who was on duty the night you were attacked owes his allegiance to your ex-husband and my cousin. He lied concerning his whereabouts from beginning to end."

Cam paused, then went on. "The guards are both silent sympathizers of those who call themselves the Hill Warriors, largely supported as we know by Hudson and Rush.

"But I have a formidable ally now, and through him I believe we can get to the bottom of this whole affair, perhaps even what happened in the United States. Tomorrow is Carnival Day. Soon I think we will have many of the answers."

He stood. "Depend on me," he said, "and may God go with us all."

Twenty-eight

Carnival Day was beautiful. Every day since Francesca, Jon and Melanie had come to Diamond Point had been beautiful. Seated in the prime minister's box in the downtown section of the island, Francesca watched the growing carnival scenes around her with awe.

Dr. Tom Barton, the prime minister, arrived with his wife to greet them. She was a very attractive, statuesque, honey-brown woman of indeterminate age. She put out her hand to Francesca. "I've been so busy," she said, "I haven't had the time to spend with you I'd like. The hospital was hit with a siege of illnesses, and I am a nurse and could help. Will you forgive me?"

"Of course," Francesca answered.

After shaking hands with Jon and Melanie, the prime minister turned again to Francesca. "I will ask you to dinner before you leave. Now that the carnival season will be over, there will be time. I intend to get to know you much better. Have you enjoyed our carnival season?"

"We have enjoyed everything," Francesca assured him. "You have a wonderful island here."

"We think so," the prime minister said. His eyes twinkled. "And we hope you'll come to like it ever better."

A look passed between the prime minister and Jon as Matt Wolpers came up with Cam Mason's wife, who touched Francesca's arm.

"How lovely you look," Alicia Mason said.

Dressed in indigo cotton with a high neckline and sleeveless, sharply indented armholes, Francesca knew she looked well and wished she felt well. Covered buttons the size of silver dollars went from her waist to her hem. Her only jewelry was a wide silver bracelet.

"Did you get the photographs?" Cam's wife asked.

"I did and thank you so much." *Ah yes, I got the photographs*, Francesca thought, but first the other photograph was delivered. *I could hardly see the lovely photographs of former carnivals you sent over. My head whirled for the rest of the day. Now it is another day, and I have to pull myself together.*

Jon caught her eye and silently questioned her: *Are you okay?* She silently assured him with a glance that she was. But she wasn't okay. She was sick with panic.

Alicia glanced at her watch. "Cam should be here by now," she said.

"He had to see someone," Matt Wolpers told her. "He may be a bit late."

The prime minister frowned. "There are several things I need him to do, including meeting a dear friend who is coming in with a party from Holland."

"I'm sure he'll be here shortly," Wolpers soothed the prime minister.

"My dear," the prime minister said to Francesca, "please tell my friend Lou that I missed him. He must be here for the next carnival. He enjoys himself so."

"I certainly will," Francesca responded. "He loves the carnival."

"And I will send him many gifts. He has the gift of life few people have."

"He's one of the best," Francesca murmured.

"Why don't we sit down?" the prime minister said. They sat around a large semicircular table covered with a snowy cloth with the ever-present cashew nuts native to Diamond Point and other snack foods in dishes spread over it. Various drink bottles were set in ice buckets.

Handed a pair of binoculars by Matt Wolpers, the three Americans used them to watch the throngs of people gathering fast. Floats were beginning to roll by, each one more gorgeous than the last.

Every imaginable costume was worn. Indian costumes of full regalia. Pirates. Dancing girls. Royalty. Fairies. Dancing dolls.

Matt Wolpers leaned over to say to them, "It is very much like the Mardi Gras in New Orleans. Some work on these costumes an entire year."

"They're fabulous." Surrounded by beauty, Francesca felt a little better.

Spread across the long viewing stand presided over by the prime minister and his wife were numbers of tables just like the one the three Americans enjoyed. Prime Minister Barton and his wife had many friends and sometimes he thought ruefully they all came to visit during the carnival season.

Jon caught Francesca's hand, and smiled reassuringly at her. She felt the pull of eyes on her and looked down to the street to see a man in the same costume of skull-and-crossbones mask and skeletal tights as her assailant had worn. A deep shudder shook her as her mind flashed back to the night in the greenhouse.

She fought to get her bearings, again feeling the phantom man's fingers on her throat. But this man bowed deeply and saluted her. She breathed a sigh of relief. It must be the man who had apologized so profusely for frightening her at the carnival a few nights before. Yes, his similarly dressed family was with him. They, too, bowed.

Jon saw immediately what was happening and pressed her hand.

"Steady," he said softly, remembering as she did the

man who had been kind enough to reassure his love when she was afraid. Jon lifted his hand in salute to the man and his family. Francesca managed a smile.

Francesca, Jon and Melanie were introduced to the others around them.

"I wish Lou and Holly could be here," she told Jon.

"Another year," he said. "Perhaps they'll be back to visit us."

Francesca didn't think so, although she murmured, "Perhaps."

"Look!" Melanie said, laughing. A golden chariot of children pulled by garland-laden, trained goats came down the street.

"Bonbini!" the children yelled as they scattered flowers in the street around them.

The children paused in front of the prime minister and his wife and bowed low. "Our beloved prime minister!" they yelled. "We love you!"

"And I love you!" the prime minister shouted back.

The children threw him kisses, and he and the people in the box returned the kisses. The goat cavalcade moved on.

"How charming," Melanie said. "I wish I could bring every child I work with here to visit. Thank you, Fran, for setting this up for me."

"You're very welcome."

Melanie leaned across Jon to murmur to Francesca, "How are you holding up?"

"I'm determined not to let it get me down."

"Good." Melanie squeezed her hand.

They watched the magnificent floats roll by and the street was covered with thousands of flower blossoms.

Finally the carnival queen's float neared them. With woven themes of Diamond Point making up her float, the radiant, pale-brown woman's tiara and jewels sparkled in the brilliant sunlight. She was resplendent in her white gauze, silver-and-gold gown. Francesca thought the floats looked a lot like the fantastic Rose Bowl floats.

The young carnival queen waved and waved as she came by. Then her float paused in front of the prime minister, and she took off her garland of red and white roses and flung it at him. A young man in front of the box caught the garland and passed it up to Matt Wolpers, who gave it to the prime minister. Then the young queen threw the prime minister a kiss that he returned.

A short time after the queen passed, Francesca smiled to see the next float. It contained a band of red-clad devils with plastic flames leaping up around them. A tall, red-costumed devil with a pitchfork rode herd on his crew. AFTER TODAY, FOR A WHILE WE ARE BANISHED! a large sign on the float read.

And behind this float came a float of angels wired into space, clad in voluminous white cotton robes with wired haloes around their heads. The sign on their float read: TOMORROW WILL BE OURS!

Steel bands and jump-up singles and couples strutted their stuff on the sidelines.

Calypso and socarengue music filled the air. Watching and listening to the merriment, Francesca began to relax a bit.

But there was one discordant note. One man's costume showed a fake dagger in his back with fake blood blobs on his white tunic. A red sign when he turned proclaimed him to be Julius Caesar.

Matt Wolpers looked at Jon and Francesca. "I suppose it takes a bit of everything for a carnival."

Francesca looked at the gleefully cavorting man with the fake dagger in his back, and she wondered if someone were going to take advantage of the carnival and plunge a *real* dagger into hers.

The prime minister leaned over and spoke to Matt, who stood.

The crowd was growing denser now. The parade was ending.

Matt Wolpers came to Jon. "I am going to ask you to go with me to find Cam. He has mild heart trouble and may have passed out coming back. I know he was to talk with Rush Mason and Winthrop Hall."

Jon nodded. "Certainly, but Francesca has to come with me. After that photograph, I can't let her out of my sight."

Matt Wolper's face creased into a smile. "I'm sure I would feel the same."

"We'll be back soon," Jon told Melanie. "Don't eat too much."

Melanie blushed like a girl. "Now how do you remember that I eat too much when I'm nervous?"

Jon looked at his mother. "I remember a lot of things." Then he added, "Mother."

Melanie's heart leaped with hope.

As they walked along the street behind the viewing stand, Matt talked. "We're going to have to go the edge of the island and go around. People are as thick as the flower petals they're throwing.

"Oh yes, I'm sure I've told you how we visit Aruba's carnival as they visit ours. Cam or I will take you there this afternoon. You'll love it, but we like ours best."

Ahead of them a man in a clown suit darted out from the crowd, crossing the street. Francesca felt a finger of dread race along her spine. The bloodied photograph had been delivered by a man dressed in a clown costume. When would this be over?

Jon knew very well what she was feeling, and he caught her hand. "Steady, sweetheart," he murmured. Matt Wolpers looked from one to the other, smiling.

They drove along the blacktopped road back to the beach, hailing merrymakers on their way to celebrate

Carnival Day. "Cam may have gone the other way around," Matt Wolpers said. "I hope he isn't feeling ill. His wife and I have been keeping our eyes on him.

"He told me he hadn't had time to talk with Rush and Win Hall the way he wanted to. Win said it was urgent that he talk with him today. I wonder what this is all about."

"He did seem pretty anxious," Jon said. "He was going to meet with Hall a little earlier, before Rush was to come. Something's going on."

"You bet something's going on," Matt said. "Something's always going on when Rush is around. I don't mind telling you he's bad news and has been for a long time."

Ahead of them a Gypsy-costumed band, rattling tambourines, playing fifes and beating drums, came into view.

"*Bonbini!* Welcome to carnival! It is a glorious day!" A handsome, brown Gypsy man with a red-print kerchief on his head saluted them. A lovely, fair-skinned Gypsy girl joined him in a jump-up dance routine. In a minute, the road was thronged with dancing Gypsy men, women and children.

Matt cut the ignition and they sat, enjoying the show. The troupe finished, bowed low and began to move on.

"Thank you," Matt called out. Then to Jon and Francesca, "They think we are all three visitors."

One of the men lagged behind the others. "No," he said, "I know you are Matthew Wolpers, aide to our prime minister. May your day end as splendidly as it has begun."

Twenty-nine

They reached the warehouse Rush owned. Matt parked near the door and they got out. Cam's Jeep was parked a short distance away.

Matt twisted the heavy knob of the warehouse's door and it opened. The building was well lit and full of new-model sports utility vehicles and other late-model vehicles. Vans of every make were well represented. There seemed to be more cars in the warehouse now than there had been the first day Francesca and Jon had visited with Cam and Melanie.

The office door was open, and they went in to find Win Hall leaning over a body, with tears streaming down his face. "I think he's dead," he said.

Cam Mason lay spread-eagled on the floor near the desk. His white-shirted chest was covered with blood that ran slowly down the sides of his body.

"Christ!" Matt exploded. "Why the hell did you do this to him?"

Win wiped his face with the back of his hands and stood. "You don't understand," he choked. "If he's dead, *I* didn't kill him. I found him like this. I've called the police. I called an ambulance."

Matt knelt quickly and felt for a pulse. He could feel none. He squatted, his body stiff with outrage.

"We shouldn't move him," Win Hall said quietly.

"Your hands are covered with blood," Matt said.

"I know. I tried to give him CPR. I was so shocked. It wasn't supposed to end like this."

"Don't leave the building," Matt said roughly. "The police are going to want to talk with you."

Hall nodded. "I know. And I want to talk with them."

Matt began to pace up and down the length of the small room. "How long ago did you call?"

"Long enough for them to be here, even on Carnival Day."

This put a different tilt on the whole story, Jon thought, his mind bleak with momentary helplessness. He glanced at Francesca and was afraid she was going to faint. She read his look.

"I'm not going to pass out," she said. But she reflected in a daze that the blood covering Cam's chest was very much like the blood on the photo she had received. She put her hand on the edge of the desk to steady herself. Jon moved closer and put his arm around her.

The ambulance came first; two policemen pulled up just after.

In a short while the ambulance attendants lifted Cam on a stretcher. "We're going to get him to the hospital in a hurry," one of the attendants said, "but I think it's a losing battle. He was hit at close range."

"He was shot then?" Matt asked.

"We won't know until later."

"I want to go with him, but I can't." Matt breathed hard. "I have to talk with you, Hall. We're going to take you in."

The police sergeant nodded. "Blood on your hands, on your shirt," he told Win Hall. "It seems like you may be who we're looking for."

"I didn't kill him," Win Hall said quietly. He turned to Matt.

"Mr. Wolpers, stay with me a little while. Talk with me here. I've got a lot to tell you that will be helpful. I think I know who *did* kill Mr. Mason, but he'll have an airtight alibi. And I haven't."

Matt Wolpers stood thinking. "What do you think, Jon? You've handled a lot more of this kind of thing than I have."

Jon glanced at the sergeant. "Get in touch with your chief. Bring Hudson and Mason in to the police station. They may skip town otherwise."

Matt nodded. He turned to Hall. "Stop for a moment while I place this call."

Hall looked at his bloody hands and sat down, his eyes reddened, more tears trickling down his cheeks.

Matt placed the call to the police chief and hung up. "Go on, Hall," he said grimly.

Win Hall got up. "First, please let me check for something in this drawer I set up here. If it's all there, it verifies everything you need to know. But I still need to talk with you, especially Lieutenant Ryson."

Jon looked at him sharply, frowning.

"I'm willing to listen," he said.

"We may be compromising the crime scene if we permit him to go in that drawer."

Matt looked at Jon, who shrugged. "The scene is already compromised. I think we'd better let him."

Win Hall wiped some of the blood from his hands with a handkerchief and tissues from the desktop. He pulled a deep lower drawer all the way out and lifted a small tape machine from under some papers.

Setting the machine on the desk, he turned the recorder on and pressed the play button.

Francesca sat in a chair beside Jon. The room seemed stifling, yet cold to her. Matt Wolpers got up and turned on the air conditioner.

It was eerie hearing Cam talk in a calm, matter-of-fact

voice. "I've found out what your game is, cousin," he said. "You and Trey are masterminding a stolen-car racket and you're considering making Diamond Point your headquarters for the Caribbean.

"But it isn't going to work. Tom Barton has moved heaven and earth to make this a crime-free island and we're going to keep it that way."

Rush's smooth voice argued, "You can't prove anything. I'm a legitimate businessman now, cuz. There's nothing in hell you can do about that."

Then Cam's voice. "I think you'll find you're wrong. I've got several people willing to testify against you. A couple of Hill Warriors—*ex*-Hill Warriors. . . ."

"You're lying."

"You'll find out soon enough I'm not."

There was silence then and when Rush spoke, his voice was strained. "Give me a break, cousin. We were friends once. . . ."

"That was long ago. You've gotten greedy, Rush, and careless. You're vain, egotistical. Vindictive. You hate your own sister just because she got more of your parents' love than you did. . . ."

"She got it *all.*" Rush's voice was guttural with hate.

"It doesn't matter. We grow up and put the past behind us."

"That's easy for you to say."

"It's possible. I never said it was easy. We're going to charge you with transporting stolen goods into Diamond Point and shipping them out."

"I'm a United States citizen."

"And a criminal there and on Diamond Point."

"Give me a break. Don't do this to me. I've got too much to lose."

"You've had more breaks than most people have had. They didn't turn bad. I've got a world of information against you. A lot of it not even on paper yet. I'll be the worst witness against you."

"You can't do this. I'm not going to let you."

"Try stopping me. You're looking at a few years in prison."

"We're family. Family doesn't hurt family."

The people in the room sat transfixed as the recorder ran on, its tone clear, distinct. There was a silence on the tape.

Then another protest. "You're my first cousin. You can't turn on me like this." Hoarse now, talking faster. "We're *family*, man!" he said again.

The statement seemed to make Cam angry. Jon could picture him talking to Rush.

"What did you ever do to uphold our family's honor?" he asked scathingly. "Since we were boys you couldn't do enough to fling mud at all of us. Stealing. Lying. Fighting. Robbing. God, man, you'd be better off if someone had jailed you long ago.

"Your sister still loves you. Your mother gave up on you a while back."

"Don't *say* that. Don't talk about my mother!"

"It's true. You've brought her nothing but shame. You've brought your entire *family* nothing but shame."

Rage filled Rush's voice. "That's a lie. I can buy and sell you. I've made a lot of money. A lot."

"And more trouble than you're worth. You're a loser, Rush. A loser and a *thief*. Like I said, you've brought us all nothing but shame."

"Let me make a deal with you. I'll go back to the United States and come back later. We can talk."

"No. Time has run out for you. You won't be going back to the States. We're going to take you in at the end of the day."

There was a long moment of silence, then the sound of something crashing. Jon noticed then the pieces of

a smashed glass ashtray in the corner. The four recorded shots were sharp and swift.

Cam said nothing more, made no outcry. And Rush
was shrill in his triumph. Shrill and vengeful.

"You're wrong, cousin," Rush said. "My time isn't
running out. *Your* time has run out."

The tape ran on and there were sounds of coughing,
of Rush's laughter. "I was always smarter than you,
cousin," he said. "You should have kept that in mind."

They listened in silence as the tape droned on. Nothing more was said.

Win Hall cleared his throat and turned the recorder
off. "Thank you for listening," he said. "I wasn't sure
the machine was working, or if Rush was going to be
suspicious. I've got something else to say."

"Go ahead." Matt Wolpers's face was anguished. His
big hands twisted in his lap.

"I need to pace again," Win Hall said.

"Go ahead." Matt thought he needed to pace, too.

"I'm good at electronics," Win Hall began. "Very
good. Electronics and photography. Too bad I didn't
make better use of my time. I've been greedy, the way
Trey and Rush are greedy. But I'm willing to go straight.
Pay my dues."

He paused a while, then turned to Francesca. "I sent
you the bloody superimposed photo," he said. "That
was bought blood. Rush told me that he had been sending Ms. Worth news and magazine clippings of obituar-
ies with the names blotted out. Mailing them from mail
drops in various cities."

Incredulous, Francesca stared at him.

"I wired the room in the orchid greenhouse. I did
that a while back when Trey and Rush suspected that
Cam might be catching on to our scheme."

Hall cleared his throat. "I'm sorry I did that wedding gown caper. I like you both"—he nodded in Francesca and Jon's direction—"but I had to go along with what Rush wanted. I didn't want to make him suspicious if I refused. Hell, I *always* went along with what Rush wanted. What Trey wanted, too."

"Do you know about the rabbit?" Jon asked.

"Sure. Rush called me and screamed with laughter about that. 'We're going to drive her crazy,' he told me. 'Break her. If that doesn't work, well, there's always the *ultimate* stroke.' "

Francesca felt a spasm of sharp fear dart through her. Jon's hand tightened on hers.

"You used the word 'caper' a minute back." Jon looked thoughtful and sad. "Does the phrase 'Caribbean Caper' mean anything to you?"

Win Hall smiled bitterly. "Sure, that's our name for the stolen-car ring."

A lump rose in Jon's throat. "What do you know about my brother's death?"

Hall shook his head. "That's something they didn't talk about to me. You see, I know now we're all rotten, but I always thought they'd draw the line at murder. They don't want to die themselves. I know I don't."

Seeing the misery in Jon's eyes, which he couldn't quite mask, Hall said, "I'm sorry. I'll help you in any way I can."

"The orchid greenhouse," Francesca spoke up. "Do you know who attacked me that night?"

"Rush. He was in no danger of being caught. Both guards are our men. The guards latched the doors from outside and had a table under the window so Rush could easily get out."

And Cam had been so trusting. He had brought the guard to apologize.

"Thank you," Jon said. "How did you come to set up the recorder in here?"

"The three of us were to meet here and Rush and I would see how much Cam knew, what he planned to do, and if he could be bribed. The thing is lately I got first-rate information that Trey and Rush were planning to replace me. I felt they were going to frame me and leave me holding the bag for what happened here on Diamond Point. They're U.S. citizens. I'm not.

"They owed me a lot of money the way I figured it, and they were behind in their payments. Way behind. I told them there was talk that someone else would replace me. They denied it, but I didn't believe them. So you see, I recorded this to save my own hide. I never thought I'd record a murder.

"Mr. Mason always treated me with respect. He wanted me to go straight the way he wanted his cousin to go straight. And he was turning me around. He thought I'd make a good policeman and said he'd help me.

"I came early to set up the recorder; then I went back home. When it was time for the meeting, I set out, but my car broke down. I walked the rest of the way, and I was too late. Mr. Mason was shot and Rush was gone."

He seemed drained then and his shoulders were hunched. He was like a car that has run out of fuel—cold and empty.

"Thank you very much," Matt Wolpers said. "You've helped us more than you could ever know."

"I'm glad. One thing I want you to know. I'd never go along with killing. I know Rush is full of hate." He broke off and looked at Francesca. "He hates you because you're a better broadcaster. You beat him at something, and he can't stand it when someone else wins."

"Then it was Rush who's tormented me all this time?"

"Yes. Trey still loves you, as much as he *can* love anyone."

Thirty

It was late that afternoon when Rush, Trey and Jersey were brought, handcuffed, into the police station. The police chief, Arnie Milton, wanted Jon to sit in on questioning the men. Jon wanted Francesca with him and Cam's wife wanted to be there when they brought Rush in.

When the men came through the door, Cam's wife was on her feet, propelling her small body toward Rush like a projectile.

"You fiend!" she screamed, beating his chest with her little fists.

"Hey, cut it out, Alicia," Rush growled. "You've got the wrong man!"

Jon caught Cam's wife before she could slump to the floor. He lifted her and took her to a small treatment room just off the main room.

Francesca went with him. Together, they put the woman on a small cot and Francesca stroked her arms, then got a sponge from the medicine cabinet. Wetting the sponge with cold water, she dampened Cam's wife's arms and put the sponge on her forehead.

The small woman lay rigid on the bed at first. As Francesca spoke soothing words, she relaxed, then collapsed.

"He would have wanted me to be brave," Alicia

sobbed, "but I *can't* be brave. I don't want to go on without him."

Francesca smoothed the woman's hair, murmured words of solace that could not prove enough.

"I will take her home," the police chief said as he came in.

"No. I don't want to go home. Cam isn't there. I want to stay here with his murderer. I want to remind him that he killed my husband."

"Then you can stay, at least a little while," the chief of police told her gently. In an aside to Jon, he said, "Mason is still swearing he didn't do it. I want you to help me question him. As far as I'm concerned, it's a cut-and-dried case with that tape recording."

"As far as I'm concerned, too," Jon answered, "but he doesn't know about the tape yet."

Matt Wolpers came in, his face haggard and drawn. He knelt beside Cam's wife. "Don't try to be brave," he said. "Feel what you're feeling. You two had so much, but your three children need you now. Cam would want you to be there for them."

Cam's wife rallied a little at the mention of her children; then she slumped back into her bottomless pit of grief.

"When will you question them?" Jon asked Chief Milton.

"In a short while. I want to let them relax as much as they can, use the gentle treatment. We're dealing with two bad men here."

"Why was the big man, Jersey, arrested?" Jon asked.

"For fighting my men when they tried to arrest the other two."

In his narrow cell, Rush banged on the bars. When a guard finally came, he told him, "I want you to send for my mother. Mrs. Estelle Mason. Do you know her?"

The guard nodded.

"Good. I thought you did. She's a well-known lady on this island. But if my sister comes with her, I don't want to see her. Is that understood?"

The guard gave a short bark of laughter. "You're not running your own show anymore, Mason, so don't be uppity with me. I'll tell the chief what you're requesting. But get used to not getting your way."

Rush was silent. When he'd been a teen, his mother wouldn't take his side, but she managed to get him out of scrapes, some of them bad. When he was a small child, she'd seemed to love him. She came from one of the island's oldest families, and she carried social weight.

Rush hunkered down on his bed, waiting for his mother to come.

"Don't hold your breath," the guard said. "You may not get your wish."

"She'll have somebody's head if I don't."

The guard grunted. He wasn't moved.

In his cell, Trey nervously sat on the edge of his cot. This was a bad break. Had Rush killed his cousin? He, Trey, sure as hell hadn't. If Rush had, he might get the death penalty. Trey groaned; he couldn't imagine life without his buddy and ally. But Rush had talked often of coming back to live on Diamond Point.

Jon came to Trey's cell door.

Trey looked up cheerfully. "I'd say come in," he said, "but as you can see, I don't have the key."

Jon looked at him steadily. He didn't know why he had come back here. Then he amended that thought: yes, he *did* know. He wanted to psych Hudson out. He wanted to know if he and Trey had killed his brother.

"I want to talk with Fran," Trey said.

The hackles rose on the back of Jon's neck at Trey's use of Francesca's nickname, at his nerve at asking to see her.

"I don't think she wants to see you."

Trey's look was cunning. "Why don't you ask her? Old loves die hard."

No need to humor him, Jon thought sourly. Then a light dawned. Faced with Francesca, Trey would probably loosen up. What had Win Hall said: *He loves her as much as he can love anyone.*

"Hadn't you better be asking for Stacy?" Jon asked.

"She'll go my bail."

"If there is the chance."

"I haven't done anything."

"That remains to be seen."

Milton gave the okay to notify Mrs. Mason that her son had been arrested. Francesca agreed that she would briefly talk with Trey. Cam's wife decided she should go home to be with her children. The police chief sent her home with a police escort.

Milton came to stand at the door of Rush's cell. He stared at him malignantly for a long while.

"You took out a wonderful man," he said quietly.

"I haven't taken anyone out."

"You're lying, you bastard. We have everything we need to convict you." Gone was his vow to be gentle. He hurt too bad.

Rush shook his head. "You've got this all wrong. Win Hall must have done this. Cam was after him."

"If he was after him, he was after you. You're all in the same bag, only Hall is a more decent man."

"He may be a murderer. I haven't been anywhere

near that warehouse. The three of us were to meet, but I got skunk drunk last night and it was eleven this morning before I could pull myself together."

The chief's ears reddened. "I didn't ask you anything about a warehouse. What makes you think we found your cousin in a warehouse?"

Rush shrugged, unnerved. He was talking too damned much.

Milton stared at Rush as if he were a snake and decided not to pursue that line of questioning for the moment. There was plenty of time. Mason wasn't going anywhere.

Francesca walked on wooden legs with Jon to Trey's cell.

He stood and came to the bars.

They stopped a little back from the cell.

"Thanks for coming, baby," Trey said, poisoned honey in his voice.

"What do you want to say to me?" Francesca felt gall rise in her throat. Jon put his arm around her. Trey steeled himself to betray nothing.

"I want to say this," Trey said evenly, under control. "I would never hurt you again. I've been too sorry about the other hurts I've dealt you."

Anger at her memories of Trey's mistreatment peppered Francesca's skin. Looking him in the eyes, she said, "I hope you're not asking my forgiveness. If you are, ask God, because I can't forgive you for a very long time."

Trey looked humble now. "It's okay, babe. I understand. But I am sorry all the same." His eyes flickered over Francesca and Jon as they stood together—against him.

Trey's face turned woebegone. "I had nothing to do

with any of this. Now the cops are saying Rush killed
his cousin, and they're trying to link me to him. Rush
can be childish, even if he is my best friend."

Francesca thought: *And you're not childish, Trey?*

Trey looked at her and smiled. "I've said my piece
and that's all I have to say for now. I love you, babe. I'll
always love you."

Stacy came around the corner with a guard as Trey
was speaking. She looked daggers at him, but he didn't
seem perturbed. Her pale skin turned a fiery red.

"Hello, Stacy," Trey said. "How are you?"

Stacy's clipped words were bullets. "I was fine until I
heard something I wasn't supposed to hear."

"That I love Francesca? That I'll always love her?"

"Never mind, Trey," Stacy huffed. "You need me now
more than I need you."

"Ah, Stace. Knock it off. A man doesn't love just one
woman. Fran came first. You're in there, too."

"Thanks for nothing," Stacy said, her voice breaking.

Jon, the police chief and a sergeant questioned Rush
in a small, windowless room of the station house. He
was all narrow smiles.

"You've got the wrong guy," he said. They hadn't told
him about the tape. He sat looking from one to the
other of the men.

"I think we've got the right guy," Milton said in a
hoarse voice. Cam Mason had been one of his closest
friends.

Jon looked steadily at Rush. The chief of police's eyes
signaled Jon to go ahead with his questions.

"You sent the clippings in Minden. And here on Diamond Point, you attacked Ms. Worth in the orchid
greenhouse and sent her the bloody photo."

"Whoa!" Rush said, laughing. "Your fancy knows no bounds."

"What do you have against Ms. Worth? That she *took* your job? You could have had a dozen more by now."

Rush's index finger circled his left eye. He wrinkled his nose. "I've got nothing against Francesca, except that she reminds me of my sister. They both think they own the world."

"And you think *you* own it," the chief of police broke in.

"Ah, this is nonsense," Rush said. "I didn't kill my cousin and I've had little to do with Francesca after I was let go. She isn't the first woman to take a station manager to bed to get what she wants. She won't be the last. Sometimes it just makes me want to be a woman."

Trained to keep cool, Jon felt anger leap in him. "You . . ." Jon began, then steadied himself.

"Listen," Rush said, loosening up. "I can prove that I didn't leave our suite until shortly before you gentlemen brought me in. We were going over to Aruba.

"I got skunk drunk last night. Trey can vouch for me. Jersey can vouch for me. Other people at the party . . ."

The police chief shook his head slowly. Finally, he cleared his throat. "I have something here I want to play for you, Mason. It may surprise you."

"Sure," Rush said, "but before you do, you ought to be checking Win Hall out. He's had a lot to say to Cam lately, and he told me Cam was on his case."

"About the Caribbean Caper?" Jon asked smoothly.

Rush's head jerked up. "I don't know what you're talking about."

Milton signaled for silence and began playing the tape. When Cam's voice came on, Jon thought he saw Rush flinch, but he couldn't be sure. *Something* was happening. Rush sat with his eyes half closed, his breathing uneven.

The men heard the tape through and sat in silence for a few moments after.

"Well," the chief of police said to Rush.

"It's a setup," Rush declared. "Win is an expert with electronics. He's got all kinds of connections on the island; he could have faked this tape. Cam's voice sounds like a million other voices."

Chief Milton looked at Rush, his head lowered like a bull readying to charge. "We have Cam's voice on other tapes," he said. "We can identify voices with certainty."

Rush looked about him.

"I think you're going up for this one," Milton told him.

"My family is prominent on this island," Rush said. "You know my grandfather was one of the men who set it all in motion. We have clout."

"Your *family* has clout. You don't. You've been in trouble since you were a kid." The chief glared at him.

"I've helped build an automobile dealership back in the States. I'm wealthy. I haven't done too bad."

"Why don't you confess?" the chief said. "If we have to try you, it's going to go really hard on you."

Rush smirked. "I'll take my chances. I haven't done a damned thing."

Rush leaned back, his eyes half closed again. He was sweating. Could they prove it was his voice and Cam's voice on the tape? One thing he felt certain of, his mother wasn't going to let him go to prison or be hit by lethal injection.

His mother had been his rock when he was a small boy. She had loved him then. He had always dreamed of making her love him again.

"Is that all?" Rush asked, grinning a little.

"Not quite," Jon said. "Did you kill my brother, Kevin?"

Rush scratched his head. "No. Word on the street was that he was killed in a drug bust gone bad."

"I know what the word on the street was," Jon snapped. "What do *you* know about his death?"

"Why nothing, Lieutenant," Rush said smoothly. "Just as I know nothing about this other stuff I'm standing accused of." He shook his head as a sly smile played about his mouth. "Nothing at all."

When they took Rush back to his cell, his mother was waiting in the hall for him. He went toward her with outstretched arms. "Mother!"

The pale, salt-and-pepper-haired dowager queen of a woman stiffened and her eyes flashed fire. She was dressed in all black as if for a funeral.

"Don't touch me, Rush!"

He drew back, painfully aware of the guard who looked at him scornfully. "Can my mother and I talk somewhere private?" he asked the guard.

"Maybe it can be arranged," the guard told him.

"There'll be no need for privacy," Estelle Mason said as she glared at her son. "I am told you have finally done what I always believed you would do. You've killed a man. Your cousin. A man after my own heart. How could you?"

Her praise of Cam cut Rush to the bone. He opened his mouth and faint words of denial tumbled out. "I didn't kill Cam. I've got an alibi."

"You're lying, as you've lied all your life."

"Mother, please!" Pleading now.

She drew a deep breath. "Laura wanted to come. I forbade her. Thank God I have one child who has done me proud."

"Mother, don't."

She had driven in the knife and his psyche was bleeding badly.

"I'm sorry," he said. He could think of nothing else. Then the words he had wanted to say for many alienated, anguished years burst from him. "Mother, when I was a child, you loved me. I know you did.

"I know I've done a lot of bad things, but I want to change now, go straight. . . ."

Estelle Mason laughed scornfully. "It's a little late for that, don't you think? I'm going to tell you something I should have told you long ago. You're right, I do despise you. When you were little and looked mostly like me and I told myself like my husband, I loved you. You were ours.

"My husband lost his head and told you another man was your father—his friend and my lover. It's the only mistake I've made in my life. When you began to look like him, my life became tormented because I hated the man who was your father. He betrayed me. He refused to marry me, but my husband was kind enough to take me back."

Hot tears stood in her eyes.

"You're trembling," Rush told her. "Please come into my cell and sit down."

"No," his mother said sadly. "I will not see you again, Rush. You sent for me, and I came to let you know I can never forgive you. . . ."

"But I didn't . . ."

"You *did* because you're a destroyer like the seed you came from. Rush, don't call me or try to get in touch with me. Laura and I will manage nicely without you. As of this day, I no longer have a son! You have brought nothing but shame and dishonor on our family, and I will tolerate it no longer."

Her words nearly knocked the breath from him. Cam

had said virtually the same thing. Rush had lost his head and shot him.

"You don't mean that. I'm changing. I'm going to change." His voice was hoarse with agony.

The woman drew a handkerchief from her purse and wiped away her bitter tears. "I was going to abort you the way your real father wanted me to do, but I decided against it. I loathe abortions, but I should have done as he asked. *I should have killed you in my womb.*"

The tears wouldn't stop, and she let them run freely, no longer caring. "Good-bye, Rush. Cam was like a son to me. May God forgive you. I know I never will."

She turned then and walked away. He had always thought her the most beautiful woman he knew. The guard looked at him, pitying him. He felt light-headed. Empty. *He was losing heart, losing courage, losing everything.*

Rush sat on his cot for the rest of the afternoon and when late afternoon had come and the raucous sounds of Carnival Day still enlivened the air, he made up his mind and sent for the chief of police.

When Milton came, he stood before Rush's cell, his eyes hot and punishing. "I want to confess to killing my cousin," Rush said, "and I want to confess to stalking Francesca Worth."

Back in Minden

Thirty-one

Two weeks later

Back in Minden, Francesca found she had trouble settling in. She was still sick over Cam Mason's murder, but she rallied a bit as she sat at a computer in the boiler room of WKRX. The room was crowded with computers, stacks of tapes, playlist slots, extra headsets and other paraphernalia needed to run the station.

She couldn't get Rush Mason out of her mind. Was it really over, and why had Trey said he loved her?

Sighing, she scrolled through an article on inner-city youth being trained to fence. She would make some calls. It would make an interesting topic for tomorrow's show, she thought.

Lou and Holly came in together. Lou's face mirrored his sadness. He had gone to Diamond Point for Cam's funeral.

"How're you holding up, Fran?" he asked, pausing by her ergonomic chair.

"I'm okay. I think the question is how're *you* holding up?"

"It's pretty painful. Cam, Matt Wolpers, Tom Barton and I have been friends since our Howard days. Alicia is taking it really hard. They married when both were young. It's a damned shame, but I always considered Rush capable of anything bad."

"So did I," Francesca said, "and we were right."

"I don't think I considered him capable of murder." Holly's face was thoughtful.

"I guess at some given point we are all capable," Lou said. "We love ourselves. We're happy and the pieces just never come together that make bad things happen. You were lucky, Fran. He swears he only wanted to stalk, not hurt you, but I don't know. Given time . . ."

Francesca shuddered. "I'm just glad it's over."

Lou cocked his head to one side. "Do you suppose Trey knew all about what Rush was doing to you?"

"I believe he did. I guess it will be awhile before we know."

Lou folded over the newspaper he carried in his hand. "Have either of you seen *The Radio Special News*?"

Both women said they hadn't. He pointed to a section that carried Francesca's photo and the caption: NO. 1 FOR THE YEAR? Francesca and Holly read the article that speculated on her excellent chances for her show being voted the number one variety show in radio broadcasting for the past year.

"Congratulations!" Lou said. Holly hugged her.

"I haven't got it yet," Francesca said. "They're just speculating."

"You will," Lou said. "You're really good, Fran. You've set this place on fire. How many times have I told you that?"

Francesca turned the page to where the article was continued. It had been her stellar performance and getting voted Female Broadcaster of the Year that had brought out Rush's virulent anger and begun the mailed clippings of dead women, the dead rabbit, the orchid greenhouse attack, then the doctored and bloody wedding photograph.

Lou walked away then and Holly turned to Francesca, who became aware of the soft, beige-leather purse Holly carried.

"I love this," Holly said. "You couldn't have brought me a lovelier present. Handmade yet. I'd never have paid what this must have cost."

"You deserve it."

Raising her hand, Holly said, "Ta-da," and turned a ring around on her finger. A lovely diamond flanked by smaller diamonds sparkled. "Of course, this beauty isn't quite in the class your ring is in, but who's comparing?"

Francesca flung her arms around her friend. "I'm so happy for you," she said.

"I'm happy for myself. It didn't happen on a moonlight-drenched, romantic island like yours did, but it's wonderful all the same."

"So Jon's buddy came around."

"Yes," Holly said, laughing. Then she grew thoughtful. "He's still scared, Fran. He said he may always be afraid, but he'll take his chances. We're going to wait awhile to get married, give him a chance to get used to the idea. His father's happy."

"How's he doing?"

"Very well. He says I lift his spirits. He was very lonely."

Francesca look at her own engagement ring. Holly saw the look of desire and doubt mirrored on her face and asked, "When are you two getting married?"

"I think we'll take it slow, too. God knows I'm still afraid, and Jon has old wounds to heal."

"His mother? Stacy?"

"Both, I believe. He doesn't talk about them."

Quietly, Holly placed her hand over Francesca's. "It's our time, Fran," she said. "Let's not let happiness slip away. Let's not let fear ruin it for us now."

* * *

Jon sat at his desk at the police station. He was thinking about coming back to work. Chief Wayne Kellem came in.

"Missing us too much?" the chief said, grinning.

"I do, but that's not why I'm here." He held up the clippings Francesca had gotten in the mail, with the added bloodied, wedding photo. "I've just been going back over these items, trying to assess what Trey Hudson might be up to."

"I'm sure glad that nightmare with Rush is over. At least now, Trey knows our eyes are trained on him. I don't think he'll try to pull anything at least for a little while."

"That's what I'm afraid of, that he'll wait and his anger will kick in later. Hudson is pure wired-essence of evil, but I do think he'll feel he's got to wait awhile. Meanwhile, what I have to do is wait, too. It's playing havoc with my life, Chief."

"Yeah," Kellem said. He came around the desk and put his hand at the edge of Jon's shoulder, then patted it.

"I wish I could be of more help to you," he said, "but I pray for you and Francesca—all the time."

"Thank you," Jon told him, thinking grimly he was going to need all the prayers he could get.

In his living room, Trey pulled Stacy down onto his lap. "Care to get something going on?" he asked, smirking.

Stacy pulled away, flinging her long hair. "I haven't forgiven you yet."

"For what?"

"You know for what! Telling Francesca you love her."

"Ah, that. I was in jail, Stacy. Even a dizzy broad like you can see what I was trying to do."

"Then tell *me* what you were trying to do. You never have explained it to my satisfaction."

Trey stood, the blood pounding in his temples. It always scared him when his temper zoomed from zero to high ten. "Listen," he snarled, "I explain nothing to anybody and if you haven't got that by now, then maybe you ought to get out."

Stacy thought tiredly that she had had it. More and more, she felt like calling his bluff, but she loved him, even if she felt like a fool for doing so. She was going to have to do something rash to turn him around, make him need her.

She stood, and went to him. Forget about Francesca. She knew what he liked. "I'm sorry, honey," she said. "I won't hassle you about your *ex*-wife again. It's just that I love you, and I get crazy at the thought of you loving Francesca."

But the blood roaring in his temples lessened only a little. Stacy was breathing hard, and he knew she was turned on. Something else was happening, too, that he didn't know about. Warlock was coming back, taking over.

He didn't let himself think of it any more than he could help it. Losing Rush was like losing a part of himself. The dumb bastard should have killed a less well-regarded person. Rush was his alter ego, half of him. Now that he had wormed his way into Trey's psyche, into his life, how would he live without him?

He was never in danger of being weak and alone. Warlock *always* came when he needed him most. But increasingly, Warlock frightened him.

He, Trey, was the host and Warlock was the guest. Now it seemed that Warlock wanted, no, *intended* to turn this around.

"Baby," Stacy cooed, running the tip of her tongue over his face.

"You want me, you got me," Trey told her. "But I warn you, I'm gonna be rough on you."

Stacy thrilled from head to toe. Trey stepped to a table and rang for Jersey. In a short time, the big man lumbered into the room. "What's it, boss?"

"Fix me the stiffest drinks you can think of. You make the choice. Put a pitcher of them in my bedroom upstairs and don't interrupt us, even if the house catches on fire."

"Sure thing, boss." He went out.

"Not just your bedroom, *our* bedroom." Stacy pouted. Trey didn't answer.

He looked at Stacy, his eyes glazing over. She felt a little fear that made her skin crawl. He wasn't rough all that often, but when he was, he was dynamite.

"Ready for me to let my demons run amok?" he asked her, grinning.

"More than ready, baby." She was gasping for breath. The next hours were going to be something. The next hours were going to be good!

Melanie and Garrett were at Francesca's house at first dark that evening.

"We just popped in," Melanie said, beaming.

"Oh, you do look happy," Francesca couldn't resist saying.

Jon nodded. "Fran's right about that. What's going on?"

"Yes, Dad, clue us in."

Garrett's face was wreathed in smiles. "I'm trying to get her to make our happiness permanent. Give me some help, you two."

A wide smile spread across Jon's face. "Sure, Mom, I'll be glad to give you away."

Surprise was sharply mirrored on Melanie's face. She looked at her son hesitantly. "Does this mean you forgive me?" Her voice trembled with hope.

Jon came to his mother, put his arms around her and kissed her cheek. "You bet it means I forgive you. I'm sorry for the pain I've caused you with my stubbornness. Can you forgive me?"

"Oh, honey, yes. I love you so much. I always have. I didn't want to hurt you, not any of you."

Jon put his finger on his mother's lips. "We'll talk about it sometime when you've had more chance to be happy."

"Thank you, son," Garrett said. "Now, we've got a movie to catch. How about dinner out tomorrow night, or the next?"

"Tomorrow's good for me. Francesca?"

"Perfect."

Melanie and Garrett left, hand in hand.

"I'll bet it's not long before wedding bells sound for those two. What about us, Walnut Love?"

"I think I want a big wedding and that takes time."

"I'm anxious, but I'll curb it."

They sat on the sofa close together. Francesca stroked his moustache gently.

"You're supposed to purr when I do that."

"I'm purring, all right. You just can't hear it."

Mrs. Addison came into the room, black tote bag in hand.

"Well, I've done all the damage I can do here," she said cheerfully. "Thanks for letting me off early."

"Never a problem," Francesca told her. "Have you got something special planned?"

Mrs. Addison blushed like a girl. "Well, a church member is taking me to a birthday party at his daughter's house. I guess you could say we're getting closer and closer."

Francesca and Jon expressed their pleasure and told her about Garrett and Melanie. She was fond of both people.

"The dishes are all stacked away from dinner. I want you to get some rest, Francesca. Already you're starting back to work too hard."

"Yes, ma'am," Francesca said meekly. "Thank you for caring."

"Thank you for helping me out," Jon said. "If she doesn't stop it, I'm going to insist she go on another vacation."

As Francesca raised her hand to her cheek, the light caught and reflected the brilliance of her engagement diamond and Mrs. Addison smiled. "The sapphire pendant. That ring. Jon, you've got excellent taste."

"Thank you again. Fran deserves the best. We all do."

With Mrs. Addison gone, Francesca and Jon settled down. Jon went to the piano and played a medley of pop tunes, then did a wild riff on "St. Louis Woman."

He got up and went to sit beside Francesca again.

"You're such a complex man," she said.

"I'll be simple if that's what you want me to be."

"I'm satisfied with you just the way you are."

"I'm glad because if I were able to create a woman for myself, you're what I'd create."

"My darling."

He lifted her hand and kissed the finger with his ring. Francesca thought she saw a brooding, wistful look on his face.

"Jon," she said suddenly, "you'd like to try living on Diamond Point for at least a while, wouldn't you?"

"Yes, I would. I see so much good I could do there. Part of their force has trained here in Minden and in D.C. But new things are going on there, and I can think of ways to combat their criminal element that they don't seem to have thought of. Why do you ask?"

"I don't really know."

"You want to say you'll go with me if that's what I want, but I'm not going to ask that of you. You love your job and you're settled here. We'll work it out."

But a shadow of pain still lay across his face. "I find Diamond Point a great place and the people are wonderful."

"The island and the people *are* wonderful."

He looked at her, liking the off-white caftan she wore. She moved closer to him. "It's cold outside," she murmured.

"I could do something about that." He pulled her close and began to stroke her, then got up, and pulled her to her feet.

Stroking the length of her back, lingering on her hips, he pressed her body close to his, and she felt the rising of his shaft hard against her and trembled.

With tiny strokes of her tongue, she brushed his moustache, then moved to the base of his ear and nibbled it. After a moment, he nibbled her ear and growled, "You're copping *my* act."

"And you know something?" she said. "It works. You're like a rock."

He leaned back, looking at her. "And who do I blame for that?"

He guided her to the bedroom door and pressed her against the wall beside it, his hands splayed on either side of her head.

"Be good to me," he whispered. "Show me love!"

"I'll show you what you're looking for," she told him, "and more. Ryson, I'm going to have you moaning for mercy."

"Big talk. I'm looking for action. You got any to offer?"

As she began to answer, the telephone rang. For a long

moment, neither of them moved. "Of all the damned times," he muttered and moved to pick up the phone.

Francesca stood where he'd left her, unwilling to accept the interruption. When he came back after a few minutes, his face was grave.

"That was the chief," he said. "They arrested a guy tonight who claims he's got information we want about Kevin's death. The chief wasn't listening too much until the guy mentioned the 'Caribbean Caper.' He says he won't talk to anyone but me."

She stroked his face. "I hope it's information you can use. Hurry back." Her hand went to her face. "Maybe I shouldn't have said 'hurry back.' Was it thoughtless of me?"

"You're talking about my grief over Kevin. No, it wasn't thoughtless for you to still want to make love. Kevin would be the first to tell me to live my life, make love to my woman. Be happy. He was that kind of guy. Maybe this will give us something to hope for.

"I'll be back soon. I'll see that you're locked in and secure." He moaned low in his throat as he kissed her.

After he'd gone, Francesca went to the downstairs bedroom and got the pastor's stone from her jewelry cabinet. She studied the smoothness of the stone and rubbed it, then dropped it into the pocket of her caftan.

Jon's kisses had set her on fire, but what the chief had had to say cooled her blood. Was something happening now that would let them know who had killed Kevin Ryson? With all her heart, Francesca hoped so.

It was true that with Rush Mason's arrest the stalking seemed to have stopped, although it was too soon to tell. But Rush had sworn he hadn't killed Kevin. They needed to know who had.

Thirty-two

Francesca walked back and forth in her living room, already missing Jon. She opened the piano and played a few chords, then walked over and restlessly looked out the window at glittering stars and the nearly full moon. Her body still tingled from Jon's loving touch. Her breasts felt ripe and she could feel his hands cupping them, his mouth on them.

She thought about her upcoming wedding, tentatively set for late October. He didn't want to wait that long, but wanted her to have what she most desired.

"Ryson," she said softly, "you have a lot coming to you from me, all of it good."

She switched on her radio station and got Ron Emerson playing pop tunes. The ultrarich sounds of Roberta Flack singing "Killing Me Softly" in her inimitable voice came through. Francesca hummed along with her. Jon wasn't killing her softly; he was bringing her alive in every cell and throughout her spirit. But had she stayed with Trey, he would have killed her softly and maybe not so softly. It angered her, just thinking about it.

She felt the pastor's stone in her pocket, took it out and stroked it. The religious man had said she was bothered. He had said, if she had trouble ahead, this could help.

She didn't see any trouble ahead. She was happy.

She brushed a crumb from her caftan.

She sat in a deep chair, simply drifting, waiting for Jon to come back, when the telephone rang.

"Hello, my own girlfriend."

"Holly!"

"You sound happy to hear from me. Is Jon not around and you're lonely?"

"How'd you guess? But I'm happy to hear from you, even when he's here."

"Not as much. Can you use a bit of company?"

"For you, always. What's going on?"

"What's going on is Keith's working tonight for a while and I'm going to the mall to do some shopping. I thought I'd drop by."

"That would make me happy. Jon went to the station house to help grill a young man who says he knows something about Kevin's death."

"Well, I hope that proves to be a break. I'll see you in about an hour."

Francesca had hardly put the phone back in its cradle when the side doorbell rang. Could it be Jon coming back for something? she wondered. Most likely. She thought for a moment, then shrugged. Thank God telemarketers didn't ring doorbells.

Going to the side kitchen door, she cut on the intercom, then looked at the TV screen that showed anyone outside the door.

Stacy Lambreth stood there, her hair and clothes rumpled, her face a study in fear.

"It's Stacy, Francesca. I've got to talk with you."

Francesca felt the start of anger. "I don't think there's anything for us to talk about, Stacy."

"There is, you know. I've got news about Kevin's death. I can help. Let me speak with Jon, *please.*"

Thinking quickly, Francesca said, "Jon's in the shower. Why didn't you simply call him?"

"Oh my God, Francesca, you don't have to invite me in, just talk to me, please!"

"You're talking to me now. Just tell me what you have to say about Kevin's death."

Francesca saw Stacy disappear from the screen. She could hear moans and knew she'd fallen where she had stood.

She didn't think very deeply about what to do next. No matter how much she disliked her, the woman was in trouble, and she had to help her. She flicked off the buzzing sensor and opened the door to pull Stacy in when the hounds of hell began their attack on her.

Slinking along the inner edge of the long side porch, Trey, with Jersey looming behind him, pointed a gun at Francesca. "Don't move," he ordered, "and don't say anything."

The earlier dream came back to her with terrifying intensity as if it would bolster the present actuality. Trey was pulling the trigger, and it wasn't supposed to be that way.

"No, Trey, don't!"

She had said those words in the dream. But he was pulling the trigger, and she was falling the way Stacy had pretended to fall.

The scene was all wrong. Jon was supposed to save her. Bursts of light filled her world; then blackness closed in the way blackness had closed in when Trey had struck her when they were still married. The way blackness had closed in on Diamond Point the night of the attack in the orchid greenhouse. The pastor's stone fell from her hand and rolled a little distance away into the kitchen.

"Cover her," Trey ordered Jersey. Stacy stood up.

"Did I do what you wanted, or did I?" She chuckled.

"Don't talk, Stacy. You did okay. You'll get your reward."

Jersey put the dark blue bedspread over Francesca, then rolled her into it and threw her over his shoulder.

"Be glad I'm strong, boss," Jersey said.

"Everybody's a goddamned conversationalist tonight," Trey growled. "Shut up and let's get this show on the road."

"Jon," Francesca murmured.

"She's saying something." Stacy touched Trey's arm.

"Forget it. She won't be saying it much longer."

At Minden's station house, Jon, his chief and Keith sat at a table with a tense young man, whose mouth seemed to perpetually smile; his eyes were cold.

"That's what you have to say?" Jon asked him. "That the man you say killed my brother's been here, but he's gone?"

"Yeah. Doesn't that help your case?"

"We've heard this before. You said you had something *new.*"

"Yeah, well. I didn't know if you knew this dude is said on the streets to be the one who killed your brother. Cops sometimes are the last to know. You guys can be *slow.*"

Jon felt the bile rising in him, started to get to his feet, but controlled himself.

"Listen, punk," Keith said. "We're not so slow we don't know when we're being jerked around. Who's putting you up to this?"

The man looked surprised, defiant. "If you don't want my help . . . Like I said, the dude's been here, but he's gone."

"I don't think he was ever here lately," Jon said flatly. "Maybe you're the one, Lawson, the one who killed him. You've been in trouble with us for a long time. It doesn't seem farfetched to me that Kevin had some-

thing on you about a couple of unsolved murders and
you took him out to keep from having your butt hauled
in and put on trial."

"I ain't killed n'body."

"I wouldn't be surprised if you had. Word on the
street is that you're the perp in at least one of our murders. Maybe we'll just keep you in here until you confess."

"You cain' do that. I know my rights."

"And I know mine," Jon rasped. "And I've got the
right to make it really hard for you. You're sweating.
What's the matter? Didn't you think about your past
crimes when you came to us, lying like the bastard you
are?"

The man smirked. "Where your respect for me, man?
Like I said, I got my *rights.*"

"Who hired or *scared* you into doing this?" the chief
asked.

The man's face hardened. "I ain't scared of nothin'
and n'body."

"That was before tonight." Jon summoned up his
best evil smile. "When I get through breaking your
bones, you're going to be happy to tell me. You'll even
confess if I want you to."

The man's mouth fell open. *Lord, this was supposed to
be just a little game. Make a fool out of the damned policeman,
the way he often had.*

And Jon sat, bluffing with the best. Chief Kellem
didn't hold with too much of the rough stuff, but this
jerk didn't need to know that.

Jon got up, got in the perp's face. "Who *sent* you?
Have you ever felt your bones break, one after the
other? Or all at once?"

"I'll get me a lawyer."

"A lawyer can't help you. I've got three men to witness that you jumped out of the window upstairs trying to escape. . . ."

The man called Lawson saw the fury in Jon's eyes and the wrath on the faces of the other two men, and he knew something bad was going to happen to him. He licked his dry lips. He was more afraid of the police than he was of the man who had sent him.

"Okay," he said. "Okay. Two men named Trey and Jersey talked to me, paid me. They said I wouldn't spend no time in jail. Now you dudes talkin' about doing somethin' bad t' me."

A cop came into the room. "Lock him up," the chief said.

"What I done 'cept lie a li'l? Why you lock me up?"

"I don't like the way you comb your hair," Chief Kellem said.

As Jon jumped to his feet the thought hit him like a flash of lightning. He said to the chief and Keith, "We've been had. I hope to God I'm wrong, but I think Hudson is going after Fran.

"I'm going home. I'll be calling. Keep me on tap and stay here until I see what's going on."

"I need to come with you," Keith yelled to Jon's back.

"No. Stay here. I'll call you."

Maybe he was wrong, he thought as he raced out the door and into the parking lot.

Driving as fast as he dared, his breath came in bursts. "Be all right, Fran. Please God, let me be wrong about this terrible feeling I've got."

"Oh-h-h. Where am I?"

Fran came awake and sat up abruptly as the room swam around her.

Someone took her hand. "You're here with me," a man said, "where you belong."

"Trey?"

"Yeah. Trey."

Francesca fought to make the room come into focus and asked the question again. They were in a bedroom furnished with opulent mahogany pieces.

"You're here in my house, on my bed and you're looking good."

Trey grinned fiendishly. "I'm one smart *hombre*. Babe, it was sharp of me to pay off one of the men who set up your security system. He shorted part of it out so I could get through."

Then grinning even more widely, he half closed his eyes. "Thank me for getting a modified stun gun to shoot you with. You're not suffering with an electrified body the way you'd be if I'd gotten the regular kind."

She could hear him, but his words swirled around her as she tried to focus. He bent and then kissed her on the mouth. His breath was hot and liquor-loaded.

The shock was like cold water; after blinking her eyes, she could see him clearly. She shifted position. "What am I doing here?"

"I brought you here. I brought you home. We're going to make love for the last time."

"You're out of your mind." His words finished the awakening shock, and she sent him a look of pure hatred.

He stroked her shoulders and her breasts in the low-cut caftan. "Don't fight me," he murmured.

The door opened quietly and Stacy came in and to the bed. "What are you doing, Trey? You said you wouldn't hurt her, that you only wanted to make her promise not to testify against you in case Rush ratted you out."

"Does it look like I'm hurting her?" He continued stroking Francesca. "I'm going to make love to her—for the last time."

Stacy turned scarlet. "You're disrespecting me. *I'm* your woman now. Leave her alone. I did my part. Now you live up to our bargain."

"I'll stroke your fur later, kitty cat," Trey said, laughing. "Don't cross me, Stacy. I'm getting sick of your whining and trying to dominate me."

Stacy looked stunned as Trey slipped off his loafers and kicked them aside. "Good Lord, Trey. You're not really going to rape her?"

"Who said anything about rape? This woman belongs to me. She's my wife."

"I'm your *ex*-wife," Francesca grated. "And I don't belong to you. You were smart enough to let me go. I divorced you."

Trey bent over her, his eyes gleaming with lust. "That was the mistake of my life, but once something belongs to me, it always belongs to me. I know that now.

"You put a spell on me." He was courting her. "I can't stop thinking about you, remembering what we had. I made a mistake in letting you go, and I'm going to correct that mistake."

Francesca drew on every shred of anger she had as she glared at him.

"I don't *want* you, Trey." Her eyes were like flint, her voice icy. It stopped him. She expected his curses and steeled herself against them.

A glint of satisfaction lay on Stacy's face. Trey got up and walked swiftly to the chest of drawers. As he turned around, the two women saw the gun in his hand.

"I'm through playing games," he told them. "You might as well know the truth early. I'm going to kill the both of you; you, Fran, to keep you from testifying against me. You saw that watch. I know all about women and their damned curiosity. There's no way you didn't look in my safe.

"But that would be my word against yours, wouldn't

it? No, I'm really sending you off because you put me out, like a stray dog. I won't stand for that."

"But we've been divorced for more than a year."

"Yeah, and things've been okay. But now you're getting married again, and I won't take that. When Rush came and told me you were going to marry Ryson, I knew I couldn't let you live. Stand up!"

Francesca swung her legs over the edge of the bed, stood up and wobbled a step or two away. She willed herself to be steady.

"What you saw at first was a stun gun," he told her. "This is a Smith and Wesson, .38 caliber. And you both know I'm an expert marksman.

"Open the door, Stacy, and don't try anything funny. I wouldn't hesitate to shoot you at this point. I've got nothing to lose."

Stacy opened the door, and Trey ordered them to turn left and go to the end of the hall and enter the long cross-room that served as upstairs study and control room.

"This is the one room in the house that can also be locked only from the outside. I don't have to tell you I have the key."

Francesca stood on shaky legs, willing herself to be strong. Waving the gun, he told her, "Walk over to that side window and stand there a minute."

She did as he asked, on badly trembling legs. "Raise the window." With effort she did so and nearly fainted when she saw two huge dogs lunge halfway up the wall at her.

Trey chuckled. "Just a warning about what's waiting for you if you got a notion to climb out and slide down that drain pipe. The front window is sealed." Going to a panel, he rang for Jersey. The big man, as always, came in a hurry.

"Yeah, boss."

"Take Stacy," Trey said, "and take care of her."

Jersey batted his eyes. "What you want me to do with her?"

"I don't care, man. Enjoy her body. Have fun. Use your imagination."

"Trey, please," Stacy begged. "I did what you asked me to do. You can't do this to me. I won't let you."

Trey drew a deep breath and waved the gun again. "Well, what the hell are you waiting for?"

Jersey slid his big arms around Stacy. She screamed and kicked his leg. Trey fired two shots at the ceiling.

"The next bullet will go into your sorry hide," Trey barked. Sobbing, Stacy let Jersey lead her away.

Trey turned his attention to Francesca. "I'm not going to tie you up. I've got no need to. Just sit down and be quiet. And pray a prayer to guide you over Jordan River when I kill you."

Watching her, Trey thought that even scared—maybe especially scared—she appealed to him. He plainly saw then what had happened. She had moved on with her life, and he couldn't.

Francesca wracked her brain trying to find some way to reach him. For a long moment, they looked at each other silently. Then the telephone rang and Trey went out, locking the door behind him.

Acting on reflex, Francesca walked over and turned off the lights, opened the blinds, quickly unzipped and stripped off her off-white caftan and waved it frantically just in case someone could see the window.

She waved the garment for several minutes, terrified that Trey would come back and shoot her immediately. Would Jon have had time to miss her? Her heart was full with praying.

On the road a block or so away Jon reflected that they were in real luck. Minden's and the county's joint

SWAT team had been practicing for several days and in tandem they were working smoothly together so far. Jon saw the garment waving in the window. Excited, he told Chief Kellem, "That looks like something Fran would do. I think she's telling us what room she's in."

"You may be right. We're all set now, the whole SWAT team. We've got to move with lightning speed."

A half block away, they heard the shot then and Jon's blood froze. He thanked God Trey's phone was listed and dialed the number. "Damn you, answer!" Jon grated. Trey answered on the seventh ring.

"You've got Francesca with you, Hudson. Don't harm her. Send her out. We've got you surrounded!"

Quite calmly Trey said, "You're going to have to come in and get her. I'm not sending her out."

Chief Kellem took the phone. "Hudson, this is Chief Kellem. You're making a big mistake. You know a SWAT team will play havoc with you. Cooperate and it will go easier on you."

Trey chuckled nastily. "Hell no. I've got an arsenal in here that will blow your SWAT team to kingdom come. Don't mess with me, Chief. We're talking about my wife here."

"Your *ex*-wife."

"What's mine is mine always."

"Cooperate with us, Hudson. It's your only hope." He said to Jon, covering the mouthpiece, "When is that crew going to cut Hudson's lights so we can move in?" The chief fretted.

Jon was sick with tension.

The chief touched base with the SWAT team located in vans along the way as they prepared to go in. In black, bulletproof uniforms and helmets, they came to Jon and the chief's black van.

The lights in Trey's house and yard went out.

"I'm going to call back and the men in the last van and I will keep talking to Hudson."

"I'm going with them," Jon said suddenly.

Chief Kellem put a hand on Jon's arm. "No."

"I happen to be wearing black."

"You're not in bulletproof gear. I can't let you go!"

But Jon was out of the van, holding close to the SWAT team, who didn't have time to argue. In his pocket, he touched his pastor's stone and said a quick prayer. They huddled low and ran toward Trey's house. It was emblazoned on his brain how he had gone into Fran's house frantically calling her name and found her pastor's stone lying near the kitchen door.

He'd wasted no time and now they were here.

Trey cursed. What in hell was wrong with the lights? He started to call Jersey and changed his mind. Grabbing a flashlight from the hall table drawer, he raced back to Francesca. He kept candles around the house for emergencies. With his cigarette lighter, he lit a few in the room where Francesca was.

She stood quietly, feeling that something was going on outside.

"Don't get any ideas," Trey grunted. "God Himself can't save you now."

They both were silent as she searched her mind for ways to escape him.

Trey took the gun and twirled it with the safety catch off.

He grinned. "I can always say it was an accident."

The SWAT team swarmed over Trey's estate. They anesthetized the dogs by shooting chemically loaded darts into their hides. The powerful medication did its job in a hurry. Jon and a SWAT team member hugged the side of the house and got in through an open window. Other agents got in through other entrances.

Jon and his cohort SWAT team member came to Jersey from the back of him as he fought with Stacy in the downstairs study.

"You big, crazy fool!" Stacy screamed. "You think I'd let you touch me?"

"You got no choice," Jersey told her. "Boss's orders. He don't want you no more."

Jumping on Jersey's back, Jon struggled with the bigger man and Jon's partner took a piece of rope from his knapsack.

"Oh, thank God," Stacy breathed. "Jon?"

"Don't talk, just help us."

"Anything."

The two men quickly tied Jersey up, then double-tied him. He was a big man.

"I can tell you where Francesca is and hurry," Stacy said.

"I think I know. The end room upstairs? To my right going up?"

"Yes, I'll go with you."

"No. You unlock the front door and let the others in."

He didn't trust her, but he had no choice.

"He was going to kill me, too," she whimpered.

Jon gave the electronic signal from his phone pad to tell the men they could get in through the front door. In the van, Wayne Kellem breathed a sigh of relief.

Thirty-three

At the top of the stairs, Jon paused, his gun steady. He hugged the wall leading to the right end of the hall. His eyes were dry with tension, his breathing labored. *God, let her be safe,* he prayed.

At the end of the hall, he paused again. What if Stacy was lying to him about where Francesca was being held? But no, sitting in the car they had seen something white waving in that window behind the open blinds, so he had come to this room.

Pausing at the door he wanted, he positioned his foot to kick the door in with his steel-tipped boots. It budged, but didn't completely give. Trying harder, he stood back and with supreme effort kicked again. The door burst in.

"Come in, Ryson," Trey said, grinning evilly. "I thought you might be fool enough to come." His gun was trained directly on Jon. "Close the door behind you."

Jon did as he asked, then turned to Francesca. "Are you okay?"

By this time, Jon's eyes were accustomed to the flickering light thrown by the fat, white candles, and he saw that Francesca's eyes were huge with fear.

Trey's gun was steady, and the thought struck both Jon and Francesca at the same time: Trey looked different! Consummate evil hardened his features. His countenance was that of a mad animal. Warlock had always flickered in and out of his persona, with some control by Trey. But now, for the first time in his life, Trey had utterly and irrevocably become Warlock!

Trey felt Warlock's power, his cunning, and he exulted.

"Stand over there in front of me," he ordered Jon, and Jon did his bidding.

"I killed your brother; now I'm going to send you to join him."

Jon wept inside with the confession, but he kept his voice steady. "Whatever you want to do to me, let Francesca go."

"Hell, no. I'm going to be charitable and let the both of you die together. Don't you want to know how and why I killed Kevin?"

"Yes." Dark anger swept through Jon, and he felt his mind clearing.

"He played the cop-gone-bad routine and he fooled us all. He set up minicameras to record our activities, caught us dead to rights, but I caught him at it and I made sure *I* did the killing.

"Beautiful watch he had on him. I'll be free to wear it when you're gone."

That, as much as anything, turned Jon's heart inside out.

Trey relaxed then. In the flickering candlelight, Jon watched to see if his countenance would change again, but no, it stayed Warlock's.

"I'm going to let you watch me kill her, Ryson. She belongs to me."

"She's your *ex*-wife, Hudson. You're divorced. She isn't yours any longer. Women aren't chattel."

Trey's voice was a half-scream. "That's where you're

wrong. Fran will always belong to me. She'll never marry you. I won't let her."

Trey became unnerved then, gasping for breath, but his gun hand stayed steady; he seemed aware only of Jon in that moment. Francesca forced a calmness she was far from feeling and picked up a heavy bronze statue from a table as she stood a bit to the side of Trey.

Swinging, she was in a perfect position to bring the statue down on Trey's head, but he moved a little to the other side and the blow only glanced his head.

Bellowing a stream of foulness, Trey began to turn when Jon's foot came up and kicked the gun out of his hand.

Moving with superhuman speed and cunning, Trey stuck out a foot and tripped Jon, causing him to lose his balance and fall.

The players moved in deadly silence. Exultation flashed through Trey. Again he was not Trey, the man, but Warlock, the god!

He moved swiftly to Francesca. He had her in his crosshairs. He would kill her before her lover's eyes and because he was Warlock, he could not be stopped. No power on earth could stop him! She was his forever!

Filled with ancestral strength he had seldom felt before, Jon knew he had to win. With lightning swiftness, he picked up the gun lying by him.

There was a flash of fire from Trey's gun, but Francesca moved aside as he had from her intended blow. Trey was close to her, but Jon's aim was on the mark. Trey's big body jerked up and he fell, dropping his gun. Jon kicked it away.

Jon handed Francesca Trey's gun, and she held it unflinchingly.

"Cover me," Jon said curtly, and she did.

Warily Jon began to examine Trey, turning him over. The SWAT team crowded in then, surrounding them.

"I think he's dead," Jon said. "I get no pulse."

He and Francesca saw with amazement that Warlock stayed imprinted on Trey's face. He died as the multiple he had most trusted, the false god he had served.

Getting up, Jon gathered Francesca close to him, and both were trembling. He took the gun and put it on the table. Each could feel the racing of the other's heart.

Triumph filled him the way she filled his arms, his heart, his soul.

"Oh, my darling," Jon whispered, "if anything had happened to you, I couldn't have stood it."

"I love you," Francesca said simply. "Thank you and I love you so much."

Oblivious of the bustling men around him, Jon pressed Francesca even closer and huskily told her, "I'm here now and you're safe in my arms. Our nightmare is over."

Thirty-four

Sitting alone at the glass-enclosed sunroom table, Francesca stared at the side door where she had been taken captive eight days ago. The memory still seized her, shook her, burrowed into her brain. It came in fits and starts.

So, Trey was dead. Neither he nor Rush would stalk her again. But as much as memories of the hellish times they had caused her tormented her mind, it was not what bothered her most at the moment.

She had come home three days ago to find a note to her from Jon.

Angel,

The office said you were away in Baltimore on assignment, as you told me you might be. I won't bother you there.

Matt Wolpers is sending a jet for me. I'm needed on Diamond Point to help them with something that could turn into a catastrophe.

I dare to go because you seem to be doing so well. My courageous woman. I will be away only a couple of days.

You won't be able to get in touch with me for at least a day, but I will get in touch with you shortly.

> My forever love,
> My life—Jon

The note lay spread out on the table in front of her, written in Jon's large scrawl. She smoothed the paper it was written on. Knowing he would worry, she had covered her continuing sharp fear that left her cold and dazed.

She would not have wanted him to pass up going to Diamond Point because of her. She was going to be just fine. And he was needed there. Sadness filled her when she thought of Cam Mason and Cam's family.

It was over, she thought now. The stalking, the clippings, the rabbit, the bloody wedding photograph, and the terrifying attacks.

She thought of everything except what concerned her most: that Jon hadn't called her. On the second day, she had called him and been referred to Matt Wolper's wife. She told Francesca that the men were tied up in meetings, run nonstop so Jon could get back quickly.

Mrs. Wolper's voice had sounded worried to Francesca, despite a forced cheerfulness. There had been no talk of serious trouble and the international news had picked up nothing. It wasn't like Jon not to call.

Leaning back, Francesca put her arms behind her head. Tomorrow she would go for an accupressure session. She had found a good person.

The door chimes sounded and she went to the front door, looked out and saw it was Raine Clymer with a large, flat portfolio under her arm.

Opening the door, Francesca hugged Raine.

"I can't wait for you to see my sketch of your wedding gown," Raine said.

"You'd make a great designer," Francesca told her.

Raine shrugged. "Being an artist is what I've always wanted to be. You've got the best designer in Vera Hawes, but when you described your gown to me, I just had to put it on water color. It's really lovely."

The two women fell silent, walking through the house.

Later, back in the sunroom, a setting sun threw its fiery rays across the glassed-in porch and Raine stopped a moment. "Magnificent. I've painted many of those."

"I'd like to purchase one."

"I'll make one a present to you. Sunrises, sunsets are two of my favorite subjects. You look bothered, Fran. I talked with you a day or so after your ordeal. Are things better now?"

"It comes and it goes." She told Raine then about Jon's trip.

Raine listened carefully. "I hope it's nothing except that he's tied up and it's taking longer than he expected."

"I get a strange feeling, that's all."

"You've been through so much."

"And come out ahead. Let's look at the sketch."

The setting sun had gone under clouds and Francesca turned on the lights as Raine opened the portfolio displaying the sketch.

Francesca drew in a quick breath. Putting her hand to her heart, she exclaimed, "It's *exactly* what I described to you. It's beautiful!"

And, indeed, the sketch was everything she had in mind, with heavy cream lace with long sleeves that ended in a point over her hands. Off-the-shoulder, closely fitted, with a trumpet-shaped bottom of lace in-

serts, the finished product would be a beauty. Francesca
was the model and carried a lily-of-the-valley bouquet.

"Jon is going to love this."

"I don't wonder. You've got excellent taste."

Francesca smiled wanly. "Now if only I could get in
touch with my bridegroom-to-be."

"I predict you'll hear sooner than later. We're two
lucky women, you and I."

"Yes."

The phone rang and Francesca rushed into the
kitchen to answer it, panting with anticipation.

"I hope you've heard something about Jon by now,"
Holly said.

"No, nothing." Francesca could have cried. It
seemed now that their intense love had been blighted
with misfortune from the beginning. How much longer
would this continue?

"You poor woman. You know, in Jon's line of work
he's going to get calls that take him to places he'd rather
not go. I hope nothing's happened on Diamond Point."

"I'm praying that nothing has. Matt's wife seemed
calm. . . . Holly, he loves Diamond Point, and I think
he wants to settle there. They're offering him so much."

"And you're not especially fond of it."

"I like it a lot, but I'm a Minden lover. There's so
much I want to do *here*. In addition to my work, I want
to pitch in with Melanie. She's a wonderful woman."

"She is."

"But I'll go with him wherever he wants to go."

"But you won't be happy about it."

"I'll make myself happy."

"You two have got such a great thing going. Are you
still having flashbacks about Trey and what he put you
through the other night?"

"Yes, but I'm dealing with it. It's so great not to have
to worry about him or Rush again. All the time I worried

that it was Trey who just wanted to frighten me. He was obsessed, Holly, like any teenager."

"I'm just so glad you're free of that creep."

Francesca laughed shakily. "Now, as I said to Raine a moment ago, if I can just find my bridegroom-to-be."

"I'm with you there. I'm saying a prayer for you, and I think no news is good news. He's almost certainly meeting back-to-back so he can get home faster."

"I hope so. It's been three days."

"Would you like me to spend the night with you or would you like to spend it at my place?"

Fran thought it over a moment. "No, I'm all right. Really." She wanted to be there when Jon called or faxed, and she didn't want Holly to know how shaken she still was. When they had come back from Diamond Point, with Rush in jail, she had been so happy. She had grieved for Cam, of course, but he would have wanted them to be happy.

Raine left early, and Francesca puttered about the house. It seemed so empty. Perhaps she should have asked Holly over. No, she had to see this through on her own.

Moving about the kitchen slowly, she made herself a grilled, sharp-cheese sandwich and a cup of hot chocolate with skim milk.

"Jon, where *are* you?" she murmured.

Francesca set the security system for night and went to bed early, carrying a mug of valerian tea with lemon juice, sweetened with stevia, a natural sweetener she had begun to use.

It was cold when she opened the window a little. She donned her pale blue, satin, fleece-lined gown. Jon always grinned when she wore it, saying, *"I'll* warm you." He was so precious.

In bed she sat up, trying to read. Reaching for the Bible, she opened it to "Song of Solomon" and read aloud.

> Stay me with flagons, comfort me with apples,
> for I am sick with love.

She and Jon were sick with love. He would do anything for her, including make a life in one place when he wanted to be in another.

Finishing the chapter, she closed the Bible and put it aside. The wind was high, whistling its wintry tune along the eaves. She drained her cup of tea and set the cup on the night table.

Weddings, she thought now. Trey had said he wouldn't let her marry Jon. That he'd never let her go.

With the lights out, she lay thinking of Jon, the thoughtful look on his face from time to time. And yes, there had been sadness, too. She loved him. She'd go with him. They'd work out their happiness somehow.

Then anger took over where she had felt pain. Surely, he could have had someone else call. Should she take time off and go to Diamond Point? But if he was staying longer because he had personal things to work out, he wouldn't want her there. Or need her there.

Pulling the covers up to her chin, she didn't want to sleep, but she fell into slumber easily, lulled by the valerian.

"Wake up, Fran!" A man's broad hands shook her awake and she felt a surge of joy. "Jon!"

But it wasn't Jon. It was Trey bending over her, grinning in the moonlight that shone through the open blinds. No, she gasped, that couldn't be.

"You're dead," she whispered hoarsely. His cold breath nearly stopped her heart.

Trey's smile was wide, lascivious, evil. "I'll never die, Fran. I'll be with you always."

"How did you get in? What do you want?"

"I can and will get in anywhere you are. I want *you*. You'll always be my wife, and I'm going to make love to you."

She fought his mad strength and screamed again. "No!" Jon would be there as soon as he knew, but Jon was away. Trey's manic Warlock strength subdued her and Trey's hot, vile, seeking mouth came down on hers. She would bite his tongue to pieces. She beat on his chest with soft fists that were not strong enough to make him release her.

"Let me *go!*"

Jerking violently on the bed, covered with cold perspiration, she saw Jon who tried to reach her, but was too far away.

She then came awake gasping for breath. Snapping on the bed lamp, she sat up. She was alone and Trey wasn't here. But neither was Jon.

She got out of bed, slid her feet into blue woolen mules and pulled on her blue woolen robe, shivering and hugging herself against the chill in her blood.

She closed the blinds, sat on the chaise longue and took Jon's photo into her hands and kissed it. "Please call," she murmured.

She settled down. All the valerian tea in the world wasn't going to help her go to sleep this night.

The second day after the dream, Francesca stopped in at the police station on her way home from the radio station. The dream still spooked her. Keith was the first person she saw.

"This is a surprise," he said.

She nodded. Keith and Holly had spent the night

before at her house. Worry over Jon and fear that she couldn't take another dream like that had rattled her. Holly was across town at a community service meeting.

"I know," she said, "but we didn't talk much last night. I was too beat."

"Still no word from Jon?"

"No. I'm beginning to get a bad feeling about this, Keith. Jon is the soul of dependability. He'd call if he could."

Keith sat with her on one of the benches in the hallway, rubbing his chin. "I can't speak for Jon," he said, "but sometimes men—and I guess women, too—need time alone to sort things out."

"You're right, of course."

"I'm sorry about what's happened to you, but it's over now." He smiled at her.

"I'm feeling a little steadier. It's Jon I'm worried about." That statement, she thought, wasn't altogether true. At moments, she felt she was coming unglued.

"Yeah. Me, too. Well, Holly and I will be over a little later, and we'll stay for as long as you want us to."

"For which I thank you."

Getting up, she realized that she had stopped by because she dreaded going into her house alone. She had gone in alone the past evening and been sick with fear. And old fears still haunted her.

Reaching home, she went in through the garage, which seemed eerily silent. Was there the sound of movement? She paused in the kitchen and listened, every cell alert.

She walked to the end of the kitchen and went out into the hall. Something fell in the bathroom. She nearly jumped out of her skin when the door opened and Jon stood there in worn black jeans, bare to the waist.

For a moment, she couldn't move. He came to her,

and hugged her fiercely, his just-showered skin damp and erotic.

She cried with relief as he covered her with kisses that searched her soul.

Her voice was choked as she asked him, "Why didn't you call?" And before he could answer, she pulled away a bit. "It's too cool in here for you to be bare. And have you eaten?"

Grinning, he kissed her again and helped her take her coat off. Throwing it aside, he murmured, "I ate on the plane. I don't need food. I need *you.*"

"And I need you. My Lord, how good you feel."

"Not as good as *you* feel. You want to know what happened, and I'll make it short. Matt sent for me to come immediately because there was trouble brewing in the hills. He needed to interface with me to get my plans and my suggestions underway.

"Three of us went to the hills of Diamond Point to talk with some insurgents who were laying foolhardy plans to take over. Our Jeep was wrecked, ran into a ravine. My leg was hurt a bit. Matt's shoulder was broken. Anyway, they treated us. They didn't let us call it that, but we were in effect hostages. They were going to use us to get their demands met for more money for their group.

"I told Matt's wife not to tell you because I knew you'd worry and try to come. And it would be dangerous. We were rescued this morning, late. Police forces from several Caribbean countries and Aruba pitched in to get us out, but it took time."

Francesca felt happy with relief. "I thought you wanted to think over moving there, taking the job they want you to take."

He pulled her close then and said against her hair, "There in the hills I had time to think. I like the stability of our Stateside law enforcement. And yes, like you re-

alized, I love Minden. I want to go back to Diamond
Point often, and they've asked me to be a consultant
and I agreed.

"Before I left, my chief talked with me about groom-
ing me over the long haul to be chief when he retires."

"That's wonderful."

He nuzzled her face. "Sweetheart, let's not wait until
October to get married."

"All right. When would you prefer?"

"I know you want everything to be perfect. What do
you say late April?"

"Or maybe even early April. Ryson, you're not the
only one who's anxious. I thought I'd die without you."

"That makes two of us. Have you been all right?"

"Yes." She would wait to tell him about the dream.

Only then did either become aware that Jon was un-
shaven. He rubbed his hands over the heavy stubble.

"I haven't taken off my beard since the day I left. I'm
a wreck."

"You look terrible. Wonderfully terrible. And I love
you to my soul."

He rubbed her face against his as she held him close.

"I'm going to change," she finally said reluctantly,
suddenly shy at wanting him so much.

In their bedroom, Francesca smiled, thinking that
she had never shed her clothes so quickly. She slipped
into a dark rose, tricot-jersey robe that hugged her figure.

Jon rapped lightly and came in.

"I can't wait all night," he said, smiling roguishly.

"You impatient man."

He was still bare from the waist up, his supple brown
skin now dry. He pulled her to him and with his body
pressing against hers, her heart melted for him.

Slipping the robe from her shoulders and unfastening it, he stroked her lightly, his heart pounding.

"I dreamed of this," he said. "It kept me going. But I've got to ask you again how you held up while I was away."

"Well enough. Keith and Holly helped. You're here and I'm fine now."

His mouth on hers was hungry, seeking everything at once. Standing there, his hands cupped her breasts, took off the filmy rose undergarments and threw them aside. Well, she thought, he wasn't alone in his hunger. She traced his moustache with her index fingertips, then tugged at the top button of his jeans.

"Ryson," she said, smiling, "you'd be frightened if you knew how much I want you now. I can't wait." Her eyes were pools of desire.

"Patience!" He was out of his jeans, kicking them aside.

"Try me," he told her.

Laughter bubbled in her throat and seemed to well from some deep spring inside her. And listening to her joyous peals of laughter, he thought he would probe the depths of her body and her soul and never let her go.

Epilogue

"Dearly beloved, we are gathered together . . ."

Early April and Jon thought this one of the most beautiful days of his life. His wedding day. Brilliant sunlight streamed through the stained-glass chapel windows. The organist continued to softly play "O Promise Me." White cattleya orchids sent by Cam Mason's wife banked the altar.

In his black business suit, he thought himself the perfect foil for Francesca's beauty. His eyes swept over her, found her entrancing in her cream, heavy-lace gown with lilies of the valley threaded into her smoothly coiffed hair. Her bridal bouquet was also lilies of the valley.

"Do you, Jon, take this woman to be your lawful . . ."

You bet I do, Jon thought, happiness and laughter rising in him before he responded.

Francesca glanced at Jon and realized he was looking at her. She smiled. So the day had come at last!

Jon finished his vows and the minister turned to Francesca, asking, "Do you, Francesca, take this man to be . . ."

Yes, she thought, she would take all of him to cherish forever.

They were flanked by Keith in a black business suit and Holly, lovely in dull rose satin. Best man and maid of honor, they would be married in December.

Francesca could feel the warmth of family and friends around her, none prouder than Garrett and Melanie, who would jump the broom in October. Melanie had laughed. "The young friends I work with would have it no other way."

Francesca and Jon had wanted the traditional service. Now as the minister intoned, "You may place the ring on her finger," Jon took the solid gold band from the ringbearer and, with slightly shaky fingers placed it, wanting to kiss her hand as he did so. In so brief a time, his mind segued ahead, even as he stood keenly aware of his wedding. He would sow his seed in this beloved woman's womb and she would bear them at least one child. His heart raced for a moment at the thought.

Dewy-eyed, Francesca looked at her groom as the minister gravely told them, "I now pronounce you man and wife." A few more words, then smiling drolly, the minister said, "You may kiss the bride."

Jon took her in his arms, and drawing her close, his lips met her slightly open mouth and drew the warm honey from it.

He lost sight of the others then. They were alone.

She was his woman.

She was now his wife.

Reluctantly, he lifted his mouth from hers to whisper, "My darling, you are my forever love."

Dear Readers,

Francesca and Jon's story is for you. Wouldn't it be great if all our troubles could end as theirs did? Writing about these two loving people was a joy.

I keenly enjoy your letters and want you to keep writing to me, letting me know what you do and do not like. Your letters delight me.

I wish you a long and happy life with the best of everything.

Best wishes,

Francine Craft
P.O. Box 44204
Washington, DC 20026

ABOUT THE AUTHOR

Francine Craft is the pen name of a Washington, DC–based writer who has enjoyed writing for many years. A native Mississippian, she has also lived in New Orleans and found it fascinating.

She has been a research assistant for a large nonprofit organization, an elementary school teacher, a business school instructor, and a federal government legal secretary. Her books have been highly praised by reviewers.

Francine's hobbies are prodigious reading, photography, and songwriting. She presently lives with a family of friends and many goldfish.

She loves to hear from her readers. You can write to her at P.O. Box 44204, Washington, DC 20026.